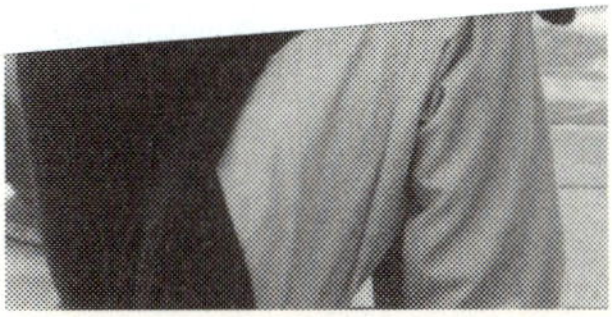

Julian Novitz was born in Christchurch and currently lives in Melbourne. His short story collection, *My Real Life and Other Stories*, won the New Zealand Society of Authors Hubert Church Best First Book Award for Fiction at the Montana New Zealand Book Awards 2005. *Holocaust Tours* is his first novel.

HOLOCAUST TOURS

JULIAN NOVITZ

For Olena, Alex, Dasha and Daphne with love and best wishes — Julian.

VINTAGE

This is a work of fiction. All the characters are fictitious and any resemblance to actual persons is coincidental.

National Library of New Zealand Cataloguing-in-Publication Data

Novitz, Julian, 1980-
Holocaust tours / Julian Novitz.
ISBN-13: 978-1-86941-728-4
ISBN-10: 1-86941-728-3
1. Holocaust, Jewish (1939-1945)—Fiction. I. Title.
NZ823.3—dc 22

A VINTAGE BOOK
published by
Random House New Zealand
18 Poland Road, Glenfield, Auckland, New Zealand
www.randomhouse.co.nz

First published 2006

ISBN-13: 978 1 86941 728 4
ISBN-10: 1 86941 728 3

Design: Elin Bruhn Termannsen
Cover design: Matthew Trbuhovic
Cover photos: Getty Images
Printed in Australia by Griffin Press

PART ONE

DANIEL

I was in Anita's bedsit when I got the message, sitting at Anita's desk, checking my email on Anita's computer. My bag was at my feet, I was ready to leave for the station, but then the name of the sender and the subject-line blinked into existence under new mail and there it was there, double-clicked open on the screen: a brief, alluring, lower-cased temptation.

```
are u back in nz??? need good people 4 big
design, wellington based. call me.
```

Name of sender: *Logan Heckle*. Subject: *job*. I leaned back in Anita's chair and sifted through the books on her desk to find my tobacco and rolling paper. Anita didn't mind me smoking, but I could only do it when she was out; she couldn't watch me light a cigarette now without squirming. She hated the fiddling around with papers and filters, the fumbling search for the latest plastic lighter, the little pucking noise my lips made as they exhaled the first draught. She said it made me look nervous, oddly fey for a man of my age and size. I had started to smoke again to keep my hands busy. Anita spent most of her days at the British Library now. She could not work at home any more, not with me around.

I finished rolling the cigarette and let it dangle unlit between my lips, stowing the tobacco and lighter in my jacket pocket. I glided the cursor over to the reply button but didn't click. I certainly needed a job but I was nowhere near New Zealand and I hadn't planned on going back. I sat at the desk for a moment longer then realised that I was hesitating. Anita would be angry if I was late. Without replying, I shut down her computer and scooped my bag off the floor. Outside the sun was already sinking and I stood on the cold slippery balcony of Anita's block of flats, looking out at a view of identically damp, dismal blocks under a low grey sky before finally lighting the cigarette I still held between my lips. My holiday was about to begin. For better or worse, it was unavoidable.

After nine years, on and off, I had already wasted more time in London than it warranted. The city had morphed from a Promised Land into a realm of crowds, traffic, rain and expensive drinks. At King's Cross Station the air was icy and pigeons fluttered around its vaulted ceiling. Crowds of irritable, joyless commuters milled between platforms and I was jostled several times on my way across to the ticket counter (only a Londoner can make "excuse me" sound like "fuck you"). I found Anita, Josh and Steve waiting for me by the counter, sipping steaming tea from cardboard cups.

"Sorry I'm late," I said. I expected Anita to be pissed off. She could be pissed off, I could be pissed off, everyone around us could be pissed off, everyone in the station, in the city.

Instead she smiled as I approached and kissed me briefly before springing back, flushed with cold and excitement. "Just glad you made it at all," she said, chucking her half-empty cup into a rubbish bin and picking up her bags, one of which I tried, unsuccessfully, to take from her. "I'm fine, I'm fine. Come on, we've got to move." She smiled at me over her shoulder, then started to weave through the crowd towards our platform.

"All right, Big Man?" Josh said, slapping my shoulder.

I hated it when he did that, I hated being called Big Man. He moved past me, following Anita.

His friend Steve lingered for a moment, finishing his tea. "How are you?" he asked.

"Fine."

"Are you ready?"

"Sure."

"You don't have to worry about Josh," said Steve. "He knows his stuff, it'll all go really well. You'll be glad to have him along on a trip like this. Trust me."

We were stopping in Nottingham first. Anita needed to revisit Beth Shalom, the first dedicated Holocaust memorial and education centre in the United Kingdom. Josh hadn't been there; he wasn't sure how he had overlooked it. "Guess I've always just focused on the larger sites," he'd said. "It's weird how some things escape you, like they just don't occur to you at all." After a night in Nottingham we would continue on up to Edinburgh. The twenty-seventh of January was the UK National Holocaust Memorial Day and the official ceremony was being held in Edinburgh that year, along with several events and exhibitions in the days leading up to it. Anita wanted to attend the main commemorative event in the town hall on the evening of the twenty-seventh, but Josh had only been able to get two tickets to it; they were difficult to come by and she couldn't pass it up. "Figured you two might be needing a break by then anyway," he said to Steve and me.

"Been to Auschwitz?" Josh asked Anita as our train sped

up through the East Midlands.

"About a year back, when I first started on my PhD. It was a mistake to go in the summer. Too many backpackers and tour trips."

"Did you get out to the new Jewish Museum in Berlin as well? Parts of that were effective. Especially the voids." He leaned forward, across the plastic table separating our seats. "You know, the voids, the empty rooms. That one, the Tower of Solitude or whatever it was called. The tall narrow freezing room. It's the dark one, the only light comes from these little pin-prick holes in the walls. You can just stand in there for five or ten minutes and contemplate the enormity. It really hits you when you're standing there."

"I found the concept really interesting," Anita said. "But I didn't get the best sense of it when I visited. It was so crowded you could only stay in there for half a minute and the queues . . ." She shook her head. "Tourists."

"I don't know," I said. "It sounds kind of tacky to me. That room."

Anita gave me a quick, disgusted look. She knew I was just stirring, just trying to wind Josh up. Josh shifted in his seat to face me and smiled indulgently. He knew it too.

"Maybe I'm not describing it well," he said. "But when I was there I really did find it very powerful. Being put in that kind of space really brings home everything you've seen in the exhibition, especially for me, being Jewish, the thoughts that were going through my head."

"I'm Jewish," I said. "Actually."

"Okay," said Josh. "All right."

"Yeah," said Steve, looking up from his newspaper briefly. "Shalom, Daniel."

Anita and I had been together for almost six months by then. We had met while I had been visiting my brother, Nathan, in

Bristol for a weekend. He was an assistant lecturer in the physics department at the university and knew Anita vaguely, through a friend who worked in the history department where Anita was doing her PhD. Though she was based in London, supporting herself by tutoring at a language school, she still commuted to Bristol every month or so to meet her supervisor. In town at the same time as me, she got invited to a party at Nathan's flat. Nathan introduced her to me as 'Anita the Holocaust historian', but she had laughed at that, shaking her head.

"The Holocaust itself isn't really my field of study," she had said. "You couldn't even begin to call me an expert on it. In fact I don't think you could call me a historian at all. What I study is the memory of the Holocaust, developments in thought about it and representations of it."

"Sounds interesting," I said.

"Sounds very interesting," said Nathan, pouring himself another drink.

"You should be interested," said Anita, sensing some ambivalence on Nathan's part. "These representations must have shaped your background in some way."

Nathan and I looked at each other, confused.

"I'm sorry," Anita said, "but Legkov is a Jewish name, right? Or have I got that wrong?"

"Oh yeah," said Nathan. "Our father was Jewish. But, you know . . ."

Anita had nodded, a little too vigorously, and took another sip of wine. "So what do you do, Daniel?" she asked me. "Nathan hasn't told me yet."

"What Daniel does," Nathan said, "takes far too long to explain." He drifted away into the thick of the party.

Anita and I laughed nervously for a moment, but then she had cocked her head to one side expectantly and I had to try to explain my life. After I did so, more or less successfully, we arranged to meet when we were both back in London. We'd had some good times for the first few months after that, while I still had a job and my own apartment. Anita was clever and attractive and I appreciated her dry, caustic humour so long as it was not directed at me. For a while we were a match.

"So you're Jewish now, are you?" Anita asked later, in our hotel room.

"Hmm?" I was sitting on the edge of the bed watching BBC World. On screen, Blair and Bush were talking about pre-emptive strikes and anticipatory defence.

"Is it because Josh said he was Jewish?"

"What does Josh have to do with anything?"

Anita grinned and sat down next to me on the bed. "Quite a lot," she said. "Probably. But I'm glad we're doing this trip with him. It's interesting being around someone so . . . I don't know . . . *enthusiastic*."

Josh's enthusiasm was one of the things which made me feel slightly uneasy about him. He reminded me of my old friend Martin, from back in New Zealand, and the gleam that would enter his eye whenever he talked about anything murderous or genocidal. Martin had been a history student and he was not my friend any more. Anita and I watched the news for a while longer. NATO was divided. Germany seemed keen to avoid war. Good for them.

"Do you like Josh?" I asked.

"I don't know. He's harmless enough, right? Hey," she said, gently running her fingertips up the curve of my spine. "Are you feeling . . ."

On the television were pictures of troops running through obstacle courses, mechanics tightening gears on tank tracks, stock footage of frightened, starving civilians in Iraq, rows of bombers in Middle Eastern airfield bases.

"Not right now," I said. "No, I don't think so."

Joshua Levit and his friend Steve had entered our lives about a month and a half ago, just after I lost my job at Deakman Games in London. I had gone down to the White Hart for one last drink with my old design team, then met Anita for a consolatory curry later in the evening. She had been in good spirits. I was not.

"Hey, I met this really odd guy today," she said.

"Odd?"

"Yeah, odd. I was at the exhibition in the Imperial War Museum again. We met there; he was interested in my research. Really interested."

"Why?"

"I don't know." Anita laughed and shrugged. "He was just odd."

A week later, when I was moodily contemplating the rent on my London flat and the dwindling savings in my bank account, the odd guy was mentioned again. "He tracked me down in the library!" Anita said one night while we were cooking dinner. "I mean, I told him I worked there a lot and he said he'd stop by, but I never expected him to come looking for me."

"Yeah," I said. "Yeah, that is weird."

"I was a little worried at first, but it was more by chance than anything else, he was just passing my table. Anyway, he bought me a coffee at lunchtime and we talked about my thesis again. He's travelled a lot; he's visited so many of the relevant sites."

"How old is this guy?"

"Older than us," Anita said, "but not that you'd notice."

By the time I actually met Josh in person I had moved in with Anita, just temporarily, just until I found a new job and a new place. It was all still going well at that stage. Josh had been stopping by the library quite regularly then and sometimes Anita would call him, arranging to meet for a drink or a coffee. "I'm not really sure how much he understands about my work," Anita said. "But he's always suggesting sites I should study, memoirs and histories I should read."

"I'd like to meet him sometime."

"I'm not sure if you'd like him."

"Why wouldn't I?" I asked.

"I just don't think you would."

But eventually Anita agreed to introduce me to her helpful Holocaust enthusiast and a couple of nights later we met Josh and his friend Steve at a pub. My dislike for Josh was automatic, almost instinctual. I disliked him right from the moment he stood up from his table to kiss Anita's cheek — a short, narrow-shouldered man with a long nose and a sharp jawline, a mass of floppy hair sprayed into a rigidly artless tangle and a smile that always seemed a notch too wide. I disliked the way he called me "Big Man" right from the start, disliked him for wincing and whistling with false sympathy when Anita let it slip that I had just lost my job, and disliked him even more for buying every round from that point on. I was more or less indifferent to Steve, a bearded, prematurely bald man who let his friend do most of the talking. Later, when we were walking back to her bedsit, Anita looked at me shyly and said, "He's fun, isn't he?"

"Yeah," I said. "Top guy. We should do this again sometime."

In Nottingham, we checked out of our hotel early, leaving our bags at the front desk. From the city centre we took a bus out to Beth Shalom, the Holocaust museum on the edge of Sherwood Forest. The Education Centre was a large red-brick farmhouse, set in two acres of memorial gardens. The grounds looked beautiful, but it was too cold to wander in them for long and we soon moved inside.

I trailed behind Josh and Anita as they strolled between the massive walls of photographs showing the men, women and children who had died in the Auschwitz-Birkenau camps and the exhibits depicting life in the Warsaw Ghetto — Stars of David, swastika armbands, ghetto identification papers, concentration camp rosters. A few photographs were new to me, but the ones that stay with you are the same ones you've seen everywhere: the piles of glasses and shoes; the naked woman with the baby, shot at from behind by the uniformed soldier; the little boy wearing a cloth cap walking forward with his hands in the air. We lingered in front of that last one for a while.

"The clearing of the Warsaw Ghetto," Anita said.

"I've always wondered who that boy was," I said.

"Everybody wonders that," said Josh.

"Nobody knows about the boy, but the guard behind him has been identified." Anita pointed to a lean, craggy-faced man holding a rifle, who stood in the background of the picture. His helmet was slanted down on his forehead, so low his eyes were almost hidden. The woman walking next to the boy in the picture, most probably his mother, was turning back to shout at the guard. "I can't remember his real name right now," Anita said. "But apparently he was so cruel the ghetto prisoners nicknamed him Frankenstein."

"Frankenstein," Josh said, nodding at the photograph. "That's the sort of thing I need. That sort of detail brings it to life for me." He turned to face Anita. "Thank you," he said, very seriously.

Steve raised his eyebrows at me and smiled, but I didn't smile back. We walked on until, at the end of the hall, we found a quote by George Santayana hanging on one of the walls. Anita and Josh had seen it before, in other Holocaust museums around the world.

    He who does not learn from history is
    doomed to repeat it.

The worst thing about history, I thought, standing next to Anita as she scribbled down a note in her diary, is that it's all in the past.

That afternoon, on the train to Edinburgh, I sat silently in our carriage and watched Josh and Anita talk.

"You've got to visit the Washington memorial," Josh was saying. "It's essential. I've been twice and I can't ever forget it, I can't get it out of my head. I think you have to go there. If you're writing about memorials you can't leave it out, it's overwhelming. The last time I was there it had this exhibition of Anne Frank's writings. The original diary pages — I couldn't believe it."

Josh had visited memorials and museums in the United States, in Europe and Israel. He had found them in out-of-the-way corners of the world — in South America, in Australia, in Africa.

"The Jewish museum in Cape Town has a good Holocaust section," he told us. "But really it's better on the history of Jewish people in the Cape. I walked out feeling quite proud of what we'd done in South Africa, actually."

From his conversation it seemed like Josh seldom stayed in one place for more than a few months. He kept a flat in London, a nominal home, but the balance of his time was spent abroad. I had asked Steve about this once and he'd grinned and said, "It's compulsive."

Steve was Josh's frequent travelling companion. They had been friends in school (they never said which school and I always imagined some strict, expensive, sub-Etonian boarding institution with cold showers and drip-nosed masters) but only met up again a few years ago. "In Berlin," Steve had told me, "quite by chance." I wasn't quite sure of the exact nature of their relationship. They were certainly close friends and seemed to know each other well, to the point of pre-empting each other's thoughts, words and actions. But I didn't think they were sleeping together and a strange wariness seemed to underlie their intimacy. They didn't talk to each other much while we travelled and were always careful to keep a distance between them, a tactic of two long-time companions perhaps, a way of making sure that they didn't get sick of each other.

Over the month I had known them I learned that Josh had money, quite a lot of it in fact, and that Steve had little or none. Neither of them did any kind of work as far as I could tell, though Steve once mentioned a teaching job he had briefly held in Asia and Josh hinted that he had previously "been in business". Anita and I had speculated about the source of Josh's wealth. She thought it was family money and was probably right, though I maintained that he had formerly overseen a ring of international heroin smugglers.

"Couldn't you just picture him slicing fingers off disloyal couriers?" I had asked her.

"No, Daniel," she'd said. "Not particularly."

It had been Josh who had suggested this trip to Edinburgh. Looking back, I could see that he had been restless and sort of stilted in London. Once we were travelling, he moved and talked much more easily. Transit was clearly his element.

"You don't have to come," Anita had said when she first told me about Josh's proposal. "I mean, of course I'd like it if you came, but don't feel like you have to."

"Can we afford a trip like this? Now?"

"It's fine," Anita had said. "Absolutely fine. Josh has already paid for the tickets, you see. He bought one extra as well, just in case you wanted to join us."

"Then I will come."

"Great."

A pause for a moment, and then I conceded: "It was very

nice of Josh, to buy us those tickets."

"Wasn't it? It's so good you're coming. You've been looking stressed out lately. Josh noticed. He thought you could use the break."

We arrived in Edinburgh at ten o'clock on the night of the twenty-fifth of January, two days before National Holocaust Memorial Day. On the way up I had been thinking about the message I'd received back in London. Logan Heckle and a job in New Zealand. What was New Zealand like now? When had I last been back?

"Here we are," Steve whispered to me as we stepped off the train. "Right in the middle of Genocide Awareness Week."

Josh had already booked the four of us into a good hotel near the centre of town. Anita picked up some flyers while we checked in.

"*The week of events and activities leading up to the National Holocaust Memorial Day is designed to heighten consciousness of similar atrocities taking place in the world today*," she read to me, later that night in our room, "*as well as to keep alive the memory of the eleven million victims of the Holocaust . . .*"

"Eleven million?"

"Six million Jews added to 'five million' non-Jews," Anita said. "Eleven million victims total." She had a beautiful way of speaking. You could smell the inverted commas on her breath.

"Is the figure accurate?" I asked.

"Hard to say. Depending on what you mean by 'victim of the Holocaust' the extra five million could be either too large or too small. Simon Wiesenthal started using eleven million instead of the six because he didn't want the Holocaust to be seen as just a problem between Jews and Nazis. It caught on pretty quick." Anita sat down on the bed. "It's all about accessibility, I guess."

I sat down behind her, putting my arms around her, kissing her neck. "I love it when you talk about your work," I said.

The next morning was bitingly cold and the pavements of Edinburgh were blanketed with a thin crust of snow. "The thing I love about Scotland, right," Josh said, "the thing I really love, is that if you're even just an inch shorter than someone, even just an inch, right, then you are required, *by Scottish law*, to call that person 'Big Man'. When I was last up this way, my time finally came. This little bloke, about five foot two, came up to me one night and said 'Awright, Big Man?' And I was tickled pink, I really was." Josh paused for a moment. "Really took the sting out of being mugged, I can tell you."

Anita laughed, but I could see from Steve's expression that this was a rather old joke. Josh had already bought us tickets to several Holocaust-related exhibits and events. That morning we saw an exhibition called "In Your Shoes, In My Shoes". School children from all around Edinburgh had drawn pictures of shoes to reflect the piles of personal effects left in the concentration camps. We got lunch in a pub after that.

While Anita was in the toilets I started to roll a smoke, but when Steve asked me for a light I realised I'd left my lighter at the hotel. We shared a forlorn moment before Josh returned to the table with his round.

"I've been thinking," he said as he sat down. "Anita really should go to the Washington memorial. She needs to see it. She can't say anything about memory until she's been to that museum, it's vital. When I was last there, one of the guides told me how he had shown a bunch of black kids around the place. After the tour, one of them said: 'Oh God, we thought we had it bad!'"

"How many people do you think died because of the slave

trade to the US?" Steve asked me, sipping at his pint.

"Toni Morrison dedicated *Beloved* to the 'Sixty Million and more' who died while being transported from Africa," I said.

"That's probably a symbolic figure," said Steve. "My money's on ten, twenty million over the course of a couple of centuries. Not quite in the same ballpark."

"Obviously." Josh grabbed my tobacco and started to roll a smoke. "We were targeted for extermination, weren't we? Nothing competes with that."

Steve and I looked at each other. "My father's Jewish," I said.

"My mother," said Steve.

"Yeah," said Josh after a moment. "Yeah, it was my father. Like that matters . . ."

Steve grinned and glanced down at his crotch. "Uncut," he said.

"This conversation is pointless," said Josh.

"Cut," I said. My mother had considered foreskins unsanitary. That was probably why she'd married my father.

Josh polished off his pint. "Do you guys have a light?" he asked. Steve and I shook our heads. The three of us sat round the table, each with an unlit cigarette between our fingers. "Then what the fuck are we doing here?"

That night I didn't have any dreams about the Holocaust, and I woke up at seven a little disappointed. I'd hoped to have at least a couple of nightmares after spending almost three weeks immersed in genocide. Josh and Anita dreamt about the Holocaust all the time, apparently. Anita had dreams about hiding, being chased and shot at. Josh's dreams were more specific; he was always naked and trapped in the gas chambers.

"In my dreams," Steve had said, "I'm always one of the guards." We didn't talk about dreams any more, after that.

I sat up in bed and turned on the television, keeping the volume down low so as not to wake Anita. The BBC was reporting on the latest martial foreplay in the Middle East. An American man was telling us that appeasement hadn't worked with Hitler and wouldn't work with Saddam Hussein. I switched over to CNN. The same man was on that channel too, telling us Europe should back a US strike on Iraq because of the sacrifices made by the American people for the sake of Europeans in the Second World War.

Next to me, Anita stirred in bed. She blinked her eyes, looking blearily at the television screen. "Then what are they doing asking Germany for help?" she said.

We went for a walk together around the central city before the others got up. The sky was still half-dark and it had started to snow again, lightly.

"Let's not go too far." Anita burrowed her hands into the pockets of her coat.

"This is nice," I said. "Just us together. No piles of corpses, no Stars of David, no glass-covered table-top recreations of the Auschwitz death camps, no . . ."

"Josh was still going on about the Washington memorial last night," said Anita. "I think it's almost a bit weird, don't you?"

I kicked at a pile of piss-coloured snow. We turned round and started to walk back the way we came. "Don't you think we need to be heading home soon?" I asked.

Anita shivered and quickened her pace. The snow was starting to fall more heavily.

"Anita, I need to find a job."

"I know."

"Could we change the tickets? Could we leave straight after the Memorial Day?"

"I can look into that." Anita stopped in the street. "Hey,"

she said and stretched up to kiss me on the side of the neck. "Thanks for coming along. It's been a lot of fun."

"You can't win," Steve told me, later that night. We had gone to a pub after dinner. Anita and Josh were at the town hall, attending the National Holocaust Day ceremony. I had already tried and failed to imagine what it might be like.

"Are you joking?" I said, rubbing more chalk onto my cue. "I'm sensing clearance here." True to my word, I knocked a maroon stripe into a corner pocket. The white bounced back to the centre of the table, all lined up for my next shot.

"That's not what I meant," Steve said. "Josh knows what she wants," he said.

"So?"

"What do you want, Daniel?"

I spent a couple of minutes getting the angles right but still managed to foul the yellow. Steve passed me my pint and I handed him the cue. "Right now I want to change my life," I said.

"I think Josh wants that too." Steve tapped his green spot over the corner pocket, blocking my orange. "It's a fairly standard desire among people with too much time on their hands."

I played my shot, then went up to the bar to get another couple of pints. "And what do you want?" I asked when I got back to the table.

Steve leaned back against the wall of the pub. He sipped at his pint. "What I want is to see a movie about the Holocaust where everyone dies. I want a movie where everyone who goes to the camps gets gassed or shot, or starves to death, or dies from diseases and infections. I don't want to see a single person still standing in the final reel as a symbol of hope or renewal or endurance." He put his glass down on a nearby table and picked up the pool cue again. "It can have one of those classic three-act structures. Act One: characters are established. Act Two: they all die. Act Three: they stay dead. No survivors."

"And what then?" I asked.

"Then?" Steve bent down over the table and effortlessly sank his green. "Then they can stop making their fucking movies about the Holocaust."

Later that night I woke up when Anita returned to our hotel room. She fumbled with the key in the lock for a while. I could hear her laughing to herself on the other side of the door. After a while she got it open and I sat up in bed.

"Shit," she said, seeing she had woken me. "Shit . . . sorry . . ."

"You're back late," I said.

"It's only twelve or so." Anita sat down heavily on the end of the bed and started to take off her boots. "I thought you and Steve might be out longer than this."

"Why'd you think that?"

"Just assumed it, I guess." She started to change out of her clothes. "You guys weren't at the hotel when Josh and I got back from the Memorial Day ceremony, so we thought you'd be having a big night. The ceremony was great, by the way. Really interesting in terms of the people there and the perspectives on —"

I switched the bedside light on. "Where were you?" I asked. "Where'd you go after the memorial thing?"

"A couple of bars," she said as she climbed into bed next to me. "Why? Don't tell me you were waiting up."

I grunted, and moved to switch the light off, but she stopped me. "Daniel, I've been talking to Josh."

"And?"

"And I'm starting to think that maybe it'd be a good idea to get more of an international perspective on Holocaust remembrance."

"Let me guess," I said. "You're off to Washington. To the Washington Holocaust Museum with its ongoing exhibition of Anne Frank's original writings and weekly lectures from the best experts in circulation. I assume Josh is going with you."

"Daniel, it's not like that. It isn't what you think."

"What is it then? If it's not what I think then tell me what it is."

"I don't think I can. But I'm not worried about Josh, I don't have to be. I can handle him."

"And how do you know that?"

Anita smiled wearily and turned off the light. I felt her stroke the side of my face and push up against me in the dark. "I've handled you, haven't I?" she said.

When I woke up the next morning, I quietly slipped out of bed to phone the station and book a seat on a train back to London. I turned on the television and watched CNN while I packed my bag. Once again I kept the sound down, but the plot was easy enough to follow. Ultimatum. War machine rumbles. Security Council in an uproar. American general makes inappropriate comparison to World War Two. Another ultimatum. American congressman makes inappropriate joke about the French. *Meanwhile back at the UN . . .*

I didn't realise that Anita was awake and watching me until I was almost packed.

"Daniel," she said as I zipped my backpack shut, "you don't have to be an arsehole."

"No one's being an arsehole," I said. "I'm being the exact opposite, I think."

It wasn't that easy to get away, of course. But in the end I still managed to get down the stairs, through the lobby and out the hotel doors. It was about seven in the morning; clear, crisp and very cold. I felt fine.

"Hey, Daniel!"

I turned to see Steve walking towards me from up the road. "Hey," I said. "You're up early."

"Couldn't sleep. Went out for cigarettes." He eyed my backpack. "I told you you couldn't win," he said, grinning.

"This isn't about Josh." I started to walk along the street, towards the bus stop. "Where is he, anyway?"

"Still asleep." Steve fell into step alongside me. "He was out pretty late last night."

"Right." I quickened my pace. We turned off down a side street. The city seemed unnaturally quiet and still. For a while the only sounds I could hear were our feet crunching on the pavement's thin carpet of snow.

"You shouldn't be mad with Anita," Steve said. "The Washington thing's a big opportunity for her. You shouldn't be mad with Josh either. Sometimes he doesn't quite know what he's doing. He just gets carried away."

I nodded.

Steve kept on talking. "I don't think he really understands how he affects other people sometimes. He has issues with empathy. And emotional distance. It's all due to a bad upbringing." Steve stopped me by grabbing my shoulder and pulling me back to face him. He was still smiling. "You see, in many ways Josh is a victim. And that means you can't hate him. Right, Big Man?"

I started to smile. Steve's smile widened and soon we were standing there in the middle of that empty street, grinning at each other like a pair of loons. Then I pulled back and punched him, quite hard. Steve dropped down onto the pavement. For a moment he was too shocked to move, but then he started to scrabble at the snow, trying to get back up. I took a step forward and he thought better of it.

"Why did you do that?" Steve looked up at me. Blood was slowly starting to dribble from his nose.

"Because Josh is still asleep," I said, but that wasn't true. Nothing was personal that morning. I had only struck Steve because he couldn't stop me. I was, after all, a big man.

Once I was back in London, I collected my things from Anita's flat before taking a bus out to Bristol. I stayed with my brother for five days and arranged a flight back to New Zealand. I had already emailed Logan Heckle and *welcme abrd, Daniel!!!* had been his response.

Nathan and his girlfriend drove me out to Heathrow and gave me a goodbye present as I was about to board my plane — a collection of Rilke's poems. I wasn't sure if that was a joke or not, Nathan's face was impassive. Once I was in the air, I flicked through the book, waiting for the inflight entertainment to start. "Archaic Torso of Apollo" had been bookmarked. The past is a deity in that poem, an ancient ruined god who still says the same thing that every god has ever said to us.

`You must change your life.`

It was time to get home. The past was the best place for history.

PART TWO

RAVINGTON

At the age of thirty-six, Lewis Ravington had come to the conclusion that he was not living a good life and was, in all probability, not a very good person. His job was ethically dubious, and as he was self-employed he could not blame anyone else. He had at various times been a bad friend, a bad son, a bad husband and a bad lover. He ate badly, slept badly and drank very badly. Rav, as his friends called him, could spend hours listing all the bad things about his life, breaking them down into sub-categories like bad things he did and things he was bad at. Bad things he had created and bad things beyond his control.

The way he went about getting laid was especially bad. Rav consoled himself with the fact that it didn't always work and he went home alone more often than not. In the scheme of things it was only a small bad thing, a tiny dark dot on the global chart of questionable behaviour. All that it involved was a cunning eye for an easy target and the slightest misrepresentation of his own person. The women certainly didn't get hurt, though quite a few might leave his bed disappointed on a variety of different levels.

When his brief, unsatisfactory marriage came to an end two years ago, Rav had found meeting single woman harder than he remembered. All his friends seemed to have settled into coupledom more successfully than he had, and all their friends were solid couples as well. No one knew of any attractive, available women around the city, or if they did they were reluctant to inflict Rav upon them. No one had parties any more, they were all too busy having kids or rewallpapering their houses. With his social networks exhausted, Rav was left to seek out alternative venues.

Fortunately Wellington was a city of varied cultural enterprise, one that could usually be relied upon for an open-mike poetry night or poetry slam competition every month or so, and those sorts of events had a way of attracting lonely women. Rav would go for the plainer, more awkward readers; they were less likely to be there with a large group of friends, and were often needy enough to take him at face value. Rav's job had helped him to perfect the look of earnest admiration that he assumed when he approached, saying how much he had enjoyed their writing, then muttering a stanza or two under his breath to show that he remembered it, then comparing her work to that of some well-established, easily recognisable poet, before stopping suddenly and laughing at his own enthusiasm in a self-deprecating way. It didn't work all the time, it didn't work half the time, but Rav still did surprisingly well. However bad Rav might be in the ethical and practical senses, he took pride in at least not being bad looking. With his spiky blond hair and lean features, he liked to think he vaguely resembled a young Sting. But there was also a fragile boyishness in his appearance and demeanour that could convince people he was genuine, even when he was being as false as a harlot's oath.

Once he had made a successful first impression Rav would try to slip his job into the conversation. Then he would take one of his printed business cards out of the top pocket of his jacket and put it down on the bar or table. *Tunnel Press* it read in gold lettering on an off-white base, with an address and phone and fax numbers printed below. And below that his name: *Lewis Ravington — Editor-in-Chief.* If Rav had picked his mark right they would listen as he described his publishing enterprise. *A boutique press* he would call it, *an unconventional press . . . moderate print runs of high-quality manuscripts . . .* Exclusive books. Poetry, fiction, philosophy, history, memoirs. A little bit of everything really. Carefully marketed to a small underground of elite readers. *Not very profitable*, he would admit with another rueful shrug, *but I'm not in it for the money.* After that, if all was going well, he would suggest they go up the road or across town to a smaller, quieter bar and discuss her interests and aspirations in greater detail (get her away from her friends, get her away from the other poets, *away* from the poets for Godsake . . .) and then perhaps to another bar and then back to his house in Seatoun where the evening would reach its culmination.

Everything Rav would say about Tunnel Press was more or less true. It was a real press, not at all made up, though in some financial years it might as well have been. It produced books, and good-looking books at that, but it didn't actually sell many, if any. It was true the books were marketed to a small underground of elite readers, but what Rav always neglected to mention was that the readers were usually the authors of said books. Tunnel was an unconventional, exclusive press, no lies there, but where conventional, inexclusive presses made their money from sales, Tunnel made its from the "author contributions", which in addition to covering printing, typesetting, design and miscellaneous costs, also covered Rav's salary under the heading "editorial consultations". Rav had started the press with a group of his friends just after university, with the aim of collectively producing books of poetry that would appeal to "the masses". The masses hadn't bought the books, the friends had trickled away, out of pocket, into real jobs, but Rav had stuck with Tunnel until he finally found a way of making it turn a profit. In any case, these aspects of the operation of Tunnel Press would not be touched upon while he was in the company of the girl in question. Or at least not until the next morning when, if Rav thought she seemed fiscally solid, he might be tempted to suggest a publishing contract.

The evening was just getting under way when Rav entered the bar. The MC, Gregory Gaut, saw Rav by the door as he was wrapping up his introduction. Gaut, a balding civil servant, considered himself to be the elder statesman of the fringe of Wellington's fringe, largely on account of the book of verse he had put out with Rav's press a few years earlier. He had fallen out with Rav since then and was now desktop-publishing his poems on his own. Annoyingly, he was also a staple figure at open poetry readings around the city and had noticed Rav's way of approaching the female readers. He scowled at Rav as he stepped down from the stage and cocked his finger at him in a you-get-the-hell-out-of-my-bar-*son* kind of way.

"Ravington," a woman said as he bought a drink at the bar. *Ra-ving-ton.* His name but long and drawn out and laced with weary contempt. She reached out and grabbed him by the corner of his jacket and pulled him round sharply, spilling half his double bourbon over his sleeve. "It's nice to see you, *Ra-ving-ton*," Grace Maher said. She was smiling. Rav knew from experience that was a bad sign.

Grace had been one of the Marxist poets who had helped establish Tunnel Press back in the day, but had abandoned Marxism quickly, and poetry even quicker, moving on to write reviews for papers and journals, then into a variety of low-paying jobs at professional presses. She had clawed and clawed and clawed, from one job to another, until at last she executed a successful *coup d'état* at a languishing art-workshop press and ensconced herself as editor. Grace was small, about five foot, and razor thin, with short hair. She was a professional. She was ruthless. She had culled the dead wood of lyrical poets and magic-realists from the press's backlist. Her fiction writers were lean and their prose was spare; never too young and never too old, they skirted the margins of success without ever being crude enough to be popular. Rav had no idea what she was doing at a poetry slam.

"Hello, Gracie," he said.

"How's business, Ra-ving-ton?"

"Business is fine," Ravington said. Behind him, on the stage, he could hear the evening's first reader launch into a poem. The reader was a man, however, and the poem was a humorous rhyming one with a political message, so he didn't turn around. "What are you doing here?" he asked Grace.

"I always try to keep my finger on the pulse," she said, stirring her drink with its plastic straw. "What about you, Ravington? Recruiting?"

"Not exactly."

"You're pathetic, Ravington."

"Shhh." Rav put a finger to his lips and gestured to the stage. "Poets."

Rav spotted his mark early in the evening, right in the first heat of the slam. A tired-looking blonde in her thirties, maybe his age or a little older. She had an accent, northern European maybe, and her first poem was all about loneliness and homesickness and her second poem was about losing love or finding love, frankly Rav's attention had been wandering, but she looked and sounded promising. By the time she had been knocked out of the slam in the third round, Rav had shaken free of Grace Maher's attention and had consumed at least two more drinks. He was in a good zone. Gregory Gaut was frowning at him again from the other side of the room and Rav flipped him off with a cocky smile and a flamboyant flick of his wrist. Childish perhaps, but he was unstoppable.

While she was buying a drink at the bar he slid up to her, his smile in third gear. "That was beautiful," he said, "what you were saying up there." He breathed in sharply as he said it, like he was sucking on a roach, and shifted his smile into fourth.

The woman looked at him blankly. "What?" she said.

"What you said. Your poem. It was beautiful. I just wanted to say it was beautiful."

She shook her head once, quickly. "What?" she said again.

On the stage behind them a younger girl, about nineteen or twenty, was reading something. Rav couldn't hear what she was saying, he was a little drunk and couldn't focus, but he was sure it was excellent. The girl on the stage was beautiful anyway. Dark hair curled around a face that one of Rav's long-time writers might have described as "luminous", a tanned stretch of lickable skin exposed between the hem of her T-shirt and the belt of her jeans. When she had walked up to the stage Rav had seen one of those boring Chinese character tattoos on the base of her spine, but he could forgive her that, he could forgive her anything. He would not approach her though. The younger ones were always with friends. They were always more confident. They still had time.

Rav turned back to his blonde poet at the bar. "Can I buy you a drink?" he said loudly. This time it seemed he was understood and she nodded once in a quick businesslike fashion Rav bought her a drink and another one for himself. On the second drink she gave him her name.

"Adja," Rav said, smiling, thinking that he might be in with a shot, thinking *what the hell sort of name is Adja?*

"Pleased to meet you, Adja."

"You liked my poem," Adja said.

"It was very striking, very moving."

Adja gave another of her curt nods. "You liked it. Okay." Her glass was empty again. Rav finished his own drink quickly and bought some more. He could see Grace Maher watching him from the other end of the bar.

"My name's Lewis," he said to Adja.

"Lewis. Okay."

"My friends call me Rav."

"Okay. Rav. Whatever."

The conversation was going strangely, Rav thought. Up close, outside the soft glow of the stage lights, Adja's face looked harder and a little worn, but Rav still couldn't tell how old she was.

"You know when I say I like your poems, I'm not just saying that, y'know. I mean, I know about poetry and . . ."

Adja stood up from the bar. "I'm going now," she said and pointed to a table on the other side of the room. "My friends . . ."

"You're here with friends? Right, of course you are. Nice meeting you. Good to talk."

Adja frowned at him. "Don't you want to come?"

"You want me to come with you?"

"Come, don't come. Whatever." Adja started to walk away. Her friends called out to her as she approached, and for the first time all evening Rav saw her smile. He turned back to finish his drink and met Grace Maher's eyes across the bar. What was the worst that could happen? He was going, he was gone.

By the time they had moved on to the third bar Rav realised he had misjudged Adja. She had been a little standoffish at first, but now she was laughing, now she laughed at everything he said. Her friends were great as well. Rav couldn't quite figure out who they were, he thought they were students perhaps, adult language students. He couldn't really understand what they were saying. But good people, good times. There were two guys and another girl or two girls and another guy or maybe more than that, he couldn't be sure, their faces all blurred into each other, but Rav thought everything was going well. They were passing round one of his business cards now and laughing at it. Rav laughed too. Sure, it was a joke. *Tunnel Press. Lewis Ravington. Editor-in-Chief.* Biggest joke in the world.

Rav got up to buy Adja another drink. He bought one for himself as well. He had lost track of how many he'd had. Adja didn't seem to need his act, she hadn't talked about her poems since he joined her and that was fine, she treated it all like a joke. When Rav sat down at the table again he realised that he had bought another round for the whole company. Rum and Coke, that's what they all seemed to be drinking. He made a couple of trips, back and forth from the bar, to pick up all the glasses. Adja smiled at him, but her friends at the table picked up their drinks without a glance in his direction. They were talking about something else now, maybe in another language — he couldn't understand what they were saying. The business card they had been passing around now lay forgotten in a sticky spill of liquor by the ashtray. Rav wanted to retrieve it, then saw that it was half-soaked through; the words *Lewis Ravington — Editor-in-Chief* were smeared into obscurity.

Rav looked around the table again. Adja was saying something but he couldn't make out what, so he just smiled and nodded, and when she laughed he laughed, easy as that. Was this the first round he'd bought or had there been others? He mumbled something to Adja, some sort of compliment, he thought, he wasn't too sure what he was saying right now. His mouth could sometimes run away on him. Whatever he said it must have been a success, because Adja threw her head back, she was laughing again, he could see down her throat. Her teeth were yellowish, smoke-stained. She was smoking a lot, Rav hadn't registered that she smoked before now. He was glad he kicked that habit a couple of years ago. One of the few good things he ever did.

They moved on to another bar, this one quiet, almost empty. It was dark; Rav couldn't see too well, he wasn't even sure if the place had windows. He had seen a sign with the bar's name on the way in. *Yukio's*. He'd never heard of it before. "It's a good place," Adja had said to him. "I have a friend here." They had lost her other friends somewhere else. Rav had heard them talking about a party and he and Adja had tried to follow them there, but they had got lost or sidetracked and wound up at Yukio's instead. Adja's friend was a short dark-haired girl working at the bar. She and Adja talked for a little while. More drinks. Rav took out his credit card again. Adja and the girl at the bar were laughing now, Rav suspected they might be laughing about him. That was fine, he could deal with that. He knew he was a joke and not even a very good one. Just a bad joke. Bad like everything about his life was bad.

He and Adja sat at a table down the back of the bar, in some sort of booth. He was talking now and Adja appeared to be listening, though she was losing interest, her smile seeming a little forced. Rav leaned back in his seat for a moment and ran his hands through his hair. He had always thought that if he ever started to go bald he would just shave all his hair off in one go, turn himself into one of those professional middle-aged skinheads he saw walking around the central city. But now he wasn't so sure. His scalp felt weird beneath his hands; strange bumps and lumps, grooves and crevices.

Rav rubbed his head again. Suddenly the shape of his skull seemed a much more pressing concern than Adja. He was not sure if she'd been talking all this while, or how long he had spent investigating the undiscovered country beyond his hairline, but now he remembered to look up and smile and nod. How was it they were still in a bar, anyway? What time was it — one, two, or three? How had he managed to stay out so long but failed to move Adja in the direction of his house? This was nonsense, nothing was making sense.

Rav was smiling and nodding at an empty space. Adja was gone. All that remained was a glass smeared with fingerprints and the smouldering stub of a cigarette in the ashtray. He could still hear her voice, like an echo or a memory; he had thought she was there when she was not. Rav looked across at her friend, the dark-haired bartender. She wasn't laughing, but Rav knew that he was still a joke, clawing fixatedly at his hair for God knows how long, then smiling and nodding at an empty space. Stupid. He got up and walked across to ask where Adja had gone, but the bartender looked away. She was not interested. He was not her problem. She wanted him to leave.

It was cold out on the street and the wind was whipping in from across the bay. Light drops of rain stung Rav's face. Ahead of him, on the street, he saw Adja. He hurried to catch up and fell into step alongside her. He said something and tried to take her arm, but she shrugged him off and walked on. He called after her, he was not sure what he said exactly, but his voice sounded shrill and plaintive in his ears and he instantly regretted saying anything. Adja turned back and shouted something, then walked quickly on round the corner, out of sight. She was gone.

Rav stood by himself on the pavement, not sure where to go or what to do. He was not even sure if the woman he had just accosted really was Adja, it may have been someone else entirely, he didn't get a good look at her face. In fact, Adja might have just emerged from the bathroom back in Yukio's and be looking for him at that moment. "He just left," her friend the bartender would be saying. "Stared into space for a while, rubbed his head, and left." Rav felt cold, lost and confused. The street around him was utterly empty, and he continued to stand still, thinking or trying to think, as the pavement darkened with flecks of rain, blown in from the sea by the Wellington wind.

Seven hours later, Lewis Ravington started to sober up. He had woken in his bed wearing his watch and one sock and with no idea how he had got home. He must have taken a cab, but he seemed to remember trying to walk it for a while, he was sure he had climbed over a wire fence at some point and that would explain the big rip on the arm of his leather jacket which lay crumpled up on the floor beside his bed. Apart from that though, he didn't remember anything. After he'd left Yukio's his night was a blank. It was probably best that way. Things were unlikely to have got any better. He looked at his watch. Eight o'clock. Still time to get to work at a half-reasonable hour. He had to proof-read the last half of a genealogy of a New Zealand high-country farming family and get started on the typesetting for *Sometime Electric Movements of Colour*, another poetry collection. Might as well get moving.

In his kitchen Rav made his coffee and looked out onto the stretch of rocky beachfront he could see from his window. A long grey sky expanded before him, signs of rain to come. Rav had inherited his Seatoun house from his grandmother and had lived there since the end of his marriage. It was a little weird living on his own, without a partner or flatmates, and sometimes in the evenings it felt like his world had shrunk down to him and his television, his bookshelves and his view of the sea. Rav wasn't lonely though. He sipped his coffee and contemplated the empty foreshore. No, he was doing just fine. Didn't score last night, but the hangover might just be survivable. The credit card bill might be a cause for concern but he was no longer worried about the bumps on his head.

And would he have been any happier this morning if Adja had been sitting at the kitchen table, looking older and more faded in the watery morning light? Would he have been happier offering toast with Marmite for breakfast and apologising for not having any milk for her coffee? Yes, he probably would have been happier. A lot happier.

The official location of Tunnel Press was a single office on the fifth floor of a building just off Lambton Quay. Pushing his way through the crowds of lawyers, financial advisers and government bureaucrats every morning made Rav feel like he was running a real business. He was young, dynamic, upwardly mobile. Self-employed, goal-focused, on the fast track to success. A motivated go-getter at the top of the corporate food chain. A straight-talking sharp-shooter who played by his own rules.

Rav stepped out of the lift into the hallway, and then through the door into his kingdom. Two desks on either side, topped by two elderly computers. A bookshelf overflowing with manuscripts and bound proofs, and a table below that for the excess material. Ms Yorke was already at her desk, hard at work, as she was when he got in every morning. There was a whiff of tobacco in the air, but Rav never saw Ms Yorke smoking. Ever since he had declared the office a smoke-free zone while he was quitting last year, Ms Yorke had always managed to put out her cigarette before Rav came in. It was quite remarkable really, considering his less-than-predictable working hours.

"Good morning, Lewis," Ms Yorke said. "You look terrible."

"Yeah."

"Poetry-slamming again?"

"Yeah."

"Any new contracts?"

"No." Rav sat down at his desk.

"Oh, Lewis," Ms Yorke said, "what terrible luck." Ms Yorke was a thin, sharp-featured woman with curled red-dyed hair, probably in her late fifties or even early sixties; Rav had never inquired about her age. She had been his drama teacher in high school and they had stayed in touch for a while after he graduated. Rav had considered a theatrical career for a while — sometimes it felt like he had considered every imaginable career at some point — and Ms Yorke had continued to be a reliable source of advice and encouragement while he continued to attend and participate in workshops, amateur theatre groups, experimental improvised productions intended to raise community awareness about whatever, and to audition for parts in professional stage plays and never, ever get any of them. He had been Ms Yorke's great hope for a while, and then her abiding failure.

So when he heard that she had been made redundant in the latest round of secondary education downsizing, Rav was moved by guilt and gratitude to offer her a part-time job at Tunnel Press three mornings a week. As it turned out, this was one of the few good decisions he had made in his business career. Ms Yorke really cared about Tunnel. She cared about the books they were publishing. The poetry, the novels, the family histories, the autobiographies, they were all important to her. Rav thought she was every bit as deluded as the authors, but he was happy to let her go above and beyond the work demanded by her salary. Ms Yorke would often come in four or even five mornings a week instead of the agreed-upon three, and happily waded through the drudge work that Rav couldn't be bothered with. People had to believe in something.

"I've emptied out the post-office box," Ms Yorke said after a while.

"Hmm?" Rav said. He had been sitting making faces at his computer screen, which he usually did for fifteen or twenty minutes every morning before turning it on.

"Fourteen new manuscripts, a good haul." Ms Yorke gestured to the pile on the table by the bookshelves.

Rav walked over and picked up the first on the pile, a thick, heavy, spiral-bound chunk of paper. The author's name was Martin Glass. Rav had never heard of him before, it wasn't one of his regulars. The title was unusual as well: *Body Disposal at Auschwitz — An Inquiry into the Mortality Rates and Crematory Procedures at the Auschwitz-Birkenau Camps*. The first ten pages were dry introductory text.

> The workings of the double-muffle coke-fired Topf furnaces used at Auschwitz for body disposal allowed for the burning of perhaps twenty corpses a day per oven. Each muffle can be considered an oven . . .

It was a history book. Not poetry, or a memoir of life in the civil service, or short stories by an angsty English major whining about how he can't get laid. The very novelty of this fact kept Rav reading for ten more pages. Then ten more. Lunchtime came and went, Ms Yorke went home. Rav kept on reading.

By the time he had finished, close to six, his morning hangover and the awful night before had faded to a distant memory. Lewis Ravington now had a plan. He wasn't sure if he had understood all he had read, but he had grasped enough to suspect that the bulky text on his desk was different from his usual stock and trade. Something might come of it. Lewis Ravington was a doer now. A thinker. A motivated go-getter.

He got up and searched through Ms Yorke's desk until he found the introductory letter that had come with the manuscript. Yes, there was a phone number. Straight-talking. Sharp-shooting. Dynamic. Rav returned to his desk and dialled the number. Fast track to success all right. He was as upwardly mobile as hell.

WASHINGTON

When Anita Clarkson was five her parents had taken her on a trip to New York. It had been the only time she had visited the United States, or any country outside Europe, and she couldn't remember much about it at all. The only thing that really stuck in her mind was the hotel. The large glass atrium over the reception area, the pool in the lobby filled with tropical fish, the neutral smell of the elevators, hallways and bedrooms. She loved the mints that appeared by magic on the freshly turned-down bed-sheets, the tiny individual plastic packets of butter and jam, the chocolate bars and Coke cans in the fridge which her parents had vetoed on the grounds of being too expensive. Every morning her father had taken her down to the hotel restaurant for breakfast and Anita had always had doughnuts. Two soft, hot American doughnuts coated in sugar and cinnamon. Nothing, now or then, could be more wonderful than doughnuts for breakfast in a hotel restaurant.

The best thing about travelling with Josh was his taste in

hotels. Anita climbed out of her double bed and opened the curtains. It was still dark outside, she had yet to get used to the time difference. She took a quick shower in the ensuite, then returned to the bedroom in a thick white fluffy bathrobe. A lot of people despised hotels, Anita knew that. They would go around looking for tiny out-of-the-way places with "character", not appreciating how refreshing characterless places could be at times. Of course the world had no shortage of other bland intermediate locations. Train stations, movie theatres and McDonald's restaurants. Airport waiting lounges and aeroplane cabins. But hotels were the best. The transitory comforts they offered were the safest and most consistent. Living through their neutral shades in mornings and evenings helped people prepare for the clashing colours of the days in between.

The hotel cafeteria was only just coming to life as Anita walked in. One customer sat by himself, by a window at the far end of the room, busily working his way through bacon, eggs, toast and French fries, a slice of pie on a separate plate. Some sort of businessman, Anita guessed. Up early for a morning meeting and making the most of his company's expense account.

She collected a plate, hot and fresh from a dishwasher, and made her way down the line of food cases, carefully examining each one. Muffins, waffles, pancakes, eggs scrambled and fried, eight different kinds of pie. Hash browns, French fries, white and brown bread toasted warm or extra crispy, gooey lumps of French toast smothered in sugar and cinnamon. All batch cooked and kept hot in the cases, waiting for the hotel guests. Anita selected two sugary doughnuts and slid her tray down towards the cashier, but then changed her mind and returned to snatch a third from the case. She helped herself to a cup of black coffee from the pot stewing at the end of the bench top. "Y'have a nice day, now," said the cashier as Anita paid.

Anita sat down at a table facing the travelling businessman.

She wanted to see out the window behind him, which looked onto the still-dark street below. The businessman glanced up at her a few times while he attacked his slice of pie and Anita had the sense of being drawn into a small private fantasy for a moment. Lonely man, disillusioned with work and life, meets pretty girl while staying in a hotel. Intimate, passionate, week-long affair ensues. Pretty girl reawakens lonely man's *joie de vivre*, and though he inevitably loses her, his life will move down a more meaningful path from then on. He'll write an opera maybe, adopt an orphan, run for Congress.

Anita ate her doughnuts and drank her coffee. Two doughnuts would have been sufficient for breakfast, but three was a total indulgence and left Anita with a glutted feeling that she had come to associate with complete bliss ever since her visit to New York as a five-year-old. An absorbing novel, an excellent film, a particularly fine orgasm, all these experiences left Anita with the same glutted feeling, as if she had just eaten too many doughnuts, all in one go, without regret. She licked her finger and ran it round the rim of her plate, scooping up the leftover sprinkles of sugar and cinnamon.

Anita heard the door to the cafeteria swing open behind her. "Morning!" Josh walked up to her table and crouched down to kiss her cheek. "Morning, love," he said again. His freshly grown stubble scraped against her skin. The lonely businessman abandoned his half-finished coffee and left the cafeteria, stiff-backed and quick-moving, looking neither left nor right.

"Did you have doughnuts again?" Josh looked disapprovingly at her empty, sugar-smeared plate. "It's kind of disrespectful. I mean, eating all this sugary crap for breakfast . . ."

"Sorry, but they weren't selling unleavened bread at the counter. Shouldn't we get going soon? You said there might be crowds."

"Oh, right. Yeah, I'll get my coat." Josh stood up from the table, looking a little disappointed. Something about him reminded Anita of the lonely businessman and his pie. Once Josh was gone Anita felt vaguely tempted to buy another doughnut, but decided not to. A too-many-doughnuts kind of feeling probably wouldn't be appropriate for the day.

Anita and Josh had been in the United States for almost a fortnight now. They had toured along the East Coast, visiting smaller memorials and museums, universities with departments of Jewish or Holocaust studies. Josh had been listless and subdued for much of this time; elements of their trip had not gone quite the way he had planned and he was quieter than he had been in the UK, almost sulky. The only time Anita ever got a sense of the old Josh had been when she had overheard one of his semi-regular phone calls to Steve. Then he was as loud and jocular and verbose as he had ever been.

Steve had come to see them off at the airport with his bandaged nose and even given Anita a hug before she and Josh boarded their flight. He had hugged Josh as well, one of those weird male-hugs-in-public, arms around each other but bodies still at least three careful inches apart, slapping each other's backs throughout the duration. Josh had feigned indifference when she asked him about Steve later. "He'll be all right," he had said. "He's got his own things to sort out." But still, they talked on the phone every forty-eight hours. Checking in, keeping in contact.

Josh had started to regain some of his old spirit as they got closer to Washington. He became happier, more talkative. He even suggested they should spend the night together again, which had surprised Anita a little.

Despite the early hour the Washington Holocaust Museum seemed to have no shortage of visitors. It felt right to show up on the steps of the museum just after dawn and approach its doors through the white mist of one's cold morning breath. Anita watched the other tourists as they wandered up to the steps in small groups to take photos, or just admire the museum's architecture — a disjointed, unsettling mix of glass and steel, brick and concrete, plunging away from each other in dips and curves, towers and elevated corridors. The big glass revolving doors at the entrance were dark and unmoving.

"Are you sure it's open?" Anita asked as they approached.

"Course. It's just quiet this time of morning. Fewer crowds."

The doors were locked. Anita consulted her guidebook. "This place only opens at ten, Josh," she said.

"The last time I was here it opened at 8:30."

"Maybe you've got it confused with some other museum," Anita said. "We could take a walk along the Mall, if you like."

Josh looked at her as if she were crazy. "We're not here to go sightseeing, Anita."

"The guidebook says there's a museum café round the corner that's open from about now. We could wait there."

"We'll just wait here," Josh said. "On the steps. In the cold. It just feels right, y'know?"

Anita's limbs felt stiff. She was bored. Josh pulled his thin jacket tight around his shoulders. He was wearing only a poloneck underneath, he wasn't dressed for the weather at all. Anita was grateful for her puffy winter coat, but the cold had a biting, tenacious quality. It burrowed down under every layer she wore, it was inescapable, no matter how tightly she huddled into herself. Josh lowered his head and folded his arms; he was muttering something, like a prayer or a curse.

Anita looked at him sideways. He was good-looking she thought, almost strikingly handsome at times, especially in profile. Probably better-looking than Daniel, in a thin, nervy sort of way. Poor Daniel. He hadn't understood anything in the end. Not about her, not about Josh. But that was all in the past.

"I'm going to take a walk," Anita said. She wandered off down 14th Street and turned onto Independence Avenue where she found a small cafeteria and bought herself a mug of soup — vegetable soup; it seemed suitably austere. She sat over her soup for an hour, flicking through the DC guide and the notebook she always carried with her, relishing the air-conditioned warmth. Josh was crazy, he would make himself sick. Anita felt excited to finally be in Washington, about to visit a museum she had been reading about for years. There was no way she could have turned down this opportunity, no way at all. She had read about the long tortuous process by which the Carter administration came to decide that a Holocaust monument and museum should be built in the Washington Mall, right in the heart of the capital. She had followed the deliberations of the museum council over the building's architecture, the layout of the permanent exhibition, the nature of the exhibits. Questions of horror, the definition of genocide, good taste, respect for the dead, Judaising or de-Judaising the Holocaust. The meaning of the word "Holocaust" itself and which of the crimes and atrocities of the Third Reich it could be applied to. Should Jewish and non-Jewish victims be remembered separately? Should other crimes against humanity be discussed? Gypsies, homosexuals, the mentally ill, Polish and Soviet citizens, where did they all fit? Daniel would not have understood any of this. He didn't have to. That was why she had left him. Or at least another part of the reason. She couldn't wait to get inside.

Back at the museum steps, fifteen minutes before the opening time, Anita rejoined Josh. He was shivering, shaking slightly, his head still bowed, frowning downwards with furious concentration. Anita touched his shoulder and he smiled at her shyly, clearly pleased with himself for having made it through the wait, having suffered through the cold without complaint. Anita remembered why she liked Josh, why she had liked him from the moment they first started travelling together. Every now and then a gentle, honest enthusiasm would reveal itself and Anita couldn't help but be touched by it. This was another thing Daniel couldn't have understood. Anita wondered why she was thinking so much about Daniel today. She returned Josh's smile. "Shall we go in?"

"Yeah," Josh said. "Yeah, I think I'm about ready."

The crowd of tourists had grown since the early hours of the morning and they had to queue for a while in the foyer of the museum. People talked in low voices, moved forward in precise, almost apologetic steps. When they reached the front she and Josh were issued with timed passes for the permanent exhibition. They were each given an ID booklet as well that contained the photograph and a brief biography of a Holocaust victim. Anita got Ilanya, a tailor's wife from Warsaw with two children. She caught a glimpse of Josh's ID, some sort of Polish academic or intellectual. Anita thought he might be disappointed at not getting a Jewish victim, but he just shoved the booklet into his pocket without interest and led her on quickly into the main hall of the building.

"This always gets me," Josh whispered. He had talked to her about this hall before; it had been something he had wanted her to see, very badly, since they first met in London. "They almost don't need the rest of the museum. This is enough. It's almost too much."

An enormous four-storey atrium served as the entrance hall to the museum; a vast, skewed, distorted space, rounded by red brick walls and penetrated with dark-grey steel structures: exposed girders, railings, supportive arches. The size of the hall and its emptiness made every footfall seem like an intrusion; a certain hush was demanded, a sense of dread, or at least awe, a slowness of pace, a deliberation of movement, a care for one's expression. Anita found herself walking the way she would in a cathedral when she hadn't come to pray on a Sunday but during the week to look at the etchings; a quiet respectful pace, with a desire to be small, to not be noticed. Josh wasn't talking any more. He walked alongside her, his head bowed slightly, as they followed a trail of tourists to the elevators that would take them up to the start of the permanent exhibition.

Anita looked back over her shoulder as they walked, back to a wide staircase that wound its way up to a brick gate on the second floor. The arch of gate was shaped to resemble that of a death camp, brick columns jutting out of the wall on either side of the opening like watchtowers. Above the gate was a sheer wall of black stone and Anita turned back on the threshold of the elevator to look up, past openings and balconies and stairways, to the small silver letters fastened into the wall near the summit of the atrium, below the glass-and-steel skylight. *You are my witnesses. Isaiah 43:10.*

A brief orientation video played on a viewscreen in the elevator as it took them up to the fourth floor. Anita pressed close to Josh in a corner; they shared the space with about thirteen other visitors. The elevator ascended slowly, timed to match the length of the video. Josh was starting to sweat a little. A thick, musty human smell rose from his body; in a way it was comforting, almost reassuring. She glanced at the viewscreen. Some details about the history of the museum. The opening day or inauguration day, whatever they called it. Elie Wiesel and President Clinton talking from their podiums. A few words about how the Holocaust must be remembered so that it can never be repeated. The visitors shifted round a little awkwardly. One child bumped himself against his mother's thigh repeatedly. The elevator reached its summit and stopped moving, bouncing slightly on its cables. There was a pause, perhaps for as long as a minute, though maybe only twenty or thirty seconds. An older man cleared his throat, a wet, organic noise. Then the doors slid open.

Josh remained quiet as they walked down the corridors, only occasionally pointing out some of the exhibits to which he felt Anita should pay particular attention. The first section dealt with pre-war Europe, the rise of the Nazi Party in Germany, the early discriminatory measures taken against German Jewish citizens. The walls of one massive three-storey tower were covered with over nine hundred photographs taken between 1890 and 1941 in Eishishok, a small Lithuanian town with a vibrant Jewish population. A placard at the room's entrance informed the visitor that the town's entire Jewish community had been massacred within two days by a mobile SS killing squad.

Anita flicked through her ID booklet as they descended from the fourth to the third floor, and got an update on Ilanya. After Poland was occupied by Germany she and her family were swiftly interned in the Warsaw Ghetto. Her younger daughter, just two years old, died four months later from influenza. Anita asked Josh if he wanted to check in on his alter ego, but he just shook his head and moved on to the next exhibit. Accounts of round-ups, deportations, killing squads, coded orders, "special treatment", railway timetables, a change in the function of some of the detention camps.

> Never shall I forget the faces of the little children, whose bodies I saw turned into wreaths of smoke beneath a silent blue sky. Never shall I forget those flames which consumed my faith forever. – Elie Wiesel.

The things I saw beggar description . . . The visual evidence and the verbal testimony of starvation, cruelty and bestiality . . . – General Dwight D. Eisenhower.

. . . our war aim does not lie in reaching certain lines but in the physical destruction of the enemy . . . Only thus shall we gain the living space which we need. Who, after all, speaks today of the annihilation of the Armenians? – Adolf Hitler.

Anita stopped and looked at a picture of a Jewish family being deported, a mother and four children in heavy coats, carrying bags and suitcases, moving quickly down a rubble-strewn street somewhere in Europe, figures in grey uniform out of focus in the background behind them. Another photo: a German killing squad lining up victims in the woods.

Photos were just photos, Anita thought. Some images stayed with you, others did not, but there was still a barrier there, another border that could not properly be crossed. Faces were just faces and though you could say that you knew they were the faces of people who had died, were about to die, were at that very moment in the process of dying, of being executed, murdered, slaughtered, something held you back from whatever it was you were supposed to feel, or what you thought you might be feeling, because you were not looking at a face, but at a two-dimensional image, a stand-in for the face of a person who was now no longer a person but a skeleton buried in an unmarked grave, or half-burned and then buried, or incinerated completely, mechanically, without ceremony, and the photo could not turn them back into what they were, they would never be people again. You can look at their eyes and think you can see fear or pain or anger or grief, but they are not really there to be seen and you are not looking at eyes, but at a flat, hard surface, a sheet of card, an opening with nothing on the other side, and those feelings are not yours to see. They existed for an instant and now they are gone. You are no witness.

Besides the photos and the words and films there were the physical exhibits, the relics. Tattered blue-and-white-striped uniforms from the camps were on display, as well as the brown uniform of an SA trooper and the white smock worn by a doctor who'd worked in Operation T4. One room contained a pile of kitchen implements, confiscated from Jewish prisoners — frying pans, knives and forks, tin bowls, rusting pots. A heap of worn leather shoes in another room, also confiscated upon internment. Elsewhere were collections of umbrellas and suitcases, prayer shawls and artificial limbs. Just like a face was a face, a shoe was a shoe. A pile of knives, of forks and spoons, pots and pans and rags. Everything people of that age could be expected to own was there, enclosed in glass, cordoned off behind museum barriers. Functional items on display, deprived of their functionality; tools and clothing, deemed too useful to be burned and destroyed, but which would now never be used again.

Josh touched Anita's shoulder as they passed a painting depicting bags of human hair, shorn from the heads of female inmates. "The museum owns the actual hair as well," he whispered. "They have it locked away somewhere. They were going to put it on display, but someone thought that would be too ghoulish, way too much."

"Do you think it would have been too much?" Anita asked.

Josh had to think for a moment. "I don't know," he said. "Yeah, maybe. A bit too much, maybe, yeah."

They were reaching the end of the exhibition now. Allied forces advanced on two fronts across Europe. Checking her ID booklet again, Anita found that Ilanya had survived to be liberated, though her husband and children had perished. She emigrated to the United States, settled in Philadelphia and eventually remarried. After some urging, Josh flicked to the end of his booklet and told her that his person, Joseph someone, had survived as well. The last few exhibits made an effort to be a little more upbeat, Anita thought. They told stories of Jewish resistance during the Nazi occupation, the struggles of the partisans, the Warsaw Ghetto uprising. There were also a number of displays about the "Righteous Gentiles" who had helped the Jews of their countries to escape. A few hundred here, a thousand somewhere else.

The last room in the permanent exhibition was a large empty amphitheatre with a viewscreen playing a movie on a continuous loop. A man was talking calmly to the camera; a woman, presumably his wife, was sitting next to him, only half in the shot.

He is divided in two, the man says. He is two people. He is a man who survived and left Europe and came to America and has a house and a wife and children and grandchildren, but he is also someone else. That person is still a prisoner, still beaten and starved, still standing on a platform and watching a young mother choose to go to her death with her children (or was that right? Maybe she chose to live, if only for a little longer, and left her children in the other crowd, the wrong crowd . . . No, his wife says, reaching out to touch his arm, that did not happen), still freezing in the barracks, still watching the dogs rip the flesh from the hands and face of his screaming bunkmate (that is enough, his wife says, no more for now, no more, please), still the same desperate person, the person who stole a ration of bread from his brother who was sick and weak and could not hold onto what was his. No, his wife says, you did not do that. You are wrong. He is confused, she says, looking at the camera.

Perhaps you could tell us a little about how you survived, says the hidden interviewer. Please tell us how it all ended.

The man shrugs. The Americans found us. His eyes glaze, his tone is perfunctory. I had a new life and it has been a good life, but what nobody understands is that the person who stole the bread still exists and there is no new life for him. But I am not sure if I should call him a person. How can a real person steal bread from their brother? He is just a thing that survives, there is nothing else he can do, he cannot die. That is why I will always be two things, the man says. A person and a survivor.

Thank you for telling us your story, says the interviewer. The man's wife stands up, ready to leave, but her husband remains in his seat, staring into the camera, deeply puzzled.

Have we really finished? I want to say more . . .

The walk through the permanent exhibition had occupied them for about two and a half hours. It was past twelve now, lunchtime, and Anita was almost light-headed with hunger. Something was wrong today, her appetite was stronger than normal. She looked at Josh as they walked out of the museum together. He seemed slightly flushed, his forehead was beaded with sweat.

"Are you feeling all right?" she asked.

"Fine." He sniffed. "No. I don't know. Not fine, probably."

They walked out of the museum, out through the entrance hall again, onto the steps. There were a few temporary exhibitions going on in side galleries that Anita wanted to investigate, but she needed a break and Josh said he could use a little fresh air.

"You see why you had to come here now?"

"Of course," Anita said. "It's been very interesting."

"It's not just interesting," Josh started to say. "It's more than that, and if you haven't understood that then maybe you need to see it again already, maybe we need to go back inside right now. Let's go, you need to see . . ."

"Josh," Anita said. "Josh, be quiet, please."

"What?"

"Just hush. Look." Anita pointed to the small plaza, down below the steps they were standing on. While they had been inside, walking through the permanent exhibition, looking at the photos, the rags, the shoes, the maps and documents, a small protest group had gathered outside the museum. It was made up of about forty or fifty people carrying signs and placards; well dressed and orderly for the most part, not chanting slogans or punching their fists in the air, just standing around quietly and talking amongst themselves. Most of the protestors seemed to be middle-aged or elderly, only a handful of younger people were scattered through their ranks. From the signs and photographs they were holding, Anita discerned that they were protesting in support of several young Israelis who had refused to join the military forces in the West Bank and Gaza Strip, conscientious objectors who had been prosecuted and imprisoned by the Israeli government. *Jews! Don't become Nazis!* read one sign. *Israel is a racist state!* read another.

Josh quietened down, his attention drawn to the small spectacle playing out below them. For a moment Anita thought he looked very calm, very solemn. "They shouldn't be here," he said, eventually. "This isn't the right place for this sort of thing."

"You don't agree with them?" Anita asked.

Josh looked back at the gateway to the museum. "You can't talk about that stuff here. It's too small to mention."

Some older protestors were already looking a little stiff; it was a cold day, and mugs and flasks of coffee were being passed around the crowd. Despite the absence of any real drama, a news crew had set up a camera on the bottom steps. Their reporter was standing nearby and Anita watched as she started to accost people walking down the steps from the museum, offering them her microphone, asking them for their thoughts on the protest. Most hurried away, but one woman in her thirties stopped and looked straight at the small, sedate crowd and the signs they were holding.

"Anti-Semites," she said into the microphone.

"But," the reporter was saying, and Anita could see she was smiling slightly, just a tremor around her lips, because this was the punchline coming up after all, this was the bit for the folks back home, "these people are all Jews."

The woman shook her head. "Anti-Semites," she said again, only louder.

The protestors heard her this time. A few people muttered to each other, some shook their heads and made clucking noises, but one man, probably in his sixties or seventies, broke free of the crowd and stormed over to confront the woman and the reporter.

"How dare you?" he shouted. He was shorter than the woman, only about five feet tall, with wispy silver hair. He was dressed in a suit and an old-fashioned Burberry overcoat. "We're Jews, all of us!"

"You are all anti-Semites," said the woman.

"Anti-Semites?" The man's eyes were wide. "You're calling us that?" He pushed the right sleeve of his overcoat up to his elbow and started to fumble with the buttons on the cuffs of his shirt. "What do you know?" he was saying. "Young lady, you don't know anything . . ."

"I know you hate Israel," the woman said.

"There!" the old man cried triumphantly, rolling his shirt-sleeve back to expose his forearm. "Look at that and tell me what you know."

"All over the world anti-Semites are trying to despoil our memories," the woman said into the reporter's microphone. She had turned from the old man but he danced around to follow her, pushing his forearm up into her face.

"Look," he insisted. "Look at what they did to us."

"Anti-Semites!" the woman shouted at the crowd. "Israel haters!"

"Just look at it," said the old man. "Look at my arm."

"I won't!" the woman screamed and twisted her head away, closing her eyes.

DANIEL

Sometimes when you come back from a long trip you find yourself gliding around on autopilot, unable to click back into the rhythms of regular life. It's a kind of fatigue that outlasts jetlag, a lingering sense of surrealism that suggests your home isn't a real place and that you can't possibly be back there. Nine years in the UK, then ten hours in a plane, twelve hours in Singapore, thirteen hours in another plane, two weeks back in Wellington, New Zealand. Sixteen days since I left Anita with Josh in Edinburgh. And two hours into my new job.

Logan Heckle had spent most of those two hours showing me around the office, half a floor of rooms up in one of the towers on The Terrace. They had a freshly rented smell, maintenance people were repainting the external doors, and the receptionist was arguing with tech-support over the set-up for her PC. Eclectic Incorporated felt like a company that had been established overnight and could vanish just as quickly. Heckle ended the tour by showing me a cubicle down the back of the large, loft-like main office.

"Now tell me, Daniel," he said, bending down to run his hands over the surface of the desk. "What do you think this is?"

"A desk," I replied, "inside a cubicle."

"No, Daniel," Heckle looked up at me. "This is your space." He put his hands on my shoulders and guided me down into my chair. "You need to make this space your own," he said into my ear. "I don't believe in depersonalisation. I don't want someone who comes in here and just works the clock. I want Daniel Legkov on my team. I want him right here. All of him." Heckle let go of my shoulders and stepped back. "I'm not sure if that last bit came out right," he said after a moment.

"Don't worry."

"Thanks, pal. Team meeting at two o'clock!" Then Heckle was gone, weaving in and out of the other cubicles to deliver brief shoulder-clapping messages to their as-yet-invisible inhabitants, before retreating back into his own office. I sat forward in my chair and ran my hands over the surface of the desk the way Heckle had done. "My space," I said. "My space, my space," and then I leaned back.

Any space in the world would do at that moment. I hadn't been able to find a flat since returning to Wellington and had spent the last two weeks sleeping on my father's couch, getting up in the night to furtively jerk off in his bathroom over memories of Anita. Everything felt more difficult now.

On my way back to New Zealand I'd had a stopover of about twelve hours in Singapore, all of which I'd spent in the airport terminal. At some point, while I was sitting by a plastic fountain and flicking through the book of Rilke's poems that had failed to last me the journey back to the southern hemisphere, I realised that I had crossed an international dateline and turned thirty slightly ahead of schedule. Singapore has a fine international terminal — lots of shops, some good restaurants, a movie theatre and even a swimming pool — but, when you got down to it, it was still just a big airport waiting lounge and a pretty lousy place to turn thirty in.

As I took an escalator up to the bar on the second storey a wave of misery swept over me and I forgot to watch my step at the top and staggered forward, bumping into an Indian man who apologised to me and walked away before I could insist that it was my fault. I was left standing stunned in the middle of a food court, commuters milling around me. I was thirty years old and all I had to show for it was about eight hundred New Zealand dollars and a collection of Rilke's poetry that I had never wanted in the first place.

I found a bar and bought myself a lager. It was tasteless and sat heavily in my stomach, but I bought another one after it. I decided I was not going to go back to New Zealand. There was nothing for me there. I was going to meet a new girl here, I thought. Bump into her by chance at the bar or in a corridor. We'd take a flight to some other place, somewhere fantastic, and we'd get our tickets upgraded to first class and we would fuck for the first time in the aeroplane toilets, but it wouldn't be cheap or tawdry or anything, because these are the first-class toilets we're talking about, and they'd probably have full-length marble spa baths and fountains, and statues of nymphs and satyrs frolicking.

Or, I thought, if that didn't happen I could stay in the waiting lounge instead, live there forever, become a beggar, a holy man. Travellers from all around the world would queue up between their flights to lay a small token from their duty-free shopping in my humble wooden food bowl. A bar of Toblerone chocolate here, a carton of cigarettes there, perhaps even a modest bottle of single-malt Scotch. And one day the cleaning staff would find me, curled up in a ball in front of the discounted Sony electronics store, cold to the touch.

When I eventually got up from the bar I felt slightly woozy. The call for my flight had sounded and I had just drunk four rather expensive handles of lager. I boarded my ten-hour flight and got up every thirty minutes to pee. In this fashion I returned to New Zealand.

I looked down at the desk and tried it again. "My space," I said, this time louder and more insistently. "My *space*."

"Yeah," said a voice from behind one of my cubicle walls, "it's your space. We get it." I heard my neighbour get out of his chair and the top of his head popped up over the side of my cubicle. All I could see was a tangle of long black hair. I watched it bob along the side of the cubicle, accompanied by a leathery creaking noise and the occasional metallic clink.

Then I saw a rather short man, maybe five or six years younger than myself, walk around the partition and stand in the opening of my space. Black jeans, black T-shirt, shoulder-length black hair, long, black leather trenchcoat. A tangle of silver wallet chains looped around his waist. He stood just outside my cubicle, looking in at me with bored, half-lidded eyes, not smiling, not saying anything.

"Hi," I said after a while. "I'm Daniel."

"Morbid," said my neighbour.

"Sorry?"

"My name," he said slowly, "is Morbid."

"So you work here?"

"Work here? I'm practically the reason this company exists." Morbid reached back into his own cubicle, pulled out a swivel chair and sat down, straddling it the wrong way round, resting his arms on the back, and leaned forward to look at me more closely. "What's your job?" he asked.

"Heckle brought me in to help work on the gameplay mechanics," I said. "I've done some scripting and design work in the past . . ." I had never worked full time on a computer game before, but while I worked at Deakman Games in London I had done some level design in their video-games division, which was how I'd met Heckle. Prior to that my specialty had been tabletop strategy and my last project in that division at Deakman had been a board game called *You Killed JFK*, where players took on the roles of the CIA, the KGB, the Mafia and the Cubans as they competed to assassinate President Kennedy and then frame everyone else for it. That project had folded, suspiciously, before it could get too far.

"Okay, right, whatever," Morbid said. He paused for a moment, clearly for dramatic effect, then leaned closer and said: "I'm the guy who designed the Eclectic AI."

"The what-and-the-what?'

"It's the reason this game is being made, the reason Logan Heckle has come all the way out to New Zealand to head up the project. It's big news. A breaking development."

"I see."

Morbid stood up. "Guess we'll talk about all this at the meeting," he said.

"Sure. Exciting times, Morbid."

Morbid grunted and wheeled his chair back round into his own cubicle.

I looked down at my desk. I could see I was doing pretty well for my first fortnight back in Wellington. A new job, friendly colleagues, a personalised workspace — life was good. I left my cubicle and walked over to one of the office windows. Eclectic Incorporated had got itself a fine view. Heckle liked a bright sunny workspace, slick furnishings, attractive business cards, a good eye-catching logo.

I hardly knew anyone in Wellington any more; leave a New Zealand city for nine years and contacts will dry up, connections will dissipate, almost everyone you know or care about will have left by the time you get back. I still thought about Karen Staunton sometimes and Martin Glass, the only two people from my past that I would have counted as good friends, for a little while at any rate. I hadn't heard from Karen since I first left New Zealand. As for Martin, I had discovered that I had no desire to speak to him again.

To my surprise I had seen him sitting in a Wellington café only a week after I had arrived back, nursing a cooling cup of coffee and absorbed in a book. I had walked right up to him, stood only a metre away from his table, just to make sure it really was him. He didn't notice me, he didn't look up and I almost said something, almost said his name, but then I changed my mind and walked away. The book he had been reading had a title like *Deadly Paperwork: German Bureaucracy and the European Holocaust*. It brought back a few memories of travelling with Anita and Josh and Steve, none of which were good. Sometimes I felt like I was being stalked by six million dead people.

Eclectic Incorporated represented the start of a bold new age in Antipodean game design, Heckle told us at the 2 p.m. meeting. It was his pleasure, his privilege to have assembled such an experienced team of programmers, graphic artists and designers, the very best New Zealand and Australia had to offer.

"We're doing the project down under because it's cheaper," Morbid whispered to me. "The game-publishers wouldn't want to cover the start-up costs in the US."

This was not completely surprising to hear considering Logan Heckle's long and chequered history in the game-design industry. At various times he had been fêted as one of the most brilliant minds in contemporary game design, at others he had been dismissed as a self-hyped fraud. He was everything that was right about the industry, and everything that was wrong. Working for him could be a boon or a curse, or a boon that became a curse, or a curse that became a boon. A job in one of

Logan Heckle's short-lived companies was a job on the cutting edge, and the cutting edge had never been a source of stable employment for anyone except him.

Heckle's association with gaming began when he was at college in the early eighties. He and his fellow computer geeks would spend long nights drinking industrial quantities of Dr Pepper while crafting basic shoot-em-up space battles and RPGs on the university mainframe. His big break came in 1985 when one of these (the cult classic *Shock Troops*, still available today on the Internet as freeware) was published by the early programming magazine *Cypher*.

Using the positive publicity from this, Heckle was able to find himself a job porting Commodore 64 games to the Apple IIe and then, as the market changed, porting Apple IIe games back to the Commodore 64, before he was picked up as a junior member of the design team at the now defunct Simulated Strategies, where he worked on classic computer wargames such as *Battle for Dagon Fell* and *Heroes of Llamsor*. In the early nineties, shortly after the release of the infamously gory *Doom* by id Software, Heckle and a band of programmers quit Simulated Strategies en masse to establish their own company, Multiverse Softworks, and quickly released one of the earliest and most innovative *Doom*-clone shoot-em-ups, *Bloodspire*.

"Sure," Heckle had said when I first asked him about this breakthrough, "the *Doom* guys came up with the thing where you shot someone with a rail gun until their body disintegrated into a red paste, but I came up with having a realistic skeleton underneath the red. Y'know how they always show the disintegrating vertebrae in shooting games now? That was all me, I started that."

Bloodspire proved to be an enormous success. Millions of copies were sold, Multiverse Softworks moved into a vast, glamorous office suite at the top of a Seattle skyscraper, and

Heckle found himself surrounded by legions of drooling fanboys, waiting for his follow-up game. He stated confidently that his next game, *Dawnstalker*, would break bold new ground in the field of interactive entertainment, offering its players a perfectly realised physics engine, breathtaking graphics, lifelike non-player characters and enemies, spouting blood and soaring entrails, shiny metallic guns, and bullet after bullet after bullet. An exhaustive marketing campaign kicked into gear almost immediately after the initial design work was begun. The first gameplay demo was unveiled at the E^3 gaming convention later that year to universal acclaim.

"I stood too proud," Heckle told me later. "I reached too high."

In the luxurious offices of Multiverse Softworks dissent was breaking out. The other designers were resentful of Heckle's hogging of the limelight. *He thinks he's some kind of f**king rock star*, one of his peers wrote in an Internet forum. *Well f**k that.* As the design work for *Dawnstalker* became more prolonged and expensive the Multiverse co-founders felt that other, equally important projects were being sidelined. Heckle had been taking a hands-off approach to the company, devoting his time to lingerie models and sportscars instead. The release date was postponed, then postponed again.

By the time the game was released, with major launch parties and advertising fanfare, the engine, graphics and design were laughably out of date, the frame rate jerked, and the unpatched bugs resulted in hourly crashes and freezes. Derided by critics, abandoned by fans, *Dawnstalker* was the joke of the gaming world, a bloated, shapeless miscarriage in the history of interactive entertainment.

Heckle desperately tried to convince the world that this was not the case, that *Dawnstalker*'s originality more than compensated for its faults. "The thing about the cutting edge," he said while taking part in a panel discussion at a gaming convention six months after the release of *Dawnstalker*, "is that it cuts both ways." Shortly after he said that he was shot three times in the chest with a nine-millimetre handgun, by a man dressed as Lara Croft who had been sitting in the front row. The cross-dressing assassin was tackled by security as he attempted to escape the hall and Heckle was rushed to hospital in a critical condition.

After a nerve-wracking forty-three hours and three operations, surgeons were able to stabilise him, but deprived of his leadership for a period of months, Multiverse Softworks underwent a final collapse. By the time he was released from hospital, Logan Heckle was unemployed and heavily in debt for medical bills. Needless to say, his days of lingerie models and penthouse office suites were over.

But despite the collapse of his company and reputation, Heckle's skills were still in demand. He drifted around the world for a while, swallowing his pride and taking jobs with a variety of minor-league European design companies, before trying to break back into the US scene. I had met him during this period, when he briefly did some consultancy work for my firm in London. Some of the games he'd worked on since *Dawnstalker* had been well received by the critics, but the triple platinum success of *Bloodspire* continued to elude him. Now here, in New Zealand, at Eclectic Incorporated, this was all about to change.

"The working title for the Eclectic project is *VirtuLife*," Heckle told us. "This game will turn the very concept of a computer game on its head. It will rock the foundations of the earth and shake the pillars of heaven."

The premise was that the player would take on the role of an individual inhabitant in a computer-generated city. They would explore the city from a first-person, three-dimensional perspective, interacting with its inhabitants who were all governed by their own, constantly evolving, artificially intelligent behaviour patterns. The player would live out a completely realistic life, guiding their avatar from childhood to old age to death. The massive variety of mundane and life-changing decisions available to the player would ensure that no two games of *VirtuLife* would ever be the same.

"This isn't going to be just your average shoot-em-up," Heckle told us. "It'll be intelligent, innovative. If we can get it into beta-testing before Christmas we'll have a sure-fire hit on our hands."

The revolutionary Eclectic graphic engine, coupled with the Eclectic AI, was going to make the gameplay superbly realistic. Once the engine was inputted with all the necessary data — the layout of the city, the seasons, the traffic, the routines of ordinary citizens — the game environment would continue to evolve organically without further input, but would also respond to the new adaptable data added by the player. "We want our players to feel like they're really in the city," said Heckle. "This means realistic traffic, people going to work and coming home, businesses opening and closing, trees growing, children playing in the park after school."

Heckle took a few questions from the team then. The cinematics designer was concerned about the slow frame rate on the Eclectic engine, but Heckle assured him the worst glitches could be smoothed out before they started the alpha tests. I raised my hand and asked exactly what level of realism we were trying to achieve.

"The most real," said Heckle.

"But would that really improve the gameplay?" I asked.

"Daniel," Heckle said, "the best games are all about escapism. And the more real the game is, the easier the escape."

RAVINGTON

Lewis Ravington had to take the bus into the city from Seatoun; he didn't have a car or even a driver's licence. When people asked him whether it was annoying to start each day with a half-hour bus ride, Rav would grin and say no, he enjoyed it, it gave him a little peace and quiet every morning, a chance to get his thoughts together, to sit back, admire the scenery, watch some people, it was all good.

He could get a little long-winded on the subject if he wasn't careful and would start rattling on about carbon monoxide, traffic congestion, civic planning, and obese children being dropped at the gates of their school by parents in four-wheel drives. He would bemoan the current climate of western decadence that had led to a culture of one-car-per-person, the streets and roads and highways clogged by lone commuters, all isolated in their self-contained steel carriages. Historic buildings were being bulldozed to make way for traffic bypasses; people were becoming more lazy, listless and selfish every day. Lewis Ravington would not be a party to this general decline. Lewis Ravington was doing his bit for the environment and the continued well-being of society. When he was on a bus, as far as Lewis Ravington was concerned, the moral high ground was officially *ocupado*.

In actual fact, Ravington had grown to hate relying on public transport. It had been all right for a while, kind of acceptable in his student days, and then in the bohemian unemployed years of his mid-twenties, but now, post-thirty, Rav felt the sting of failure more acutely while waiting at the bus stop in the morning than at any other time of day. Grown-ups didn't take the bus. Kids and pensioners took the bus; the unemployable and the mentally ill.

What sort of man fiddles around with timetables and route maps and scuttles down to the corner every morning and waits to be picked up, standing underneath a rusting metal sign or sitting on a cracked wooden bench? A real man leaves his house in the morning purposefully, determinedly; he opens his electric garage door and walks into his cool dark domain of tools and garbage bags, running his fingertips down the sleek, smooth bonnet of his automobile, before clicking off the alarm and opening the locks and sliding into his leather-upholstered seat. He cruises into work, sunlight flickering through his windows, traffic lights turning green as he approaches, the best easy-listening hits of the eighties playing on his radio. All this while Rav bumped and swerved his way into town, wedged between a schoolkid in a damp anorak and a senile grandfather who insisted on talking about his pet camel while referring to Rav as "Susan".

Ravington's ex-wife had once tried to teach him to drive, but their lessons had always ended first with shouting ("Clutch! Clutch! Remember your fucking clutch!"), and then with tears and recriminations, mostly from Ravington. Rav's garage was full of empty cardboard boxes and old newspapers.

He longed to be one of those guys who knew all about makes and models and fuel efficiency, who could spend entire weekends *tinkering under the bonnet*, who went out for long, lonely drives round the hills in the evenings *just to clear their heads*. The responsibility, the respectability, the stable, grounded regularity of car ownership seemed forever beyond his grasp.

More often than not the humiliating morning bus ride left Rav in a foul mood by the time he'd made it into the office of Tunnel Press, ducking through the crowds of more successful professionals on Lambton Quay, riding the lift in the company of dentists and accountants, then walking in to be taunted by the scent of Ms Yorke's last cigarette.

"Busy day today, Lewis," Ms Yorke said, as he sat down at his desk. "We absolutely need to start on the typesetting for Malcolm Gurney's high-country farming memoirs, can't wait any longer. Three new manuscripts just came in and you should really take a look at them — there's a utopian science fiction prose-poem that I thought was rather good — and Laura Temple wants to have a launch for *Sometime Electric Movements of Colour*, and Mr Glass has sent the proofs for his book back —"

"Glass's book?" Rav said, looking up. "Let me see those, will you?"

Ms Yorke lifted the heavy folder off her desk and passed it to Rav. "The second cheque from Mr Glass's Australian friend came through, by the way. I called Mike at the printers and he says he should be able to slot us in in the near future provided we're all ready."

"Good," said Rav, opening the folder and turning the pages. *Body Disposal at Auschwitz — An Inquiry into the Mortality Rates and Crematory Procedures at the Auschwitz-Birkenau Camps.*

Page proofs were always so exciting, he thought. The

memoirs, the novels, the poetry, the family genealogies, they all looked so good when they were properly formatted and paragraphed. Rav loved to turn the pages without reading the words, just admiring the look and shape of the sentences, the elegant section breaks, the tasteful choice of font. To be honest, these were the only times he ever had a sense of achievement or job satisfaction, apart from occasionally bedding an aspirant poet. He was holding onto something that looked all right, something that had potential.

He never felt that way when he saw the actual bound book. By then, of course, he had always collected his final cheque and the experience was deflatory; what he was holding was not so much a book as it was his own fraudulence given material form. But the page proofs were different. If Rav held them in just the right way and didn't look at them too closely, then he felt like something real.

Glass's book was longer than the fiction and poetry Rav usually published. Close to three hundred pages, not including the bibliography and footnotes. The printing costs would be higher, but Glass's financial backer in Australia seemed to be happy to pay for everything.

Rav hefted the pages and flicked through them again. Chunks of dry-looking text, photographs, diagrams, lists of figures, lengthy quotations from primary documents. Rav felt good. Unmistakably, unusually good. It wasn't just the page-proof factor, it was something else. *Body Disposal at Auschwitz* was a real book. There was merit, there was interest, there was controversy. This book would be noticed.

In Rav's lock-up halfway across town there were boxes of unsold books waiting for the remaindering furnace. Gregory Gaut's poetry collection *Love and Rhyme,* the first volumes of several never-to-be-completed science fiction and fantasy sagas, and about 300 copies of *A Journey Heartwards* — the biography of a deceased Motueka real-estate agent written by his dutiful eldest daughter. Their authors had gotten wise to Rav's game and had refused to buy up the "remaining unsold copies" themselves. Rav would sometimes go down there to sort out the next furnace-load and spend an hour or so wondering over his backlist. Had the world ever really needed to hear about the day-to-day existence of a loving, hard-working father and husband? Or about trade embargos on the planet Reptillion? Or Gregory Gaut's lonely middle-aged lusting?

```
Tsk, my eyes!
Look not here nor there,
Lest the visible panty-line,
you espy.
```

Shouldn't Ravington feel good now? He was publishing a real book, a book that was worthy of a little consideration and respect. It was about the Holocaust. Body disposal at Auschwitz. New facts, new findings, new figures. Potentially problematic, potentially controversial. The right book for a daring publisher on the cutting edge. Tunnel Press was working the way it should.

Ravington remembered his first meeting with Martin Glass. He hadn't sent out the usual acceptance form, but called him personally and asked if he could meet him for lunch. There was a bar/café/restaurant inside the Mobil-in-the-Park building that was Rav's favourite environment for wining and dining prospective authors. It was a lunchtime hang-out for city workers, and the surrounding sea of suits made the concept of a Tunnel Press book deal seem more serious and professional.

Rav had been a little surprised when Glass eventually showed up. He had been expecting someone older. Some balding, doddering professor type maybe, shuffling through the café with the dog end of a cigarette dangling from his nicotine-stained fingers. But instead Rav was confronted by a tall, slender man about his age with longish light-brown hair and glasses.

"Mr Ravington?"

"Rav, please, my friends all just call me Rav. Sit down, sit down."

Glass had joined Rav at the table, smiling shyly as he pulled out his chair.

"Your book, Martin," Rav said, "it's an incredible piece of work. What I wanted to tell you, the reason I asked you here, is that Tunnel Press would like to publish your book. We'd be honoured, in fact."

"Thank you," Glass said. "That's excellent news." Then he cocked his head to one side politely, waiting for Rav to continue.

Ravington was momentarily thrown by this response. At that very table, in that very same café, Rav had witnessed laughter, tears, explosions of joy, heartbreaking gratitude. "Right then," he said after a moment. "It's great to have you on board. Like I said, I thought your book was incredible. Are you a professional historian?"

"I was a student for a while in the UK," Glass said. "This book started off as a PhD thesis while I was studying with Marion Pryor." He paused as if that name should mean something. Rav nodded vigorously. "But I'm not a professional historian," Glass continued. "I left the university system, it wasn't for me. The book really started coming together while I was travelling in Europe, visiting the Auschwitz site and consulting archival material."

"Did you send your book anywhere else before Tunnel?" Rav asked. Not to Grace Maher, he hoped. He wasn't picking up another one of her rejections or cast-offs. Not this time. Not again.

"Tunnel Press was my first choice. I saw your advertisement in *New Zealand Books*. You know, *Authors! Publish your works*!"

Ravington was sizing Glass up now, he couldn't help it. He was well dressed, sporting an expensive-looking brown moleskin jacket, but then he had been a student and travelled in Europe for a while, so he was probably out of pocket. Rav had been hoping for an older guy. Some eccentric old pensioner with bundles of cash hidden under the floorboards, willing to commit everything he had to ensuring that *Body Disposal at Auschwitz* would see the light of day. Rav hated himself for thinking this way, it was loathsome, parasitic. He wished he didn't have to raise the next question.

"Now, because Tunnel Press is committed to publishing challenging non-commercial works," Rav began, "we do require a certain level of author investment. You should think about this carefully, but to be frank I wouldn't worry too much. It's money you can make back on royalties."

"That's fine," Glass said.

Another unusual reaction. The matter of author investment usually had to be approached delicately. Again at that very table, in that very same café, Rav had witnessed anger, disappointment, raised voices and additional tears. This was usually the point where he had to rev his speech up into its fastest and smoothest gear, pull out anecdotes about the great works of the past that had been first published out of the pockets of their authors, explain the need for sharing the risks of publication, restate his confidence in the book on the table.

"I mean," Glass was saying, "I don't really have the money myself . . ."

Not good, thought Rav.

". . . but I have a colleague in Australia who's prepared to invest in *Body Disposal*. He's sort of a non-professional historian too, but he knows a few things about publishing and is willing to help me out. His name's Nigel Wilton." Again, Glass paused as if the name should have some significance.

"Well, I'll need to sort out a separate contract with him, but that won't be a problem." Rav had worked out these sorts of arrangements before, cutting an outside party into the book deal. Uncles, aunts, parents, grandparents, long-suffering husbands and wives, boyfriends and girlfriends, it didn't make any difference. "Martin," Rav said, offering the young, non-professional historian his hand, "allow me to welcome you to the Tunnel Press family."

He hadn't seen Glass again after that meeting, though they had corresponded, swapping signed contracts in the post, and emails regarding the book's format. The royalties broke down to the straight fifty–fifty deal Rav offered all his authors. *Just like the deal Tolkien had with Allen and Unwin*, he would tell them. Of course there was also Nigel Wilton, Glass's Australian friend, who had to be cut in as well. Rav had swapped a few emails with him and sent out another set of contracts.

Dear Mr Ravington, (Wilton had written in his first email)

> Truly Tunnel Press deserves its reputation for courage in the pursuit of general excellence. I am delighted that you have accepted the work of my friend and colleague Martin Glass. It is a bold, uncompromising study, and I would have published it myself, if my current difficulties had not made such a course of action inadvisable.

Ravington had doubts about Wilton. He had looked into his background and not liked everything that he had found. A highly publicised Melbourne court case, links to unpleasant-sounding groups. But still, a cheque was a cheque, and Rav had written back: *Cheers, Nigel, you're very welcome.* Wilton's first cheque went entirely on "editorial expenses" — i.e. rent on the Tunnel Press office space, Ms Yorke's salary, a fair bit of running-around money for Rav. The second cheque, which had just come through, would be used to print the agreed first run of one thousand copies. And if there was a little money left over for more "editorial expenses" at the end of the day, then that was all to the good. The third cheque (which was apparently in the post, last he had heard from Nigel Wilton) had taken some negotiation. This was one for promotional expenses; Rav had agreed to exploit his meagre network of contacts in the book world to ensure that *Body Disposal at Auschwitz* would be stocked in a few decent bookstores. Perhaps this time it would actually be possible. This book would not fester away inside Ravington's lock-up, it couldn't. Controversy leads to debate which leads to sales. It was an easy calculation to make. The involvement of Nigel Wilton was perhaps a little distasteful, but unavoidable and in the end a small price to pay for a book that would be noticed, mentioned, demanded, critiqued. It might not be much to show for ten years spent in publishing, but at least it would be something.

"All right," Rav said, looking up from the proofs on his desk and grinning at Ms Yorke on the other side of the room. "I think we're about ready to go to print."

FROM SHOAH TO REBIRTH

"How long is this going to take?"

"Not long. A couple of hours maybe. You can wait that long, can't you?"

Anita and Steve walked down the Avenue of the Righteous Among the Nations, between the carob trees planted to honour the Gentiles who had risked their lives to help save Jews under Nazi occupation. The end of the walk was marked by a small rickety row-boat, standing on display. It had been used by Danish fishermen to help deliver six hundred Jews from the shores of Nazi-occupied Denmark. From there the path led them up a flight of steps to the Warsaw Ghetto Square.

"I'm surprised Josh didn't want to see this with you," Steve said.

"I don't pretend to understand what he's up to. Besides, he's seen Yad Vashem before and it's not one of his favourites." Anita paused for a moment beside the reproduction of Rapoport's ghetto uprising monument, the stone soldiers looming above them. "He favours the Washington museum above all others."

They moved inside, into the lobby of the historical museum, where a massive, four-panelled wall sculpture confronted them. *M'shoah l'tkumah*. From Shoah to Rebirth. In the first panel distorted aluminium figures were set against a black background. The smoking chimney of a factory, two menorah overturned, a dead fish floating on its side. The figure in the second panel clasped a spear in one hand and a ladder in the other. A boat in the third panel carried a lion who set his paws on the ground. In the fourth, the overturned candlesticks had been righted and they burned brightly.

Steve had arrived in the city that morning on the bus from Tel Aviv. Josh had sent him an email from the States last week, saying that he and Anita were extending their tour and travelling on to Jerusalem. Steve could come and join them there, Josh had written, if he wanted to, if he had nothing else going on. Steve had no particular desire to visit Israel, but his circumstances in London were strained and he was eager to join up with Josh again, even if Anita had to be around as well. His taxi driver from the bus station had asked half-jokingly what in God's name had possessed him to visit Jerusalem now.

"I'm here to see a friend," Steve had said.

"Your friend is Israeli?"

"A tourist," Steve said.

"Ah," said the driver. "A British Jew, like you. I knew it. I can always tell a British Jew. What's the matter with your friend? Caught Jerusalem Syndrome?"

"What's Jerusalem Syndrome?"

"People get it their first night in Jerusalem. They get to their hotel, see the sheets on their bed and bang! It hits them."

"What hits them?"

The driver twisted round in his seat and grinned at Steve. "They think they're the Messiah," he said. "They go into their room, sane as anything, then half an hour later they come out wearing their bed-sheets like a robe, a toga, and promising to bring peace to the world or fight a war against the devil or something. Crazy talk. Only ever happens with tourists. There are clinics full of them."

Steve had not been happy when he arrived at the hotel. Josh had checked him in on the budget accommodation floor. His room was a grimy cubicle that overlooked the fire escape and a small square of alleyway; the noise of a dehumidifier droned in the background. Josh was nowhere to be found, but Steve had caught Anita by chance, breezing through the foyer on her way out into the city. She had no idea where Josh was, he was usually out at that time of the day. He would be back in the evening. Steve was welcome to join her if he wanted.

And that was how Steve had wound up following Anita to a bus stop outside the Jaffa Gate and sitting silently next to her while she wrote in her notebook as they rode through East Jerusalem and up past Mount Herzel on the road to Yad Vashem, Israel's national Holocaust museum, occasional bumps jostling them against each other, causing their knees to touch or their shoulders to connect. Another Holocaust museum. It was all Steve needed. He had waited for Anita to tell him about Josh, but now his patience was wearing thin.

"Anita," he said, catching her by her arm before she could move deeper into the museum, "what's going on with Josh? Where is he?"

"I'm not sure how best to put it." She frowned and contemplatively cocked her head to one side, her lips parted slightly as she pondered what to say next.

Steve's feelings towards Anita slipped down a notch, from disdain to dislike. Josh's behaviour was a puzzle to her, a thorny problem, it was difficult to explain. But she could be confident in the knowledge that she was not the one who had to unravel it. She could leave tomorrow, and Steve would have to stay.

Whatever was going on he would have to fix it, like he had always done, ever since he and Josh had been at school together.

"Well," Anita said eventually, "Josh has started donating sperm."

"What?"

"That's why I can't take you to him. He could be in any number of clinics."

"Why is he donating sperm? Why here?"

"I'm not entirely sure. He says it has something to do with him being Half-Jewish," Anita said, "but I don't know really."

"What do you mean, Half-Jewish?" Josh had never admitted to that before unless pushed. He had always been just Jewish, plain and simple. Steve could be Jewish as well sometimes, when it suited Josh.

"Come on," Anita said, and this time she took his arm, pulling him towards the entrance of the historical exhibition. "Let's keep moving."

"But I don't understand —"

"Come on!"

Steve followed her. There was nothing else he could do.

Anita hoped the man hadn't seen her. She hoped he wouldn't talk to her, not here. It would be too much in this place, she could not bear it. She had glanced at him twice while talking to Steve, making sure it was the same person. A tall wiry man in his mid-to-late sixties holding the hand of a little boy, maybe eight or nine years old, standing together near the doors, looking up at *M'shoah l'tkumah*. A baseball cap covered his graying hair and sunglasses hid his eyes. She hurried Steve on, further into the museum. Lippman. Mr Lippman. That was what Josh had called him. She could not talk to that man here.

She had met him while she was trying to find out what

Josh was doing and why he was doing it. She'd felt responsible for Josh by then, enough to at least make a single guilty attempt to check his behaviour. Anita had followed Josh to one of his clinics and found him talking to Lippman as they both loitered in the waiting room, while awkward, quiet young men were led in and out of cubicles. Perhaps Lippman worked there, perhaps he was a donor himself, though he seemed too old for that.

Josh had been delighted to see her and waved her over to join them, while the young men in the room coughed and looked away or grinned at her nervously. It was so good that she was there, Josh had just been talking about her. Mr Lippman's father had been in Treblinka. Josh was sure Lippman and Anita would have a lot to talk about, they would have many insights to share.

From Anita's point of view things had deteriorated from there. She had avoided talking with survivors over the course of her study and that aversion extended to their families as well. She didn't want to talk to them or their children or their grandchildren — she was not investigating the experience itself but the representation of that experience; how it was presented, muted, accentuated, diluted, exploited. Encounters with survivors and their families were unnecessary, potentially even harmful.

Yet in the back of her mind she sometimes suspected that she just disliked rubbing up against a first-hand experience of any kind. She was afraid of her understandings being dwarfed by recollections, afraid that she would be forced to dismiss her own contentions as insufficient and incomplete — or worse, childlike. Meeting Lippman once was bad enough, but what horrible luck to come across him here, in Yad Vashem of all places. She hoped he had not seen her. She hoped she could avoid him.

The first two sections of the historical exhibition were nothing new for Steve. He had travelled with Josh after all, for a long time, on many occasions. Gutted shops on the day after *Kristallnacht*, a Jew having his beard cut off by laughing Germans, these images surging into photo displays of mounds of tangled bodies, shootings, graves, medical experiments. Somehow, though, it all reminded him of a dream he'd had on his flight out from Heathrow, the red-eye to Tel Aviv. It had been about zombies, about the living dead. A strangely vivid dream to have while twisted half-sideways in his seat, drooling onto his collar. The dead rising up to devour the living, civilisation collapsing, hordes of corpses lurching through the ruins of cities. Josh loved that kind of horror stuff; along with Holocaust movies he enjoyed watching anything even vaguely apocalyptic.

In Steve's dream the dead had woken up again, but they weren't rotting, not yet, and you couldn't tell them from the living and they were hiding out amongst us. You could only tell if a person was alive or dead when you got right up close to them, close enough to touch if they were alive, or close enough for them to grab and eat you if they were dead. At first, everyone in the world was wary, keeping their distance — the dead did not want to be found out and the living did not want to be eaten. Then the balance slowly started to shift, the dead ate more and more and suddenly they were no longer afraid and started to revel in their connection to each other, hugging and fondling at every opportunity, and it was only the handful of living people left who were still afraid of getting too close. The dead wandered through art galleries, borrowed books from libraries, taught courses at universities and held dinner parties in their apartments. Steve accepted an invitation and met a girl there he thought might also be alive, but when he got close to her he found out she was dead after all and she bit him and soon Steve was being chased through the apartment building by its dead residents. He escaped through a window, out into the city, and everyone was after him, everyone was chasing him, but then things switched around and Steve realised that he was dead after all. A pale, cold, slack-jawed, lurching corpse hunted by perfect smooth-skinned living people. He woke up just as his plane started its descent, with a sense that the world had changed utterly and it hadn't made any difference.

Anita also found herself less than engrossed by the photography and exhibits. Her mind was wandering, she occasionally caught herself ducking her head to catch a glimpse of her reflection in the glass casings of photographs, checking her hair and teeth before registering the black-and-white horror. Perhaps she was reaching saturation point after all the museums she had seen. She would need to head for home soon, to get back to her writing and the book that was taking shape inside her heard.

Anita transferred her drifting attention from the exhibits to the other visitors in the museum. There were a few tourists, like her, but also schoolchildren with their teachers, groups of young Defence Force soldiers on national service, and a troop of Pentecostal pastors from the States all wearing badges with *Hi my name is X . . .* The tourists, the visitors and the pastors all moved with that slow, thoughtful, slightly trepid gait which Anita had seen in other museums, but the Israelis, particularly the khaki-clad soldiers, seemed to have a slightly quicker, more confident step. It was not as if they were louder or less respectful, just that everything they saw seemed to belong to them. Their history, their stories, their suffering. Where were the uncertainty, the sense of intrusion, the hesitance, the whispers? Where were the witnesses? Israelis do not bear witness. They are part of this history, they are the end result.

There had been a turning point in each of the exhibitions

Anita had previously seen, a point where the horror is exhausted, a point where another photo of corpses or emaciated prisoners or the testimony of gassings or shootings or starvation could only numb the visitor. The story then inevitably turned to the liberation of the camps, the salvation of the few that remained. Yad Vashem, however, had a different turning point. The Warsaw Ghetto revolt, the partisan bands in the woods — Jewish men and women, boys and girls, posing grimly with carbines and hand grenades, not led to their death like sheep but fighting, struggling, shedding blood, enduring, winning. From there the exhibition led to photos of survivors coming ashore at Haifa and Caesarea.

Anita looked back over her shoulder and saw Lippman not too far behind. He was holding the boy up to examine a picture of the Warsaw Ghetto gates more closely. She remembered the way he had smiled and raised a single hairy eyebrow when Josh told him she was a Holocaust researcher, an expert. *Really?* he had said, his deep, thick, throaty voice oozing with cynicism. What was he doing here? Why did he have to be here?

Anita hurried Steve through the final room of the exhibition, the Hall of Names. "What's the rush?" he started to say. "I thought you wanted to see . . ." But by then they had passed the Baal Shem Tov's gilded words — *Forgetting lengthens the period of exile! In remembrance lies the secret of deliverance* — and were outside, stepping into blinding bright light, ascending the steps up to the Hall of Remembrance Plaza, backed by the Jerusalem hills that were now spotted with new neighbourhoods of shiny white houses. Steve took in the view, feeling hot, harried and irritable. Josh was out there somewhere, in the city or just beyond it, donating sperm.

Steve felt like he'd been here before, the situation felt familiar. He had to find Josh, to drag him back from the edge of his latest madness. It was expected, it was what he had always done. Steve wondered how many other people in the city that day had a similar mission. How many relatives, how many spouses, how many friends came to Jerusalem every year to find someone who had gone mad — who had caught the "Jerusalem Syndrome" the cab driver had been talking about, or had just found some sort of meaning in the city and were now, despite all claim of logic, duty and sanity, determined to hold onto it? Josh wouldn't be the first person driven mad by Jerusalem, Steve thought. Not by a long margin.

"Why is Josh donating sperm?" he asked Anita again as they walked down another path, away from the square. "What's the point of it?"

"You'll have to ask him tonight. We're all having dinner. But he seems to think that it furthers the cause of Half-Jewishness in some way."

"What cause? There's no such thing as Half-Jewishness," said Steve.

"Josh seems to think there is now. And I kind of think Daniel did too in a way . . ."

Daniel, Steve thought. *Poor old abandoned Daniel.* Then he thought *poor old Steve*, instead. His nose hadn't healed properly yet. It still ached in cold weather and sometimes whistled slightly when he breathed through it. He hadn't seen that blow coming, hadn't expected it. Daniel had not seemed like the violent type.

"I've tried to keep an eye on Josh while we've been in the city," Anita continued, "but it isn't easy. He's not really interested in me any more. He's got something else on his mind."

Steve smirked but didn't say anything. Had it really come as a surprise to her? He had been abandoned by Josh himself, not just in Edinburgh but times before that as well. He knew what it was like to be carried along on that wave of enthusiasm, then dropped suddenly and unceremoniously as Josh spun around to chase after some new obsession. He felt no sympathy for Anita. She'd had a good ride.

They walked into the centre of the complex, through more squares and plazas, past the children's memorial, the Jewish soldiers' monument. At the heart of Yad Vashem, framed between two walls of black concrete, rose a tall, three-sided, stainless-steel pillar. Near its base was an inscription in Hebrew. Anita had the translation in her guidebook.

> Now and forever in memory of those who rebelled in the camps and the ghettos, who fought in the woods, in the underground and with the Allied forces, of those who braved their way to Eretz Israel and those who died sanctifying the name of God.

"Miss Clarkson."

Anita turned to see Lippman and the boy were standing behind them. She knew he had seen her right back at the start of the exhibition. He had followed her, dogged her steps, and caught up with her at last.

"I thought it might be you," he said, smiling. "We met the other day in Morasha. Your friend Joshua introduced us."

Lippman stepped forward, leading the boy by the hand to stand with them at the base of the pillar. "I am Lippman," he said to Steve. "And this is my son Mordecai."

"Yes," Steve said. "I'm Steve." He offered his hand. "I'm here to see Josh."

"You are a friend of his?" Lippman gave Steve a brief, dry-palmed handshake. "It has been interesting getting to know him. He may turn out to be the father of my first grandchild after all. Though it is all a matter of chance, they say."

"Do you have a daughter who is a patient?" Anita asked.

"I'm sorry, Josh didn't tell me . . ."

"We got distracted talking about other things, I recall. Talking to you, talking about your 'research', I thought it would be good to bring Mordecai here today, while we are in the city. He is probably old enough to see this now."

Lippman craned his head back, looking up at the monument above them. "The Pillar of Heroism," he said, and placed a gentle hand on the head of his silent son. "Do you know what my son asked me when he first saw this from the Warsaw Ghetto Plaza?" he asked, turning back to Steve and Anita, raising an eyebrow, inviting them to share whatever joke was coming. "He asked me if this was supposed to be a chimney. A chimney like the ones in Birkenau or Belsen. I had to explain to him that this wasn't for the Jews who had died, that this pillar is for the Jews who fought." He waved an arm, gesturing to the rest of Yad Vashem. "We have other things for the Jews who were murdered in the camps. The rest of the world remembers them as well — the museums in Washington, London and Berlin are there to remember all the dead Jews."

Lippman patted his son on the back and muttered a few words in Hebrew. The boy nodded and walked around to climb on the rocks behind the pillar. Lippman pulled a packet of cigarettes from his pocket and offered one to Steve before lighting up. "They are closing some parts of Yad Vashem now," he said. "There must be renovations, there must be changes. They are worried about the museum in Washington — people like your friend Joshua seem to think it is better. That will not do, the best museum cannot be in America. We must have it here, apparently."

Lippman looked up at the pillar again, his cigarette dangling forgotten in his fingers. "Perhaps we should have built a chimney there," he said. "A giant chimney reaching up to the heavens, like my boy thought he saw. The rest of the world would have liked that more, maybe. Yes, a chimney instead of a pillar and the world would be happier with us, I think."

"We have to go now," Anita said. "We have to get back to the hotel."

"Of course. Your friend Joshua has invited me to join him for a drink this evening. I hope I will see you again, Miss Clarkson. I would love to talk more about this research you like to do."

Anita nodded at Lippman and took a few steps back before she turned and walked away, towards one of the paths which wound away from the Pillar of Heroism.

"I hope they do not try to turn Yad Vashem into another Washington," Lippman said as she left. He looked at Steve, smiling slightly. "That would not do for me, I think. It would not make me proud." Lippman nodded once, sharply, dismissively, then walked away himself, round to the rocks and grass, joining his son who was playing on the other side of the pillar.

MARTIN GLASS

Martin is at home when the package arrives. He does not have a job at the moment. He reads, he watches television, he takes the occasional walk around the neighbourhood, he waits. Nigel Wilton sends him some cash every now and then, enough to keep him going. Martin lives in a one-bedroom flat up in Highbury. He has a view of the city when he opens his front door, all the way down to the bay, past the towers of The Terrace and grey Te Aro. The outside air is crisp and cold, with a touch of smoke; it is good to be back in Wellington again.

The package he has been waiting for is too big to fit in the mailbox and the postman has left it on Martin's top step, not quite all the way under the guttering. One of its corners is damp from the brief burst of rain that morning. Martin sees the return address as he picks it up, marked clearly on the back in black Vivid: *Lewis Ravington, Editor-in-Chief, Tunnel Press*. He takes the package inside and leaves it on the kitchen table, then rummages through his drawers, looking for a knife sharp enough to slice it open.

Living alone suits Martin. He hasn't shared his home with anyone, not a partner or even a flatmate, since the house in Karori. That had been enough for him, all the communal living he would ever need. Sometimes he wonders about his old flatmates, Daniel and Karen. He has been following Karen's career for a while, ever since he returned to New Zealand, hunting up her freelance articles and feature stories. She seems to be doing well for herself as a journalist. He doesn't know and cannot imagine what Daniel has been doing since he disappeared from the university scene, but he saw him once, not so long ago, at a café in central Wellington. Daniel hovered by his table, peering at him, but Martin refused to look up. He had been reading one of his history books, but he'd put those away for the time being. He was reading *The Sayings of Master Rinzai* now, underlining his favourite passages.

> When you meet the Buddha, kill the Buddha. When you meet your ancestor, kill your ancestor. When you meet the disciple of the Buddha, kill the disciple. When you meet your father and mother, kill your father and mother. When you meet your kin, kill your kin. Only thus will you attain deliverance.

It is interesting to know that Daniel is back in Wellington. He will have to keep that in mind.

Martin finds the kitchen knife he has been looking for and cuts the package open. Five copies of *Body Disposal at Auschwitz* are tucked inside a box between crumpled scraps of torn newspaper. Plain, serious-looking covers, joyless academic font. The last seventy pages all footnotes and bibliography. Martin is satisfied with what he sees. Five more copies will now almost certainly be on their way to Nigel Wilton in Australia. Martin picks up one of the books and turns it over in his hands. He has let Lewis Ravington compose the blurb.

> This authoritative investigation of the crematory procedures in the Auschwitz-Birkenau camps . . . meticulous . . . incisive . . .

Martin sits down at the table, flicks through the book once more, then returns it to the box. He will not think about it for now. Wilton and his friends in Australia and New Zealand are probably doing more thinking now than they have done in their lives. Poor old Lewis Ravington isn't thinking hard enough. He wonders what Karen will think, or Daniel. He should try to get in touch with Karen again. She might be useful.

> When you meet the Buddha, kill the Buddha . . .

Martin remembers the early days, his years at the University of Manchester when his project, his investigation had first started to take shape. Marion Pryor, his supervisor, had been a useful teacher. An aging, failing, flailing hyper-relativist, slipping out of sight, no longer controversial, no longer relevant, reduced to a largely honorary position and one less than completely worshipful graduate student. "All history is constructed as narrative," she had tried to convince him, as if he needed convincing, as if there were anyone left in the world who believed that historians were something other than storytellers, something more than novelists who hid behind footnotes and citations. "The order of past events, the chain of causation, can never be discovered by a historian." Causation is the creation of the historian, their invention, their act of storytelling, their claim to the best possible story to tell. Marion taught Martin to love history. That is what he has to thank her for, the only thing.

`When you meet your ancestor, kill your ancestor . . .`

Through school and undergraduate university, history was just a subject for Martin. Primary sources, secondary materials, political, social and economic factors, debate, evidence, counter-evidence, interpretation, reinterpretation, orthodoxy, revisionism, re-revisionism, dates, dates, dates and timelines. When that is all you see then it's fine, perfectly respectable, a solid discipline to cool your heels in while you wait for the rest of your life to appear. But when you move past all that, when you realise what history really is, that is when the fun starts. That is when you begin to fall in love.

`When you meet your mother and father, kill your mother and father . . .`

The phone starts to ring in Martin's living room. Martin does not get up from his seat. It is only Wilton, most probably. Who else would want to talk to him? He decides to let it ring. He doesn't feel like talking to his ally in Australia. The answer machine clicks on and Martin hears Wilton's voice murmuring hollowly and mechanically in his living room.

". . . the battle's about to start, Martin. We won't let you down . . . I'm rallying the troops . . . you've got our support . . ."

Presumably Wilton's copies of the book have arrived. He has paid for them, after all. Them and one thousand other copies. Wilton's conviction cannot be faulted and now he is rallying the troops because a battle is about to start. History is a battleground and that is why Martin loves it. Historians do not fight wars of truth and meaning, they fight the same wars as everyone else, wars of likes and wants and needs. Martin spent his time in England and on the continent trying to figure out what people could be made to like and want, trying to find the story he thought they needed. He looks at the box on the table before him and carefully folds its cardboard shutters flat, resealing them for the moment with a scrap of torn masking tape. It is almost time to see if he has found the right one.

`Only thus will you attain deliverance.`

DANIEL

I wound up sharing an apartment with Morbid, the long-haired trenchcoat-wearing inhabitant of the cubicle next to mine at Eclectic Inc, after a disheartening two-week search for accommodation in central Wellington. Student flats, hippy flats, straight-edge flats, young Christian professional flats, lawyer flats, flats with couples, flats with children. After all this I was more than willing to accept the offer of the spare room in Morbid's apartment: a dingy little hole on the eleventh floor of a building on The Terrace, the sort of place a real-estate agent would call "spacious two-bedroom living".

The second bedroom had previously been a walk-in closet for Morbid's surplus electronic equipment — broken TVs, old game consoles, and outdated computers all the way down to a dusty Commodore 64 — but once all that had been cleared out there was space for a bed. As flatmates went, Morbid wasn't too bad. He spent most of his time in his room with his custom-built, heavily modified, big black behemoth of a PC, emerging occasionally to watch DVDs or play PS2 in the lounge.

One morning, when Morbid and I were leaving for work at Eclectic Inc, I found a package waiting for me under our letterbox in the apartment foyer. I picked it up and took it with me. The offices of Eclectic Inc were only a block away from Morbid's apartment, which was good, because Morbid liked to get to work early and I had fallen into this pattern as well, despite Heckle's generally relaxed time-keeping policy.

Morbid was obsessed with the *VirtuLife* project. "I don't see it as a game," he told me once while we were domestically deathmatching on the PS2. "It's more like conceptual computer art. It has the potential to be more real than real life, an internally evolving world of choice and consequence. That's what we have the power to create. The Eclectic engine gives us this, Daniel. We finally have the technology to create a world that will feel real."

The cinematics and character-modelling were proceeding smoothly, so it was possible Morbid's hopes might bear fruit. Speculation was already mounting on several online game forums.

> Voidkiller386: heard some dudes called eclectic are working some new game or something. its about being a real person in a real world like can you have guns and stuff????
> Bygonator: It's called VirtuLife, dumbass, and yes you can probably have guns, but people are going to play it because it's an INTERESTING GAME. So f*** off back to playing Grand Theft Auto, retard.
> Linkmaster: Bygonator takes it up the chocy starfish :)

I spent the first few hours working on non-player character behaviour routines for the Eclectic AI, conversation trees and action-flowcharts, before I remembered the package I'd received that morning. I flipped it round, but the sender hadn't left any details on the back.

I leaned back in my swivel chair, clicked the web browser closed, and opened my parcel. Inside was a bulky-looking paperback with a plain black cover. *Body Disposal at Auschwitz — An Inquiry into the Mortality Rates and Crematory Procedures at the Auschwitz-Birkenau Camps* read the title. Below that: *Martin Glass.*

I examined the book for a while, turning it over and reading the blurb without fully registering a single word. *Incisive . . . detailed . . . authoritative . . .* Martin had written a book. I flicked through it once. Pages of small, austere type; diagrams; photographs (not plates in the middle of the book but copied into the text itself); footnotes and bibliography at the back, in smaller print.

I checked its flyleaf. Nothing was written there; I couldn't find any hint as to who had sent it. Perhaps it had been Martin himself, but I was inclined to dismiss that thought. Why would he want me to read his book? We hadn't been in touch in years. Next to me I could hear Morbid stirring in his cubicle. That peculiar Morbid sound — leather coat rustling, silver wallet chains clinking. I turned the book over in my hands, thinking about Martin and how we had once been friends.

I knew Martin during the last few years of high school and my two abortive years at university. We met and became friends in the sixth form, Martin having transferred down from some hick town in the upper North Island. He was in Wellington without friends or family, boarding privately in his first year, flatting on his own the year after that. He never talked about his family or his home town; he would mention receiving a cheque or a parcel of clothes in the mail every now and then, but apart from that they might as well not have existed. I envied his independence, his apparent self-sufficiency. My home life had become particularly claustrophobic by the time I was sixteen, my parents bickering, my little brother always underfoot. I would have liked to have cut them all away, coolly and calmly, the way Martin seemed to have done.

We shared a desk for a period, hung out at lunchtime and after school. We became friends not because we had much in common but because of chance and proximity; there was no point in being anything else. Looking back, I sometimes liked to valorise my high-school days and imagined that Martin and I were outsiders, cynics observing mundane teenage follies from the fringe, but that was not really the case. We were middle-rankers of the school set, adolescent yes-men, not popular or unpopular, just guys hanging around. We both graduated with average grades, average attendance records, acceptable appearances, and *sans* virginity, but only barely. Martin, I think, came away with second prize in a speech competition and I picked up a badge for being on the third XV.

We carried on to university for want of any better options and that was where our ways began to part. I continued my average to mediocre performances, hopping between courses in computer science and economics, which I hoped might get me a job somewhere further down the track, and arts courses that looked like easy points towards a degree. Martin, however, began to flourish. He found a natural home in the university history department — his course work was excellent and he had a real appetite for the subject matter.

He would sometimes let his enthusiasms carry him away when we met, and lecture me about the persecution of the Protestant Huguenots in France by the Catholics and the persecution of Catholics in England by the Protestants; New Zealand's colonial history and the tyranny of the British Raj in

India; the sack of Constantinople in the Fourth Crusade and its fall, years later, to Muslim armies — conquest and cruelty all across human history. I would let him talk for a while, then I'd look at him and raise my eyebrows and smirk. He would fall silent then, slipping back into the façade of the stoic coolness we both affected. I regret that now. I should have let him talk more, I think I enjoyed it. I had no direction or fixations of my own back then and it was good to hear him trying to make sense of things, struggling to figure everything out.

When I dropped out of uni not long into my third year I had every intention of going back. I was just dead broke, having cut myself off from my parents, possibly in an unconscious emulation of Martin. I needed work, I needed a new place to live. Fortunately Martin had just discovered the cheapest flat in Wellington out somewhere in Karori. I secured a low-paying full-time job with a removal company run by a friend of an uncle and arranged to move in.

The Karori flat turned out to be the biggest dive I had ever set eyes on. Peeling wallpaper, rickety stairs, entire rooms where the floorboards had more or less rotted away, a bathroom smeared with years of grime and equipped with only the most rudimentary, creaking plumbing. Four bedrooms, three of them inhabitable. There were five of us in the place, splitting the rent. I shared the largest room with a guy called Peter, partitioning it as best we could. Lance, a big hairy guy with an annoying grin and a bad sense of humour, took the small boxroom on the second floor. Martin and his girlfriend, Karen, had the bedroom across the hall from mine.

I was a little jealous of Martin and Karen. They had been together for almost two years by then and Karen was every lonely high-school geek's wet dream of what he might find at university; all sarcasm and cigarette smoke, knitted wool hats and disillusioned Eliotism. I felt a little frustrated that Martin, who had seemed so like me all through high school, had sprung away and seemed to be enjoying a range of satisfactions I couldn't seem to grasp for myself. I wasn't bad looking back then. I still played some sport and kept in shape. I went for runs and did push-ups and stomach crunches. Now, of course, my abdomen has lost its shape and my arse is on the brink of collapsing into a big gooey wad of dough and my widow's peak has eroded to the point where it's almost just a tuft, a brave little island at the summit of my scalp. Back in those days, though, I could step out of the shower in the morning and feel pretty good about myself. But while I had successfully kept my virginity from growing back all through university, longer-term relationships, the committed kind Martin and Karen seemed to have, continued to elude me. I suppose they still do.

When Martin and Karen broke up, suddenly, a little way into the year, I was slightly shocked. It came unexpectedly, without any dramatics, just a few muffled, angry conversations in their bedroom, some cold silences in the kitchen and lounge, and then Karen was taking over Lance's room on the second floor and he was camping out in the lounge because nobody particularly wanted to share with him. Up until then it had been a good flat. We all seemed to be working hard — Martin and Karen at university, the rest of us at our jobs — and we'd collapse in the living room at the end of the day, with barely enough energy left to cook a meal of baked beans on toast, or to make the walk down to the fish-and-chip shop if it was a Friday night. On the rare days when the weather was good we'd sprawl around in the garden. Lance sitting by himself under the fence, Martin and Peter quietly continuing an argument begun in one of their history tutorials, Karen and me lying on our bellies on the grass, playing cards.

But the atmosphere changed as Martin and Karen's relationship briefly spiralled and then crashed. Part of me revelled in my mate's misfortune. Part of me was a little saddened that something that had seemed so stable and desirable could collapse so quickly.

Karen couldn't afford to move out, and living under the same roof soon took a toll on both her and Martin. The Karori flat became a treacherous terrain of awkward silences, closed doors, entrances and exits, underhanded jibes and bitter asides. Lance, Peter and I kept our heads down. Conversations became muted, then abortive. I spent more and more time out of the house, wandering the streets around our flat, the central city, the botanical gardens, the walk along Oriental Parade. It was the height of winter by then and the city had a grey deserted feel. I decided not to go back to university as I had planned, but to use my savings to buy a one-way ticket to Europe instead. Wellington felt like the end of the world, the death of all possibility.

One Saturday night I got back to the flat around ten in the evening. The cold was starting to eat through my parka and the Wellington drizzle had grown more pervasive; I could feel it oozing down my neck and under my jumper, icy cold above my buttocks and in the small of my back. I had forgotten that Lance and Peter had been planning to throw a party that night and so I was surprised when I walked through the gate to find a bunch of strangers sitting around drinking on the porch. I vaguely remembered a few of them from the classes I had once shared with Peter, but that seemed like a lifetime ago.

I brushed past the people on the porch without saying a word and entered the house. A couple were leaning against the wall in the hallway. One of them was a friend of Lance's, a guy called Ash. He was in his mid-forties, his grey-blond hair balding on top but long on the sides, falling to his shoulders. His companion was a short plump girl with dyed black hair and garish make-up. I didn't say anything to either of them, but Ash grinned when he saw me and pushed open the door to the kitchen, ushering me through. Inside the room was crowded and smoky. The door that connected the kitchen to the downstairs lounge was open, and dark, heavy music played on a borrowed stereo. I stood there like a zombie for a minute or so, half-recognised faces around me, half-heard snatches of conversation, until Peter found me and drew me away, talking, laughing, to the kitchen table. We had a few drinks. Eventually I asked where Martin was and wandered out to the garden to find him.

He was leaning against the wall of the house, watching one of our guests pee on the rockery we had constructed out of broken concrete chunks at the bottom of the garden. "What do you think of all this?" he asked.

I shrugged, a little drunkenly.

"Yeah," said Martin, "I don't think much of it either. I hope we haven't chased you out of the house this week. I hope you haven't felt uncomfortable here."

I shook my head.

"Because the last thing anyone wants to do, Daniel, is make you feel uncomfortable."

I straightened up, away from the wall, and gestured to the open doorway. "Is Karen about?"

It was Martin's turn to shrug.

"I just didn't see her inside," I said.

"She's probably hiding upstairs," said Martin. "She doesn't like this, she doesn't feel sociable."

"Would you mind if I . . ."

Martin laughed, his breath misting in the cold air. "Go on up the stairs, see if she's there. Doesn't matter to me. Couldn't matter less to me. Go on up the stairs, you'll find her all right."

I left him in the garden and walked through the back hallway. I bumped into Lance's friend Ash again on my way to the stairs. He smiled at me and his face seemed to blur around the edges. I blinked and tried to decide if that made him look younger or older.

"Some fucking Walpurgis Night, huh kid?" he said.

I grunted and then, suddenly angry, pushed him out of my way. I heard him laugh behind me as I climbed up the stairs. Maybe a few other people were laughing as well.

What happened after that I almost don't remember. I found Karen upstairs and she was upset and drunk, just like Martin was, I think, down below. She and I sat talking in the dirty damp hallway for a few hours. I couldn't tell you how we got from there to the mattress in her small boxroom. The details of our progression seem hazy and uncertain, almost unreal. The only thing I remember vividly was the cold nauseous feeling that seemed to grow in the pit of my stomach, the sense that somehow everything was wrong.

Martin was pissed off, of course, filled with a cold, contained fury that I barely remember because I moved out so soon after that and was on my way overseas a week later. Friends falling out over a girl, drifting apart. A typical story, conclusive and easily understood. These things happen.

But I still remember those months in the flat as a good time in my life even though they ended badly. With this in mind, I took *Body Disposal at Auschwitz* home with me when I left the Eclectic offices later that night.

MARTIN GLASS

The furnaces, the muffles. That is what *Body Disposal at Auschwitz* comes down to, everything is reduced to the economies of coke and clinker. The double-muffle, triple-muffle, eight-muffle coke-fuelled furnaces built by the firm of Topf and Sons for Kremas I, II, III, IV and V. The furnace and rotary dampers, the chimneys and the hearths charged with coke. The corpses could only be introduced once the muffles of the furnaces had been brought to the good red heat of 800 degrees. The pulsed air-blowers on their sides had to be run on and off in twenty-minute intervals to ensure that the cremation chambers didn't receive too much or too little fresh air.

Martin has been scrupulous in his study. He has included blueprints, construction contracts, plans and documents, extensive footnotes, and references to treatises on the science of cremation. He has estimated the average time corpse disposal would have taken. He has calculated the daily disposal capacities of the camp complex of Auschwitz-Birkenau at every stage in its construction history. He has examined these figures alongside the accepted death toll for the camp in his conclusion. He has discussed the camp's typhus epidemic of 1942 and noted that the expansion of the camp's crematory capacities was completed the following year. He had warned Lewis Ravington that the conclusions he'd reached might be controversial.

"Of course," Ravington had said. "I can see that. I'm not sure if I agree with you. I'm not sure if I know enough to agree with you. But you should put it out there, you should take the chance. Controversy isn't to be feared."

Nigel Wilton had said something similar, back when Martin had first approached him for assistance. "Brave, courageous, dedicated work," Wilton had said. "A beautiful vindication."

So Martin knows he has found a story that pleases both of them, each in their own way, a story built out of the humblest facts. The fact that it took something in the region of twenty minutes to reduce the body of a forty-seven pound child to chalky white ash. Fifty minutes for a 144-pound woman and a 227-pound man in close to an hour. One must bear in mind that most of the burning occurred in the first thirty minutes. Once the optimum temperature of 1100 degrees was reached in the first half-hour there would have been a rapid fall-away in heat efficiency, and the remaining body mass, often not much larger that a football in diameter, took longer, more intense burning to remove. Martin knows his story will be a success. It is needed, it is wanted, and he has applied a perfect historical methodology to find it. Some facts were emphasised, some were muted, and some were just lost altogether. Martin knows this is often the case with history. To keep a grip on some things, you have to let others slip by.

After each incineration, the temperature in the furnace of the oven would rise. The corpses and airflow had to be carefully regulated to prevent the heat from rising above 1100 degrees which was dangerous for the working of the furnace. Crematory science was a precise art, especially when it was dealt with on such a large scale, in the midst of so much death.

Martin often thinks about the architect of the Auschwitz-Birkenau furnaces; he has spent so much time immersed in the fruits of the man's labours that he can't help thinking about him. Kurt Prüfer, the chief engineer at the Erfurt construction firm of Topf and Sons, the head of the *Krematorium im Bau*. He had started out as a humble construction worker, rising up through the ranks, struggling his way to education. The boom that Germany experienced as the Nazi Party cemented its grip on the country had depended on people like him. Experienced, practical minds in the trades and industries, ready to seize the rewards being offered by the new regime.

Martin would not call Prüfer a genius — that would be going too far, that would be romanticising the man in a way that even Prüfer himself might not have cared for. His surviving correspondence suggests a brisk, efficient man of few words, a man who did not mess around with niceties, a man who always got straight to the point. Not a genius, perhaps, but a problem-solver, a man of precise, straight-lined thoughts.

He had replaced the ailing coke-fired cremation furnace at Dachau with a new design, a furnace with two muffles that could be fuelled and maintained simultaneously. Buchenwald was quick to commission a similar design from him, then expanded their facilities in 1942 with two of Topf and Sons' very first triple-muffle furnaces. Mauthausen received two double-muffle furnaces, one in 1940 for its Gusen annex camp, then another for the main camp which was completed in 1944. Then two double-muffle furnaces installed in 1940 and early 1941 at Auschwitz. Five triple-muffle furnaces (Kremas II and III) later constructed at Birkenau. In 1942 two eight-muffle furnaces were commissioned for Kremas IV and

V. Eight individual muffles to the oven, requiring only two fireboxes to fuel them. So many more bodies disposed of, so much more economy in labour and price. In December 1942 Prüfer had received a 450-Reichsmark bonus from Topf and Sons for the number of furnaces he had sold to the SS, an unprecedented sum.

Martin has been careful to chronicle Kurt Prüfer's eventual fall from grace. He makes much of it in *Body Disposal at Auschwitz*; it factors heavily in his equations, is a key element of the story he wants to tell. By May 1943 Krema II was put out of commission with a broken chimney. Krema IV had suffered damage to both its chimney and the machinery of its furnace and was declared irreparable. No more furnaces were commissioned from Topf and Sons. Instead smaller single-muffle "pocket" furnaces produced by Topf's major competitor Kori were installed in the Auschwitz III sub-camps of Blechhammer and Trzebinia.

After Germany's capitulation, Kurt Prüfer was eventually arrested in East Berlin in March 1946. One of the directors of Topf and Sons committed suicide. The other fled to West Berlin and re-established the firm with a subsidy from the Wiesbaden Chamber of Commerce after its "unjust expropriation" by the communists. It is all there in *Body Disposal*, the whole history of Kurt Prüfer and Topf and Sons. From the blueprints to the construction contracts to the operating instructions to arrest warrants, death certificates and subsidy applications. Everything slides into Martin's narrative or slips behind it. He decides what should be kept and what must fall away.

Remember that most of the burning is done in the first thirty minutes. Remember that once the ideal temperature of 1100 degrees is reached the remaining human body mass will take considerably longer to burn away. Things slow down, things get harder by that stage. Remember all of this, Martin thinks. And remember that when the remains of the corpses fell through the chamotte grid to the ash-collection channel below they would be pulled forward using a scraper towards the ash-removal door. Remember that it would then take a further twenty minutes for all remaining matter to be consumed, and even after that the ashes would need to be stored for a while, to allow them to cool, while further corpses were fed into the chamber above. It is important to note that every evening the furnace fire-bars needed to be cleaned of clinker and cinder. And one should not forget that at the end of the day, when the furnace was empty, the air valves, doors and damper needed to be closed so the furnace would not cool down. These things can be vital, Martin thinks. They can make all the difference, if you let them.

RAVINGTON

There were times when Ravington thought life became too much to bear. His bad job, his bad habits, the general overwhelming cheap drab badness of his existence would rise up in his mind like bile in the back of his throat and he would be struck still with panic for a moment. What sort of life was this for a man? A shabby office, a torn leather jacket, an erratic, dubious income. A scam instead of a career, a bus pass instead of a driver's licence, a dark swirling mess of guilt and envy in the place of courage and conscience. These moments tended to strike when he first arrived at work and often there was nothing else to do but turn the Tunnel Press office over to the care of Ms Yorke and spend the rest of the day hiding from self-knowledge at a booth in one of the pubs on Cuba Street. A pint of stout and a day spent poring over the sports pages could resolve almost any existential crisis.

This time it only took an hour and a couple of pints for Rav to feel calmer. He could live another day as Lewis

Ravington after all. All he'd been feeling was a sense of listlessness post the publication of *Body Disposal at Auschwitz*. It had been an anticlimax of sorts. Not that Rav shouldn't have been used to that by now. His life was full of anticlimaxes. He had known them himself and seen them unfold in the eyes of his authors.

The book had been proofed, printed, bound and sent out into the world to vanish without a trace. Apart from the fact that Rav had gone out of his way to get it into bookstores and libraries, its trajectory was no different from any volume in his back catalogue. No reviews, no reported sales, nothing. Not even a mention in a magazine or newspaper to say that Tunnel Press had published a book that might be worth reading. And now it was back to the autobiographies and poetry collections.

Sometime Electric Movements of Colour would be out next month. The launch would be something to look forward to, something indeed. The friends and family gathered in the second-hand bookstore in the Hutt that Rav had a deal with; the author, weeping, thanking Mum and Dad and Grandma and Grandpa for all their love and support; the drinks, the chips and the dip; the ritualistic book-signing; and Rav, standing there, right in the middle of it all, a smile fixed to his face, feeling bad.

Rav looked up and saw a woman sitting at the bar, watching him. She was tall, blonde, vaguely familiar, drinking some kind of cocktail. It was . . . who was it . . . ?

The woman saw she had caught his attention, then got up from the bar and walked over to his table. "I am Adja," she said, looking down at him, unsmiling.

Adja . . . thought Ravington. *Adja* . . . The woman he had met after that poetry slam, the woman who had given him the slip — or had he given her the slip, or had he just lost her over the course of the night? He didn't know, he couldn't tell, it was all too confusing and too long ago.

Adja sat down opposite him without waiting to be invited. Seeing her now, she looked older than Rav had thought.

"How have you been?" Rav asked.

Adja shrugged.

"Good? Bad?"

Another shrug. Rav was not enjoying this. The pub was his sanctuary, the place where he rested and healed. He did not want to be disturbed here, especially not by her, a woman he had dishonestly and ineffectually tried to seduce.

Adja reached into her purse and took out a liquor-stained, half-torn calling card. She put it down on the table and slid it across to Ravington. Rav looked at it dutifully. *Tunnel Press*, it read. Then below that: *Lewis Ravington — Editor-in-Chief.*

"Ah . . . yes . . ." he started to say.

"I want to talk to you," Adja said. "You help me with something, maybe . . ."

Not now, Rav thought. *Not today*. He couldn't face any more of this, not another minute. His cell phone rang. He answered like a drowning man lunging for a lifeline.

"Hello, Lewis," Ms Yorke said. "Just thought you might like to know that a reporter called our office. She'd like to come in and have a chat about Mr Glass's book, wants to get some background from you."

"For Glass's book? For *Body Disposal*?" Rav was grinning. Adja was looking at him strangely, but he couldn't stop grinning. "When is she coming in? No, never mind, I'll come back to the office now. See you soon."

He turned off his phone and started to struggle his way out of the booth.

"Your help . . ." Adja started to say.

"Yeah. Sorry." Rav looked down at her and decided he wasn't going to let another author onto his lists. Not her. Not today. He would do a good thing and disappoint her, he was turning a corner, he was starting to be good. "I don't think I can help you with anything."

Despair in the morning, moral equilibrium in the afternoon. His day was back on track.

Ms Yorke was waiting for him at the office. "I'm just popping out for lunch," she said, picking up her handbag.

"Fine," said Rav. "That's great. Do that. Take two hours. Take three."

He sat down at his desk then stood up again. He walked over to straighten the piles of manuscripts on the table under the window. A reporter was coming to see him. The details were all written down on the note Ms Yorke had left for him. Karen Staunton. Two o'clock. Another hour to wait. Sixty minutes. That was okay. Rav could do that.

Things were changing now. The end of his badness was in sight, it was tangible, he could see it bobbing just below the horizon of his existence. Perhaps *Body Disposal* would be the start of something new. Perhaps with the right media attention Tunnel Press could become a viable, quirky, alternative publishing house, something other than a sick joke. This was a great new time, a new age.

There was a knock at the door. Rav spun around, knocking over a stack of spiral-bound high-country farming memoirs. The reporter? Too early. Rav walked over and opened the door.

Two men were standing in the hallway outside the Tunnel Press office. One was in his mid to late thirties and had a shaven head and a thick, severely shaped beard. He stood a little taller than Rav and kept his shoulders square, trying to take up as much space as possible. The other was an older man, slightly portly, wearing a jumper and worn-looking track pants. He sported a grey-flecked beard, cut close around his mouth, and his hair was sharply receded.

Rav looked down at Ms Yorke's note, which he still held

in his hand. *Karen Staunton*. That was who he was expecting. Rav looked back up at the two men. The older one smiled at him.

"Can I . . . help you?" Ravington said.

"This is the Tunnel Press office?" asked the older man.

"Yes?"

"And you are Lewis Ravington?"

Rav took a step back, trying to collect himself, trying to figure out who these men might be. Debt collectors? Disgruntled memoirists?

The strangers took Rav's retreat as an invitation to step inside. "It's a pleasure to meet you, in that case," said the older man. "A true pleasure." He looked around the small, cramped office and rolled his shoulders. "I must say, seeing you in this environment is a surprise, Mr Ravington. But perhaps that's foolish of me. It's only natural to find a man of your intelligence and talents trapped in a dire little room like this. They hound us, you know, right to the very margins. Isn't that so, Eric?"

"They do, Mr Wilton," the younger, taller man said, glaring down at Ravington. "They certainly do."

"Wait . . ." Rav stumbled over details in his mind. The name on the cheques below those nice, round comforting figures. "Wilton? You're Nigel Wilton?"

"In the flesh, Mr Ravington." Wilton took hold of Rav's unresisting hand and shook it. "It is so very good to meet you. We have a lot to talk about. A great deal, in fact."

His companion, Eric, kicked the door shut behind them.

"If perhaps we could make ourselves comfortable, Mr Ravington?"

Rav scurried back to sit behind his desk and waved Wilton to a chair. He had not anticipated this, not contemplated the possibility of a face-to-face meeting. Wilton had paid for the books and they had been printed. In accordance with the terms and conditions of the Tunnel Press mission, their business had been concluded. This meeting served no purpose, he could not understand it.

Wilton sat down in the chair opposite Ravington. His friend stood silently at his shoulder. "I suppose the first order of business is to congratulate you, Mr Ravington."

"Thanks," said Rav. Hadn't Wilton already congratulated him once before? Why did he feel the need to do it again? Why did it have to be in person? Why did he have to be here?

Nobody said anything more for a moment. Then Wilton twisted round in his chair and smiled up at his larger companion. "You know what I think? I think Mr Ravington doesn't quite know what he's got himself into."

Eric smiled for the first time, a quick flash of his teeth, which disappeared almost immediately.

"No," Wilton continued, "he probably doesn't. None of us do at first. You see, Mr Ravington, a man like you acts without considering the consequences of his actions. You decide on the best path to take, the truthful path, and will not even consider following another. It's an admirable trait, but one that's rare in today's world. One that is liable to get you into trouble."

"Trouble with you?" Ravington didn't like the direction this conversation was taking. He didn't like the fact that the conversation was taking place at all. It had been a bad idea to come back from the pub; he ought to have hidden there all afternoon, reporter or no reporter. Going back to the office was always a bad idea. Nothing good ever came of it. He should lock its doors, board up its windows and leave, never come back, go to Africa, join the International Red Cross or the French Foreign Legion. Get a new life, become a new person, be good.

Wilton and Eric exchanged another look. Wilton laughed. Eric rolled his eyes. "Trouble with us?" said Wilton.

"Of course not. We're your friends, Mr Ravington . . . Lewis — you don't mind if I call you Lewis?"

"Most people call me Rav."

"Rav, certainly. No, we only came here to make your acquaintance, to thank you and express our admiration. We're on our way to see Martin this afternoon, that's the main reason for my visit here. The days ahead may be difficult for him. We must never forget our friends, Rav —"

"We're done here," said Eric. "Come on, Mr Wilton, we're just wasting time." He looked down at Rav, still grim, still standing, still scowling. "He's not one of us."

"But that's why we're here, that's why we're talking to him. You'll have to forgive my friend," Wilton said to Rav. "Eric Stapp is a good man. He's the head of a small organisation over here, the New Zealanders for National Solidarity, and I'm proud to say that I was something of a mentor to him back in the early days, much as I am to our friend Martin now." Wilton leaned back in his chair to smile up at his companion. "What I want Eric to understand is that there's more than one way to fight a battle. We have to evolve, we have to adapt, we have to adopt the tactics of the enemy." Wilton turned back to face Ravington. "We need people like you, Rav, people who are new to the fight, who fall into it without thinking. You're about to find out what the world is really like; it's not a simple, honest place. But you'll weather it, you'll endure it, and in the end you'll emerge from the storm, proud and upright, to stand alongside us. Do you know why, Rav?"

"No."

"You must know."

"I don't."

"Because you are good," Wilton said, with absolute conviction.

"Excuse me?" someone said, knocking on the open office door.

Rav looked up from his desk, shaking off his bafflement to see a woman standing in the doorway, longish red hair pulled back in an unbecoming ponytail, carrying a leather note-satchel, wearing a navy suit-and-skirt combination and sensible-girl glasses. The reporter. She had come at last.

"Mr Ravington?" the woman said. Then, when Rav nodded, "I'm Karen Staunton. Sorry, I know I'm a bit early. I can come back in a bit —"

"No!" Rav stood up so quickly he clicked his kneecap on the edge of an open desk drawer. "Please, Karen, hi, come in. I was just finishing up here."

Wilton and Eric Stapp looked at each other once, then Wilton slowly rose up from the chair. "I didn't know you were expecting company, Rav," he said. "We won't keep you any longer."

Wilton walked out of the office, but Stapp paused on the threshold. He looked over at the dusty pile of new manuscripts on the table by the window and at the bookshelf stuffed with bound proofs, then back to Rav. He opened his mouth, as if he was on the cusp of saying something, but then Wilton called "Coming Eric?" from the hallway and Stapp shook his head, glared, and stalked out, swinging the door shut behind him.

"Just some people dropping by," Rav said to Karen after a moment. "No one important. Sit down, please."

Karen took the chair Nigel Wilton had recently vacated and removed a spiral-bound notebook and a ballpoint from her satchel. She folded the cover back, crossed her legs and smiled at him. A row of brushed-and-flossed, yearly-dentist-visit teeth between perfect lips. Rav smiled back. "I won't take up much of your time," she said. "Just a few background questions. *Body Disposal at Auschwitz* is an unusual publication for Tunnel Press, isn't it?"

"Yeah, we don't usually publish works of European history,

but the quality and controversial nature of *Body Disposal* convinced us to make an exception."

"Could you tell me something about Martin Glass's background?"

"He was a history student in the UK for a number of years, never finished his PhD. That's probably why he came to us in the end. We're prepared to consider publishing research that evolves beyond traditional academic domains and spheres."

"Who are 'us', exactly?"

"Tunnel Press." Rav looked around his office, a little defensively. "Other people do work here," he said. The interview wasn't going quite the way Rav had imagined it would. He'd hoped for a little gushing, a few serious questions about the role of the independent publisher in society, and maybe, just maybe, an opening to suggest that they move to a less formal setting, the wine-bar around the corner, then perhaps dinner after that.

"Anyway," Rav said, "a lot of rigmarole goes on with academic publishing, you know," he had to sound knowledgeable, had to sound confident, "and Martin's research does challenge aspects of the orthodox thinking in these matters."

"So you fully endorse his methodology and the conclusions that he reaches?"

"What do you mean?"

"For example, what interested me was his claim that the double-muffle coke-fuelled Topf furnaces used in some of the Auschwitz crematoria were only capable of disposing of up to twenty bodies a day. It's a controversial claim, Mr Ravington."

"Call me Rav."

"Sorry, Rav. And what about Glass's in-depth discussion of the 1942 typhus epidemic in Chapter Five? You don't think that some of the conclusions he reaches there may have barred him from approaching better-established publishers?" Her perfect, pleasant smile remained fixed on her lips. Rav felt himself stiffen behind his desk.

"I have absolute confidence in the quality of Martin's research," he said. "He makes his case. It's up to the reader to decide whether or not they accept it."

"Can I ask if you hold any strong political beliefs, Rav?"

He could see what she was getting at. He had expected something like this, but it certainly wasn't fair. Rav liked to consider himself fashionably left-of-centre, like almost everyone else in central Wellington, but to be honest he couldn't really back that up with anything other than his brief flirtation with Marxism at university and a history of indifferent Labour-voting. Trade barriers: didn't care. Globalisation: take it or leave it. Taxes: barely noticed them, one way or the other. There were times when he thought the Maoris were getting a bit of an easy deal, but then he was pretty much convinced that everyone who wasn't Lewis Ravington got an easy deal. "I don't really feel comfortable answering that," he said, at length.

"Of course, Rav." Karen then asked a few general questions about Tunnel Press. Rav was on more familiar ground there; he happily threw around words like "boutique" and "unconventional" for the next fifteen minutes, ripping through his regular spiel about "moderate print-runs" and "high-quality manuscripts". He felt the interview had got back to a good zone when Karen closed her notebook and thanked him for his time. Rav got up from his desk to see her to the door. "Where's your article going to be printed?" he asked as she stepped out into the hallway.

"This is a freelance piece. I haven't decided on a magazine yet."

Rav must have looked a little crestfallen, because Karen was quick to reassure him that her article would see the light of day. "I don't think anyone's going to be turning it down once it's done."

"Be seeing you then."

Rav stepped back into his office. He couldn't decide whether he'd been right to come back from the pub, whether it had been worth it after all. The visit from Wilton and Stapp had been unpleasant, he didn't like to be reminded of that connection. Then again, the books Wilton had paid for had been produced and some of them distributed, so the end of his association with Tunnel Press was in sight. The interview with Karen Staunton had been a little difficult, but Rav had never been interviewed before and one interview was better than nothing at all.

He wasn't certain of anything, not even close to certain, but by Lewis Ravington's standards this might yet turn out to be a good day.

DANIEL

Voidkiller386: So you can do anything in this game?
Pieboy: yup anything u do in real life
Linkmaster: bullshit, you won't be able to do anything
it's all just hype
Voidkiller386: can you have sex?
Pieboy: yup
Linkmaster: hype hype hype hype hype
Voidkiller386: I wanna have sex!!!
Linkmaster: (post deleted by moderator)
Pieboy: yup

I clicked my web browser closed. Internet speculation for *VirtuLife* was mounting. We had posted several new screenshots on the Eclectic website last night, along with an updated FAQ and a couple of developer diaries. The hype was powerful, chatrooms were ablaze. But the mood at the office was currently not so great.

Word had just come in that Styx, our publishers, wanted us to scrap the "childhood" and "adolescence" sections of the game. We had mainly been focused on attuning the Eclectic engine to the "developmental maturity" levels anyway, optimising the players' experience as they glided around our virtual city, between their virtual jobs and their virtual houses, their virtual families and virtual friends, but some members of the design team were unhappy.

"This is bullshit. Complete fucking bullshit," Morbid had said.

"Your contributions are always appreciated," said Heckle. "Okay, so we start in with the player trying to find their first job. We'll come up with some sort of general background for the upbringing and education of all the player-avatars . . ."

Morbid had sulked off not long after this discussion, the first time he had ever left the Eclectic offices early. I stuck around for a while in the evening, having nowhere else to go, listlessly playing with one of the rudimentary *VirtuLife* demo levels we had put together.

> You are sitting in your office. It is getting late. Around you people are packing up, getting ready to go home. You (Option A selected) decide to work on for a bit. Your boss has been dropping hints about "tight schedules" after all . . .

Perhaps it had been a mistake for me to come back to New Zealand. I didn't know anyone in Wellington and the closest I'd come to getting laid since I got back was hearing Morbid talk about how his half-orc necromancer got into some pretty intense role-playing with an elven fire-mage at his D&D night. I found myself thinking about Anita a lot, wondering if I should have given up so easily in Edinburgh. Maybe I should have tried to stick it out in London, maybe I should have gone somewhere else altogether.

```
While working late you start to feel lonely
and isolated (life-satisfaction levels
dropping) and start questioning the life
choices you have made up to this point.
(Reload saved game?)
```

I had read Martin's book. *Body Disposal at Auschwitz — An Inquiry into Mortality Rates and Crematory Procedures at the Auschwitz-Birkenau Camps.* I had read it, skimmed it, flicked between the diagrams. It didn't have anything to say about deportations, round-ups and Special Treatment. Next to nothing about daily life in the camps. It was a Holocaust history purged of horror, of suffering, of abjectness, purged of all the numbing stories and images I had seen while I was with Anita. Just corpses, camp populations and crematoria. The changes in the camp architecture, the expansions, the building contracts and schedules.

```
The workings of the double-muffle coke-
fired Topf furnaces used at Auschwitz for
body disposal allowed for the burning of
perhaps twenty corpses a day per oven (each
muffle can be considered an oven).
```

How many corpses can you burn in a day? How many in a double-muffle furnace? How many in three double-muffles? How many in eight single-muffles? How many in fifty-two ovens, when the crematorium is running at full capacity and there are no breakdowns or fuel shortages?

```
The full fifty-two ovens did not become
```

operational until the middle of 1943. Prior to that there were only three double-muffle furnaces in the main camp.

Can you burn 1.1 million corpses between 1942 and 1945 — assuming, of course, that you are working with only two double-muffle furnaces in Auschwitz I prior to 1942, the new double-muffle furnace only being added in the spring of that year, and the four new crematoria constructed later that summer at Birkenau consisting of five triple-muffle furnaces each in Kremas II and III, and one eight-muffle furnace in both Krema IV and Krema V; fifty-two ovens in total, all operational by July 1943?

Wartime shortages of the wood and coke necessary to fuel these furnaces also have to be considered in the estimation of the average daily crematory capacity of the Auschwitz-Birkenau Camps.

If you can't, then what happened to all the bodies? Then again, if all the people are gone, who cares about that?

I reopened my web browser and checked the game forums again. They were still talking about *VirtuLife*. That was gratifying.

Voidkiller386: can u kil people in the game???
Linkmaster: killing isn't the point of the game. It's all about living a real life.
Voidkiller386: u can go on shooting sprees in real life cant you??? shotgun @ mall *bdam bdam bdam*
Scratch77: LOL

Of course the game wasn't about shooting, or killing, or

murdering. But blood and decapitation, gunshots, recoil, exit wounds and bodily mutilation had all been pixilated on the character models and mapped into the physics engine. "Violence is part of real life," Heckle had said. "It needs to be addressed in *VirtuLife*." With that in mind, I loaded up *VirtuLife* Build again for some further play-testing.

(Reload saved game Daniel01). You decide to leave work earlier than normal (Option C selected). Your boss is a little disappointed, but there will be time to catch up on your project later. There are more important things in your life, after all . . .

Martin and Karen and the Karori flat. Anita and Josh and Steve and Edinburgh. I had been thinking a lot about the past lately and I knew this wasn't healthy.

Back at the apartment, your (options: girlfriend / boyfriend) **girlfriend** is waiting for you.

"I'm so glad you could get home early," she says. (Bonus points – quality time – life-satisfaction level increases). "I've been waiting for you. What shall we do?"

It wasn't good to get hung up on stuff; you couldn't change the way things had gone. I always liked to think that I lived my life looking forwards. I was someone who focused on the real world, on my current life.

(Conversation option selected.) "Great!" she says. "What do you want to talk about?"

"Why did you leave me in Edinburgh?" you

ask. "What the hell happened?"

"What?" she responds.

(ERROR – incompatible option selected. Please choose again.)

"Why did you (ERROR) ditch me? Who the hell are you?" (ERROR ERROR)

"I'm Ani(ERROR)ta," she says. "And I've never left you, I've been here all this time."

Best not to think about things too much. No point in pondering the whys and wherefores. Live and let live. Bygones be bygones.

"Lying bitch!" you shout and lunge forward, wrapping your hands (ERROR ERROR option incompatible ERROR) around her throat.

"No . . . stop . . ."

(Bonus points – quality time – life-satisfaction level increases).

Don't ask too many questions. Think about where you are, not how you got there. Sometimes you just have to let things go. Accept what you've got and what you may have lost. It's not so hard, not really. These things happen.

"Enough lying! Give me the truth!"

"Stop! Please!"

ERROR

"Not until I'm finished with you . . ."

"ERROR . . . Daniel . . . ERROR . . . please . . ."

ERROR

MARTIN GLASS

"You've changed," he says and gets up to put on the kettle.

"You haven't." She is sitting at the kitchen table, fiddling with a notebook and her tape recorder. Her presence in his home is somewhat disconcerting. He tries to tell himself that this is what he's been hoping for.

"Coffee?" he asks.

"I don't drink it."

"No, of course not." He has forgotten about that. It seems like the sort of detail he'd be able to hold onto after all the evenings, mornings and afternoons they'd spent together. But memory was fallible, after all. If it wasn't then no one would have any use for history.

"Tea then?"

"No milk in it, please."

He makes the tea quickly, burning his palm on the kettle steam, unable to shake the feeling that she is watching him, that her eyes are on his back, but when he turns round she is flicking through her notebook and looks up with a start as he puts the tea cup down by her elbow. Again he is surprised at how awkward he feels in her presence. He thought he would be calm, completely in control.

She sips her tea and smiles at him as he sits back down opposite her. He remembers a line from a poem she used to like, something about serving tea to friends. T. S. Eliot. *Portrait of a Lady.* She once tripped him up with that poem; he'd insisted that Eliot hadn't written it, had never written a poem by that title, that it was a novel by James, Henry James. And she had baited him on and on, knowing that he was wrong, drawing him out, letting him insist he was right to make him feel like an idiot when she finally produced her *Collected Works* and showed him the contents page. They'd had a big argument after that, furious, intense and ridiculous. One of their last.

"I visited your publisher," she says. "Couldn't you get anyone else to pick it up?"

"Tunnel Press was my first choice."

"Tunnel Press has never been anyone's first choice. I'm not sure I believe that the course of history changes with you."

"Believe what you like." He is irritable, letting her rile him. Things aren't going the way he planned. It is something you can't always factor ahead of time — how much people change, year to year, day to day.

"Your publisher — Ravington, Rav — he had some friends visiting when I dropped in to see him."

He knows who she's talking about. Wilton and Stapp. They'd been around earlier that afternoon, he'd had to shoo them away before she arrived. He keeps his face carefully neutral. She is good at provoking him. He knows this now and he has to adapt. He has to regain control.

"Nigel Wilton and Eric Stapp," she says. "I didn't get their names, but I'm pretty sure that's who they were. They have something of a reputation, you know."

He nods and takes a sip of tea.

"They're not the sort of people you'd want to be associated with." She looks concerned. He is not falling for it. "Why did you call me exactly? Are you really sure you want me to write about you and your book? You know I won't be kind, you know I'll be completely objective." She smiles again. It is a beautiful smile. Another thing he had remembered imperfectly.

"Have we started the interview or are we still doing small talk?" he asks.

Karen sighs and turns to a blank page in her notebook, creasing it back, as neat as a schoolgirl. She looks up at him, but she still hasn't turned on the tape recorder. She is going to try and get something out of him before she starts, something for free. "This is kind of weird, isn't it?"

He shrugs. He is starting to catch onto her, starting to adapt.

"I mean you and me," she says. "Meeting again like this. I almost didn't want to come."

"It's a small country. You're the only journalist I know."

"Did you know," she says, writing his name at the top of her open page, underlining it twice, "that Daniel is back in town as well?"

He doesn't say anything. He waits.

"He's working at some sort of computer company downtown," she continues. "Isn't that a trip? We could all get together again, have a reunion."

It is perverse, she is perverse, she'll do anything to unsettle him. He can't believe it, can't believe she'd mention Daniel. He isn't sure of the person she has become, not sure if he still understands her. She is playing a game with him and is prepared to hazard very high stakes. It hurts to be callous, but he can play the game too. He can play it better. "Are you going to ask me a real question now?"

"Of course," she says and turns on her tape recorder. "You studied history with Marion Pryor in the UK."

Naturally she begins with a statement, not a question. "You've heard of her?" he asks.

"She was quite famous in certain circles. Was she a good teacher?"

"She shaped my approach to history. But I didn't stay with her long."

"Do you consider yourself to be a historical revisionist?"

"If by revisionist you mean denier, then no. My book makes no claims about the Holocaust," he says. "The only claims it makes are about the mechanical workings of the furnaces at Auschwitz-Birkenau. Nothing more."

"But the conclusions you reach about the furnaces are at odds with the testimony of survivors, guards and officials. Are you saying they were mistaken? Or are you saying they were lying?"

"You're putting words in my mouth," he says. "I don't have anything to say about mistakes or lies. All I talk about are the furnaces, their physical capabilities, their limitations."

"You're claiming that fewer than the established figure of 1.1 million actually died at Auschwitz."

"No," he says. "I make no such claim."

"But you do claim that it is possible they did not?"

He smiles. She is a tenacious questioner, but he will not give ground. "I have nothing to say about possibilities. Facts are my only concern. Facts about furnaces. I'll leave it to you and the rest of my readers to talk about possibilities."

They pause here, eyeing each other warily. He keeps quiet, unwilling to volunteer anything more, waiting for her next assault. He knows it is coming. He has her now, he has lured her in.

She turns another page in her notebook, then looks up at

him and smiles again. "Martin," she says, "I've often wondered why we didn't stay friends."

He doesn't know what to say to that. She fights a good fight, plays a good game. She has changed.

JERUSALEM SYNDROME

Before in-vitro fertilisation can begin, eggs must be surgically extracted from a woman's hyper-stimulated ovaries. Nomi was young, so this stage of things wouldn't be a problem. Younger women usually responded well to the hormone treatment — they usually produced more ova of a better quality. Everyone at the clinic remarked on Nomi's youth. She was barely thirty, they would say. Her fertility problems were unusual in a woman of her age.

Attempts at standard insemination over the last year had failed but prior to those problems coming to light the clinic staff had remarked on her youth in a different, slightly suspicious way. *Why hasn't she found a man?* they had been thinking. *Why doesn't she want to find a man? What is wrong with her?*

Lippman wouldn't have minded knowing the answer to these questions himself. She could still find a husband, there was still time. Lippman didn't think Nomi was a bad-looking girl. Her waist was a little thick, maybe, her thighs a little heavy, but she could attract a man if she tried. They had argued over this, or rather Lippman had argued, had railed, and Nomi had weathered it. He had no idea his daughter could be so resolute. He would have preferred shouting, anger, tears. This was the only option, she had told him. Take it or leave it.

The procedure would take place under full anaesthetic, the patient lying on her back, her feet up in stirrups, the lights in the operating room turned down because eggs are photosensitive. A probe with a hollow needle attached would be used to pierce the vaginal wall and collect the eggs from the ovarian follicles. Lippman had been there while the doctor talked Nomi through it. The doctor, a bright-eyed woman with steely-grey hair, had explained that she would use an ultrasound image of the ovaries to guide her as she collected the eggs. She assured them that she could perform the collection without causing uteral bleeding and thus rendering Nomi a niddah. If Nomi was in niddah then she would not be able to receive the embryo transfer two days later, she would have to wait seven days in order to be clean and that would be too long. A child conceived in niddah would be a ben-niddah and that would not do. It reassured Lippman to know that the doctors were thinking about these things. The clinic had been recommended to him. Nothing they did there broke the Halakha.

Lippman put down the pamphlet he'd been studying and got up from the kitchen table. He walked into the living room of his daughter's West Jerusalem apartment, where Nomi and Mordecai were sitting on the floor, poring over the glossy pages of a computer-game magazine. He stood in the doorway for a moment, watching them. Mordecai pointed excitedly at some article and Nomi laughed, poking her half-brother in his ribs, then leaning closer to whisper into his ear. Of course he had made the right decision. He just had to look at the two of them to see how right it was. Remember *g'milut hasidim.*

Loving-kindness. He could not deny his daughter.

Lippman cleared his throat and told them that he was going out for a little while. Just to see some people while they were in the city. He would not be back late.

Nomi nodded and returned her attention to the magazine article, which Mordecai was explaining to her. The boy didn't even look up when Lippman patted him on the head to say goodbye. He had not told Nomi about Joshua, hadn't told her that he was meeting him again tonight. Nomi was having her harvest tomorrow. He did not want her to feel upset or angry on the eve of an operation.

Lippman collected his jacket from a hook by the door and stepped out onto the stairway. He had to see this young man again, had to know him, just a little. It would have been too difficult to explain to Nomi. He could not properly explain it to himself.

The hug came as a surprise to Steve. Physical affection, particularly in public, had never been one of Josh's favourite things. After embracing him for a long moment Josh put his hands on Steve's shoulders and pushed him back, holding him at arm's length, considering him. "It's great to see you," he said.

Josh looked good. Tanned, healthy, flushed with energy. Positively glowing. Steve said "You weren't around when I arrived. I've been worried . . ."

"Sorry, yeah. Let's get a drink, I'll tell you what's going on." Steve allowed himself to be led over to the hotel bar. "I've found something here," Josh was saying as he signalled for a couple of beers. "I've been thinking and something's clicked, my ideas are coming together. And it's great that you're here now because you can be part of it too. This is for you as well, Steve. It's for all of us."

"Us?"

"Half-Jews."

Steve sipped his beer. "Okay," he said. "You've kind of lost me."

"Being in Israel, in the Jewish homeland, it's helped me to understand myself better. I know who I am now. I always used to think of myself as Jewish. I thought that was who I was, yeah? It defined me. But being here, talking to people, seeing the sights and the history, now I know I'm not."

Steve took a deeper swallow of his beer and continued to listen.

"I don't have the background, I don't have the religion, I don't have the right parentage. I've been denying that for a long time, but I can't escape it here. Yet discovering what I'm not has helped me to discover what I am." Josh put his hand on Steve's shoulder and leaned closer. "A Half-Jew," he said. "I am Half-Jewish."

Steve was about to ask more — he was particularly interested to hear what this had to do with the sperm donations Anita had talked about — but a man appeared behind them, coughing to attract their attention. Steve turned to see Lippman, the man who had recognised Anita at Yad Vashem. In the soft lighting of the hotel bar he seemed older than when he had stood beneath the Pillar of Heroism in the midday sun. His eyes, unguarded by sunglasses, were small, slit-like, squinty. "Sorry to interrupt your conversation," he said.

Anita had just emerged from the lifts and was crossing the lobby towards the hotel bar when she saw Lippman approach Josh and Steve. She paused, hesitating by a plastic pot-plant as they started to speak. Anita had been prepared for one more night with Steve and Josh before she took the early bus to Tel Aviv the next day. Talk to them, have a drink, have dinner, see that Josh was safe in Steve's care, then be on her way. She had forgotten Josh had invited Lippman to join them at the hotel. She didn't like being in Lippman's company. She disliked the relaxed, loose-limbed confidence of his movements and his half-mocking tone, the assurance of a man who always knew what you were thinking and why your thoughts would always be wrong.

There was an Israeli phrase Anita had encountered over the course of her stay, in the conversations that almost inevitably descended into arguments: "I shall show you where the fish pees." To know "where the fish pees" was to have the most focused, detailed and refined knowledge of what was at stake. "Where the fish pees" was a point or distinction so small it was barely perceptible, and yet so crucial that it could unravel every claim and counter-claim made about the fish itself. You cannot argue with someone who knows where the fish pees.

Anita's studies were going well, the tour with Josh had been useful. She was not so worried about her PhD any more; that would come, the material was all there. Her thoughts had turned to writing some sort of popular book now — a guide to Holocaust sites and memorials perhaps. A book with an accessible hypothesis, a few thought-provoking claims and questions, a large number of photographs. There was something to be made there, a future could be carved out.

But being near Lippman risked all of this. She had theories, thoughts, perspectives. She had faith in them — they were solid, substantial, important and interesting. Yet here was Lippman with his swagger, his almost sneering smile. Lippman with his real stories about his real father who had been in the camps. Lippman ready to tell her where the fish pees.

Lippman considered Joshua. The man had donated at Nomi's clinic. Lippman wasn't sure if all the sperm collected at the clinic was used there, or if it went into some sort of central sperm bank. But there was a chance that he was looking at the raw DNA of his future grandchild. A small chance, a tiny chance, but he would take it, he had to.

The three of them moved to a table in a corner of the bar, where Anita joined them. The young British friend of Joshua, the woman who claimed to be a Holocaust researcher. She sat down, looking sideways at Lippman. The other friend, Steve, seemed nervous as well; they weren't happy to see Lippman in their nice hotel. He was a bad old Israeli, he lived in Judea, he never apologised. He was everything *Economist* editorials had taught them to despise, the sort of person these young humane British children bemoaned at their dinner parties. They were all wonderfully humane, yes, wonderfully compassionate, these British children. Joshua pulled out Anita's chair for her. He had manners.

"Steve said he was worried about me," Joshua said to Anita. "I've been telling him how I've never been better, yeah?"

Nomi would have this man's son, Lippman thought. He could not imagine a granddaughter, not looking at Joshua Levit. The son might grow up to have the father's slightly wide eyes, large grin, and tendency to speak too fast. But he might remember to pull out a chair for a lady, once in a while. That would be something.

Josh was talking a little too much. He knew he could do that sometimes. A familiar look was starting to form on Steve's face. Slightly raised eyebrows, eyeballs just poised to roll.

"So when you've got one side saying you are not Jewish and the other saying that you are not *not* Jewish," Josh said, "where does that leave you? With an identity. An identity that is as real and as valid as anyone else's."

Josh was glad Lippman had come along that evening. He could express his ideas in front of that man, an old man, an orthodox Jew, a man whose father had been in Treblinka. If Josh could assert his Half-Jewishness in front of Lippman he could do so in front of anyone. He could claim his Half-

Jewishness back, could make it his own.

He and Lippman had sat together in the clinic waiting room. Lippman had been waiting in some other part of the hospital, perhaps he was a patient, perhaps he knew a patient, but he had wandered into the donors' waiting room, looking around for a long while before making the decision to sit down beside Josh and introduce himself. Josh felt as if they should have shaken hands but they didn't. Ahead of them, one by one, donors were being called up by the nurse to take their turn in the cubicle.

Josh started to talk about Washington, about Yad Vashem. He mentioned Anita and her research. Lippman hadn't said much, even then. He had just nodded a few times, mentioned his father had been at Treblinka. Then Lippman said, "You're not Jewish, I suppose, if you are here." He had sounded a little wistful.

Josh had replied, "I'm Half-Jewish." It was the first time he had used the term and it felt right in his mouth, absolutely right. He could not be Jewish, not when he was talking to a man like Lippman, but he could be Half-Jewish, he could claim that much for himself.

Lippman considered him for a moment. He had not stormed *There is no such thing!* Instead he had simply nodded, and said, "I thought you looked Jewish. A little, perhaps." And it happened there, at that moment. Josh was reborn half a Jew.

"Maybe we should order something to eat," Anita suggested.

Lippman waved a hand. "You order if you like. I have already eaten."

The clinic where Nomi was being treated had been recommended to Lippman. He had insisted she go there, his one condition for helping her with the mandatory interviews that would decide whether she was fit for artificial insemination. She was not too young to have a child, but young enough that awkward questions could be asked about why she wanted to have it on her own. Lippman had a few questions himself, but he had vouched for his daughter, told the social workers and psychiatrists he supported her decision. That or no grandchild, what choice did he have? But he had been allowed his condition; that she should go to a clinic where they observed the Halakha, where they made sure no child born would be a mamzer or ben-niddah. Not much of a condition. A husband, now that would have been a condition. But the clinic was something.

Because the clinic observed the Halakha, it only used Gentile sperm. Lippman had been shocked when he'd been told that, but apparently it was right, it was proper. A Jew was prohibited from masturbation, from spilling seed needlessly, but the Halakha didn't care where or how a Gentile spilt his. Also, the child born from an anonymous Jewish donor might unknowingly grow up to marry a half-sibling, whereas under the Halakha two children who shared a Gentile father were not considered to be related at all; the father did not exist. Bizarrely, perversely, Gentile sperm turned out to be the best.

Where did this Gentile sperm come from? He had been assured they did not take sperm from Arabs, but how could he be certain? Some places didn't care — a Gentile was a Gentile — others only got their sperm from the United States in frozen packaged deliveries. Lippman had wandered into the donor waiting room one day at Nomi's recommended clinic, to see what was on offer. Students mostly. European Kibbutz volunteers, big and healthy and fair-haired. English, Scandinavians, Germans. These were the men who would help to father the next generation of the Jewish state. Better than an Arab, but not by much.

If Lippman could he would have called the whole thing off. But they had gone too far, it was too late, and Nomi was stubborn. They said that Gentile sperm was the best, that it was all right by the Halakha, but Lippman had done research and found dissent. He had read Rabbi Amsel's views on impure sperm and eternal pollution, Rav Waldenburg's warnings about the spiritual destruction that "these creatures" would bring to Israel, Rabbi Teitelbaum's exhortations to not allow the pure lineage of the House of Jacob to be contaminated. It might be better to use Gentile sperm but it was not a good thing. The child could still be a Jew, but a Gentile father was a misfortune at some level.

A grandchild or no grandchild. A Gentile father or no father. There were no easy answers.

And then in that waiting room, surrounded by Europe's fit, healthy and happy young heirs, he had met Joshua.

"Half-Jews, huh?" Steve said, once they had ordered. "That's what we are now. Great, fine."

"It's not about the world defining us as part-Jewish, or non-Jewish, it's about us defining ourselves. Half-Jewishness should be something anyone with a single Jewish parent can have if they want it. It's a culture, a past, an identity."

"So what exactly does this have to do with the sperm donations?" Steve asked.

"Half-Jews were persecuted as much as anyone else in the Holocaust," Josh continued, ignoring Steve's question. "It's the crucible of Half-Jewish experience. You know, you hear all about the gypsies now and the queers too, but the Half-Jews don't get mentioned at all. Their existence is denied. Reclaiming our place in the Holocaust is the key to asserting our Half-Jewish selves."

"Yes, but about the sperm . . ."

Lippman was following the conversation, looking back and forth between Josh and Steve. Anita couldn't tell if he was amused, bored or perplexed. What was he doing here? It was not hard to see why Josh had invited him along. He did that, he seized on people with enthusiasm and drew them into his life. But why had Lippman accepted the invitation? He couldn't be fascinated by Josh's new Half-Jew movement, or charmed by his enthusiasms.

Anita looked at Lippman and suspected he was here for her. He had stalked her through Yad Vashem and had been waiting for her at her restaurant table. He would tell her that a Christian girl could know nothing about the Holocaust, that her research was worth nothing, that she understood nothing. He would invoke his dead father and the sacredness of the event. She was an intruder — she didn't know where the fish peed, couldn't even see the fish.

She looked at Lippman and wondered how she could resist him. How did one break a monopoly on memory? He was a settler, that had been mentioned before. He lived in a settlement in Judea, the West Bank. This could be her hook then, her defence against survivor stories and stories about survivors.

"How is your research going, Miss Clarkson?" Lippman asked then.

"Very well, thank you." The disenfranchisement of Palestinians. Squalid villages. Military harassment. Collective punishments. Jews acting like Nazis. That was where her fish would pee.

"You found your visit to Yad Vashem useful?"

"I did."

"Good. I will be interested to see if you can learn anything new."

The mention of the Holocaust sidetracked Joshua. "I've found this site, right?" he said, leaning closer to Steve. "This website. I've got a printout in my room, I'll show you later. It's vile. It's an attack on memory. I'm thinking this sort of thing needs to be checked out, it needs to be investigated."

"But Josh, the sperm . . . ?"

Lippman watched Joshua. Was the man mad? Lippman had known a number of madmen. His own father might have been one. It hadn't made any difference, he had still been a good father, Lippman had still loved him. There was no guarantee that Joshua would be the father of Nomi's child, of course. The sperm was doled out secretly; it wasn't quite a lottery, but only the doctors and nurses knew who got what. Apparently they made 'sensible choices', but there was only the smallest chance that the seed would come from Joshua Levit, this man he knew, however slightly, and not from a European kibbutznik or some under-the-radar Arab. Have they not done enough to us, that they must now father our children?

Lippman asked Anita a few polite questions about her research and she gave him short stiff responses. He teased her a little, saying that he hoped she would find "something new", but kept his face straight. She was welcome to whatever she found — she could have it all, it was no use to him.

Lippman remembered how he used to lie about his father. At school he told the other boys his father had escaped Treblinka, hidden in the woods, fought with the partisans. Lippman was ashamed to have had a father who'd just survived. What did he have to do to survive? What sort of person must he have been? Sabon was what the boys had called his father when they found out he'd never escaped from Treblinka, never fought, never picked up a pistol or a carbine. Sabon, soap. If you did not fight then you were nothing, you were human dust.

Things changed later. People wanted to listen, they thought they needed the stories. But Lippman's father would not talk, he had finished with it. No Sabon in Israel.

"Did you know," Josh was saying, "that soon there will be more Half-Jews in the United States than there will be Jews?

We're talking about a major cultural and ethnic group here, one that goes unrecognised, one that doesn't even recognise itself." Josh was trying to make his point, but he couldn't shake the feeling that he was the only one involved, that nothing was getting through. Lippman seemed to be listening, but Steve still had that familiar look of wearied indulgence on his face.

Steve had never felt the true pull of the sites they'd visited. He wouldn't appreciate what Josh had found here in Israel, in the last place in the world where Half-Jews would be welcomed. Being here, seeing Jews in the streets on the buses, driving taxis, delivering mail, he had rubbed up against it every day, the fact that he wasn't Jewish, the fact that he was something else.

Steve was still questioning him about the sperm donations. Josh was trying to dodge that one — not because he was embarrassed, but because no one else at the table could be expected to understand. The more donations he made, the more children would be born in Israel with only one Jewish parent. That parent would be the mother and so the children would be Jewish, but by Josh's definition they would be Half-Jewish as well. He had lived a life being neither one thing nor the other. Now he could beget children who were two things at once. Be fruitful and multiply.

Anita looked at Lippman while Steve and Josh continued to talk across each other. She resented the jibe about "learning something new". He would come at her again, she could feel it. He would challenge her authority and knowledge, her moral right to her subject matter. Anita had her counter-argument ready, she knew how to subvert his claims to Holocaust ownership. Her fish peed with the Palestinian people, the 1948 partition agreement, Ben-Gurion's ultimate intentions. He might come back with something about

Biblical precedent, but she would then mention natural justice and they would keep going from there.

Lippman sipped the beer he could not taste and continued to watch Joshua talk. Nomi lived a quiet life, she was all on her own. Did she see anyone? Just a few girlfriends, she had said when he asked. Perhaps he should have paid more attention since her mother died, since he moved out to Judea. But he had a new family now, a new child of his own.

And that was the problem; how could he deny her what God had given him? He could not be cruel, he could not be suspicious, he could not ask for answers to his questions. All he could ask for was Joshua Levit; this strange man's seed was all he could pray for.

Forced expulsion, Anita was thinking. War-like neighbours. Oppressors — terrorists. Bulldozed homes — suicide bombers. The Sabra and Chatila camp massacres — the Munich Olympics. The arguments and counter-arguments were unfolding in her head, like the opening moves in a game of chess.

"Thank you for your company," Lippman said, standing up when their food arrived. "I really must be going now."

Josh looked surprised. "But you only just got here. I wanted you to have a proper talk with Anita."

"My daughter is having an operation tomorrow. I would have loved to have had a proper talk with Miss Clarkson, but I cannot stay out too late. Very nice to have met you all." Lippman nodded to the three of them, then walked out of the bar.

"Strange man," said Steve.

"Sorry," Josh said to Anita. "Guess I've been talking too much. I really did want you two to talk."

Anita leaned over and put a hand on Josh's arm. "It's okay," she said. "Really."

They ate dinner. Josh talked a little more about Half-Jewishness, about bringing Half-Jews out into the light of history, making them tall, making them proud. After dinner he took Steve and Anita up to his room to show them the printout from the website he'd found. Something called *The Online Forum for the Academic Analysis of the Holocaust.* An advertisement for a book about body disposal. Steve couldn't figure what it was all about. He was feeling tired.

"It's an attack — not just on Jewish history, but on Half-Jewish history as well," Josh was saying. "Any attack on the Holocaust is an attack on Half-Jews. It's our defining historical moment."

Anita was yawning. She had to get up early the next day so she would say goodbye now. She bent down over Josh, who was sitting on the bed, and kissed his cheek. "Stay in touch. Let me know what you find out in New Zealand."

Josh nodded absently, he didn't seem to register that his tour with Anita was over and she was leaving. She walked out of the room without glancing in Steve's direction. Then the door closed and Steve was alone with Josh.

He sat down next to him on the bed, still tired, almost numb. Josh was talking about Half-Jewish unity. About drive and direction, about a spiritual and cultural homeland that could be found in the landscape of the Holocaust.

"It's being published in New Zealand," Josh said. "This book, this thing. That's how far denial has spread — right down to the arse-end of the earth. Nobody's watching this, not yet. I have to go there, it's like a sign, it's like my chance to fight it."

Steve hunched over, putting his head in his hands as Josh talked on. He had followed Josh far enough, he thought. To the east, to the Holy City. But this was the end now. Josh had abandoned him in Edinburgh, now Steve would return the favour in Jerusalem.

Lippman paused outside his daughter's apartment building, watching his taxi weave away into the night. He wasn't really sure what he'd expected to find. Joshua Levit. Of course there was no such thing as half a Jew; of course a Half-Jew could never be recognised in the Halakha. Joshua could protest all he liked, but this Half-Jew culture he talked of never existed, would never exist, could never exist as long as Jews were Jews.

But half a Jew was better than nothing Jewish at all, and if this was it — if there would be no husband for Nomi and no real father for his grandchild — then Lippman was prepared to say that Joshua Levit was a Half-Jew, the only one in all existence. He, Lippman, named him as such and would pray that the madman's sperm found its way to his daughter's ova.

And what else could Lippman do other than deny his daughter? *G'milut hasidim.* That was a mitzvah. The most important of all.

BREAKING THE STORY

Karen Staunton woke up as the sun rose. Her windows had no curtains and a shaft of sunlight scorched her into consciousness. She rolled over, burying her face in her pillow for a moment, before climbing out of bed to start her day.

Karen's bedroom was being dismantled. A pile of drafts, photocopies and a partially submerged iBook occupied the pale patch of carpet where her desk used to be. Karen's clothes, torn from the recently departed wardrobe, were now piled on the floor in "keep" and "chuck" piles. Her shelves had been passed on to a friend, one of those perpetual postgraduate students, and the only books left were the ones she couldn't sell or give away — an out of date epistemology textbook from university, a copy of T. S. Eliot's *The Cocktail Party*, a couple of issues of *Landfall*. She had already got rid of the small things, the ornaments, knick-knacks and art prints. The souvenirs from holidays, the framed photographs, the postcards stuck to the wall above her bed. The scented candles, the stuffed animals her last boyfriend had given her. The first thing she had done, before deciding on a destination or thinking about a job or investigating flights, had been to dismantle her memories of the last three years. She had ripped them down, all in one go, and not looked back.

Karen wrapped herself in her blue dressing gown (destined for the "chuck" pile eventually, but not today) and walked down the hallway to the kitchen. Her flatmate was not up yet; she was sleeping through the sunny morning, content and safe in a room that still had curtains, a large dark oak wardrobe, and walls plastered with movie posters and framed enlargements of the cute cherubs from Raphael's paintings. Karen looked out the window while making some coffee; she could see right down onto Oriental Parade and out across the harbour. The sky was crystalline and the bay was still, one of the perfect Wellington mornings that can spring out and hit you, even in the heart of winter.

Her article would be out today. Karen took her coffee back into her bedroom and sat down on the floor in front of her laptop, tucking her legs underneath her. She logged onto Nigel Wilton's website, his online forum, and checked his latest post. Smiling to herself, she forwarded the link to Daniel Legkov's email address. You know people who know people, you talk, word gets around, contact details are passed on. It was almost impossible to not know who was in Wellington, who was coming and who was going, and now Daniel Legkov was like a canker underneath her tongue, a nick in her gumline, an abscess in the roof of her mouth. She had sent him Martin's book not too long ago. Next he'd get the website, and then the article. He would see it all eventually.

Karen stood up and arched her back. She blinked her eyes in the bright sunlight, heavy motes of dust floating around her face. It looked like it would be a good day.

Martin Glass found a thick envelope wedged half inside his letterbox and sat down on the scrap of grass by his doorstep to open it. Flicking through the pages of the magazine inside, he quickly located Karen's piece. The article was not exactly true and not exactly false. Nigel Wilton and Eric Stapp appeared as ominous forces, lurking around the edges of Karen's references. Ravington came across as a bit of a fool. Martin Glass didn't come across as anything at all.

There was a photo of the cover of his book and the photo of him that Ravington had taken of him for "publicity purposes" standing outside, eyes half-hidden by the sun's glare on his glasses — but there was little in the article specifically about him, only a few out-of-context quotes from his meeting with Karen and the barest sketch of his background. He wondered why she'd made the whole thing so impersonal — he had expected her to revel in their secret connection, to lace the article with subtle observations about him and his character. But she had held back from that, left him almost faceless, a cipher. He wasn't sure whether to be offended or grateful.

Martin thought about the magazine, thought about it sitting in bookstores and supermarket check-out shelves all across the country. It was a national publication, read by thousands each week, it would get everywhere. He imagined readers flicking through, stumbling on Karen's article and his slightly blurred photo. It was good that he had found her again, that they had found each other. *Body Disposal at Auschwitz* had looked like it would sink without a trace. She had helped him, even if she didn't believe it. Still, he felt uneasy, thinking about all those magazines and all those people. He wasn't quite sure he was prepared for what would be coming. Martin stood up and walked back inside to wait for Nigel Wilton to call him.

Lewis Ravington arrived at the Tunnel Press office at eleven that morning. He was in a good mood, having spent the last night at Adja's flat on the other side of the city. She had called him and in a moment of weakness he had agreed to talk about her poetry. That one thing had led to the inevitable other thing and now he was looking for a spare publishing contract. He was a bad person.

While sorting through the piles he saw that Ms Yorke had left a copy of the magazine on his desk, opened to the page of Karen's article. A hint of Ms Yorke's cigarette smoke still lingered in the air, but she was gone.

Nigel Wilton did not trust journalists. He never had, not since they pilloried him during his court case in Melbourne. They seemed fine when you talked to them, smiling and nodding, taking their little notes so that you could "get your side of the story across". And then you opened the newspaper or magazine to see lies, packs of them, distortions, half-truths, mangled quotations. Nigel Wilton was a man dedicated to the truth. He was dedicated to reality, to objective, empirical, dispassionate observation. That thing the cops used to say on *Dragnet*, "Just the facts, ma'am", that was him. But journalists attacked him, they tore him down, they shredded him.

And now here was another journalist, that Staunton girl. And here was her article, alerting New Zealand to "a hidden threat", to an "assault on truth and memory rapidly entering the mainstream". She had mentioned him and Eric Stapp and their connection to Martin's book. She'd even had the gall to talk about the court action in Melbourne that had been brought to silence him. Clearly she had "researched" him, which meant that she'd harked back to the work of earlier journalists and propagated the same old lies.

Wilton picked up his phone to call Martin. These things had to be weathered, you had to keep on standing and never budge from the light of the truth. Wilton had known this was coming, he had seen it before, had suffered. But he had to stand, he could do no other. God help him.

Alone on an aeroplane, bored with inflight entertainment, suffering from a full bladder yet unwilling to join the after-dinner toilet queue, Joshua Levit hasn't had the opportunity to read Karen's article. But somehow it will be the first thing he finds when he touches down in Auckland, and before he makes his connecting flight to Wellington he will have read it. And then he will know that his fears and hopes have been confirmed. A small fight in a small country — half a fight really, perhaps even half a country — but his, all his.

Sometime after all of this, at eleven in the evening, Daniel Legkov remained oblivious. It was his natural state.

DANIEL

"Gamers are bloodthirsty creatures," Logan Heckle said shortly after we arrived at our third bar of the night, one of the fake Irish pubs on Courtenay Place. It was getting close to midnight and most of the office party had trickled away by then. Only Heckle, Morbid and I were left, and Morbid was no longer in a fit state for communication. "We're running into some problems with the Styx Softworks marketing department. A completely immersive real-world virtual environment isn't quite the innocuous game premise we had supposed."

Next to us Morbid finished his pint and silently slipped the glass into the pocket of his trenchcoat.

"We've been aiming for an M rating, but the ratings board are now talking about an AO," Heckle continued. "Styx Softworks are worried — an AO rating would mean no distribution in Wal-Mart. It's the kiss of death for a computer game."

I got up to buy another round. When I returned to the

table Morbid had appropriated my old glass as well and was reaching across the table for Heckle's empty.

"Let's be frank," Heckle said as I put his pint in front of him. "You can do some pretty hairy things in real life, can't you? Maybe trying to simulate every possible action wasn't the best idea."

I nodded, remembering the time I had put into the Alpha game-testing.

```
Your hands find her throat, her hair, you
force her down to the floor of the kitchen.
  "Daniel! Stop!"
  "Look at me. Karen, look at me."
  ERROR.  Selected  name  *Anita*  ERROR.
Shutting down.
```

"And none of this is helped by the talk on the game forums," Heckle was saying. "A lot of gamers love the idea of getting this pristine virtual world to fuck around with, they love it so much they're threatening to boycott it if we take the blood and violence out of the engine."

"This is good," Morbid said, once again jerking upright and the table. His eyes cleared for a moment. "This is all good," he said again, then drained his pint and hid the glass inside the folds of his trenchcoat along with the others.

We stood up to leave. On the way out I brushed shoulders with a blond-haired man in a leather jacket who was sitting at the bar.

"Sorry, mate," I said, but he just gazed past me, his eyes wide and vacant. He had been sitting there all evening, drinking, not talking to anyone.

Outside we started to walk down to the second fake Irish pub on Courtenay Place. "So we can't take the violence out of *VirtuLife* or we'll lose our players," Heckle said. "And we can't make them choose not to be violent."

"Choices," Morbid says, staggering along behind us. "You can't take away the choices. *VirtuLife* is all about making choices and observing their consequences. No two *VirtuLives* need ever be the same."

Heckle and I stopped outside the second fake Irish pub, not sure whether we wanted to go in or to call it a night. Morbid had no such hesitations and walked forward quickly, but the bouncer stopped him.

"Gamers are always going to want to try things like throwing hand grenades at ambulances, or dropping preschoolers off tall buildings," Heckle said. "Just because it's possible to do these things in *VirtuLife*. If everything's possible then we've got no control."

"Maybe real life is always going to be rated Adults Only," I said.

Ahead of us, Morbid was arguing with the bouncer. "I'm fine," he said, swaying slightly from side to side. "Really. Super-fine."

"Sorry, mate," said the bouncer.

"Want to split a cab?" Heckle asked.

"Maybe," I said. "In a minute." I thought about play-testing *VirtuLife* again.

```
She is drunk upstairs while the party in
the ERROR Karori Street ERROR flat
continues below. You sit against the wall
beside her in the hallway and ERROR ERROR
ERROR talk about things you can(ERROR)'t
really remember, but they seem important at
the time.
"Daniel," she says, though she will not
look at you and later she leads you ERROR
you follow her ERROR into the bedroom.
```

There were times when the game felt almost uncannily real but there was still something missing. Maybe it was a glitch in the Eclectic engine or a quirk of my gaming style, but somehow playing *VirtuLife* felt more like manipulating a dream or a memory than living in a real world.

"Look," I heard Morbid say, "all I want to do is sample the authentic Irish ambience that your bar does so well."

"On your bike, mate," said the bouncer.

"It's because *VirtuLife* doesn't have a story," I said to Heckle. "If we had a plot then we could direct the players to only be violent in appropriate ways. Without a plot they get to do whatever they want."

Behind us, Morbid's argument with the bouncer had come to a head. "No, you look," the bouncer was saying. "There is no way that you are getting inside."

"Right," Morbid said, sweeping his trenchcoat back and shoving his hands in his pockets in a fluid, disgusted motion. The four pint-glasses he had stolen earlier fell out and smashed on the pavement at the bouncer's feet. "Well," Morbid said, after a brief pause, "I guess this will just have to be your loss."

Later in the evening, I managed to haul Morbid back to the apartment on The Terrace and drop him down on the black bed-sheets of his big black double bed in his black-wallpapered room. The impact of his body caused an elaborately constructed string mobile of cute beanbag animals impaled on spikes, letter openers, paperclips and broken nail-scissors to jiggle slightly on the cord attaching it to the ceiling. I stepped out and quietly closed the door behind me.

In the kitchen I took a tub of chocolate-and-caramel éclair ice-cream out of the freezer and sat down with it at my laptop to check my emails. One message was from an email address I didn't recognise, stairway@hotmail, and contained only a link to a website: ofaah.com. The site turned out to be something called *The Online Forum for the Academic Analysis of the Holocaust*. I glanced over the latest moderator comment.

```
The tide is changing, my friends. I am turning over moderation of this site to AussieFootSoldier for the next few weeks as significant developments concerning our New Zealand colleague, Martin Glass, will be occupying my attention for some time. Remember, copies of his book are available from Tunnel Press, NZ (link below) and I urge you to purchase. Experience has taught us that challenges to the exterminationist orthodoxy rarely pass without terrible retribution. I would like to thank each and every one of you for your warm wishes, moral support and much-needed financial assistance over this time.

Nigel Wilton.
```

Martin Glass. Our New Zealand colleague. Presenting a challenge to the exterminationist orthodoxy. I looked round for my copy of Martin's book, but couldn't find it. What exactly was its challenge to the "exterminationist orthodoxy"? How many bodies could a Topf double-muffle coke-fuelled furnace burn if a Topf furnace could burn bodies?

"What are you looking at?"

I twisted round in my seat to see Morbid standing behind me in the doorway. Several strands of his long hair were stuck to the corner of his mouth. "Something to do with the Holocaust," I said.

Morbid looked at me blankly.

"The Holocaust," I said again.

Morbid shrugged and sat down opposite me at the kitchen table.

"You don't know what the Holocaust is?" I asked.

"I've *heard* of it," said Morbid.

"Didn't they ever cover this in school?"

"I never paid much attention in school."

"You know about Nazi Germany, right?"

"Yeah. Hitler and stuff." Morbid shrugged again as my eyes widened. "I'm just not all that into history."

I started to mumble about railcars, gassings, concentration camps.

"Concentration camps? Right, I think I've been to one of those."

"You've been to a camp, but you don't know what the Holocaust is?"

"I think it was a half-hour stop on this bus tour I was doing across Europe a few years back. Fuck, I must have been the only guy on that bus not to get laid in Germany or Poland . . ."

The kitchen felt like a small pool of cold, stale light in the middle of a great, overwhelmingly shabby sort of darkness. I was adrift on a black ocean and the sticky, melting tub of chocolate-and-caramel éclair ice-cream was the only thing keeping me afloat. Somewhere down below us, on The Terrace, a car's tyres screeched. Then it revved away into the night.

"I don't know why you're getting so worked up about this," Morbid said. "I don't see how it's my fault if I don't know something."

"It's not just something," I said.

"What is it then?"

"Go back to bed, Morbid."

"Does it have anything to do with that thing about Hitler being half Jewish?"

"Go back to bed."

Morbid grunted and stood up, stumbled out of the

kitchen. "I live in the now!" I heard him shout as he collapsed back into his bedroom.

I returned to my email and tapped out a reply to stairway@hotmail. *Who are you?* I sat back in my chair to wait for a reply and picked up the sweaty tub of ice-cream, scooping another spoonful of the sweet gooey mess into my mouth.

MARTIN GLASS

Back when they were in university Martin had once tried to talk to Daniel about the Holocaust, tried to explain his wonder at its scale and logistics. Martin was still raw back then, even with a head full of brutal knowledge.

"Yeah," Daniel had said, cutting him off mid-spiel. "Well, I'm half Jewish, y'know?"

Martin had felt this claim somehow cast his own interests into shadow, stripped him of any right to talk authoritatively in his friend's presence. He might have read more, he might have known more, but somehow Daniel had a link to the event that went beyond all that, dismissing Martin's knowledge and reading and attempts at understanding.

Martin had been almost delighted to discover, years later, that there was no such thing as a Half-Jew at all. Jewish descent is traced through the maternal line only and is like a binary, you are either a one or a zero. This came after the Karori flat and its history, and Martin's discovery had felt like a small pyrrhic victory over Daniel, a reclamation of compromised moral ground. But then still later, after a few years spent studying with Marion Pryor and a few more in Europe laying the groundwork for a new history, Martin started to think harder about the term and its meanings. It flitted around the edges of his study, weaving in and out of the primary and secondary sources, flourishing momentarily then fading away.

After a brief investigation Martin discovered that Half-Jewishness was undergoing a contemporary renaissance. He found online communities, websites, messageboards, books and articles, children of Jewish fathers and Gentile mothers talking about what it meant to be born Half-Jewish. He even came across a tongue-in-cheek petition for the foundation of a Half-Jewish homeland on Governors Island, off the coast of New York.

Something about this pleases Martin. He likes the idea of people arguing for a middle ground between the zero and the one, for a decimal place, for a nought-point-five. Martin's study of history, its writing and its rewriting, has gifted him with an appreciation of unreal objects, of the tangibility of their non-existence, their substance and weight.

Take the Half-Jew. There is no trace of him in Scripture. The great Jews of Biblical times took Gentile wives (Judah married a Canaanite, Joseph an Egyptian, Moses a Midianite and an Ethiopian, David a Philistine, and Solomon seemed to shag just about everything that came within his general radius), but no Half-Jews resulted from these unions, only whole and complete and indisputably Jewish children. By the Common Era, Jewish descent had been restricted to the maternal line alone, thus discouraging young Jewish men from wandering too far and also protecting the community rights of Jewish women who had been raped during the frequent pogroms of the Middle Ages. "Born Jews" were considered to be only those born of a Jewish womb with a Jewish soul. You cannot split a soul in two so you cannot be a half a Jew. There is no sign of the Half-Jew in antiquity, no sign in the Middle Ages. What gives him half-life? When does he spring into half-being?

You have to go forward, Martin thinks. To the nineteenth century, where the dark days of religious *Judenfeindschaft* — or Jew-hatred — had given way to rational, scientific, racial *Antisemitismus*. Wilhelm Marr's seminal text of 1879, *The Victory of Judaism over Germanism*, breathed life into the concept of the Half-Jew. Following Marr's new philosophy of anti-Semitism, the child of a union between a Jew and Gentile would inherit a half-share of the qualities possessed by those of the Semitic race, whatever their professed religion. This new anti-Semitism was a triumph of thought and language, Martin thinks. No longer would the people of a rational, enlightened Europe have to be troubled by their converted or secular Jewish neighbours. A Jew was a Jew and they could go on hating them — for being cunning and calculating, for being mentally inferior, for polluting the arts with their unhealthy visions, for being uniformly inartistic, for keeping to themselves, for being too well assimilated, for corrupting European bloodlines, for breeding Half-Jews.

Wilhelm Marr's *Antisemitismus* may have set the stage for Half-Jewishness but it was the 1935 laws of Nuremberg that broke the binary decisively. One Jewish parent resulted in a Mischling, first class. One Jewish grandparent and you had a Mischling, second class. Half-breeds. It amuses Martin to read about contemporary claims to Half-Jewishness when the first- and second-class Mischlinge of National Socialist Germany were so desperate to convince the world that no such thing existed. He has read about the advocacy group "Reich League of Christian-German State Citizens of Non-Aryan or not Completely Aryan Origins, Inc", informally known as the Paulus Bund, that was dedicated to improving the status of

Mischlinge in Nazi Germany and convincing the state that they were loyal servants of the Reich. He knows the stories of young Mischlinge men who tried to redeem themselves as Germans through service in the *Wehrmacht*, who were even granted *Deutschblütigkeitserklärung* or "Aryanisation certificates" by Hitler himself. However most Mischlinge slowly became isolated in German society, spared the full force of Nazi persecution, but pushed into menial jobs. The laws governing questions of race and interbreeding prohibited them from marrying full Jews in the first case and "full blood" Germans in the second. Who would want to claim to be Half-Jewish in that time and place? Well . . . a Jew perhaps, Martin thinks. They might see the appeal in having halfness over wholeness under those particular circumstances, in that particular case.

After 1945, Martin can find little trace of Half-Jews in history. They disappear from Europe, happy to slip out of focus, to shake off categorisation, to fall back into the oblivion of the undefined. They were possible in some minds, impossible in others, uncertain in their own. In Germany they had been half-victim and half-collaborator, reluctant March Violets, dissenters by default. The former Mischlinge kept their stories to themselves, they had no one to tell them to. They had suffered, but had not suffered enough. While others had died, they had lived half-lives. They had a half-share of pain and a half-share of guilt.

But now this is changing. As Daniel had, more and more people were stepping forward to say, "Well, I'm half Jewish." It is possible to be Half-Jewish in the way that a person could be Half-Irish or Half-Italian, or so it is claimed. Religious Jews are generally uncomfortable with this and still maintain that Half-Jews do not exist at all. Acknowledging their existence would change what it means to be Jewish. Martin is sometimes surprised at the virulence of their objections, and wonders if historic feelings of suspicion and resentment don't play into it at some level. There is a sense that these so-called "Half-Jews" are freeloaders, opportunists and fair-weather friends. They are happy enough to be descendants of the tribes of Israel in the good times, but when the going gets tough they disappear.

"Jews are such intelligent, hard-working folk."

"I happen to be Half-Jewish myself."

"Jews are money-grubbing conspirators bent on world domination."

"Actually, you know, I'm only half Jewish."

There are also many old stories with nasty stings in their tails, stories about how the most brutal anti-Semites of the Old World of Europe and the neighbourhoods of the United States would turn out to be of mixed parentage themselves. There is a satisfying irony to this; that the most hate-filled person is the person who hates something about himself. Martin thinks this could be why that old rumour about Hitler's "half Jewishness" has survived for so long. Who can resist a twist like that? There is no evidence for it, just hearsay and idle speculation, but at the story level, it offers great satisfaction.

Perhaps religious Jews cannot quite shake the suspicion that the person who claims to be Half-Jewish might turn out to be just another species of Gentile enemy. Martin can see why the Half-Jew must be denied. Another enemy can be dealt with, but not one that lays claim to half of what you are.

Thinking back to Daniel, Martin isn't sure if he ever described himself as Half-Jewish again, apart from that one conversation about the Holocaust. Daniel may just have been trying to change the subject, to pre-empt the discussion by claiming knowledge he neither had nor wanted to possess. He might never have used the term before and never have used it since, never given it any thought even when it passed his lips. But Martin thinks about these things. He has to, he cannot help it.

He wonders about the Half-Jew. What sort of life does he lead today? Perhaps he enjoys having a Seder, but feels uncomfortable with Yom Kippur. He may not mind opening presents under a Christmas tree, but feels a little alienated when people celebrate Easter. He might be religious, in a vague "spiritual" sort of way, comfortable in most houses of worship, though with a tendency to censor the liturgy to suit his tastes. He does not care for passages relating to salvation or chosen-ness. He is undogmatic. The thought of taking communion makes him feel queasy, but he loves a good church choir. He smiles when he hears Shabbat music and can hum along passably, but Hebrew, spoken or written, excludes him. He may or may not have a foreskin, but if he has one he has probably enjoyed it far too much to ever think of giving it up. He is probably not a bad person, on the whole, though God knows he has his faults, just like everyone else.

RAVINGTON

Ms Yorke had resigned without notice. She was gone, she would not answer Ravington's calls. The two books of poetry and the high-country farming memoir lined up for printing later in the year had been called off by their authors, the cheques cancelled. Ravington sat in the Tunnel Press offices with the blinds pulled down. The ancient computers, the scarred wooden desks, the discarded piles of dusty proofs all dark and shadowy.

Tunnel Press had thrived on a lack of publicity, had depended on not being talked about. It wasn't a tunnel, it was a hole with one entrance and no exit. Its custom was generated by tiny advertisements at the bottom of magazine classified pages, business cards slid along a bar to a fellow drinker or left on a bedside table in the early hours of the morning. Tunnel Press had depended on no one knowing what Tunnel Press was. He had hoped for notice, but notice of a respectful kind, a kind that would have obscured the day-to-day functionings of the press rather than casting them into a dreary, dreadful light.

> In the past, the press has relied on author contributions for most of its revenue, contributions often generated by inflated sales projections according to former Tunnel Press author and Wellington littérateur Gregory Gaut.

Gaut, Karen Staunton, Martin Glass, damn them all.

> Financial assistance in this case appears to have come from an Australian organisation called the Centre for Academic Analysis of the Holocaust. Nigel Wilton, its chairman and sole member, recently had a civil action brought against him in the Melbourne High Court for distributing anti-Semitic pamphlets.

Who had told the Staunton woman about Nigel Wilton? Had she recognised him in the office? That was a disaster, an absolute disaster. He should have seen it coming. Taking money from an eccentric Australian neo-fascist is not something an independent press lives down, not when it's decided to publish controversial books about the Holocaust. Grace Maher would be laughing. Rav would laugh with her — he might as well, there was nothing else he could do. Tunnel Press was crumbling. Adja was the only poet who would return his calls and her book wouldn't cover the office rent for another month. Sales figures on Martin Glass's book had gone through the roof, naturally, but most of the money from that was owed to Nigel Wilton. Of all the times in his life to publish a book that actually sold.

"Everything in Karen's article is a matter of emphasis and interpretation," Martin had said, when Rav called him after he'd seen the magazine lying open on Ms Yorke's empty desk. "I make no statements about the Holocaust as a concept or as a fact. I only talk about the population of the camp and the number and quality of its furnaces."

"But she says that the conclusions you reach about them amount to Holocaust denial," Rav had said. "She says you're a Holocaust denier."

"Would you have published my book if that was true, Rav?" had been Martin's response.

Wilton had left a message on the Tunnel Press answering machine. He bemoaned the article, but revelled in the new sales figures.

Ravington had started smoking again. He'd found Ms Yorke's old ashtray in the bottom drawer of her desk. Tunnel Press had always been there. From the days of his early twenties drift through to his failed marriage through to his existence as the roving predator at open-mike poetry slams, Tunnel had been the one constant factor in his life. If you looked him in the eyes and asked him who he was, Rav had always been able to snap back: "Lewis Ravington, editor-in-chief." He had hated it, he had hated saying it and being the person who said it — hated it for longer than he could remember.

But if you took that away from him, what would he be? What could Ravington do?

WILTON

The living room in Eric Stapp's flat was dominated by a large swastika flag hanging on one of the walls. A little over the top, Nigel Wilton thought. Counterproductive to the general aims of their mission, a symbol that was likely to alienate the mainstream. He had suggested as much to Eric when he first saw it, but Eric had just raised his eyebrows incredulously and said, "It makes a statement." Each to their own, thought Wilton. It would have been hypocritical of him to try to restrict Eric's freedom of expression.

"While the tone of the recent article is upsetting, we must look at it in perspective," Wilton said. Around him, in the living room, sat the members of the NZNS — New Zealanders for National Solidarity. An excellent group, Wilton thought. He had enjoyed getting to know them over the last few weeks.

"In truth, any publicity for our cause is better than none at all. While the article was undoubtedly biased, it still may expose people to the fact that there are differing points of view on the historical verifiability of the Holocaust."

A few members of the NZNS nodded their heads. Others looked a little dubious. Wilton could understand the sentiment.

```
Wilton is an associate of several neo-
fascist groups based in Australia and New
Zealand, including New Zealanders for
National Solidarity, a splinter group of
the better-known New Zealand Patriots'
League. Eric Stapp, the leader of the NZNS,
has been convicted twice for assault, in
the Palmerston North District Court.
```

Typical slanders and inaccuracies. Journalists had no respect for the intricacies of language. Dredging up a couple of youthful misunderstandings from Eric's past was shameless. And then there were the statements Karen Staunton had made about him. The trial in Melbourne had been a farce. To call him an anti-Semite was to grossly misunderstand his goals.

Wilton could remember visiting the Holocaust museum in Melbourne, moving quietly between the exhibits, watching the guides talk to groups of visiting schoolchildren. All the guides were "survivors", elderly men and women who had been in the camps. Wilton had glided along, past the walls of photos, many misleading and unrepresentative, others clearly faked, and past the documents in glass cases, often incomplete, euphemistic, and universally open to interpretation. He felt sorry for the guides, he felt sorry for all of these "survivors". That was the thing that the journalists had never reported, no matter how many times he tried to make it clear.

Of course the prisoners of the camps had suffered, of course their stories were terrible. These things happen in war.

Cities get bombed, civilians killed, potential dissidents rounded up and imprisoned in camps with insufficient food and medical supplies. Tens of millions died in World War Two. Wilton felt sympathy for each and every one.

But where were the memorials for Dresden? Why weren't they scattered all across the world? Narrow ancient streets, dense neighbourhoods of wooden houses rushed with walls of flame, incendiary bombs dropped in patterns for maximum conflagration. Why hadn't a legacy of guilt been foisted upon the Allied nations responsible for such an attack? War is terrible. People die.

He had walked through that pathetic little museum, watching the guides with sympathetic eyes. Some of Wilton's fellow revisionists directed their vitriol towards the Jews themselves, hating them for their role in the perpetuation of a lie. Wilton respected his colleagues; they were entitled to their opinions. But Wilton was no anti-Semite. He just wanted to expose Jews to the truth, to help them understand the real history of their race. They had suffered but there was no genocide, no deliberate extermination. Everyone suffered; they were like everyone else. The news he brought them was good.

MARTIN GLASS

Martin Glass has been screening his calls. His father has left one hesitant message on his answer machine, asking if the things Karen said in her article were true. Martin decides to send him a copy of *Body Disposal.* He has a brief conversation with Lewis Ravington soon after that. Martin leaves his flat before Nigel Wilton or Eric Stapp can call again. Wilton had been afraid that *Body Disposal* was too innocuous, too refined in its arguments, to garner any attention. That has all changed now. Thank you, Karen.

> Glass's book reaches the conclusion that the Topf furnaces installed in the Auschwitz-Birkenau camp complex were incapable of disposing of the remains of the 1.1 million prisoners allegedly murdered there between 1942 and 1945. Furthermore, he asserts that the expansion of the camp's

```
crematory facilities in 1943 might be
better explained as a response to the
typhus epidemic that had swept the camp
than as a signal of genocidal intent.
```

Martin has spent the day walking the old suburbs of Wellington, stopping every now and then to look into the dairy storefronts and see copies of the magazine, Karen's article listed on its cover: *Holocaust Denial in New Zealand?* He has missed her over the years; there were a couple of girls in the UK, but nothing serious, nothing that ever came close.

Martin remembers the first girl he ever slept with, shortly after moving to Wellington. He remembers that her skin had smelt of candied-fruit perfume, she had pressed her freshly chapsticked lips against his and laughed softly as she guided his hands. Martin didn't tell anyone about her, but somehow word got out and he noticed a flicker in Daniel's eyes when they eventually talked about it. It wasn't that he was jealous of Martin's fairly inexplicable success, rather he was sizing up the differences between the two of them at that moment and finding himself wanting. This was how their friendship would continue; Daniel had chosen to be just by Martin's shoulder, always pushing to get ahead.

Martin would not sleep with anyone else until he met Karen, halfway through his first year at university. He found her in a tutorial, an Introduction to Early Modern Europe; he liked to think of their eyes meeting while woodcuts depicting torture, persecution, the Black Death and witch trials flicked on the overhead projector above their heads. She had been a pale, bony, chain-smoking redhead, fuelled by delusions of poetry, not quite pretty, not exactly pleasant or welcoming, but still nervously pursued by a fair number of English and Creative Writing majors, whose euphemistic come-ons she generally ignored.

She and Martin had argued when they met, first in the classes they shared, then between classes, at parties, over lunch in the cafeteria. She accused him of a morbid curiosity — he lingered too long over history's bloody details. It was not scholarly, she said. It was salacious, almost sadistic. She had been half joking when she said this, but only half.

Karen was a little wary of him initially, a little suspicious of the attraction she felt. She had seen friends fall into a certain pattern with certain men, sniping and bickering then falling all over each other, misreading fractiousness as desire when in fact they simply did not like each other. Novels and films have a lot to answer for.

But she and Martin kept arguing about writers and historians, theories and counter-theories and then, Martin thinks, they were in love and he was weaning her off poetry and hand-rolled cigarettes. He had been naïve back then, he supposes, to have enjoyed it so much: being an influence, shaping his girlfriend's thoughts. All positions were relative, all perceptions constructed. He should have been able to see that it wasn't going to end well. "You suffocate me," she had said one evening when they were lying on their mattress in the Karori flat.

"I can stop," he had replied, but he couldn't really. He was too young, not quite yet in full control of his own thoughts. They spilled out and dragged everything down.

It had taken only two years of undergraduate history to fascinate him with human cruelty. He watched it swell through the ages, growing to match our capacities and ambitions at every turn. Karen spent more and more time out of the flat, away from him. Daniel lurked in the background, wandering listlessly through the Karori house and waiting for everything to break down irrevocably.

Martin read Hannah Ardent's account of the Adolf Eichmann trial in Jerusalem. He enjoyed her talk of the banality of evil. Evil was everywhere, commonplace, workaday, in everyone and everything. If you could call it banal then the sweep of human history started to make some sense. That was what he had thought then, that there was a pattern to everything, that the true story would always be the right one. All historians went through that phase. He was sure of it.

Martin's life had been dead in the water by the time Peter and Lance threw their party. He and Karen had argued and it was not a good argument; this one was long, bitter and final. Karen had got drunk at the party then retreated upstairs.

Outside in the garden, Martin had leaned against the wall of the house, staring blankly into the night. Daniel found him there, sensing pain, sensing weakness.

"Is Karen about?" he asked.

Martin had told him she was upstairs. That was bad enough, but Daniel had to push him, had to make him part of it, and had asked "You don't mind?" and Martin had told him no, he didn't, he no longer minded, he no longer had any stake or claim in what became of Karen. Daniel couldn't act on his own, he couldn't just go and do what he wanted. He had to bring Martin into it, because Martin had always been a part of it. He had to make him complicit.

Martin remembers waking up the next morning in his sleeping bag. He and Karen had never got around to buying a bed together and she had dragged the mattress they'd once shared up to the boxroom on the second floor. Martin's head had fallen off his pillow in the night and he woke with his cheek stuck to the damp, warped floorboards of his room.

He wriggled upright and fumbled for his glasses, climbed out of his bag and walked down the hall to empty his bladder. He bent over the bathroom sink to drink icy winter water straight from the tap.

No one else was stirring as he climbed the stairs to the

second storey. Martin always woke up too early after he had been drinking. Alcohol made him restless. Something to do with blood sugar he supposed.

The door to Karen's room was open and inside Martin could see Daniel lying asleep alone, naked on the bare mattress. He quietly turned and walked back downstairs. These things happen, he told himself. He would not let it affect him. He was finished with Karen. Finished with Daniel as well. These things just happen.

Outside, on his way down to the dairy for a carton of chocolate milk and a mince pie, he saw Karen sitting on a bench in the park across the road. He was about to walk past her but she looked up at him and Martin thought that she might have been crying; he has never been very good at telling, but her face seemed strangely slack and soft. He was tempted to ignore her and carry on to the dairy, but instead he crossed the road and sat next to her on the bench. She was still hungover, dressed in last night's clothes and outside in the morning cold without any shoes.

He didn't ask her about Daniel, he didn't ask about what had happened the night before. But he did mention walking upstairs to find Daniel asleep and naked in her room. That was the way things were now. He wouldn't pretend to understand it, but he would not make a big thing out of it either. They were over now, he was done.

Karen's face hardened, she looked at him spitefully, sitting next to her on the bench, all stiff-backed hurt and wounded dignity, and she told him what had happened with Daniel, spitting it out in a half-drunken spiel, then slumping over on the bench, her face gone slack again.

Everyone should have a moment like that, Martin thinks, years later. A moment where their life changes, where they realise how little they understand about the world. Those moments can help you a lot in the long run.

Unable to think of anything else to do, Martin had reached down and lifted one of Karen's bare feet from the damp grass, holding it, warming it between his hands.

Martin's head was filled with stories of human cruelty. Invasions, conquests, annexations. Massacres, expulsions, cleansings. The greatest myth we hold to is that evil is something exceptional, something beyond us. But when it touches you, when you see it first hand, when you are made complicit in it, that is when you see it as a mundane reality, a force perpetuated through endless repetition.

Karen disappeared after that morning, heading back up north to stay with her parents for a while. Martin was left in the flat with Daniel, who was already packing, already preparing to leave. They had circled each other for a while, exchanging curt greetings, discussing matters of rent and bond, the damages caused by Lance and Peter's party.

"Look, mate," Daniel had said, pre-empting Martin at one moment, "I'm sorry about what happened with Karen. It was just . . . you know. Just shit. Sorry."

Martin had reeled for a moment. Daniel was apologising to him. He was making it into something between them, dragging Martin in deeper.

"I know it was out of order," Daniel continued. "But I was drunk and shit. Sorry."

This was a fraudulent narrative. Martin refused to be drawn into it. How was it? he had asked. How would you describe it?

Daniel's eyes had widened. He took a step back, uncertain.

Sensual? Martin continued. Satisfying, gentle? Making love or a fucking? Not gentle? Aggressive maybe? Forceful? Stop me when I find the right adjective because I want to know . . .

"What the hell do you mean by forceful?"

Pushing her legs back and fucking her, Martin wanted to say, but Peter was looking through the kitchen door, watching their argument, and he couldn't say it in front of him. He felt ashamed about that later, another sign of his own complicity.

"Don't try to make this into something it's not," Daniel had said, backing away. He moved out of the kitchen, past Peter, then turned back in the hallway. "I was drunk," he said again, before heading on up the stairs.

Two weeks later, after Daniel had left, Karen returned to collect her things. Martin had tried to talk to her then, but her story had changed. It was nothing, she said now. She had been emotional before, unbalanced, still drunk. What she'd told him wasn't true. That wasn't how things had been. Martin hadn't been able to understand and they had argued one more time before she left.

She and Daniel forgot, they said that things weren't as they had been, and they continued on and lived their lives. Martin remembered and the thoughts still lingered. It took him a long time to figure out that their path was the correct one, that they had each done the only sane thing. That realisation had led him to Marion Pryor in the UK and from there to the ruins of Europe and *Body Disposal at Auschwitz.*

They had been right, of course they had been right. Evil serves us best when we deny its banality, when we see it as something exceptional, something that can never touch or take hold of us. Our best stories keep it in the distance, turn it into something far-away.

DANIEL

Battlelines were being drawn in the Eclectic offices. Dissent ran high. There was no such thing as a neutral party, no middle ground.

"Real lives," Morbid said, "do not have plots."

The mood in the meeting room was tense. The project was changing in front of us, morphing in our grip. "Real games sell, Morbid," said Heckle. "Real games don't get screwed over by the ratings board. We need to rein in the player's freedom."

"I thought freedom was what *VirtuLife* was all about."

What we had been suspecting for some time had come to pass. No ratings board anywhere in the world was going to give a game that simulated real life anything less than an AO. Considering the current talk on the game forums, this attitude was unsurprising.

Voidkiller386: wouldnt it be cool if you could tear out peoples intestines and make them into ropeladers????

RealSnake: yeah or macramé potplant holders LOL

I was thinking about Karen's article. I had read through it earlier that day, in between testing the old builds of *VirtuLife* in my office cubicle.

```
Karen ERROR Anita in ERROR ERROR room
leading you into the room ERROR following
her ERROR neck ERROR ropey trails of saliva
ERROR a big man ERROR wanted to know what
it was like to see ERROR could do to stop
me.
```

Karen's article suggested that *Body Disposal* was a flawed and misleading history, a work of Holocaust denial possibly funded by white nationalists. Martin's conclusions about the crematory capacities of the Auschwitz-Birkenau camps appeared to preclude the fact that 1.1 million people were murdered there. What I had found on the *ofaah* site still troubled me. Every message I had sent to stairway@hotmail.com went unanswered.

"How about some kind of plot with terrorists?" one of the development staff asked. "Like, the player's avatar is leading this completely real life in the city, but his job is to be a terrorist hunter or something. Plenty of acceptable violence there."

A few people muttered approvingly. I had my copy of *Body Disposal* in my lap and I flicked it open, looking at the publisher's details. Tunnel Press. Their offices weren't too far from Eclectic, just a couple of blocks away.

"That's not good for the long term," said Heckle. "It's fine to have terrorists in games now, but by the time *VirtuLife* hits the stores there might have been another big attack and people would have started looking for something to get outraged about."

I snapped *Body Disposal at Auschwitz* shut. “What about Nazis?” I said. Everyone in the room looked at me. “No ratings board will have a problem with the players killing them.”

“Keep going,” Heckle said.

“We could have the player find out that his parents were killed by an escaped Nazi war criminal. In addition to living a completely real life, in a completely real city, he has to uncover an underground cell of neo-Nazi terrorists to avenge his parents’ death.”

Morbid’s eyes were wide with disbelief. “Fucking hell,” he started to say. “What kind of crap —”

“You think this will work?” said Heckle.

“Ultimately *VirtuLife* is about the search for individual identity,” I said. “Reconciling oneself with the past in order to make a better future. Nazi-hunting fits the game’s themes.”

“Yeah,” someone else said. “Terrorists are popular at the moment, but these ones won’t be real enough to offend anyone.”

Heckle grinned and pointed his finger at me, pistol-like. “You may be onto something here, Daniel. Show me a breakdown of that plotline and we’ll make a decision.”

I couldn’t see him, because I was facing in the opposite direction, but I could feel Morbid’s eyes burning into the back of my neck. Time to get out of the office.

Tunnel Press turned out to be a single room on the sixth floor of a Lambton Quay building. It was occupied by a solitary blonde man in his thirties, sitting at a desk, smoking his way through a pack of special filters.

“What?” He looked up at me with bloodshot eyes as I opened the door. “What do you want? What is it now?” There was a little sign on his desk saying *Editor-in-Chief*. “If you’re from the New Zealand Jewish Council, I’ve already —’

“I’m not.”

The editor shrugged. "Didn't think you looked Jewish anyway."

I told him I was wondering if he could help me get in touch with Martin Glass.

"Glass, Glass. Fuck Martin Glass. He fucks things up. He'll fuck you up." He fumbled through the Rolodex on his desk, then scribbled down a number and an address on a scrap of paper. "But here y'go. If you're one of his neo-Nazi pals, then tell him I say hi. And if you're out to murder him . . ." The editor grinned. "Then that's just super too."

When I got back to the Eclectic offices all the partitioning cubicle walls had been removed from the main office. Down the back, my desk and computer stood stripped and exposed. I stopped the head of the cinematics team as he walked past. "What the hell happened here?"

"Heckle got rid of our cubicles. He says we're entering a new phase of the project. No more barriers."

I sat down at my desk. Morbid walked over from the water cooler and sat down at his desk, the one next to mine. He looked across at me. He made no pretence of turning on his computer or flicking through the charts and printouts that cluttered his workspace. His eyes, wide and unblinking, bored into me. I got up and walked over to Heckle's office to tell him I was taking the afternoon off.

"Okay, but I want that plot breakdown done ASAP. Nazis, Daniel. Goddamn Nazis. How do you do it?"

"What can I say? It's a gift."

Martin lived in a one-bedroom flat up in Highbury, on a steep hill above the university. The glass sliding door that led into the living room was half open. I knocked, but got no answer.

"Martin?" I called, stepping inside. "Hello? Martin?"

The living room was haphazardly furnished with chairs, a

couch and a table, all of which could have been purchased from the local recycling centre. I called Martin's name a third time and pushed open the door to his bedroom. A single bed, a desk, a chair, and an older-model PC.

One of the books on Martin's desk was open with words underlined and I bent over to look at it more closely. It was one of those poorly printed Buddhist chapbooks. I had seen shaven-headed, placid-featured young men, with torn brown jerseys pulled down over their saffron robes, peddling similar books around the central city on Saturdays.

> `When you meet the Buddha, kill the Buddha. When you meet your ancestor, kill your ancestor . . .`

Next to it was a closed, black-bound notebook. I flicked it open with my index finger. *Martin Glass* was written in neat looping letters on the first page. Then, below that, a Latin inscription: *Eritis sicut Deus, scientes bonum et malum.*

"What are you doing here?" I looked up from the desk to see a tall man with a shaven head and a beard standing in the doorway. "What the hell are you doing here?" he asked again.

"What am I doing here?" I said. "What are you doing here?"

The man's nostrils flared and he took a step towards me, but then Martin appeared behind him in the doorway. He hadn't changed much since our university days. A little thinner maybe, hair a little longer, more fashionable glasses, but that was it. He looked at me, considered me for a long moment, then said. "It's all right, Eric. This is Daniel Legkov. I've told you about him."

"Oh Christ — sorry mate." The bearded man stepped forward and offered me his hand. "Can't be too careful, y'know, that's all."

We all walked out into the living room. Another man was waiting there, this one older and slightly overweight. He also shook my hand. I looked over his shoulder at Martin and lifted my eyebrows.

"Daniel," Martin said, "please meet my friends Eric Stapp and Nigel Wilton."

I recognised both of the names from Karen's article. The leader of the New Zealanders for National Solidarity and a man convicted for the distribution of anti-Semitic pamphlets in Melbourne. "You're Australian, aren't you?" I said to Nigel Wilton.

"That's right, Daniel," Wilton said. "Came out here from Melbourne to lend this fellow," he slapped Martin on the back, "a bit of support. An honest man can't take a single step in this world without making enemies. I think it's very decent of you to come to Martin at this time. He's told me a lot about you, about how much he used to value your friendship. You two probably need a little time to get reacquainted. Please, enjoy the gift," he said to Martin, "just as I've enjoyed our little walk and talk. We'll be back soon."

Wilton walked out the sliding door. Stapp put a hand on Martin's shoulder and leaned close to whisper something into his ear, then he left too, dragging the door shut behind him.

Martin moved over to the window and watched the pair of them walk away down the hill. Once they were gone he turned to face me. "It's good to see you again," he said. "I'd heard you were back in town."

"You're keeping some interesting company these days," I said, nodding at the door Wilton and Stapp had left through. "That's what I read in Karen's article, anyway."

"You don't need to worry about them." Martin sat down on his couch and waved me over to an armchair. "They're basically harmless. Here, look at what Wilton gave me." He reached down and picked up a cardboard shoebox that was on the floor near the couch. "I was just heading down to the dairy when I met Stapp and Wilton coming up the road to present me with an offering." He opened the box. "A token of their appreciation."

Inside the box, half submerged in soft wrapping paper, was a gun. A squat handgun with a narrow, elongated barrel.

"It's a Luger," Martin said. "Wilton brought it out for me from Australia, from his artefact collection. Apparently it once belonged to an *SS Kommandoführer*. I don't know if it's still in working order, but God knows how he got it through Customs."

Fascinated, I leaned forward to look at the Luger more closely. "Wilton has another one back at home, in better shape," Martin said. "That one has its original holster and everything. Hell of a thing to own." He looked down at the gun, then back up at me. "You can touch it if you like."

I extended a finger and ran it down the cool barrel, looping under the trigger-guard.

"Little piece of history right there," said Martin. I pulled my hand away and he quickly replaced the lid of the box. "Hell of a thing to own," he said again.

"I read your book," I said.

He picked up a magazine lying next to him on the couch. I saw it was the issue that had carried Karen's article. "You'll find," he said "that celebrity has not changed me."

"I think Karen's been emailing me. I think she sent me your book."

"What did you make of it?"

I had spent the last day flicking back and forth, reading, re-reading, thinking harder, remembering the facts and figures I had picked up over the months I had been with Anita, back in the UK.

"Karen's put an interesting spin on things," Martin said,

when I did not answer him. "Everyone's entitled to make their own interpretations."

"What's your interpretation?"

"I don't have one. I just state the facts." Martin paused for a moment, holding my gaze. Then he laughed and flopped back on the couch. "Nine years, man. It's good to see you again, you're looking well. You got any questions?"

JOSH

Josh slid his credit card into the payphone. He had to wait through eight rings before the Bristol end picked up.

"What?"

"Anita?" said Josh.

"What?" Anita said again.

"It's Josh," said Josh.

"Josh," said Anita. "*Time difference.*"

Josh twisted away from the phone booth, looking down the grey rain-flecked Wellington street behind him. He was on the move. No time to go back to his hotel room, no time to wait until this evening, he needed to talk to Anita now. "It's all happening here," he said. "This place is a hotbed." He had the magazine he'd bought at the airport in his hand.

"For God's sake," Anita said on the other end of the phone. "It's three in the morning."

"You said you wanted me to let you know what's going on down here," Josh said, somewhat reproachfully. "Well, now

I'm letting you know." He started to summarise the article. Martin Glass, Tunnel Press, *Body Disposal at Auschwitz.*

"Is Steve with you, Josh?" Anita asked after a few minutes. "Can I talk to him, please?"

"Steve? Steve's gone. He couldn't hack it, you know? I'm fighting this on my own. Have you got Daniel's address? I might need some back-up when I start poking around for real."

"I don't know if it's such a good idea for you to see Daniel," Anita said slowly.

"That's all in the past now," Josh said. "Edinburgh and stuff. He'll understand when I talk to him. I can bring him round, I know it."

"Josh . . ." Anita said again. He heard her sigh, then fumble with the notebook she kept beside her bed. "I got it from his brother," she said sleepily after she'd read the address out and he'd copied it onto his palm. "Just thought I might want to write to him. Explain a few things. Still haven't . . . probably won't . . ."

Josh could hear her nestling back beneath her bedclothes. For a moment he remembered her smooth pale skin, the way she'd gently slide her soft hairless leg over his while they lay alongside each other in the dark.

"Thanks," Josh said. "But I want you to do something else for me." He rustled through the article again. "It says here —"

"Please, Josh, it's three in the morning."

"It says here that Glass, the guy who wrote the book, studied under someone called Marion Pryor in the UK." Anita stirred. He imagined her sitting up in bed. "You know the name?"

"It's familiar."

"I want you to check her out," Josh started to say. "Look into her work and background . . ." but Anita quickly grunted her agreement and hung up. Josh thought about calling her back — there was too much going on for her to be sleeping — then decided against it. He walked down a street and found a post office, where he express-mailed one of his copies of *Body Disposal at Auschwitz* to Anita at her new flat in Bristol. He hadn't forgotten about her work, her research. She needed to be aware of what was going on here.

Josh looked down at his remaining copy as he left the post office, bending its plain black cover over in his hands. It had the address of the Tunnel Press office on its inside front cover and he thought about heading over there, but he was too shaky, too angry — he hadn't slept much on the plane, and hadn't rested his head since he touched down in Wellington. Best to get hold of Daniel first, get an ally, someone who knew the terrain.

Josh had not cared much for Daniel when he first met him. It wasn't exactly that he disliked anything about him, just that he'd seen him as an obstacle between him and Anita, an impediment to Anita's research. But things were different now. They were Half-Jews. Daniel would listen. Josh would make him see.

RAVINGTON

Lewis Ravington sat in his office until the sky outside darkened. He fielded a couple of abusive phone calls, leaning back in his chair, cradling the receiver between his ear and shoulder, nodding quietly at every insult and expletive until the caller got bored and hung up.

He started in his seat when someone knocked on his door round about seven; another visitor, he couldn't bear it. Rav breathed in deeply, calming himself, then looked to see Adja peering at him from behind the half-open door. He wouldn't be able to publish her poems as he had promised. There was no way he could maintain his business for more than another month at best, he had no more resources. Tunnel Press was sunk. He knew that, she knew that, so why was she still here? He stood up from his desk and walked over to her.

"I . . ." he started to say, but she put a finger up to his lips.

"I know," she said and moved closer, her sympathetic eyes glimmering in the murky office twilight. She knew, she knew everything, she understood. Rav sighed, a long, shuddering exhalation that pushed all the torment and tension of the last few days from his lungs. Then he reached out, pulling her to him, feeling the warmth and richness of her body as it pressed against his. She knew everything. She knew Ravington was a charlatan and a parasite. She knew he had tried to redeem his existence, if only partially, by publishing a real book, a book he had thought might really be worthy and noticeable. A book about the Holocaust. She knew that his attempted redemption had ruined him.

But if a woman like Adja could know all this and still come to him in the darkness of his soon-to-be vacated office, if she could know all this and still think that he was worth holding in her arms, then perhaps there was still hope for Lewis Ravington. Perhaps, like Adja, the rest of the world might one day come to understand that, bad as Ravington was, his failing wasn't born out of that badness alone, but out of innocence also, and a one-time, half-hearted desire to do something good.

"You *know*," he whispered into Adja's neck.

"Of course," she said matter-of-factly. "The Jew-bastards got you. They get us all."

The rain was falling fast in Seatoun by the time Ravington got home. He had let Adja drive him. He hadn't said anything at the office — it had been a hard day after all, he had been at a loss for words. Adja turned off her engine outside his house and looked at him, smiling slightly, expecting to be asked in for tea or coffee or whatever. He wanted to tell her to go, to get away, he wanted nothing to do with her. But it was late and he was tired and it seemed so much easier to just be polite for a few minutes.

"Would you like a cup of . . . ?"

"Yes."

Inside he put on the kettle and rummaged through his

pantry for some biscuits. Adja seated herself on his couch. She crossed her legs and shook out her hair. She was still smiling. Rav hesitated in the doorway of the kitchen. He couldn't stand hearing things like what she'd said at the office. That sort of racism was completely vile. But it had been one hell of a day. Adja uncrossed her legs then crossed them again. He didn't need any more stress. He was only human. Perhaps they could have a talk about it in the morning.

As Rav started to move towards the couch someone knocked on his front door. "Shit," he said. "Hold on a sec." He ducked out into the hallway and did a double-take when he saw Eric Stapp of the NZNS standing on his step in the rain.

"Gidday," Stapp said, after Ravington had hurriedly opened his door.

"Eric," Rav said. "Hi." He stepped back, allowing the tall, damp form of Eric Stapp to enter his house.

Stapp looked around the hallway and sniffed. "Nice place. Didn't think you'd be at your office so I came here."

Neither of them said anything for a moment. Ravington rocked back on his heels and coughed, perturbed by Stapp's unblinking gaze and unchanging expression.

"That article about Mr Glass's book," Stapp said at length. "It said you publish poems."

"Right, well, yes . . ." Ravington couldn't exactly deny that. Poetry was his stock in trade.

Stapp slowly extended an arm, pushing a plain brown envelope towards Rav. "I've written some poems," he said.

"Really?" Rav stared at the envelope, slightly horrified, until Stapp's scowl deepened and he hastily accepted it, tearing open its sealed lip to examine the small bundle of paper within.

"Most of it's free verse," Stapp said after a while. "And, you know, some rhyming stuff."

"Right."

"I tried writing a sonnet once."

"Really?"

"Thought I'd swing by your office sometime," said Stapp. "have a talk about them." Stapp looked down at Ravington, who held the envelope full of poetry in both hands, and nodded once. Rav nodded back. Stapp turned and walked out the door, pulling it shut behind him.

Rav watched him walk down the path to the gate, then get into a car. He considered the envelope again. What else could he have done? What could he have said? He was only human, he really was.

Lewis Ravington walked out of the hallway, returning to his lounge and to Adja on his couch.

MARTIN GLASS

You have a camp. You have a massive complex of camps encompassing Auschwitz I and, at the edge of the village of Birkenau, Auschwitz II. Between the two is the train station of Auschwitz, still used by civilians from the city of Auschwitz (known as Oswiecim before the Nazi occupation) but also a waypoint for the trainloads of prisoners being transported. Plans show that only three-fifths of the intended complex were fully realised during the course of World War Two. So if you have all this space, and all these people going into this space, what's going to happen to the people? Why don't they come back out?

"You know a bit more than I thought you would," Martin says. "These are good questions. I'm a little surprised."

"I had a girlfriend who was kind of into this stuff," Daniel says. He has changed a lot since Martin last saw him. His hairline has receded sharply and his large frame is running to fat. His cheeks are covered by a day's growth of beard and his face has a broad blank look to it, but his steady gaze is a little unnerving. Martin finds it bizarre to be facing him after all this time, sitting here in his home talking about the Holocaust. There are so many other things they could be talking about, but this is what Daniel is here for; he has come for the conversation that Martin remembers him avoiding all those years ago through a claim to Half-Jewishness.

The Holocaust, World War Two, the Nazis. What a subject, but everyone keeps coming back to it, no one can help it — even Daniel has been sucked into it now. Martin looks at him and longs to tell him what it all comes down to, the truth of it all, the source of all this endless fascination. What is a war, anyway? What is a massacre, an atrocity, a crime against humanity? World War Two, all of it — from the fall of Warsaw and Paris, to the Blitz, to Stalingrad, to Pearl Harbor, to the camps in Europe, to Dresden, to D-Day, to Berlin, to Enola Gay and Little Boy — was a continuation of a trend, a little larger in scale, but nothing that hadn't happened before. There are so many other wars and crimes, Martin thinks, but somehow we never let them come close. Nobody does it better for us than the Nazi. The communist lacks style. The global capitalist is too impersonal. The terrorist is too random and sporadic in his attacks; he doesn't have the sweeping monumentalism we desire. The Nazi is uncomplicated, unconflicted, clear-eyed in his cruelty. He is terrible. He is beautiful. We love him.

"The people go into the space," Daniel says again, "and they don't come out. How do you account for them in your study?"

"I don't," says Martin. "I don't need to — they are not my concern. All I'm really concerned about is the Topf coke-fuelled furnaces in the crematorium. How they worked, how well they were maintained, how much they could burn in a day, an hour, a year. I've looked at the plans of the camp, the blueprints of the furnaces and the crematoria. I've looked at the aerial photographs, the official documents and the reports."

Daniel leans forward as Martin says all this. He is fascinated, Martin can see that; he is being drawn in deeper and deeper, just like everyone else, everyone in the world.

Martin finds himself thinking about the *Wehrmacht* and *Waffen SS*. No ordinary army, no ordinary soldiers. Straight, sharp uniforms with clear lines and creases. Symbols and decorations, badges, collar runes and death's head rings. Hitler's war was fought by Hugo Boss. Boots, buttons, caps, coats, gloves. Chains, collar studs, helmets, medals. Full decorations worn in battle. Rank after rank of fit young men in grey, in black, in camo. Glimmering pins and insignias. That is what keeps drawing us back. Of course it was evil. We should call it evil, but no one should dare to call it banal.

"What about the testimonies of the victims?" Daniel asks. "You can't just ignore them. They must factor in somewhere."

"Memory is a tricky thing, Daniel. Testimonies alone cannot be trusted. There are no surviving documents dealing with day-to-day crematory procedures, or requests for the necessary overhauls of the furnaces. The blueprints and aerial photography of the camp do not necessarily confirm that the gas chambers were used for executions. No one has been able to produce a written order explicitly demanding the execution of the Jewish prisoners. I simply state the facts as I see them and omit what I consider to be speculative or inconclusive."

Martin finds himself reaching over and picking up the cardboard shoebox sitting on the coffee table. He slips a hand under the lid, running his fingers up and down the cool metal barrel of Wilton's gift. Daniel raises his eyebrows but says nothing. The Luger pistol had most probably been taken as a trophy during the war; even in defeat the uniformed Nazi was coveted for his beauty. What GI, British or Russian grunt did not long to loot his fallen corpse, to seize that perfect helmet as a trophy? To tear away a badge or a pin. Rip the iron cross from under his neck. When Wilton first gave it to him Martin thought the pistol was a ridiculous gift, but now he finds it entrancing. A perfect sidearm, a gorgeous object. He cannot stop touching it.

"How much can you remember about your life, Daniel?" he asks. "Memory can't always be trusted. The dead are the only real witnesses. They don't forget, or misremember, or exaggerate. But they're not going to tell us what they know."

Daniel coughs. "It's getting pretty late. I ought to make a move. Work in the morning and all that."

Martin nods. He is meeting another journalist tomorrow, doing an interview for another magazine, a cheaper rival of the one that printed Karen's article. There will be other interviews and other journalists after that, he thinks, for a while at least. Controversies and camps and furnaces aside, it is the thought of the Nazis that will attract them; they cannot resist them, no one can. The marches, the uniforms, the unthinking arrogance, the offhand cruelty, we need it all, we love it. Little wonder that the SS officer with all his tight, crisply packaged darkness has become a quintessential image of S&M role-play.

And all those movies about World War Two, those portentous American epics about courage under fire, those European art-house flicks with the Holocaust as a backdrop, sometimes Martin thinks that they are all an excuse to reach that moment when our Nazi enters. The door swings open and he walks into the room, polished boots clicking on the floor, coat-tails flapping behind him. The hush falls and he pulls off one leather glove with a snap. "So," he says, and for a moment the entire cinema audience is enraptured, because this is what they have been waiting for, this is their perfect villain in his moment of perfect beauty.

Martin marvels at how we can watch these films, telling

ourselves that we are there to see an act of witness, or a meditation on the loss and horror of war, or a deep serious drama about man's inhumanity to man, and yet still secretly revel in every flash of jackboot that crosses the screen. We watch for all these things, for all the right reasons, but also to see our beautiful Nazis again. This is why Daniel has come back to pick up their old conversation, Martin thinks as he sees him to the door. This is why he will come back again.

Outside the flat, Daniel pauses. He turns and asks, "Martin, why are you doing this?"

"I'm a historian," Martin replies.

"Karen wrote the article about you. She's been sending things to me. Does this have anything to do with what happened back in . . ."

"You shouldn't think about that so much, Daniel," Martin says quickly. "Don't let that be your defining moment." Then he slides his door shut.

Inside his flat, alone, he sits back down on the couch and takes the Luger pistol out of its box and holds it in his lap. Such a strange weapon, so sculpted and stylish with its long thin barrel and its elegant stock. Its standardised use speaks volumes for the National Socialist aesthetic. Deadliness combined with a certain vulgar beauty to create a lasting appeal. Much has been made of the fact that Adolf Hitler was a bad painter, Martin thinks. It is one of those little ironic stories: a failed Austrian watercolourist brings about the nightfall of European civilisation. But Hitler was not a failed artist, far from it; painting was simply not his medium. Martin remembers a passage from *Mein Kampf*:

I myself, meanwhile, after innumerable attempts, had laid down a final form: a flag with a red background, a white disc, and a black swastika in the middle. After `long trials, I also found a definite proportion between the size of the white disc, as well as the shape and thickness of the swastika.`

Dedication, rigour, creative intensity. A logo for the ages. The swoosh, the golden arches and the apple might have longer marketing vectors, but they can never match the swastika as a symbol of brand loyalty. Aesthetics had been the name of the game, the first weapon of engagement. Marches, rallies, monuments, night-time book burnings. Call it evil, if you think you can use that word, but evil never looked so good.

Martin looks at his watch and realises how late it is. He should get some rest, he has a full day planned tomorrow. He should sleep and try to stop thinking these thoughts, if only for a little while, for a few hours at the most. But there is a strangely elongated object sitting in his lap, brutal yet beautiful, and he cannot bring himself to stop touching it.

DANIEL

It was close to ten by the time I got back to the apartment on The Terrace. Martin and I had talked on into the evening, about camps and trains and deportation timelines. We did not speak about what we had been doing for the past few years, we did not reminisce about the Karori flat. The Holocaust had felt like the easiest subject for us.

I leaned back in the lift as I rode it up to the ninth floor, resting my head against the wall. I could barely wait to get into the Eclectic offices tomorrow. The plot of *VirtuLife* was starting to unwind in my head.

The player's parents had survived Auschwitz; let's say they met in Auschwitz, some kind of heartbreaking love story of glances between wires, we can tell it all through flashback cut-scenes. Then years later they recognise one of the camp officials who tortured them. The aging ex-Nazi has them murdered to protect his secret and then the player has to hunt him down through the constantly evolving, breathtakingly realistic cityscape we had designed. Living a real life had been our starting point, our initial premise, but we had always known that it would never be enough. The game needed a story that would make it more than real.

I got out of the lift and walked down the hall, half-hoping that Morbid would be asleep by now, or at least locked away, brooding in his bedroom. Perfect plotless freedom had been his aim for *VirtuLife* and the Eclectic engine. He would find my back-story tyrannical, he would never accept that the player's actions could and should be guided by references to past events. He lived in the now, and wanted to know what sort of real lives we might all live if those real lives weren't really our own. But games like this had to come with a story. Stories staved off chaos, stories made their own consequences.

My hopes were dashed when I opened the door. Morbid was wide awake and in the living room, perched on the arm of the couch and talking to a visitor who was sprawled in the La-Z-Boy. Morbid looked up as I entered and fixed me with his long blank stare of hurt, betrayal and hatred.

The visitor craned his neck round the side of the chair and grinned at me. "Hey there, Big Man," said Joshua Levit.

Oh no.

Apparently taking Anita to the Washington Holocaust memorial had been a big success for Josh. Upon seeing its size, the range of its exhibits, and the attitudes of its guides and its visitors, Anita had decided to broaden the scope of her studies.

"You know I always thought that just focusing on the UK was a little too narrow," Josh told me as he slumped in Morbid's La-Z-Boy. "Every country thinks about the Holocaust in a different way, yeah? How can you understand Holocaust remembrance in one country if you're not prepared to compare it to another?"

And what country could provide more material for a

comparative perspective than the United States of America? What country had more Holocaust museums, better Holocaust education programmes, and a population more obsessed with the gory details of genocide and the Nazi regime? And what other country could support not just memorials, not just museums and education centres, but a whole industry of movies about the Holocaust, TV mini-series and documentaries, books and novels and short stories and poetry? What other country could also have an industry devoted to Holocaust denial, churning out poorly bound books and cheaply printed journals full of theories about Zionist conspiracies, all of which somehow made their way into the hands of eager buyers? Where else but the USA?

"It sounds like a good trip," I said. "Hell, it sounds like taking your little sister to Disneyland."

He and Anita had spent more than a month hopping around the East Coast, just as he, Anita, Steve and I had hopped around the UK at the start of the year.

"Anita loved the universities. Lots of courses about the Holocaust. We even found an entire department of Holocaust Studies at one place."

Morbid got up from the couch. "I'll just put on the fucking kettle then, shall I?" he said, walking into the kitchen.

Josh ignored him; he was in full swing. After their US tour Josh had managed to convince Anita to travel just a little further, to Jerusalem. He had visited before, he told me, but he'd always felt uncomfortable, unwelcome there. He hadn't been sure why until he returned with Anita, until he somehow found himself spreading his seed between a range of Jerusalem fertility clinics. Revelation had struck while he sat in waiting rooms, not meeting the gaze of his fellow donors, or it had come to him in the little cubicles themselves, while he sat poised on the edge of a bed, juggling his manhood and a small plastic container, an open skin-magazine balanced in his lap.

"I came to accept that I am not Jewish," he said. "I came to realise that it was something that I never really wanted to be."

But Josh was Half-Jewish. The popularity of his sperm donations and his own satisfaction in them came out of being not quite one thing and not quite the other. He was learning to love the grey area he had defined, an identity of the in-between. He suggested I should learn to love it too. My life would make more sense if I did.

"I've never really given it that much thought."

Josh smiled. He leaned forward in the La-Z-Boy. "Daniel," he said, "it's okay. I get what this is about."

"What?"

"You're resisting me because of what happened back in Edinburgh. What happened with Anita."

"Forget it."

"I admit it was bad — I admitted that at the time I failed to understand the connection we shared and the loyalty we owed each other . . ."

Morbid returned with three cups of coffee. He shoved one in my direction, sloshing its scalding contents over the edge of my hand. After passing the other to Josh he leaned against the wall next to the door to his room and bowed his head, his dark hair falling over his face like a curtain, his eyes still on me.

Josh was leaning forward in his seat, holding his coffee in both hands, sipping and looking up at me with searching eyes over the rim of his cup. I couldn't bring myself to feel angry with him any more, couldn't bring myself to feel anything at all. Here was the strange little British man for whom Anita had abandoned me in Edinburgh. I had never wanted to see him again. Yet here he was.

"What brings you to New Zealand?" I asked.

Josh reached into the bag at the foot of his chair and pulled out a crumpled copy of the magazine that had run Karen's article on Martin. Apparently he had stumbled upon Nigel

Wilton's website, *The Online Forum for the Academic Analysis of the Holocaust*, while he had been busy donating sperm in Israel. Joshua Levit was no slouch when it came to the history of the European Holocaust. He'd known right away that there was something wrong with the extracts from Martin's book that he found posted there. He wasn't able to find out much about Martin, but he had dug into Wilton's background before touching down in Wellington.

"He's a borderline neo-Nazi based in Melbourne. A few months ago someone brought a civil case against him because of the pamphlets he'd been printing. He defended himself at the trial, like David Irving all over again."

"What happened to him?"

"A fine, a slap on the wrist. He was saying the Germans were the true victims of the Second World War, that the Holocaust was just fabricated to gloss over Allied atrocities and to keep the German people downtrodden. This guy is a neo-Nazi intellectual, he's dangerous. That's why I'm here."

"So you're . . . what? A Nazi hunter now?" I said. "Like Laurence Olivier in *The Boys from Brazil*?"

"More a neo-Nazi hunter, but yeah."

"Was Laurence Olivier hunting Nazis or neo-Nazis? I mean, what's the distinction?"

"They were ex-Nazis in that movie," said Josh.

"But 'ex-Nazi' or 'former Nazi' would imply that they'd given up their Nazi ways and just gone into hiding. The Nazis in *The Boys from Brazil* were operating as a covert organisation. They must have been neo-Nazis."

"Neo-Nazi means that you adopted the Nazi credo sometime after the end of World War Two. The Nazis in *The Boys from Brazil* were wanted war criminals. That's why Laurence Olivier was hunting them. If you're uncomfortable with 'ex-Nazi' then I guess we can just settle on plain old Nazi . . ." Josh paused and shook his head. "Anyway, I have to find out what's going on here," he said. "People need to know about these things. This sort of thing goes on all the time. I just saw it was happening in New Zealand and I guess I just felt like I should come here, because I had met you back in the UK and it felt like some kind of sign — because you're Half-Jewish like me and this is a denial of history, and people deny Half-Jews like us all the time, they deny our historical existence and suffering. It just felt like I should come here, it felt right . . ." His spiel trailed off into a sigh and he slumped forward, massaging his eyeballs with his fingertips. I waited for him to say more but he did not. He was done, he was completely burnt out.

Josh had to keep moving, I understood that now. If he ever stopped, even for a moment, then he would be caught, he would be overwhelmed. If he slowed down then he would be forced to see everything that he did not have in his life, he would be forced to admit that he was only part of a person, half of a man. I looked at him, and to my very great surprise found that I was not completely unsympathetic.

"You look tired," I said. "I would get some rest if I were you."

"Yeah," said Josh, sniffing, standing up. "Big day tomorrow. We'll catch up again soon, Big Man. Got lots to talk about, there's lots going on."

I saw him to the door. When he was gone, I turned back into the living room. Morbid was still staring at me.

"You know, the thing at work with the Nazis — it was nothing personal, right?" I said but my flatmate did not reply. We maintained a silent stand-off for a long while. Then the intercom buzzed behind me and I groaned, thinking it might be Josh again with some vital piece of information he had forgotten to share, but this was not the case.

"Mr Legkov?" said a deep voice I didn't quite recognise.

"Yes?"

"This is Eric Stapp. We met briefly at Martin Glass's flat this afternoon." I was feeling washed out, almost light-headed; I hadn't eaten since lunchtime. It all just kept on coming.

I heard Stapp exhale a burst of intercom static. Then he said: "I'm here on behalf of Mr Nigel Wilton. He appreciated meeting you this afternoon and would very much like to talk to you, Mr Legkov, if only for a little while."

"What? Right now?"

"Maybe you could just come downstairs. We'll not take up much of your time."

I glanced back over my shoulder at Morbid. Neither his position nor expression had changed. The New Zealanders for National Solidarity or an angry goth-boy programmer. I didn't really have a choice.

Eric Stapp was waiting for me just outside my apartment complex, leaning against the window pane under the awning to keep out of the rain. His black, spade-shaped beard glistened with moisture, and beads of water trailed down the sides of his bare scalp. As soon as I stepped out the door he pushed away from the glass and started to walk down the street.

"Where are you going?" I called after him.

"Mr Wilton is waiting for you," said Stapp, turning back. "He isn't far." He started walking again and I stood for a moment, wondering if I shouldn't pack it in and retreat back inside, until the door clicked shut behind me and I hurried after him into the rain. The new *VirtuLife* plot was still running in my head, connections being made, events falling into place.

`Game options:` **`Select:`** `follow mysterious figure through the silent night-time streets to a clandestine meeting point.`

Stapp led me down from The Terrace and into town. "This way, Mr Legkov," he'd say every few seconds. Or: "Not far now."

Eventually we stopped at a pub on Cuba Street. Out the front a noisy cover band played for a handful of half-interested patrons, but Stapp ushered me past all that, into the dark interior.

"This is it, Mr Legkov," he said, pointing me to a booth at the back. "We're here."

Nigel Wilton was sitting inside the booth, at the head of a table littered with half-finished pints and greasy potato-chip packets. He smiled broadly and stood up when he saw me. Three other men shared the booth with him. One of them was a stocky, clean-shaven young man the same size as Stapp. Another was a plump, bald man whose skin looked as pink and sticky as a marshmallow; he stared down at his pint glass with a glum, unchanging expression. The third was a scrawny-looking guy in khakis, about my age.

> The trail leads to a mansion on the outskirts of town. Cars have converged on the gravel courtyard outside. Sleek limousines pull up, depositing conspirators in evening dress at the door. Your only hope of unravelling the mystery of your past is to infiltrate this secretive gathering.

"Daniel!" Wilton said. "I hope you don't mind meeting us here. We thought it might be better than descending on you *en masse*, as it were. Martin was kind enough to give us your address."

The plump bald man shuffled along to make room for me and I slid into the booth. Stapp immediately squashed in next to me. I wriggled, trying to get enough room to breathe, then pulled my arms free.

"I understand that this must be a difficult time for you, Daniel," Wilton said. "You're confused at the moment. You don't know who to trust. What I want, Daniel, is for you to feel you can trust us."

"Welcome, Daniel," said the plump man sitting next to me.

"Welcome," said Stapp.

"Yes, welcome, Daniel," said the guy in khakis.

"Yeah," said the younger man, who was glaring at me.

I reached across the table and pulled a handful of potato chips from one of the open bags. I was reluctant to eat in front of them, I always felt vulnerable when I ate in front of people — but my stomach felt like it was collapsing inwards.

A sumptuous banquet is laid out in the dining hall but you are far too nervous to eat. "New blood, eh?" says the man you followed, appearing from behind you as if out of nowhere. He is tall and cruelly handsome, sporting an eyepatch and a widow's peak. He has "chief henchman" written all over him. An expectant hush falls over the crowd. Something is about to happen.

"We don't want much, Daniel." Wilton said. "We don't want you to do anything for us. But we'd like you to help Martin. We'd like you to help your friend." He leaned forward. "You've been his friend, his best friend, all through high school and university. He talks about you in the warmest possible terms. Martin needs your support now more than ever."

"We had a falling out," I said. "Quite some time ago."

"Is that what you tell yourself now?" Wilton said, his eyes misting slightly. "Martin still considers you to be his friend. You just spent most of the afternoon and evening talking with him — how can you not be his friend?"

"I was curious about his book."

"Good." Wilton gave me a broad smile and gestured for me to help myself to more chips. "People like you should be curious. I financed that book for a reason, Daniel. Could 1.1 million people really have died at Auschwitz? Martin's book proves that they couldn't, that the crematoria were not capable of disposing of so many corpses. He reached this conclusion without bias or prejudice. You must know that. He is your friend."

"You need to go further, Daniel," the plump man said suddenly. "You need to make an open show of support."

"Yeah," said the guy in khakis. "Take a stand, man."

Wilton and Stapp glared at them and they fell silent, shifted back into their seats. Wilton did not want to move so fast with me.

`At last a door at the other end of the room opens and, after some ceremony, an elderly man in a wheelchair enters the room. It is the same man you saw in the photographs you found in your dead parents' apartment; you recognise the tell-tale scar that runs down one side of his face. To your horror you see that he is dressed in a black SS uniform, complete with a blood-red armband and swastika. He pulls off one black leather glove with a snap. "So," he says.`

"The first thing you should know, Daniel, is that this is not about the Jews," Wilton told me. "We have nothing against Jews."

I self-consciously stuffed another handful of chips into my mouth.

"But look what happens to us when we speak out, when we challenge even a small facet of the conventional understanding." He pulled a copy of Karen's article out from under the table and tossed it down in front of me. "We get attacked and vilified in the media. They do not respond with counter-argument, they are not interested in historical debate, just rejections and accusations."

Wilton glanced at my face to make sure I was following him, then pressed on. "Think about it, Daniel. Death camps, gas chambers, lampshades made out of human skin, bodies turned into soap; this is the stuff of hysterical wartime propaganda. Why is it being taught as fact in our universities and schools? Why do people and governments spend fortunes on memorials and museums?"

A hush had fallen over the table. Everyone's attention was fixed on Wilton.

"Certain powers in the world have a vested interest in discrediting the history of the Nazi government," he said after a sufficiently dramatic pause. "Now I'm no fan of Hitler —"

"Yeah," interjected the young man sitting across from me. "Hitler was smart and all but he was, you know, a faggot."

Stapp shot him a warning look and he shut up. Wilton continued without acknowledging the interruption.

". . . And in fact my dad went to fight in Europe and I'm proud of that," he said. But Wilton also took pride in strong leadership and a sense of national unity, he told me. The stories about the Holocaust had been perpetuated in order to make us reject strong, effective governments and sentiments of national pride. They were raised above the level of history, raised to the level of religious myth. Infinitely enduring, all-encompassing, unchallengeable.

"Ladies and gentlemen," the elderly Nazi, or ex-Nazi, or neo-Nazi says. "We gather

> together at the dawn of a new era, an age wherein the weakness and falsities of the past will be swept aside . . ."

"Businessmen are behind this, Daniel," Wilton insisted. "Globalists, international bankers. They're not all Jewish, not necessarily, but they don't like strong governments. They just want to be able to slip in with their multinationals and local branches and dummy companies and bleed a country dry."

> "Our scientists in Brazil are almost ready to begin the final phase of construction. Soon our Doomsday Weapon will be ready and the world will tremble at our feet . . ."

"They seized on the hysterical Holocaust rumours circulating after World War Two. You bet they did. They used them to garner support for the United Nations, their most useful tool in their battle to undermine the autonomy of individual governments. They entrenched the concept of genocide as an indisputable pretext for interference in the internal affairs of a sovereign nation, perpetuating the Holocaust myth to further their own ends. Weakened states and borders, multiculturalism . . ."

> "Nothing can stop us now!" shouts the wheelchair-bound Nazi, his speech reaching its crescendo. "Ladies and gentlemen, the Fourth Reich is nigh!"

Wilton paused for breath. His forehead glistened in the harsh light of the bulb dangling above our booth and he took a sip of beer to moisten his mouth. He tapped the article open in front of me. "We're not neo-Nazis, Daniel," he said. "Don't pay any attention to what's implied here. My connections in Australia, Eric's group here in New Zealand — we are not fascists. We are just free-thinking people who want to take pride in our national identity again. We want the truth about the Holocaust to be known, but even in these so-called democracies we're not allowed to speak out. We are silenced, derided, persecuted, banished from universities and scholarly debates. We can't allow this to happen to Martin as well. I'm out here to watch his back, to lend him my support. You could do that too. You could make a difference for your friend and the world."

> `Game options: Selection: a – battle the Nazi conspiracy that your innocent inquiries into your own past origins have inadvertently uncovered; b – Slip into one of those cool black uniforms and get down with all the goose-stepping fun.`

"Legkov is a Jewish name, isn't it?" Wilton said. "If we were all the rabid anti-Semites people would have you believe we are, then we wouldn't be sitting here with you having this pleasant conversation, would we? We're not asking for a lot here. We just want one little book to be treated fairly. You should be more open about your friendship with Martin, your lifelong friendship. Even a small gesture of support from a young man like you, a young man with a Jewish background, could be powerful."

"Martin and I do not have a lifelong friendship," I said. "And I have never considered myself to be Jewish."

"Daniel . . ." Wilton shook his head sadly. "I am prepared to agree that some of the actions of the global Jewish community have been less than admirable, but that's no cause for you to go cutting yourself off entirely. The Hebrew people have had a long and noble history. You should take pride in it."

I stood up quickly, surprising Stapp and the plump man on either side of me. Stapp met my eyes for a moment, then pulled his knees back, allowing me to push past him. This was enough. I already had more than I needed.

A flicker of dismay crossed Wilton's features; he probably had a sense of having gone a little too far, said a little too much for our first conversation, but he kept on talking as I struggled away from him. "One of the aims of our movement is to recapture our pride in our own identity, and that extends to people like you as well."

Free of the booth, I started to walk out to the front of the pub, where the band was wrapping up its set with a Nirvana cover.

"Judaism is where you have your origins, Daniel," Wilton called as I hurried away from him. "It's part of who you are."

RAVINGTON

```
Rise up, rise up, Aryan man,
Turn your anger into hate.
Rise up, rise up, Aryan man,
Take back your land before it's too late.
```

Ravington had read Eric Stapp's poetry lying in bed, Adja curled up beside him, her long blonde hair spilling over the pillow, a trickle of morning sunlight dappling the freckled skin on the tip of her shoulder. Rav was already panicking. He had never turned down a book before, he didn't know how it was done. And how exactly did you phrase a polite rejection to a man like Eric Stapp?

Rav looked over at Adja. Still asleep. He wasn't sure about her — that "Jew-bastards" thing had thrown him — but she hadn't said anything particularly anti-Semitic during the rest of the evening. Perhaps it had been a one-time slip, an aberration. And anyway, she was European.

Ravington slipped out of bed and walked downstairs to make coffee. He prepared two cups, intending to take them upstairs, to maybe have a meaningful morning talk with Adja about Kiwi values and ethnic slurs, but she soon joined him, already fully dressed, brushing her hair into place with her fingertips.

She shook her head at the offered cup of coffee. "Late for work," she said and kissed him, pushing close, slipped a cool, long-fingered hand down into his boxers to cup his testicles for a moment, then pulling away. Ravington noticed that she was holding the paper-clipped sheaf of Stapp's poetry in her other hand. "You publishing these?" she asked, putting them down on the table.

"I'm . . . I mean, I can't . . . Did you look at them?"

Adja shrugged.

"Did you like them?"

Adja shrugged again and Ravington was happy. If she didn't like Stapp's *Aryan Man* sequence perhaps there was hope for her yet. "Have to go," she said, and walked out, smiling back at him over her shoulder.

No need for that meaningful talk, Rav thought. She would come right all on her own, he was sure of it.

Ravington drank his coffee, then caught his bitterly resented bus to Tunnel Press. He stopped at the post office on the way there, checking his box out of habit, and was surprised to find three packages waiting for him. Once he was in the office, sitting at his desk, lighting the morning's first cigarette, he tore them open. The covering letter in the first one read:

Dear Mr Ravington,

I have been informed that you are an unusually bold publisher with an interest in important and controversial matters. Please

> find enclosed my extensively footnoted 128-page policy analysis of why all non-European immigration to New Zealand should be halted within six years . . .

The second had a US postmark.

> Dear Mr Ravington,
> I saw your press recommended on the ofaah.com website and thought I'd give you a try!!! Enclosed is a copy of "The Spawn of Ham" a sci-fi epic set in the wastelands of America in 2026. It deals with the aftermath of a vicious RACE WAR in which a heroic WHITE ENCLAVE battles to hold out against BLACK HORDES seeking their ultimate destruction . . .

The third appeared to be another volume of far-right poetry entitled *The Sword of God*. Ravington leaned back in his chair and fumbled for a second cigarette. Wilton and Glass, what had they done to him? How many more of these things could he expect?

Bored, with little else to do except start packing up his office supplies, Ravington spent the morning and early afternoon half engrossed in *The Spawn of Ham*. Some time around three o'clock Eric Stapp entered the office without knocking. His entrance was swift: one moment Rav was reading about a perilous journey by an Aryan convoy to the ruins of Bismarck, North Dakota, the next the door had banged back against the wall and he looked up to see Eric Stapp standing over his desk.

"Mr Ravington," Stapp said.

Ravington nodded as Stapp seated himself. He hadn't seen Stapp sit before. He had been a looming, shadow-casting presence. Now they were eye-level, facing each other across the desk. Rav wasn't sure if this made him feel more or less comfortable.

"So what did you think?" Stapp asked. His expression had changed slightly. He wasn't quite so impassive and granite-like, and while he was not exactly smiling, his eyes had widened slightly and his lips were parted.

```
Keep strong, Aryan man,
Hold true to the dream.
Keep strong, Aryan man,
A nation proud, brave and clean.
```

"Your work feels deeply personal," Lewis Ravington said. "Very emotional. Have you been writing for long?"

"Nah. The last few years maybe." Stapp leaned back in his chair, his eyes flicking around the room, avoiding Ravington. "Did you like them?" he asked.

Rav paused, unsure exactly what he could say about the *Aryan Man* sequence. "I did find some of them quite affecting."

"Shit," Stapp said and for a moment Rav thought he sounded angry, but then Stapp said "shit" again, in a softer tone, and shook his head. "I didn't really think they were any good," he said. "Just getting my thoughts down, expressing them. And yeah, my emotions. Anger and some other stuff, yeah . . ."

Some other stuff? Rav tried to think what that might be. There were plenty of exhortations for Aryan men to rise up, a rather long poem about the *leeches that bleed / our country / into dryness*, another called "Crush Every Parasite". And yet in the midst of all the raging, stomping, rhyming anger there were quieter moments, a few tiny flecks of regret and melancholy. One poem began:

```
My whole life
fell apart
in the moment
I broke
my son's nose
```

"Never shown this stuff to anyone before," Stapp said.

"Eric," said Ravington as gently as he could, "I'm afraid that Tunnel Press is running into some difficulties at the moment and I can't think about taking on any new authors . . ."

"Shit!" Stapp said, and Rav was again worried that this might be an angry "shit", but instead it turned out to merely be an incredulous one. "I don't want to publish anything. It's private," Stapp said. "My private thoughts. Shit, I don't know why I write them down. I don't know why I'm showing them to you." Stapp was starting to sound angry now, though thankfully not with Ravington. He rubbed his head hard, scratching at his stubble and then looked away again, out the window, to Rav's small, slit-like view of the central city. "Stuff just spills out sometimes. You seemed like a guy who'd understand that."

Ravington nodded. He was thinking of Stapp's broken-nose poem again.

```
I apologised
a thousand times
in a thousand ways
but no redemption
```

"I've got to go." Stapp stood up."Got stuff to do. But thanks for looking at the poems. It helps to have someone read it, someone who understands."

Ravington nodded again. Perhaps Stapp was just like every other writer who'd ever sat across from him in that chair. Beyond the egos, beyond the claims to imminent fame and glory, beyond the small, self-deprecating smiles and nervous hopes for success, beyond all that was the simple desire to be read, to have their words and thoughts go to places beyond them. Ravington knew that desire well — he had exploited it, made his living off it. To him it was the most familiar thing in the world. And he had seen weaker rhyming structures.

"If you liked the poems . . ." Stapp hesitated at the door of the office. "If you liked them . . . I could show you some more."

This was some sort of karmic pay-off, Rav thought. He had to be Stapp's reader. It was his lot in life; he was Lewis Ravington, editor-in-chief.

Stapp left the office. Rav lit another cigarette, took a few drags to calm his nerves, then returned his attention to *The Spawn of Ham*. Once he had finished the novel, he picked up *The Sword of God* and started to read that too. He would read them all. Until he finally left the Tunnel Press office he would read everything that came his way. There was nothing else he could do.

Rav read on and on as the afternoon slipped into evening. What more could he expect? Could there be poetry after *Body Disposal at Auschwitz*? Ravington would have to see.

MARTIN GLASS

Martin's inbox had been full of new emails when he checked his computer that morning. Congratulatory messages from around the world, a few invitations to submit to certain journals, a request for him to present his work and take part in panel discussions at a conference for "historical revisionists" later that year. Wilton must have passed on his contact details to others in his community.

> Dear Martin Glass,
> I have just ordered several copies of your book. Few people in the world have the courage to speak out on the myth of the HoloHoax . . .

This is how it begins. Supporters and detractors, magazine articles, journalists at his door.

Mr Glass
I've not read your work yet but I intend to. It's time the world woke up to the fact that the only true genocide is the genocide facing the WHITE RACE, soon to be overrun and outbred . . .

Genocide is an interesting word. It has always fascinated Martin and driven his historical studies, and it is on his mind again while he waits to meet the latest journalist at the Aro Street café.

The Greek-derived "geno", meaning "race" or "tribe", and "cide" from the Latin *caedere* or "killing". The two terms were first joined as "genocide" by Raphael Lemkin, a Jewish lawyer who fled Europe for America in the early forties, a man determined to give a name to "the crime with no name". He had petitioned the newly formed United Nations to declare genocide an international crime, prosecutable in any nation, and this eventually resulted in the 1948 Convention on the Prevention and Punishment of the Crime of Genocide. The Soviet Union had agreed to its terms with the proviso that any mention of "political groups" be removed (it still had business to settle with more than a few "counter-revolutionaries"), but the United States refused to ratify it, fearful of the day when one of its own nationals might be tried for the crime thanks to the body it had helped to establish.

The journalist arrives at Martin's table, apologising for being late. He is a tall, curly-haired man, a little older than Martin, with a broad, reassuring face and pleasantly straight features. He sits down, orders a coffee, and opens a shorthand notebook. Martin talked to him on the phone the other night, but cannot remember his name now. It does not really matter anyway; he already has the interview planned out in his head, what he will be asked and how he will answer. As they make introductory small-talk, Martin remembers that Lemkin had been a historian as well as a lawyer, that he had planned to write a four-volume history of genocide from antiquity to the modern age. To Martin that sounded like a grand scheme, to insert a new word so far back into the past, but sadly Lemkin's history received no interest from publishers and was never completed. Lemkin had died in 1959, the year in which the film adaptation of *The Diary of Anne Frank* was nominated for eight Academy Awards; seven people attended his funeral. The United States eventually ratified the 1948 genocide convention twenty-nine years after Lemkin's death, but only with stringent "reservations", which effectively meant that the US could never be charged with genocide in the International Court of Justice unless the US itself consented to be charged. The 1988 Genocide Convention Implementation Act made the crime of genocide punishable in the US by life imprisonment and fines of up to $1 million.

"Yes, I do feel that the scope of my book has been misrepresented in the recent article," Martin says in answer to the journalist's inevitable first question. "The attempt to define my study as a work of Holocaust denial is very misleading. At no point in my book do I deny the existence of the Holocaust. It is a historical fact that Jews in Europe were horribly persecuted by the Nazi government. It is also a fact that many died as a result of this persecution. My book does not dispute this."

The interview is going smoothly. Martin has rehearsed these points, he barely needs to keep half a mind on the conversation.

"I realise that my findings are likely to be controversial," is his response to the next question, "but I feel it is the duty of a conscientious historian to never accept any historical theory unquestioningly. Our first duty must always be to the evidence. I do suggest that it was possible that fewer than the accepted figure of 1.1 million died at Auschwitz-Birkenau. I suggest this possibility, but I do not claim it as fact. The only fact I claim is that it took something in the region of fifty to sixty minutes to completely incinerate an adult body in one of the Topf furnaces used in the Auschwitz-Birkenau camps. That is it. That is the whole deal."

Lemkin's word is used quite easily today, Martin thinks. It can be invoked in a host of different contexts: Nigeria, Bengal, Burundi, Indonesia, Cambodia, Iraq, East Timor, Yugoslavia, Rwanda. Often it will not be used immediately, but only after a suitable time has passed, after the killing has stopped.

"I'm going to get a little technical here," Martin says, "but try to bear with me. The workings of the double-muffle coke-fired Topf furnaces used at Auschwitz allowed for the burning of perhaps twenty corpses a day per muffle. The full fifty-two furnaces did not become operational until June 1943. Prior to that there were only three double-muffle ovens in the main camp, allowing for six furnaces total. So we can see that it would have been highly unlikely that so many corpses could have been disposed of over the time period in question, even if every oven was burning its full capacity of corpses every day. Now when we factor in wartime shortages of the wood and coke necessary to fuel these furnaces . . ."

Martin had discovered that Lemkin's word had been tactfully avoided by the US State Department's Bureau of Near Eastern Affairs when describing the 1987–1988 Anfal campaign against the Kurdish people in Iraq. He finds this interesting. In 1994 The Office of the US Secretary of Defense had been wary of using the "genocide" term to describe Rwandan events. It could commit the United States to actually do something . . .

Next question. "My book just deals with the physical, primary evidence surrounding crematory capacities and recorded death rates. That is all. I do, however, venture the typhus epidemic of 1942 as a possible explanation for the expansion of the crematory facilities. Whether it was a contributing factor or an alternative to the gas-chamber hypothesis will be for other historians to judge."

Whatever its meaning in language or law, the word "genocide" came into existence in the wake of the Nazi government and World War Two. In political terms that makes it dangerous and difficult; its use can commit nations to condemnation and intervention. Martin believes this explains the rise of "ethnic cleansing" as an alternative phrase. It is less confrontational, less all-encompassing, less committed. It sounds like something that is manageable, that can be defeated by a little diplomacy or an international peace-keeping effort. In 1993, at the inauguration ceremony for the Washington DC Holocaust Memorial, Elie Wiesel had said: "I have been in the former Yugoslavia, last fall. I cannot sleep since for what I have seen. As a Jew I am saying that." But when asked about this later by reporters, President Clinton had responded: "I think the Holocaust is on a whole different level. I think it is without precedent or peer in human history." Uniqueness is often preferred, direct comparisons can be so awkward.

"Of course I would be happy to discuss *The Online Forum for the Academic Analysis of the Holocaust*," says Martin. "The coordinators of the site consider themselves ideologically neutral — it is a discussion board for people of all points of view. I will admit that distasteful views have been expressed on the site. Ever since the founding of the Holocaust-revisionist school of history by Paul Rassinier shortly after the end of the Second World War its objectives have often been subverted by anti-Semitic groups. This does not mean that every unorthodox study of the European Holocaust should be immediately equated with anti-Semitism. Rassinier himself was a former Nazi prison-camp internee. My point is that all historical theories of the event should be considered on their merits and not be censured by these kinds of accusation. It's a freedom-of-speech issue."

Martin is familiar with the debate among historians and social scientists over the uniqueness of the Holocaust. Can other historical events be compared to it? Was it the first genocide in history? Will it be considered the last, until some other act of mass murder exceeds its established high score? Call an event ethnic cleansing, then call it genocide a few years later, but "Holocaust" is always lurking behind these terms. Sometimes we long to make the connection, sometimes we strive against it, but it is still the most powerful word, it cuts the deepest.

In any case, Martin knows that Lemkin's more general word eventually had its day in court, fifty years after the convention on genocide had been drafted. Perhaps that might have brought the dead lawyer some satisfaction. In 1998 Jean-Paul Akayesu was found guilty of genocide for the systematic rape of Tutsi women in Rwanda's Taba commune. In 2001, former Serbian President Slobodan Milosevic became the first national leader to be charged with genocide before an international war crimes tribunal. His wife, Mirjana Markovic, naturally denounced the tribunal as a "concentration camp with gas chambers for Serbs".

The journalist has bought four coffees, two for Martin and two for himself, and has been filling pages of his notebook with quick, spidery scribbles. "We'll be sending the photographer round tomorrow," he said.

Martin nodded. The journalist looked at him and Martin knew that this was the moment, this was when he had to make the real sell.

"So your book and its findings were in no way motivated by any anti-Semitic agenda?" the journalist asks.

"Of course not," Martin replies, "and I very much resent that implication in the last article. In fact . . ." he started to say and almost didn't finish because he thought it might be going a little too far, but then found that he couldn't resist it, that it was too perfect, too delicious. "In fact," he says, "some of my best friends have been Jews."

Genocide. From the Greek *genos* and the Latin *caedere*. Clear, crisp and beautiful, difficult to misspell, mispronounce or confuse. Poor Lemkin, thinks Martin Glass. If only he were alive now. How well his four-volume history would have sold. It was a shame he couldn't live this long, a shame he couldn't live long enough to see how well his word would catch on. Honestly, Raphael, we love it now. We simply cannot get enough of it.

DANIEL

```
Game options selected: You leave work early
to spend quality time with your girlfriend,
but are unable to keep thoughts of the
sudden and mysterious death of your parents
out of your head. You swear to find whoever
is responsible and make them pay.
  "Are you all right, Daniel?" your girlfriend
asks. "You look a little distracted . . ."
```

Work at Eclectic Inc had kicked into high gear. Heckle had liked my Nazi-hunting plot level-breakdown. He had been delighted with it in fact. There was already talk of giving the game-city a late-sixties Cold War makeover, to tie in with my idea of the player's parents being Holocaust survivors. A bunch of programmers had started playing the board game *Axis & Allies* during downtime, and several scripters had watched a DVD of *Schindler's List* in the break room, trying to get into the right mindset. By the water cooler, near my desk, a born-again Marxist graphic artist was lecturing some of my workmates about the Holocaust.

"The tightened financial situation in post-war Germany meant that resources would have to be redistributed within the upper echelons of the capitalist hierarchy . . ."

I had come up with a good idea. My stock in the Eclectic offices had gone up. Thank God for Nazis. I had checked the game-forums again and the rumoured changes were meeting with approval.

> Voidkiller386: i heard there only going to let u kil nazi terrorists in teh game now but u can still kil them any way u want!!! roxors!

"The Jews, as a distinct group within the bourgeoisie, provided the most obvious target," the Marxist graphic artist continued. "The Nazi doctrine of Aryan racial superiority was ultimately just an excuse for a massive economic restructuring of German society."

Morbid still hated me, of course, which made sharing a small apartment with him awkward. We had successfully avoided each other for much of the past week — or I had avoided him, working late every night at the Eclectic offices. I could feel his eyes on me now though, watching me work from the exposed cubicleless desk next to mine. I had distorted the artistic project of his life into clichéd pulp trash; the grudge was not about to dissipate any time soon. But the final version of his Eclectic engine was a thing of beauty, even I had to admit that. The first-person perspectives were fully three-dimensional, the environments completely naturalistic. If a player's avatar went out in the rain, it got wet. The water would bead and roll down its body. A certain amount of pre-rendered moisture would affix to the avatar and continue to drip off it for a time afterwards. Winds ebbed and flowed, clouds moved in the sky.

"Of course, it wasn't enough to just strip the Jewish bourgeoisie of their wealth and privilege. Under the Nazi regime, the efficiency of the capitalist system was elevated above all other goods, even human life . . ."

Martin's latest magazine interview had caused a stir when it appeared a few weeks ago. It was in a magazine with a slightly larger circulation, and was placed a little bit further up in the list of features. *A Call for Free and Open Debate: Controversial Holocaust Historian Martin Glass Speaks Out.* There was a photo of him standing outside his small flat, hands in the pockets of his jacket, staring unsmilingly past the camera. I knew that Josh had seen the magazine. He had not been happy. I was never at home when he called, but he had left angry, slightly incoherent answerphone messages.

The article was too sympathetic. Martin was too devious. Paul Rassinier hadn't founded any historical school, he'd been an anti-Semitic fuck. We need to do something, Big Man, people have to know what's going on.

> "You seem so distant lately," says your girlfriend. "So cold." How can she understand what you saw in the mansion that night? Your quest to unravel the neo-Nazi conspiracy is what drives you. No matter how real the rest of your life is, this has become more real, it is your obsession.
>
> "I never see you," says Karen. "Daniel, why do you never call?"

I clicked out of the Alpha game level, opened my email and composed a brief message to stairway@hotmail.com. *You sent me Martin's book. You sent me the link to the website. We need to meet. I need to know what you're thinking. Please.*

". . . so that's what that Glass guy is trying to cover up in that book of his. When he denies that the Nazis murdered the Jews he denies the inherent barbarism and inhumanity of capitalist thought."

When I returned to the game I found that it had been auto-playing itself. The scenario had moved on, it had broken down, degenerated into something unrecognisable.

> `Your girlfriend turns away, walks into her room and you follow her. "I'm not (ERROR) your girlfriend," she says. "No," you say, "you left me in Edinburgh," and you reach out and ERROR ERROR ERROR Karen's hair fills your face, your eyes, fine red strands stick to the corners of your mouth and the trails of saliva on her neck ERROR Nothing is personal ERROR couldn't stop you ERROR you are, after all, a big man.`

"Hey, Daniel."

I jerked up from the computer, hastily clicking the degenerating game-scenario closed. The Marxist graphic artist was standing over me. "What do think of this?" He passed me a printout of some concept art. It was a 3D design for the escaped Nazi war criminal (he now had a name; Heckle and I had decided on "Herr Kommandant von Wolfen"). The Marxist graphic artist had got von Wolfen just right — sinister wizened features, shiny metal wheelchair, crisp black SS uniform. Only one thing puzzled me.

"What's this?" I asked, tapping the picture.

"We've given von Wolfen a mechanical claw-arm," the Marxist graphic artist said. "It was Heckle's idea. He thought it would make him a bit scarier."

"I like it." From his desk, Morbid was still glaring at me.

"Heckle wants to see you in his office," said the Marxist graphic artist.

"Cheers."

"He thinks this game is going to sell big."

"It may."

"He's thinking Platinum title."

"Well, Heckle would know."

"Fuckin' A," said the Marxist graphic designer and returned to his desk.

Heckle was on the phone when I tapped his open door. He waved me to a chair. "Lots of games have addressed Nazism in some way," he was saying. "*Medal of Honor, Brothers in Arms, Secret Weapons of the Luftwaffe, Return to Castle Wolfenstein*; the Nazi enemy is a recurring motif throughout the history of video games. But *VirtuLife* is going to be the first game to really address the consequences and the history of the Nazi regime. It plunges new depths of emotion and memory. When we combine that with the kicking graphics and extreme gameplay, we've got our marketing pitch sorted."

Heckle hung up, and swivelled round in his seat to face me. "Everything's go, Daniel," he said, grinning. "Styx Softworks love your new direction. They'd always been a bit iffy about the open-endedness of *VirtuLife* anyway. It's hard to sell a game without a story."

"Glad I could come up with one."

"The graphic engine is in place. All we have to do is revamp environments and the AI scripting and we'll be ready to move on to post-production. I'm going to get you onto a new contract." Heckle handed me a thick manila folder. "Have a look over that tonight. I want you on this project right till the end."

When I got back to my desk there was a new message waiting for me in my inbox. *Need a lift to the airport next*

Thurs, stairway@hotmail had written. *We can talk then, if you like*. I wrote the date down in my diary along with the address Karen had sent me, then returned to my game.

KAREN

I guess it's no big deal to talk about, it didn't affect me much one way or the other. I'm on my way out now, I'm leaving, so I couldn't care less really, it just doesn't matter. It was like everything else. Just stuff that happened to me and a few other people. But if we're going to talk, let's start with Martin.

Martin was my first serious boyfriend. I'd had a guy almost all the way through high school, but he was a wanker, he didn't count. Martin was exactly the sort of guy I'd spent half my first year at uni looking for — quiet, smart, pretty-looking. I had my eye on him from the moment I first saw him in my history tute, but it took two classes before he'd look back at me. No, sorry, screw starting with Martin, let's go back a little further, let's start with me.

In high school I wasn't much to talk about. I was just about every girl in a blazer you ever knew. Hand always up in class, pleasant to everyone, a well-scrubbed tease in plaid skirts, boyfriend on the second XV who lied to his friends about the things I was prepared to do for him. Captain of the girls' water-polo team, stage manager for the drama club, chairperson of the Leavers' Ball committee. I lived in a two-storey house in suburban Napier with two parents, two cars and two dogs. I liked Jesus for a while when I was fifteen and horses for a little longer after that.

At university in Wellington, in my hall, I transformed from every nice girl in a blazer into every undergrad pseud in op-shop rags. I pretended to understand *Finnegan's Wake* and learned how to smoke. There was no shortage of flaccid arts-major pricks hanging around me, eager to impress with their knowledge of Pindar's Orphism, and I had to sleep with a couple before I found one I really liked.

Though Martin swore it wasn't the case, I'm certain I was his first. I was the one who decided when the time was right, who guided him into me. He was passive, gentle, nervous, and I wrapped my arms around his thin, shaking body.

He probably told you that we argued a lot. He wanted to show me how clever he was and I would let him harass me into sharing his viewpoints, seeing the world his way. I hadn't yet made a firm commitment to an identity at that stage — blazer-girl, op-shop poet, hard-thinking theory-chick, it was all the same. The quiet moments with Martin were nicer. Long afternoons in the botanical gardens, dozy Sunday mornings, that's what I like to remember.

I got on well with Daniel. I liked him. He was so different from Martin — big, slow on his feet, slow to talk. He and Martin had known each other in high school, had fallen in with each other and never fallen out. I was no longer on speaking terms with any of my high-school girlfriends, even the ones who had moved to Wellington. I guess I was kind of amazed at the ease of male friendships: low-key, adaptable, little maintenance required. The stakes seemed generally lower.

I don't really want to talk about breaking up with Martin. I'm not holding back anything juicy. No shouting, not too many tears. Just a gradual decline and an eventual halt. A few sad days. A raw bruised feeling that lingered. Naturally Lance and Peter chose this time to throw a party. A bunch of near-strangers flooding the property that had been our own private world for months on end. The whole thing threw me off balance. I should have moved out long before then; being around Martin every day had me on edge. I got really drunk really fast, screamed at Martin (or maybe it was Peter, or some guy called Ash — I screamed at someone) then ran upstairs to hide.

And later Daniel found a way to raise the stakes.

Martin has his own theory about what happened. I think he's held onto it ever since. He got angry with me for telling him that he was wrong, later on. For a while it seemed easiest to just go along with what Martin said, the way I had back in the early days, when we first started going out.

We saw each other again a few times over the years. But it was impossible to be with him, impossible to be friends. He kept coming back to that night — he kept coming back to Daniel, and kept getting angry with me. Not just for not agreeing with him, but for being the way I was — happy, healthy, ambitious, never needing to pause for breath or recovery. He could not reconcile it, he couldn't write my present-day self into his story of us, of him and me and Daniel. He was young, and in some respects quite stupid. I think he has retained that to a certain extent. He is exactly the same when I see him; the years have not changed him enough.

Last questions. What has all this got to do with what's going on right now? Absolutely nothing whatsoever. Whatever's happening now is all about what's happening now, if you catch my drift. The boys might tell you something different, but they're grasping for an illusionary cause, the convenient answer, an easy excuse. You probably wouldn't agree with me. You're entitled to your own opinion.

The flat, the party, what happened afterwards, it was all just stuff. It was not a defining moment. I refuse to see it that way. You can't make me.

And that's all I'm prepared to say about it.

JOSH

When he first found the address he wasn't sure what to do. He had walked up to its location on the street, a nondescript little bungalow on the side of a hill. The blinds were shut and he could not see inside. He lingered by the letterbox, then walked on down the street. A cul-de-sac opened onto a small park and he sat down on a bench, watching children play on a swing set in the early evening twilight.

Josh hadn't been idle since arriving in Wellington. He had been biding his time, following the events in the media and familiarising himself with Martin's work. He had thoroughly explored *The Online Forum for the Academic Analysis of the Holocaust*, tracing the website's links back to organisations with names like "Legion of White Decency" or "League of British Fascists", reading the articles and forum discussion threads.

`The Leuchter Report finds no trace of`

```
cyanide in the ruins of the Auschwitz gas
chambers . . . Witness testimonies were
clearly fabricated . . . Confessions easily
coerced . . . The invention of a global-
Zionist conspiracy . . . Coincidentally,
most of the orthodox Holocaust historians
who have sought to discredit these findings
are Jewish themselves . . .
```

Extracts from Martin Glass's book had been posted on ofaah.com and Josh had read them again as well. The conclusions about the overall crematory capacities, and the account of the 1942 typhus epidemic that he claimed could have accounted for many of the deaths. In the book itself they had been half hidden in a mess of dates and figures and documents, but exposed on the website, where Josh had first seen them, they hit like a blow upon a bruise.

Josh had found advertisements for the book on other far-right websites, editorials praising its "intellectual honesty" and links to Tunnel Press for orders. But before the book, before *Body Disposal at Auschwitz*, he could find no trace of Martin Glass. Glass had not posted any stand-alone articles on ofaah.com or ranted in its forums.

Josh had gone to the local library and dug back through their stacks, looking for every book that had ever been published by Tunnel Press. Poetry, poetry, autobiography, poetry. Apart from Glass's book, none of them dealt with an even vaguely academic subject. A first-time Holocaust denier, publishing a book with a press which itself had no previous association with Holocaust denial. This wasn't the usual madness. This was something different, something new.

Josh found himself sitting on the bench for more than an hour. It was almost nightfall by the time he stood up and the children in the park had morphed into listless adolescents who played on the swings in a desultory, ironic fashion. He started to walk back down the street. His adrenaline was ebbing; righteous anger could only take him so far. Washington had exhausted him, Jerusalem had exhausted him, and now here he was, tired out and alone at the end of the world.

Josh had visited the Tunnel Press offices and found its editor sitting at a dusty desk in a single room with half of its contents packed up in boxes around him. The editor looked up from the manuscript he was reading and said: "Here about Martin Glass? Have his address, have his phone number. Call him, stalk him, interview him, invite him to join your gun club."

The editor handed Josh a slip of paper from a pile on his desk. All of Martin Glass's details were there — phone number, email, home address, the lot. Josh looked at it for a moment, dumbfounded. "Are you sure you should be doing this?" he found himself asking.

"I'm not sure about anything," the editor said. "If you have a manuscript you can drop it off on the table by the door. I'm reading everything."

Now Josh was walking past the address again. The blinds were still drawn, no lights in the windows. Josh hadn't doubted himself while guiding Anita through the Holocaust memorials of the New World. He hadn't doubted himself while donating sperm in Israel and talking to Lippman about his new Half-Jewish identity. But now, on the doorstep of the man he had designated his enemy, he found himself doubting his mission. What could he do about Martin Glass? Talk to him? Argue with him? He would knock on the door at least. He had come all this way. All he could do was knock on the door and see what happened next.

Before he could get across the garden to the sliding door of the apartment someone called "Hey!" from behind him and two men were getting out of a car parked on the other side of the street and walking towards him — a plump squishy man in a suit and a small, feral-looking man in khakis. "What the hell are you doing here?" the man in khakis shouted. "What the hell do you want?"

Josh's self-doubt vanished and he turned around to face them. Just as he had been losing energy a confrontation presented itself. He almost felt relieved.

WILTON AND JOSH

Nigel Wilton was just getting back into his rented car when he got the call. He had driven up to the top of Mount Victoria to admire the view. A splendid city, Wellington. He was pleased to have the chance to visit.

"Mr Wilton?" It was Shane, one of the boys from the NZNS. "We've got an intruder on Glass's property. Doesn't look like a friendly."

"I can be there in ten minutes," Wilton said before hanging up and reversing out of his park. Eric Stapp had raised the question of organising protection for Martin. There had been no sign of him being under threat, not yet, but it paid to be cautious and Wilton had to agree; Martin and his work were important, vital in fact.

One had to start with the details, Wilton could see that now. Body-disposal records, the camp population numbers, the mechanical workings of the furnaces. In the past revisionists had been too bold and sweeping. Martin's book was where revisionism should begin. *Body Disposal at Auschwitz* might serve as the groundwork for a larger study, a more complete history. The way forward was to fight the small battles, let the little ideas and challenges build into the larger ones. This was the point he had to get across to the NZNS and his other allies. If accepted, even marginally, then *Body Disposal at Auschwitz* could be the rock upon which all would be built.

Wilton pulled up outside Martin's home and got out of the car. Shane and Warren were arguing loudly with a man on the lawn. It looked like Martin was out. He had been happy enough to have the NZNS watching his house, but he was adept at giving them the slip, disappearing unexpectedly.

Wilton strode up the path, gently motioning with his hands for Warren and Shane to stand down. The NZNS boys tended to be a little too forceful. Wilton could understand that, he had been rather impassioned himself when he was younger, but it was not the right way. The challenge was to never conform to people's expectations. "How may I help you?" he asked the angry-looking man on the lawn.

"I want to talk to Martin Glass." Wilton detected a strong British twang to his voice. "I want to talk to him about his fucking book."

"We're friends of Martin's," Wilton said. "We're keeping an eye on things here. Martin is very busy at the moment. If you have comments or concerns however, you might find them addressed in the interview that was published earlier this week. I don't know if you've seen a copy yet . . ." Wilton had been pleased with the new article. Much fairer. Martin had done an excellent job with the interview. Perhaps he'd been distracted a little in the earlier one, been thrown off balance by that appalling girl, Karen Staunton.

"Yeah, I've read that fucking interview!" the British man practically shouted. Wilton wondered if he was Jewish. He looked it a little, so perhaps. It didn't really matter, but it was always interesting to know.

Josh could feel the anger seeping through him. It was a wave of sweetness, it was delicious, it was good to have it back. The older man had made a mistake mentioning that article. It had been full of distortions, half-truths and outright lies. *A freedom of speech issue.*

"Please," the older man with the beard was saying, "please, your language." Behind him Fat Man and Khakis were fuming. Josh knew their type, they were itching to move in on him, itching to shout back. The older man kept them in check though.

"Who the hell are you anyway?" Josh said again. "What business is it of yours what street I walk down?"

The man with the beard pushed his shoulders back, straightening up until he had gained a half-inch or so on Josh. "My name is Nigel Wilton. As I said before, I am a friend of Martin's."

"I know exactly who you are." Josh should have guessed who would have been watching Martin Glass's house. "I've read all about you."

"Then you should know that my friends and I are here to see that Martin Glass does not suffer the same misguided persecution and censure that I did in Melbourne."

"That's right," said Khakis, and Fat Man nodded in a slow, deliberate fashion. They both started to move closer and Josh almost grinned with anticipation. He had provoked them. He had done it. It was time for them to show Josh who they really were. He already knew, of course. He had known all along.

"I get you," the short British man was saying as Warren and Shane stepped forward to stand shoulder to shoulder with

Wilton. "I've seen anti-Semites like you all over the world. I should know, I'm Half-Jewish."

That explains it then, thought Wilton. Ever so slightly, he felt himself lose a hold on his temper. Here was another man standing in front of him thinking he had the right to throw insults, thinking he had a moral authority that excused him everything, perversely proud of his Jewish blood because somehow it allowed him a claim to eternal victimhood. Wilton knew he had to be patient, he knew he had to hold his anger in. The tiresome British man had been taught to think that way, it wasn't really his fault. But it still infuriated Wilton, he couldn't help that. Why did these people have to persist in their claims? Did they really think it was such a wonderful thing to be a victim?

He, Nigel Wilton, knew what it was to be a victim. He was the one who had been persecuted, hounded, dragged before inept judges like Christ before Pilate. Nigel Wilton could have told them that it wasn't quite so nice, not quite so pleasant to be a victim as they seemed to think it was, certainly not to be *their* victim. But he still persisted, he still turned the other cheek and tried to make them see in spite of themselves.

"I am in no way, and never have been, an anti-Semite," Wilton said, carefully keeping his voice level and calm. "Neither are my associates. Neither is Martin Glass." He hoped Shane and Warren would have the good sense to follow his example and keep their cool. Anything else would be playing into the hands of their enemies. Of course they had a right to be angry when confronted with a man like this. The Jews had started a cult of victimhood, the Blacks and the Asians and the Aboriginals had all followed them, and suddenly everything had fallen down on the backs of men like him and Shane and Warren. They were the real victims, they always had been.

"Sure he isn't," the British man sneered. "He's got the

oldest line of all. *Some of my best friends are Jews . . .*"

"That is true actually. I know that for a fact." Wilton wondered what a British Jew was doing here on Martin's doorstep. There could be any number of reasons, but he was suspicious nonetheless. Poor Lewis Ravington had already fielded complaints from the New Zealand Jewish Council; Wilton feared that the jaws of a global conspiracy might be closing around Martin Glass's neck.

"Name one, then," the British Jew was saying. "Name just one."

Nigel Wilton drew in another deep breath. He had to take a risk, he thought. He had to play what he hoped was his trump card. Martin had talked at length and with great sentimentality about his friendship with Daniel Legkov. Perhaps bringing the fight to Daniel's doorstep was the only way to make him stand up publicly as Martin Glass's Jewish friend and supporter. He was needed, he was necessary. He could be part of Nigel Wilton's plan.

JOSH

"I can give you a name of one of Martin Glass's Jewish friends," Wilton said. "I can give you a phone number, an address, everything. He would be proud to attest to Martin's good character." And he did give Josh everything, but it turned out to be nothing he didn't have already.

"I see. Right." Josh took a few steps back, his posture weakening.

"Would you like me to write that down for you?"

"No. No, that's okay . . ."

"It's no trouble, really." Wilton was pushing him, pressing home his momentary advantage. Khakis and Fat Man exchanged satisfied glances. Josh knew that he had to fall back, regroup. He ducked around the small group of neo-fascists and started to walk back towards the gate. "I'll look into this," he said. "And then —" his voice sounded hollow, weak and pathetic "— then I'll be back."

He walked quickly away, hurrying down the street. Behind

him, he could hear Khakis and Fat Man laughing and Wilton saying loudly, "Argument. Calm and reasoned argument. That's how you deal with them. They have no defence against it."

They could laugh. Josh would let them. It was no hurt to him, no wound or blow, they could laugh as much as they liked. He knew what they were, he would expose them. And now he had the name that would help him do that. Daniel Legkov. His contact in New Zealand, his hoped-for ally, his fellow Half-Jew. Daniel knew Martin Glass, he was his friend.

Josh was struggling to take this in his stride, but he could. Given enough time he could force everything to make sense. His years of intermittent wanderings with Steve, then his last months in America and Israel with Anita . . . these journeys had led him to his history, back to the past, back to the event. Here in New Zealand, they had led him to a false history, a distorted past, a negated event. He would find something here, Joshua Levit thought as he walked. Something that would build on what he had found in Jerusalem, in Washington, in Berlin, and on the fields of Birkenau.

At the end of it all, after this final tour, he would be able to put everything together. The empty room in the Berlin museum, the drawings of children's shoes in Edinburgh, the protest on the steps of Washington memorial, his sperm donations in Jerusalem, and this anti-history in New Zealand. He would know what his place was, how the past had brought him to the present, what it meant for him to be Half-Jewish and what it meant for him to be Joshua Levit. All he had to do was keep moving. He could not slow down.

ABOVE JERUSALEM

Steve wakes up on an aeroplane in a panic, not quite knowing where he is. It is a night-time flight out of the Middle East; they are probably somewhere over Europe now. His watch says 3 a.m., but they must have changed time zones, so he doesn't know what time it is exactly. It is a small plane for such a long flight, not much better than an Airbus; he can feel the engine juddering through his seat. Every now and then the plane dips and banks slightly. A little turbulence perhaps, but not enough to be worth an announcement. Does the pilot even speak English, anyway? Of course he does; all pilots speak English.

The plane is half empty; passengers are spotted throughout at irregular intervals. There would be space for Steve to stretch out down the back if he wanted, if he could muster the energy to get out of his seat. He dozes off again and dreams about the end of the world and zombies; he is always dreaming about zombies now, the living dead. A zombie girl kisses her fingertip, then pushes it deep into a wound in Steve's side. He wakes up with a jerk and looks around. He is still tired, all his energy has gone.

Steve had meant to return to England directly. When Josh took off on his bizarre quest to the southern hemisphere Steve had intended to stay on for only a few days in Jerusalem, then go back to Tel Aviv then return to London. He had thought that he would settle down for a while now that Josh was gone, get a job and a flat and some kind of life, take a moment to reassess things. Instead he had lingered in Israel, then ventured into Jordan and up to Turkey, before looping back to Tel Aviv for a few more days and flying out at midnight.

Again he had intended to fly back to London, but found himself changing his much-delayed ticket and boarding a flight bound for Berlin instead. He doesn't know why, he cannot afford it. Josh had left him some money, but that is running out quickly. Steve has booked a room in an overpriced hostel near Zoo Station. He can already picture himself sitting at the hostel bar in the evening, nursing a beer, rationing his cigarettes, killing time until it is late enough for him to sleep and then wake early on the following day to kill more time over coffee and newspapers. Steve has no real appetite left for travel. He feels old, he needs to start his life. But he still cannot bring himself to go home, not yet, and so he keeps moving. Even with Josh gone, he has no choice.

Steve starts in his seat and realises he had drifted off again. He is sitting by the aisle and wishes he was by the window — that way he could rest his head against the pane and sleep more comfortably. There is a man in the window seat on Steve's row. He has black hair and dusky skin and is wearing a charcoal-grey suit. He is in his mid-fifties maybe, hunched over, reading a book. Steve wishes he could remember boarding the plane. He should have looked at all the passengers before sitting down, made sure he knew who he was flying with. He feels an impulse to say a word, to attract his fellow passenger's attention somehow, but his mouth is bone dry. Where is the stewardess with the water? Stupid cheap flight. Stupid stewardess.

He remembers his first trip to Berlin, years ago, when he had stayed in a barn-like backpackers in northern Mitte, drank, fucked, met people, partied, had a good time. He had been travelling with friends on a post-university binge, but they went home and he'd stayed on and there, in Berlin, he had met Joshua Levit again. Steve had avoided tourism and sight-seeing for most of his stay in the city — there were other attractions demanding his time — but one morning he found himself feeling guilty about all the museums and galleries and historic curiosities mentioned in his guidebook. He decided to see what was left of the New Synagogue, once the centre of Berlin's Jewish community. As it was not too far from his back-packers and close enough to a café he quite liked, failing to visit it would be inexcusable.

While he examined old photographs and a model of the synagogue and fragments from its destroyed dome, Josh had approached and tapped Steve's shoulder. Steve almost failed to recognise him — it had been four years since they left school — but Josh was grinning, delighted to have found him. They talked, and left the small museum together to get reacquainted over a meal that Josh wound up paying for. Steve had enjoyed the food and let Josh's talk wash over him; all he had to do was nod and murmur in the right places.

They met several more times over the next few days, and when Josh invited Steve to join him on a trip to Dachau he had accepted. He was almost out of money but didn't want to go home yet, couldn't bear the thought of a job and a flat and a life. It was easy to take money from Josh, almost like falling back into the routine of their schooldays, and that was it, that was how the first Holocaust Tour began.

Steve jerks upright in his aeroplane seat. He is dreaming.

He fell asleep again without even noticing. Everyone on the flight is sleeping. The man in his row is slumped over against the window pane. His book has spilled out of his lap and is lying open on the seat between them. A man wearing a suit on a night-time flight, there is something suspicious about that. Steve misses Josh, there is nothing worse than travelling alone. He looks at his watch but can't make out the time. The flight feels like it has gone on forever, like it will never end. He doesn't remember boarding, but remembers the security at Tel Aviv. The searches, the pat-downs, the detectors, the X-rays. He is as safe as he ever needs to be on this flight. This plane is probably the safest in all the world.

Several years after that meeting Steve and Josh had visited Berlin again. The new Jewish museum had opened and they had spent a day exploring its strangely skewed architecture, wandering up and down corridors representing continuity and exile, location and dislocation, memory and the Holocaust. The corridors intersected, twisted and spiralled away, joined, broke apart, rejoined, terminated with exits and empty dead ends. The axis of the Holocaust cut a sheer line across the other museum paths and led into an empty, lightless tower, its heavy door manned by a museum attendant.

Steve remembers Josh talking about that visit to the tower on their train ride to Edinburgh earlier in the year. Anita had found the use of empty space interesting; Daniel had dismissed it as tacky. Steve hadn't said anything then, he would have been too embarrassed, but when he'd taken his turn in the chamber he had breathed the cold in, reached out for a moment to steady himself against the rough, irregular wall, then had sat down cross-legged on the concrete floor and bowed his head. He had sat in the dark for minutes, listening to the wind whip through the slits in the tower wall high above him. Eventually the door creaked open again, somewhere to his left — he had forgotten where the exit was — and Steve stumbled to his feet, pushing his way out before the new visitors could enter, not wanting to share the space with anybody. He had waited until the door closed again behind him, then opened his eyes to the rest of the museum and walked away, following its paths through glass-enclosed displays, hoping to find Josh.

Steve wakes up again with something sweet and hard in his mouth. It clicks against his teeth. A boiled sweet. He cannot remember accepting or unwrapping it. He thinks about Anita, safely back in London or Bristol now, working on her book. She hadn't let herself get caught up, not the way he had. Steve wishes he could go home, wishes he had a home he could go back to. The plane rocks beneath him, rolling, swerving and bumping, but only slightly, only gently, and while Steve has his eyes closed he can almost believe that he is not in a plane at all, but in the back seat of his father's car, asleep, a child again, being driven home after a long trip in the country. When he opens his eyes he is in the back seat of a taxi, being driven away from Heathrow. London is burning around him and the dead stagger through the streets. Zombies again. Steve wakes up. He has sucked his sweet into a jagged-edged spike. It tears at the roof of his mouth, drawing blood.

When he and Josh last visited Berlin, construction on the city's Holocaust memorial had only just begun. They had seen the construction site, Josh had read about what was planned. An uneven field of tall concrete slabs, two thousand seven hundred of them, right in the heart of the city between Potsdamer Platz and the Brandenburg Gate. Josh had been excited by the scale of the project. He could already picture the eerie expanse of sheer faceless slabs laid out in a grid pattern, a graveyard surrounded by the buildings of Berlin's businesses and government.

"I've got to come back here once it's done," he said. "I hope they get it right. They have to."

Even though Steve is now returning to Berlin without

Josh, he looks forward to checking on the site and seeing what progress has been made. Perhaps it will be complete by the time he gets there, perhaps he will be able to look down the rows of slabs to see a flicker of light between them at the other end of the field. Perhaps he will be able to walk in amongst them, through their undulating terrain, until they loom high above his head and he is lost in their shadows. Perhaps he will realise that the tour has not ended for him, that it goes on forever, that it endures, it is inescapable. Steve can see himself walking in the field, in the graveyard, and he can see that Josh is there too, passing between the rows of slabs, flickering in and out of his vision. They both walk and turn, backwards and forwards, moving up and down the grid in an ever-tightening pattern, coming closer and closer until at last they meet in the centre and Josh throws back his arms to embrace Steve and Steve opens his eyes again and wakes up.

DANIEL

I couldn't stop thinking about the Luger pistol Martin had shown me, his present from Nigel Wilton. Its long sleek barrel, its pebbled grip, its elegant trigger-guard. It was a bizarre thing to have in a shoebox on the floor, tucked in the space between the couch and the wall. Wilton had mentioned that his father had been in the war. I wondered if this was how it had come to be in his possession, if his father had taken it somewhere in Africa, or France, or Italy, and passed it down to his son, who would then pass it on to my old friend as a thank-you gift for his attempt to rewrite the history in which it had played a small part. I wondered when the gun would be fired again and who it would kill. A gun hanging on the wall in Act One must be fired by Act Four. Wasn't that the rule? If it was never fired then what was the good of the gun?

I knew a thing or two about narratives now, I had introduced one into *VirtuLife* — I was Eclectic Inc's expert on "linear, story-based, in-game progression". More and more of the story had fallen into place with each day of design-work and by the end of it all *VirtuLife* was no longer *VirtuLife*; Heckle and I had rechristened it *Nazi Hunter*. The story had consumed everything, it had taken over all of us, just as Morbid had feared.

My flatmate wasn't in attendance on the day the last of the Beta Code was completed and we started closing the Eclectic offices down. He was also not present at the party later in the week, where we got smashed on alcoholic punch and crates of beer in the empty office loft. Heckle had thanked all the programmers and scripters and cinematic designers and assured them that this had been the most innovative electronic entertainment project ever undertaken in the South Pacific. He was proud. We had made history. Morbid would not have agreed. History would have been his game — history would have been *VirtuLife* — and we had not made that.

"See you in two weeks," Heckle said as I left the empty office. Of the New Zealand team only I and the Marxist graphic artist would be travelling with Heckle to the United States, to join the *Nazi Hunter* post-production team that was being set up at Styx Game Studios. I was going places, Heckle had told me. I was his key guy.

When I got home I opened my laptop on the kitchen table and listened to my answerphone messages while it powered up. There were several from Josh which I immediately deleted, and one from my brother in Bristol, telling me that he had proposed to his girlfriend and she had accepted. One from Karen confirmed I was driving her to the airport tomorrow, as I'd promised.

My laptop whirred into life, illuminating the kitchen with the pale glow of its screen. I had saved a primitive, unfinished build of the original *VirtuLife* on its hard drive. Technically this was illegal — it was industrial espionage or something — but I couldn't leave the game alone. As the slick, linear, marketable story of *Nazi Hunter* took shape something kept pulling me back to the scratchy inconsistencies of Morbid's earlier design.

```
Option B selected: you return to your
apartment/house/ERROR dingy Karori flat.
She is waiting with dinner readERROR she is
drunk, slumped against a wall upstairs
while the party continues below. "How was
your day at the office?" she askERROR "You
aren't my boyfriend," she says . . .
```

I heard a long slow creak as a door opened and there was barely enough time to shut down *VirtuLife* before I saw Morbid slowly emerge from his room. He paused for a moment, then sprang across the lounge towards me like a Marilyn Manson jack-in-the-box.

"Listen . . ." he said, looming over the kitchen table.

"You missed a good party," I said.

"I want you out of here," said Morbid. "Soon as you can, you find a new place."

"Won't be a problem." I was surprised he had waited this long to kick me out. The bonus he'd just been paid would probably help cover my rent money.

"Good. Your weird mate's been calling for you."

"I know."

"And your brother is . . ."

"Getting married, yeah."

"Well, that's it then." Morbid turned and started to walk back towards his room.

"Hey," I called, and he turned back. "You know this'll work out right? You've got a reference from Logan Heckle. You can take that anywhere in the world. You'll be a success."

Morbid stopped in the kitchen doorway and slowly turned

back to face me. "Nazis," he said softly. "Swastika-wearing, goose-stepping, *so-you-thought-you-vould-escape-my-death-khamp-Allied-svine* Nazis. Was that the best you could come up with?"

"The game was a mess without a story, Morbid. We had no control over what would happen."

"No control was the whole point." He walked back into his room, slamming the door shut behind him. I felt like calling after him, trying to convince him that the story I had grafted onto his game was still true to real life. *Nazi Hunter* was about the conflict between the past and the present. But I didn't need to convince Morbid, I didn't even need to convince myself. I could save all that stuff for later, for the marketing executives, for the advertisers, for feature writers at computer-game magazines. Unable to sleep, I re-booted the creaky old *VirtuLife* build and played Morbid's game until morning.

```
"Some fucking Walpurgis Night, huh kid?"
says the older man called Ash as you walk
on up the stairs.
```

Karen's flat was on a little windy road on the hillside above Oriental Parade. I saw her waiting for me when I pulled up in my father's car, a duffle bag and suitcase next to her on the curb. I got out but she waved away my offers of assistance and hauled first one bag and then the other into the boot.

"That it?" I asked.

"That's everything," she said. "It's good to see you again, Daniel." Without saying anything else, she walked round to the passenger door. I had expected her to have changed more in eleven years — I knew I had. But she might have just walked straight out the door of our old Karori flat. Long red hair pulled back tightly across her scalp, faded jeans, a floral-patterned blouse with wide flapping sleeves, pale perfect skin unblemished by wrinkles, sagging or roughness. She looked across at me over the gleaming roof of my father's car. "I don't want to be rude, but I am in a bit of a hurry."

I walked back to the driver's side and climbed in. "Where are you going?" I asked once I had three-point-turned out of her street and onto the main road.

"Out of New Zealand," Karen replied. Her head was bent against the car window pane and she watched the suburban houses and gardens flick past with half-lidded eyes. "I'm leaving."

"I'm doing that myself in a bit," I said. I shifted the car into first as the hill got steeper. It only took about twenty minutes to get to the airport from here. Fifteen if the traffic was good and you were lucky with the lights. There were things I had to know. Events to clarify or confirm. "What made you want to get in touch with me?"

Karen shrugged and lazily rolled her head back to look out the window again. "Heard you were in town," she said. Her voice sounded bored and nasal. "I did a small piece on that company you work for, back at the start of the year. Wasn't too hard to get your email. I heard you were here and thought you might want to know what Martin was up to, that he was back here as well."

`You sit together and talk in the upstairs hall, for a few hours, you are not sure how long exactly or exactly what you say, you are both a bit drunk ERROR she says "You're not my boyfriend," and you both laugh ERROR and you laugh though you're not sure why it's funny and later she leads you into ERROR she walks into the bedroom at the end of the hall and after a while you rise unsteadily to your feet.`

"You and Martin were always such good friends," Karen said. She was smiling now — not at me, but to herself as she stared out the window. "I always thought it was a shame that the two of you fell out."

I wondered if Karen had thought about this meeting, wondered how hard she might have prepared for it. I pictured her carefully considering her clothes, applying subtle make-up, getting her hair just right, before stepping out onto the pavement with her bags to wait for me. We had been driving for five minutes. I had a quarter-hour left at the most. "Do you remember much about what happened?" I asked.

"How much do you remember?" said Karen.

"Not much, that's kind of why I was asking, I mean, it's hard after all this time . . ."

"Then why does it matter?"

No, you think to yourself. That's not how it's going to go tonight. You push the door open and it bangs against the inside wall. Karen is sitting on a mattress next to an open window. The night breeze riffles the mildewed curtains. You sit down next to her and lean close and kiss her below her jaw, then slowly run your tongue up and down the side of her neck. She tenses and wriggles but you pin one of her arms to her side and pull her closer. A cold, nauseous feeling is growing in your gut.

"Maybe it doesn't." The one clear and unmistakable memory I had was of the morning after, being woken by a cold gust across my chest, rain outside, the window above the bed blowing open and shut. Sitting up to find Karen already gone, shivering on the bare mattress, noticing its patterns of scabby crusts and floral stains. Pulling the window closed and looking out, down onto the garden below, beer cans and bottles scattered around the weed-conquered flowerbeds, a couple of broken folding chairs that had been thrown off the porch, someone's jersey, a shoe and a single sock left out on the lawn, sodden in the rain.

"What have you been up to, Daniel? What have you done with your life?"

"I don't know. Travelled, worked. The usual, I guess." Ten minutes left, maybe less. "Where did you say you were going again?"

"Away. For a good long while."

I glanced at Karen and again wondered how much effort she had put into preparing for this twenty-minute drive, into pretending to be the person she had been eleven years ago. "I am starting to worry," I said. "About what happened between us, I mean. It's all come back over the last few weeks and Martin clearly thinks there was more to it. What I am saying is that I am starting to think about it again . . ."

> Karen's hair fills your face, your eyes, fine red strands stick to the corners of your mouth and the trails of saliva left on her neck. Her breath quickens, she is too small to push back against your weight. Her small breasts are clammy with cooling sweat.

"Martin can think what he likes," said Karen.

"The problem for me is that I'm starting to look back and I think I'm starting to see what he sees . . ." I was losing control of my voice. There was little time left and I was losing control.

When you reach down to unbutton her jeans Karen stops you. She holds onto your hands long enough to know that you are not going to remove them. She lets go. You feel her body relax and interlock with yours. Everything is wrong here, you think.

I wanted to say more, I think I wanted to argue and insist but by then we had reached the airport and I was pulling into the line of cars outside the International Terminal.

"Let me tell you what I remember," said Karen. "Martin once told me something about the word 'repentance'. He's probably forgotten about it by now but he said that repentance in the religious sense is often misunderstood. The word that was translated from the New Testament as 'repentance' is the Greek *meta-noria*, which means 'change of mind'. *Meta* is 'transference', you know, like in 'metaphor', transference of meaning."

I double-parked the car outside the terminal. Our time was up. This was all that I was going to get.

Karen half-opened her door and put one foot out. "I've looked back and changed my mind a bunch of times, Daniel," she said, and she turned then and looked back at me with clear green eyes. "And if you're really worried then you should remember that there's no such thing as repentance, that it's not possible. All you can do is say that the past was something other than what you thought it was at the time."

She paused there for a moment, half in and half out of my father's double-parked car and that was my real window, my opening to say something, but I couldn't, I didn't have any words, and Karen's eyes narrowed and she said, "Good luck with that, anyway", and then she was gone, slamming the door shut behind her and retrieving her bags from the boot. I wanted to wait and watch her walk into the terminal, but someone hooted their horn behind me and I had to drive on. Again I wondered how long she had prepared for our meeting.

RAVINGTON

Falgorth, son of Numeroth, looked down from the battlements of Fort Peloroth, gazing with disdain upon the bestial tribal hordes below. The wind whipped their brutish cries up to him as the sun rose over the peaks to the east. Lianora, daughter of Teflinan, joined him, delicately resting a thin-boned hand on his shoulder.

"Thousands of them and barely a hundred here fighting fit," she said, all the poise of her noble lineage unable to keep the tremor from her voice. "How can the colours of Fort Peloroth fly another day?"

Falgorth, son of Numeroth, grinned and fingered the hilt of Naidel, the razor-edged runic broadsword sheathed at his side. "I trust in the strength of our bloodlines," he said. "We shall sweep through the ranks of these subhumans like the scythe of the Reaper himself."

And then did Falgorth, son of Numeroth, blow his silver runic horn and summon the knights of Fort Peloroth from their barracks in the inner keep . . .

"What are you reading, Rav?"

Ravington looked up from *Blade of Night's Edge, Book the First in the Chronicles of the Pelorthi* (kind of like Tolkien, only slightly more overt with its racial themes) to see Eric Stapp standing over his desk. The door had been open, he hadn't even heard him come in.

"Just another book," Ravington said. "Another one I got in the post."

Most of the Tunnel Press office had been packed up now. Rav usually stopped between manuscripts to chuck a couple of folders of page proofs into a cardboard box. Adja was going to come by with her car tomorrow and take the boxes to the dump. After that she would help him clear out his lock-up. He had already sold the two office computers and found a buyer for his third-hand furniture. By this time next week Tunnel Press would be no more, just a name on a few long-filed tax returns, a logo on the spines of books marked down to ten dollars in well-meaning bookstores, then five dollars, then two dollars, a brief ignoble blot in the history of publishing. But until that day came Lewis Ravington was determined to keep reading.

"You look a mess," said Eric Stapp. "I'd clean myself up if I were you."

Adja had said something similar the last time she had stopped by. Rav hadn't changed his clothes in two days, hadn't showered for some time longer. His hair was clumped and tangled, his stubble out of control.

"A man's appearance is an outward sign of his self-respect," Eric Stapp said. "And a man's self-respect often depends on his appearance."

Rav slumped back in his chair to look up at Stapp. The leader of the NZNS certainly looked more respectable than he did now. Stapp's collared shirt was buttoned all the way to the top and tucked into his crisply pressed trousers. His shoes were polished, his beard neatly trimmed and the stubble on his scalp of an exact consistency.

"Why read the books if you're not going to publish them?" Stapp asked softly. "Why are you just letting everything slide?"

Rav shrugged and returned his attention to *Blade of Night's Edge.*

"Incoming!" cried Bevolth, son of Humvolth, as an arc of primitive stone-headed arrows soared over the parapet. They rebounded against the solid steel shields of the knights of Peloroth.

"Let them come!" Falgorth, son of Numeroth, howled in his bloodlust. "Let the scum break themselves upon our ranks. Stand true, sons of the West!"

He still had several other manuscripts piled up on the desk. *Towards a New Understanding of Eugenics* was one of them. *We Were Here First: the Volkish Wanderings of the Northern European* was another. It would be a busy afternoon.

Eric Stapp cleared his throat. "C'mon," he said. "I want to buy you some lunch."

Ravington allowed himself to be led out of the office, out of his building and across the street to a bakery, where Eric Stapp bought them steak-and-cheese pies and cans of Coke.

"Did you read the last lot of poems I gave you?" he asked once they were seated.

Rav nodded as he chewed his pie. He had read everything.

```
I try to repent,
And pray to God above,
For another embrace
With my Aryan dove.
```

"You don't think the last stuff was too emotional, do you?"

"Not at all." Ravington was getting used to Stapp's presence. He had dropped by the office a couple of times since the first visit and would usually stay for ten or fifteen minutes, volunteer a few more poems, listen to Rav's judiciously noncommittal comments, then beat a hasty retreat. Rav could not continue to be intimidated by a man who was so easily embarrassed.

"It's getting into some personal stuff, I guess." Stapp did not touch his own pie. It sat forgotten on his plate, next to his unopened Coke can. "Stuff about my wife and my son, I guess."

"Your sense of loss is palpable and powerful." Ravington's pie tasted delicious. The coke was delicious as well. He couldn't remember the last time he'd eaten. He couldn't remember the last time he had tasted anything that wasn't a cigarette.

"Drinking, drugs. I was a wreck back then, I lost so much."

"Your past is the touchstone of your poetry."

"They took me away from my wife and kid in handcuffs. I've barely seen them since then."

"The attempt to understand the past and reconcile yourself to it is what gives your poetry its tension and strength."

"You get this stuff," Stapp said, blinking, his eyes watering. "You understand. I knew you would."

"It's my job to understand, Eric." Rav produced one of his business cards, one of the last he had left, and put it down on the table. "I'm Lewis Ravington, editor-in-chief."

"I think you're a good man, Rav."

"Thank you, Eric."

"I think you're broken, though. I think you've been trampled on."

Rav had finished his pie. He waited to hear what Stapp had to say next. He was eager to get back to the office, strangely keen to find out what the future held for Falgorth, son of Numeroth, and the knights of Fort Peloroth.

"I see it in your eyes, Rav. I used to see it in my own when I could bear to look in the mirror. You've got no love for yourself."

Was this true? Ravington had never thought about it before. What did it mean, exactly, to love oneself?

"Men like you and me, Rav, we have to take back our self-respect in order to change. We have to stand up straight and be proud of who we are."

Ravington thought his ex-wife, Carol, might have loved him once. Not any more obviously, but he couldn't say for certain that she had never loved him. His mother had loved him. His father might have as well, in a way.

"It changed me, Rav. It gave me the strength and the discipline I have now. It gave me a code, it gave me honour. It can do the same for you."

In his more sentimental moments Ravington had thought that Ms Yorke might have loved him, in a doting, maiden-aunt kind of way. But she had abandoned him.

"We're trying to get more people like you involved. You know, entrepreneurs. The independent businessman needs the help and support of other people like him."

A few nights ago Ravington had whispered "I love you" into Adja's ear as they lay together in the dark. Thinking back, he wasn't sure what he had meant by that. Perhaps just that she was the only person close to him, the only person he could touch. If that wasn't love, then what was? But she hadn't responded and had not mentioned his words since then.

"The government gives the ethnics support, gives them subsidies, gives them everything but the knife they'll use to cut our throats in the dark. Guys like you and me get nothing, we just get everything taken away."

What good was it loving yourself if no one loved you? What good was it if you didn't love anyone else? Ravington tried to tell Stapp that he should stop talking, that he didn't want to hear any more. But his lips weren't moving properly. There was a pain growing in the back of his head.

"It's like Mr Wilton says. We're the real victims. It'll keep happening, mate, there'll be more and more of them and less and less of us."

They were victims? Ravington could accept that. The world was big enough for everyone to be a victim. Everyone could be the victim of everyone else, one way or the other, everyone could be accommodated. The pain in Ravington's head crept along the inside of his skull, a tentacled, electric agony that burrowed its way into everything. Stapp's face flickered in front of him. Rav tried to reach for his can of Coke — he was thirsty all of a sudden — but his arm jerked uselessly by his side, he couldn't lift it up.

"It would be a shame to see that press of yours go under. You've done so much good work with Mr Glass's book and everything else. I'm sure we could find a way to help you publish a few more books and get back on your feet. We've got to look out for each other."

Ravington wanted to thank Eric Stapp for his offer. He wanted to say that he didn't want to see Tunnel Press go under either. He wanted to admit that he loved being Lewis Ravington, editor-in-chief, and that by extension he loved the press and its office and the manuscripts that came in and the books that came out, and that really he did have a lot of love in his life even if he didn't understand what Eric Stapp meant by loving oneself, but his lips were still not working properly and he felt them stretch and curl upwards over his face.

"Rav?" he heard Stapp ask.

Ravington almost felt relieved as he fell off his chair. Yes, he could say. Yes, this is bad. His head felt as if it had been pierced by a volley of stone-headed arrows. Eric Stapp shouted something as Rav hit the floor and moved towards him, upsetting the table, but Rav did not care.

The pain could not go on forever, he had not been as bad as that. It would have to stop soon, even if he had to stop with it. Of course, he wanted to say. I wasn't such a bad man. I read a few books that no one else would read, I was of some use. But now Tunnel Press is going under and I have to go under too. Of course. How utterly proper.

ANITA

Summer had hit Bristol, hit it hard, and the city was sinking in a sea of noise and sweat. Anita now spent most of her time in her office at the university, arriving early in the morning and never leaving before sunset. In the evenings she stayed home alone, reading or watching television, every window in her small flat open, mild breezes rustling her curtains. On getting back from Israel she had decided not to look for another flat in London, but to pick up her possessions from her parents' house and travel back to Bristol, to be closer to the university while finishing her thesis. She now lived on the same street as Daniel's brother, Nathan, and his partner Bridget.

Nathan was still teaching at the university; he and Anita sometimes saw each other as they walked through the cramped little avenues between buildings. Once, when they met at lunchtime in a café across the street from the Wills Memorial, Anita had tried to broach the subject of Daniel. How was he? Was he okay?

Nathan had answered so quickly he had almost interrupted her initial question. His brother was doing well, he had a new job. Anita shouldn't worry about their break-up. Stuff happens, Nathan had said. A wistful, worried look had passed over his features. Sometimes . . . Nathan had said. Well, sometimes things just surprise you.

Two days later, when they bumped into each other again, Nathan had grinned and hugged her, then told her how he had proposed to Bridget the night before and how she had said yes, and then he hugged Anita again. She had promised to join them for a celebratory drink, but had not got round to it yet.

The chapters of her book were falling together in her head and on the page. The National Holocaust Memorial Day in Edinburgh, the Washington DC Holocaust museum, Yad Vashem in Jerusalem. She wrote about maps of memory spiralling back into the past, their preservation, their transmission, the narratives they could be woven into, the ends they could be made to serve. A publishing house in London had been intrigued by a sample of her work; they would like to hear more about her project. Everything was going the way she had hoped, the way she had planned.

The wider life of the university history department failed to engage her. She was not interested in tutoring classes and had stopped going to seminars and reading groups. The only departmental event that managed to catch her eye was an evening guest lecture. It was to be given by Professor Marion Pryor.

Anita had read *Body Disposal at Auschwitz — An Inquiry into the Death Rates and Crematory Procedures at the Auschwitz-Birkenau Camps* by Martin Glass. She had ripped through it in a day, amused by its meticulous academic format and the subtlety of its argument. It was a work of denial — she had seen enough of them before — but this one was so small and low-key that it almost slipped under the radar. Its challenge was oblique, it came at you sideways. It pointed no fingers, accused no one of being a deliberate deceiver. It just left you with the quiet impression that the past could not really have been how it was.

The book had arrived in the post five days after her strange, rather frantic conversation with Josh, when he had called her from New Zealand at three in the morning. When Anita had left him in Jerusalem she'd only the vaguest idea about what he was going to do next. He had waved something at her, talked about a website and an "assault on truth and memory", but by then she hadn't cared. Getting away from Josh had been vital. His enthusiasm had threatened to drown out her own and she needed to preserve her appetite for her work. They had boarded their planes and flown off to two different islands, at opposite ends of the world. She hadn't expected to think of him again for a long time. But then he resurfaced to drop something golden in her lap.

Marion Pryor was no longer a particularly fashionable historical theorist. She was still a name, but not a Memorial Lecture Hall name, nor a Library Reading Room name. You might recognise her name as worthy and distinguished, rather good and useful in its way, but not a name that would ever excite you, not a name that would change your life. Enough, however, to fill a lower seminar room at six in the evening, people standing at the back, a few undergrads crouched down by the feet of the table at the front, all ready to do their duty and sit through a half-hour paper and another half-hour discussion before the guest was whisked away to dinner with a faculty member, then put back on a train and returned to her distinguished chair of semi-retirement at the University of Wherever.

Anita had arrived early enough to get a seat and she watched Marion Pryor while all the usual history department suspects trickled into the room. Pryor was a rather stout grey-haired lady in her sixties whose full, heavy cheeks sagged her face a little, dragging the corners of her mouth down into a disapproving anti-smile. She raised her eyebrows and pulled her lips into a pleasant flatline as the department's self-defined cultural historian began his introduction. He praised her most famous or least forgotten book, *Narrative and the Structures of Life*, as "groundbreaking", though this last statement was more good manners on his part than the truth. The book had been more of a ground-chipper or a ground-bruiser. It had got down to the dirt a little earlier than the heavy-duty shovellers, but it hadn't made as big a hole in the landscape as it had intended, it had only softened up the turf.

Marion Pryor thanked the cultural historian and stood up behind her table. She was an old-school presenter, someone who liked to deliver from her feet, who liked that small touch of formality and drama. She cleared her throat, then made a joke about the weather. One of the older faculty members coughed politely. Marion Pryor began her paper.

What sorts of narratives did historians use to bring order to all their dates and facts and events? Marion Pryor was interested in the whys and wherefores of this construction, and believed she had identified its three basic modes. The Classical Design mode involved stories with causality, closed endings, linear time, an external conflict, a single, active protagonist. The second mode, Minimalism, created stories with open endings and passive protagonists. The stories of the third mode, Anti-Structure, were based around patterns of coincidence and non-linear time.

The second and third modes of narrative construction were undoubtedly more true to the ways our lives unfold in the real world, Pryor believed. Things just happen and our explanations of them can never be complete. But the solid, practical stories of history and historians seldom strayed from the Classical Design. Nation states serve as heroes and villains. Events occur as the causal result of other events. All manner of straight stories with resolvable plots and active protagonists can be made out of documents, artefacts and testimonials. They will prove to be popular or unpopular, depending on the time and place in which they are told. Causality is just another literary device.

Marion Pryor believed that minimalist and anti-structuralist narratives get us close to the chaos and disorder of existence, but do not make for good history. We look to classically designed narratives for our explanations. They take us furthest from reality but are the most real to us. We all see ourselves as the protagonists of our own lives, and so while these stories create worlds that we will never see they also show us a humanity that we are all able to recognise. The stories of history do not attempt to mirror the structures of real life, but those of the human mind. This is where their truth and falsity lies — not in some outside world, but in the patterns and connections of our own thoughts.

There were a few polite questions at the end of the paper. A couple of modern theorists were mentioned, some older ones suggested as influences. People were starting to think about dinner now, or the pub. An hour was just enough time to spend in the presence of a name like Marion Pryor. The cultural historian thanked her for the insightful paper and formally dismissed the gathering. When the last lingering postgrad exited and the cultural historian excused himself to fetch his jacket from his office, Anita had her window of opportunity.

"Hello," said Anita, walking over. "I'd like to ask a question. It's about Martin Glass."

Marion Pryor cocked her head attentively. "Martin was my

last graduate student," she said. "That was a few years ago now. How do you know him?"

Anita reached into her bag and removed the copy of *Body Disposal at Auschwitz* she had brought with her. She passed it to Marion Pryor, who examined its cover and smiled slightly. "He disappeared rather suddenly," she said. "Never finished his degree. That wasn't a surprise in itself though, I had a sense that he wasn't going to go the distance." She flicked through *Body Disposal.* "I didn't think he would disappear entirely, of course. He wasn't the cleverest student I ever saw, but he had a sense of adventure. I'd hoped it might take him somewhere."

She looked up at Anita, holding the book. "I suppose I was expecting something a little more sweeping from him than this. Silly of me, really."

"Actually its conclusions are kind of controversial," Anita said, "if you look at them closely."

"Well," said Marion Pryor, "I do enjoy looking at things closely. I'm not unfond of controversy either. I always thought I never quite got my share of it."

Anita glanced at the open door. She though she could hear footsteps in the corridor, the cultural historian returning for his obligatory dinner-date perhaps. "There's controversial and there's controversial," she said. "Controversial theories about the concept of history itself are one thing. Controversial claims about how many bodies the furnaces at Auschwitz could burn are another."

"Are they?" said Marion Pryor. "I don't think so."

"Books like this have a way of getting around," said Anita. "There are people who will go out of their way to promote them. You might not be too pleased to be connected with its author."

The cultural historian walked back into the room with his jacket. "Are you ready?" he asked Marion Pryor. "I've made a reservation at the Indian place you liked last time."

"Just a second, Godfrey." Pryor snapped *Body Disposal* shut and gave it back to Anita. "Thank you for bringing this to my attention," she said. "I am so pleased for Martin. And really, dear, don't be concerned about me." Marion Pryor smiled beatifically. "If all that can be said of me, in the twilight of my career, is that I introduced a little chaos into the world, that I upset a few complacent narratives, then I shall be very glad indeed. Now you must excuse me."

She took the arm of the cultural historian and walked out into the corridor, leaving Anita and *Body Disposal at Auschwitz* alone in the lower seminar room. Anita looked down again at the plain black cover of the book, then returned it to her bag. She needed to get back home to write.

MARTIN GLASS

Martin Glass's answering machine has five messages on it when he gets home. Wilton has called twice. The first time he says that he is thinking of taking the remaining copies of *Body Disposal at Auschwitz* in lieu of debts owed to him by Tunnel Press. He will sell them from his website. Martin need not worry, Wilton intends to see that everything is square; all the percentages will still be paid. His second call is to give Martin the terrible news about the publisher Lewis Ravington, their friend and ally, just terrible news. Eric Stapp is with him at the hospital. Wilton still hopes to arrange for the transfer of the remaining copies, but now is not the time, perhaps later. Has Martin heard anything more from that Jewish friend of his?

Two of the other phone calls are abusive. Martin has received hatemail as well — not quite as much as he had initially expected, but still steadily increasing in quantity. Martin isn't troubled by it, he already has plans to move. The last message is from yet another journalist, asking for a comment for a piece he is writing on the anniversary of the liberation of Buchenwald. The journalist is desperate for a little controversy, the respectful, mournful tone is chafing him. A comment from Martin Glass might be just what he needs.

Martin deletes all the messages. The journalist will call again, other journalists will call after him, and this will go on for a while, but he will not have another call from Karen. Martin Glass looks at his watch and wonders where she is flying to. Against his better judgment, he had called her at home yesterday. She had told him that there wasn't any need for them to see each other before she left. Martin had agreed, he'd had no other choice. All he could do was thank her for her help.

"Martin," Karen had said, her tone softening slightly, "what are you doing? Your book and those people and all this crap. I'm worried about you."

And Martin had hung up then, because the last thing he wanted to hear was her saying that she was worried about him, though if that was all he could get then he would take it. And now she is gone.

Martin sits on his couch and re-opens the cardboard box on his coffee table. The Luger pistol is still there; he runs a finger down the cool metal length of its barrel. Pistolen-08. Nine millimeters. 6.75 calibre. Things like this can fetch over a thousand American dollars on eBay. People are willing to pay a premium on history. It is more than a simple gift from Nigel Wilton, it is a pledge of loyalty, a commitment. Martin suspects that Wilton is already thinking about a book of his own. He would not be surprised if Wilton is already working on it; *Body Disposal at Auschwitz* has shown him the way.

Martin stands up and walks over to the window. The sun

is setting and its last shafts of light sink the homes on the hillside below him into shadow. He has no plans at the moment. Wilton keeps asking him about the next step, but that has nothing to do with Martin, there is no next step for him. Wilton and others like him will continue his work. Perhaps they will learn to be less crude in their polemics, less obvious in their constructions. Then perhaps other people will continue that work after them, people who are not like Wilton at all.

One of the earlier abusive messages called him an anti-Semite. The caller had used the word several times — Martin was an anti-Semite, he was anti-Semitic, he had written his history because he hated Jews. If Martin had been home, he might have remonstrated with the caller. *Judenfeindschaft* is as ancient as the hills, *Antisemitismus* is a product of the modern age. Martin does not consider himself to be an adherent of either philosophy, but he is interested in words, in their meanings and their origins, and he believes their connotations should not be confused.

Given a chance, Nigel Wilton would protest that he is neither anti-Semitic nor a hater of Jews. Wilton with his memorabilia collection back in Melbourne, his books of military history, his pushes, fronts and bulges, his illustrated hard-backed guides to the uniforms and accoutrements of the German army. Wilton loves the boots, the attitude, the thrill, the triumph of the will.

When Karen hinted that he was a neo-Nazi in her article, Martin thought that it was a delicious overstatement, one that Wilton would secretly enjoy. "Neo-Nazi" suggested a level of ideological sophistication that Wilton does not possess. He is a fan, an enthusiast. The ordered, symmetrical, tightly packed images of power; the marches, the rallies, the ranks of fit young men intent on remaking the world in their own image, Wilton will redeem it all if he can.

It is little wonder Eric Stapp and the NZNS support him in his efforts. They would do anything to share in such beauty. He will make it safe for them to hate again and safe for them to love themselves.

The phone rings and Martin wonders if it might be yet another call from Wilton. Another link to his website, another positive response from some dubious far-right group or organisation, another meeting of the NZNS that Martin really should attend. Martin is glad to think it will be over soon. He hopes that whatever has happened to Lewis Ravington is not serious. He hopes it is not his fault.

"Hello?" Martin says, picking up the phone.

"Martin, it's Daniel. I've been trying to get hold of you."

"Everyone's been trying to get hold of me." Martin wonders what has happened, what has prompted this phone call.

"I'd like to talk to you," Daniel says.

"That's certainly possible," says Martin. "Yes, I think we can arrange that."

Martin is not like Wilton or Stapp. He is not trying to redeem or rehabilitate anything. His goal demands a lighter touch, more patience, a more focused ambition. History cannot be changed overnight. Martin thinks that Daniel might be the one person capable of understanding what he is doing. Karen might have been able to as well, but she has fled, she doesn't want to know.

It will take some time for the rest of the world to see, decades or centuries perhaps, but in the end it will be inevitable. Things cannot go on as they are. Denial can really be quite healthy.

DANIEL

```
Loading . . . Loading . . . Game Options
Selected.
  "Why did you leave me in Edinburgh?" she
asks.
  "I'm not your girlfriend," you reply.
  "ERROR!" she shouts. "ERROR!" and grabs
you ERROR pushing you down ERROR.
  Loading . . . Loading . . . LOADING
ERROR. No life selected.
```

The primitive build of the original *VirtuLife* saved on my laptop was breaking down. Its untested programming structures were incomplete; they could not sustain the choices I had made. I closed the bug-riddled software, knowing it would not take me anywhere.

After dropping Karen at the airport I'd spent most of the day driving around the city, visiting a few old sites. In Karori I tried to find the street I'd lived on with Martin and Karen, but I had forgotten its name and the neighbourhood felt unfamiliar. There had been a lot of development in the area, and the streets were now lined with clean symmetrical houses and well-tended gardens. It looked like another world, and whatever life I had once lived there was beyond my reach.

When I got home I'd found a message from Josh waiting for me on the answering machine: I knew Martin Glass, Josh knew that I knew him. There was no hiding it, I couldn't protect him. Josh had asked me to arrange a meeting. He had demanded it — he wanted to see that man, he wanted to meet him face to face. "Help me, Big Man, don't try and stop me, this is how it has to go, this is the way it has to end."

I deleted the message, then called Martin and arranged to meet him myself later that evening. He suggested sometime around eight or nine; I could come to his flat. After that I sat at the kitchen table and played the build of *VirtuLife* stored on my laptop until the incomplete program degenerated into no kind of life that could be recognised as real. Morbid emerged from his bedroom just as the last trace of his lofty non-linear ambitions fizzled out on my laptop screen.

"I still want you out of here," he said when he saw me sitting at the kitchen table.

"I'm working on it," I said.

"You got a call while you were out."

"I know. Josh."

"Not your weird mate. Some chick."

"Who . . . ?" I started to say, but at that moment the phone rang again.

"I want you gone," Morbid said, before retreating back into his bedroom. His door slammed shut yet again and I picked up the phone. "Hello?" I said into the receiver.

"Daniel? Is that you?" A woman's voice, British.

"Hello?" I said again.

"I've been trying to get hold of you."

It was Anita. It took a while for me to make the connection. It had been months since I'd last heard her voice and her physical reality had receded from my memory of her. She had become more of a concept than a person. The ex-girlfriend. The last woman I had slept with. The woman who'd left me in Edinburgh.

"I can't talk for long, Daniel."

"No." I slowly slid down the wall, into a crouching position. "No, obviously not. I mean, you're calling from London, right? The tolls must be pretty expensive."

"Actually, I've moved back to Bristol."

I started to twist the phone cord around my fist.

"I don't have much time to talk," Anita said again. "I was wondering if you could do me a favour. Josh has told me you know a man named Martin Glass."

"So you're still in touch with Josh. He said your trip went well."

"Yes, we're still in touch. He's been telling me about what he's found in New Zealand, about Martin Glass and his book."

"You must have given him my address and phone number," I said. "It's almost funny, Anita. First you ditch me for the creep, then you dump him in my lap months down the track. It's more than funny, it's a farce."

"I'm interested in Martin Glass, I'd like to know more about him."

"For your research, right?"

"Can you take Josh to see Glass?" Anita asked. "Just a brief visit, and he'll keep his cool, he's promised. I'd like him to ask some questions for me. It could be very useful."

"When you left me in Edinburgh I thought at least I'd never have to hear about your fucking research ever again."

"I didn't leave you in Edinburgh," Anita said quietly.

"What?" By now the phone cord was wrapped so tightly

around my fist that its curled loops were stretched straight.

"You left me, Daniel. Don't you remember?" Anita asked.

"You were going to leave me though. I remember that. You can't say it wasn't your intention."

Anita didn't say anything for a while. I thought I could hear her breathing on the other end of the phone, but perhaps that was merely static on a bad international line. "Okay, Daniel," she said eventually, "just forget it. I told Josh it was a stupid idea for me to ask. I'm sorry, you know. I'm sorry I called." She hung up.

I listened to the dial tone for a while, then let the phone cord go. The loops sprang away from my hand and I flexed my fingers, looking at the livid marks that criss-crossed my skin. After a few minutes, once I'd calmed down, I picked up the phone again and dialled the number Josh had given me for his hotel.

WILTON

"Good man, Eric," said Wilton when Eric Stapp called him on his mobile. Stapp was outside the hospital; he'd been with Lewis Ravington for a few hours. They took care of their own.

"He's recovered, pretty much," Stapp said. "A bit woozy, he threw up a few times, but nothing seems to be wrong. He'll be in overnight."

Wilton looked at his watch, it was getting close to ten. "Head home, Eric," he said. "Get some rest."

"Yeah," Stapp said. Then: "It makes me angry."

"Of course it does, Eric."

"A guy stands up, tries to do something right, and he gets run into the ground. Business gone, health gone. It isn't right."

"Get some rest now, Eric."

"I just called Rav's woman," Stapp said. "I'll go home when she gets here."

Wilton could feel his eyes misting. "Okay, Eric," he said. "Okay," and turned off his phone. This was what they were about, this was the heart of White Nationalism. This was the terrible spectre that had the politically correct elites so terrified. One man sticking by another in a time of adversity. People like Eric and Wilton simply stood up for the oldest traditions of loyalty, mateship and solidarity, the traditions upon which their countries had been founded.

Was this really so frightening? All the ethnics stuck together. They could be trusted to close ranks at the drop of a hat. They swept through countries, taking over neighbourhoods and shops and businesses, hiring each other, living in their own little enclaves. But when men like Eric and him did this, when they tried to carve out a space for themselves, to demand the respect and pride that had once been theirs, then they were monsters, they were demons, they were beyond redemption. The last thing anyone wanted was for white men to come together, to preserve their national identities and borders. Progress meant turning every country on the planet into a mongrel, weak and mixed and conflicted. All "diversity" meant was money in the pockets of the global elites.

"How is Mr Ravington?" Martin asked, returning from the kitchen with two steaming mugs.

"All right, it seems," Wilton said, accepting the offered tea gratefully. "Thank God it wasn't something more serious."

Martin nodded and moved over to the window, looking out onto the dark hillside of houses below him. Wilton had come by that evening to try and talk to Martin about the conspiracy of globalists and bankers, the way he had with Martin's Jewish friend. He thought it was time to alert Martin to the wider issues at stake, time to draw him into the deeper, darker terrain of the struggle. But Martin had seemed edgy, unwilling to listen. Wilton had to make Martin understand that the truth meant nothing to their enemies; history in their hands was merely a weapon of oppression.

He hoped, however, that Martin didn't think he was

making an anti-Semitic point when he talked about the globalists and bankers. It wasn't an exclusively Jewish conspiracy. Asians and Arabs were involved too. And yes, some white men who cared nothing for loyalty or fellowship. Wilton was not anti-Semitic, he was not anti anything. He was pro-strength, pro-unity, pro-*truth*. And he would willingly extend his hand in friendship to anyone, of whatever race or creed, who was pro-truth as well. No Jew or ethnic had presented themselves to him yet, but Wilton was prepared to keep his hand open and waiting. He had high hopes for them, despite all he had suffered. He really did.

JOSH

Daniel had said barely a word since picking him up at his hotel, but Josh was trying to be friendly nonetheless. He was aware that the tone of his last few phone calls may have been unsettling and he was trying to make up for that. Sometimes things ran away on him, he just got swept along.

"It's good that you talked to Anita," he said.

No response from Daniel. He kept his eyes on the road ahead of them, his hands firmly on the wheel. Josh still couldn't imagine what Anita ever saw in this man with his big, fleshy body, his hairline receding back over a sloping brow, his blank-eyed, simmering hostility. Josh tried to remind himself that they were the same at some level — they had both grown up Half-Jewish, after all. It might be hard to see the connection but there had to be one. If not, then to be Half-Jewish was to have no identity at all.

"It looks like Anita's book is coming along well," Josh said. Again, no response. "I've been to a lot of places," he continued.

"I've learned a lot about the Holocaust and I just get this feeling about Anita and the work she's doing, like she's putting everything into a pattern, making it all fit together. I mean, maybe she's going to show us the lessons we need to learn."

Daniel still refused to look at him. Josh was trying, he was really trying. A gesture was needed perhaps. Maybe Daniel was owed some sort of explanation.

"That's why I had to take her places, yeah?" Josh said. "Because I saw that potential, her research had to be completed. I was acting with the best of intentions. It's important to me — you understand that, Daniel. It really is." Josh twisted in the passenger seat, looking away out the window. "I think she needs to know what's going on here as well," he said, more to himself than anyone else. "Your mate Glass, these deniers. She's writing about memory and these people want to destroy it."

"Can I ask you a question, Josh?" Daniel said.

Josh straightened up, turning back to face his driver. "Yeah, of course," he said. "Ask anything."

"Why do we only make movies about Holocaust survivors?"

"What?"

"That *Pianist* movie is about a guy who survives the Holocaust. The wife and the kid survive in *Life is Beautiful.* I watched *Schindler's List* recently and I don't think it had a single character with a name — or even more than a couple of lines of dialogue — who died. *He who saves but one life saves the world entire.* That's nice, you know, but I don't think it's really the case. Maybe I've missed the point, but it seems to me that if you save but one life then you've saved one life and the world is still falling apart."

Daniel shifted round slightly, facing Josh, smiling rather cruelly. "Believe me, Josh," he said, "I like hearing survivor stories. I get off on the endurance of the human spirit as much as the next man. But what about all the people who weren't saved? Proportionally, when there are so many of them and so few survivors, shouldn't we be hearing more about the dead? When do they get their film? Why can't we see the dead?"

Josh looked at him, stunned. At least now he knew he'd had nothing to feel guilty about in Edinburgh. He'd been right to get Anita away from this man.

As if he could sense what Josh was thinking, Daniel pulled the car to the side of the road suddenly, halting it with a savage jerk that threw Josh back in his seat. "We're here," he said, and then he killed the engine.

MARTIN GLASS

Martin often thinks about Raphael Lemkin's uncompleted four-volume history of genocide, especially now that his own work is nearing its end, now that he is ready to leave it to others. Martin likes to think that if Lemkin had completed his history it would have been a masterwork of historical revision. Lemkin would have shown us all that the past was not what we thought it was, that it was not even how it had seemed at the time.

When he hears Daniel knock on the glass, Martin pulls back his curtain and unlocks his sliding door. Daniel hasn't come alone. A short, wiry, grim-faced man stands next to him on the doorstep. Martin thinks the stranger looks a little older than Daniel, but he can't place his age, not exactly.

"This is Joshua Levit," says Daniel. "He wanted to meet you. He's read your book."

"Nice to meet you," Martin says. He steps back to allow them both inside. Wilton looks up from the couch and carefully puts his second cup of tea down on the coffee table. "Daniel," he says, nodding. "Good to see you again. And I think we've met," he says to the other, still silent visitor, "but I don't believe you gave me your name."

"I see you're not alone, either," says Daniel to Martin.

"Don't mind me," says Wilton. "I wouldn't want to intrude on your conversation. But I am so pleased to see you here, Daniel. I'm glad you took some of what I said to heart."

"You're really in thick," Joshua Levit says, looking at Daniel with disbelieving eyes. "You're in thick with all of them. I can't believe it."

Raphael Lemkin's unrealised work is still on Martin's mind; he can't focus properly on the conversation, not yet. He thinks that the 1915 persecution and massacre of the Armenian population of Turkey would have been a good first step for Lemkin on the road backwards. Between one and two million Armenians murdered by the Turkish government, an excellent pre-Holocaust candidate. Then something on the Atlantic slave trade, perhaps; it would have deserved at least an honourable mention. The colonisation of the Americas — North and South — the Caribbean, the Pacific and Australia would have provided chapter upon chapter. Four volumes might not have been enough to document it all. Martin cannot leave the thought of this unwritten history alone, not while he is surrounded by people in his living room who have gathered to discuss the much smaller, more specific history he has written himself.

"I'm not in with anyone," Daniel is saying to Joshua Levit. "Martin and I were at university together. We used to be friends."

"Still are friends," says Nigel Wilton.

"He told me to go to you," says Joshua Levit, pointing to Wilton. "He said you were a supporter of Glass. That you were his good Jewish friend."

Daniel straightens up, squaring his shoulders, glaring down at Wilton. "You said what?"

"I could tell you were close to doing the right thing, Daniel, so close. I just hoped if I gave you a little push, a little nudge, you'd understand the fight Martin has got himself into. You needed to meet the kind of person who'd want to attack him, to bring him down."

"I already knew Josh," Daniel says to Wilton. "And you don't have any right sending people to talk to me."

"But clearly it was the right thing to do. You've brought this gentleman to see Martin, to debate the historical issues as they stand."

"There's nothing to debate," said Joshua Levit.

"That's a disappointing attitude, Mr Levit."

Martin wonders if he even needs to be there. Once set in motion the conversations and arguments could all roll along without his input. This thought brings him a little satisfaction. Soon he will be able to remove himself entirely, he can be free of this history, it will unfold without him. Martin is not surprised that Raphael Lemkin never found a publisher for his work on genocide or even managed to finish it. For all his good intentions, Lemkin was writing the wrong history, the one no one needed to hear. It would have gone too far, it would have pushed Lemkin's new word back into too many inconvenient places. Religious persecution in Europe, the witch craze, the execution of heretics, the pogroms, the sack of Jerusalem in the First Crusade. Scale and intention get smaller the further back one goes, the results are less spectacular.

Though perhaps Lemkin's study would have shown that genocide was the product of a more modern age, Martin thinks, when humanity possessed greater ambitions and capacities, it came with the broadening of minds and imaginations, with the sense that everything was possible. *When the Enlightenment Attacks* would have been a good title for his book.

"I do have some questions for you," Joshua Levit says. It takes Martin a moment to realise that he is being addressed. The focus is back on him, escape is not so easy.

"That's good," says Nigel Wilton, stepping forward. "That's fine, that's perfectly appropriate. We all have questions, Mr Levit. We'll try to answer yours if you promise to try to answer ours."

How much farther back could Lemkin have gone? Martin is still carried away by his train of thought. He can't stop it, can't stop himself. Mongol invasions, the massacre of Christians in Nero's Rome, the sacking of Carthage. Back further even, to the Bible, to Numbers 31:17–18:

> Now therefore kill every male among the little ones, and kill every woman that hath known man by lying with him. But all the women children, that have not known a man by lying with him, keep alive for yourselves.

How would Moses have squared up against the convention on genocide? How would God? He had ordered or tacitly endorsed the genocide of the Amalekites, the Canaanites, the Bashanites, the Amorites, the Hazorites, the Perizzites and the Ammonites as well as the bloody destruction of the cities of Jericho and Ai and Succoth and countless others. He had personally massacred the Zamzummims and Horims and smitten the city of Sihon, not to mention old Sodom and Gomorrah. He had confessed to at one time wiping out every man, woman and child on the planet, save for one drunk and his dysfunctional, incestuous family. Could Lemkin's new word have called Him to account?

"We're not going to answer any questions of yours," Daniel says to Nigel Wilton. "You're going to leave."

"What?"

"You heard me. I've had enough of you."

Wilton looks over at Martin, his eyes large and worried. "Should I . . . ?" he starts to say. Then, "Martin? Are you all right?"

There is no statute of limitations on the crime of genocide, Martin thinks, and the United Nations convention is presumably a piece of retroactive legislation. No national leader, public official or private individual could be excluded from prosecution under its terms and the Divine Creator surely fell under one of those categories. Why hadn't the case against God been put before the Hague? He would be easier to try than Milosevic had been.

"Yes," Martin says eventually. "Perhaps it would be best if you left."

Wilton grunts and gets up from the couch. He collects his coat and walks out into the night. Daniel and Joshua Levit shift slightly on their feet and Martin knows that he must try to focus on them and the questions they have, try to see them as real and meaningful. Just a little more effort and then he can stop.

A dictated confession, thinks Martin as he asks his guests to sit down. Thousands of pages of documentary evidence attested to be absolutely and indisputably true by leading religious authorities all around the world. Will no one speak up for the Zamzummims? God was going down, He could serve any number of consecutive life sentences and that pretty beard of His, those sensitive, all-knowing eyes, that long flowing head of hair, they wouldn't be doing Him any favours in the Big House.

But this was the problem really, this was why Lemkin's history could never be written. His new word could crawl back too far, it could undermine too many foundations. Now that we have the word and its meaning, now that we know the crime and it has been named and know that our capacities and ambitions can be so very great, we do our best to disavow all knowledge, present and prior. *Eritis sicut Deus, scientes bonum et malum.*

DANIEL

The first thing I noticed when I entered Martin's flat was his gift from Wilton, the cardboard shoebox, still sitting on the coffee table. Its lid was on and I couldn't see the Luger pistol nestled inside, but my eyes were still drawn to the box. When Josh moved past the coffee table, to sit down on the couch after Wilton had left, he nudged it with his knee and I almost winced.

"Are you from the UK?" Martin asked Josh once we were all seated. "You're a long way from home."

"I travel a bit, yeah."

"And you know Daniel?"

"We met on a tour of Holocaust memorials in the UK," I interjected. "When it was over Josh swept my girlfriend, Anita, off to Washington DC. He's here on her behalf tonight. She's interested in you." I took a small pleasure in seeing Martin look surprised for a few moments, but he recovered quickly.

"I'm here for myself as well," Josh said. "Wanted to see you face to face. See what sort of a man does a thing like this. Lying about the past."

"Is this satisfying?" Martin asked.

"What?"

"Seeing me face to face, like you said before."

"It is," Josh said, staring at Martin intently. "It really is. This is my past you're trying to mess around with, my identity. I'm Half-Jewish."

"Like Daniel," said Martin.

"No, not like me," I said.

Josh gave me a long cold look, then turned back to Martin. "Your estimate of the burning time is incorrect," he said. "It could take an hour to burn an adult body completely, but after twenty minutes the body would have broken down enough to allow a second corpse to be placed in the furnace and then another above it. They could have got through many more bodies than you suggest in your book."

"That's speculation," Martin responds quickly. "I make allowances for body-stacking in my calculations, but estimate crematory capacities more conservatively than most because I also consider the demands of basic maintenance, breakdowns and fuel shortages. As there is no clear documentation left dealing with crematory procedures, I think my figures are as accurate as they can be."

A new *VirtuLife* scenario was unwinding inside my head. I could see the game-level mapping itself out before me, previous player-choices building into a resolution that would ultimately make sense.

`You leave Martin's flat late in the evening and drive home, dropping Josh back at his hotel on your way. But Josh leaves the hotel moments later and takes a cab back to Martin's neighbourhood. He waits near the` flat until all the lights go out, then stealthily makes his approach.

"What about the open-air burnings?" Josh asked. "Witness testimony shows that there were a significant number of open-air burnings of corpses on makeshift outdoor pyres at Auschwitz, just as there were at Bergen-Belsen and Belzec, Sobibor and Treblinka. Couldn't outdoor burnings account for your supposed shortfall between the accepted death toll and the camp's crematory capacities?"

I was a little surprised. I'd had no idea Josh knew his stuff so well.

"There's no concrete evidence," said Martin. "No reliable photography. No official records. The witnesses may have been mistaken or misguided."

Josh had intended to break in, but discovers that Martin tends to leave his front door unlocked. Martin is in the bathroom when Josh slides his front door back, slips inside and makes straight for the coffee table. He had seen the box earlier, registered its contents. When Martin returns to the living room, he sees his former guest, a short, scrawny virtual stranger holding the Luger in his gloved hand.

"What about the memoirs of the camp commandant, Rudolf Höss? He describes the open-air burnings in great detail. Would they do for a document?" A cold clear glaze had descended over Josh's usually volatile features. He wanted to take Martin down. I was trying to follow their conversation but my eyes kept wandering back to the shoebox on Martin's coffee table. Josh knocked its lid slightly askew. I could see a faint metallic glint from within.

"Those memoirs were written while Höss was a captive of the Allies. He could have been coerced into including details about open-air burnings. Or his memoirs could have been rewritten before being released."

Josh looked like he would lose his temper for a moment. He struggled to control himself, then said: "Right. Let's look at your typhus theory then. You suggest that a typhus epidemic may have been the reason behind the expansion of the camp's crematory facilities, that's your alternative scenario, yeah? But testimonies by some prisoners indicated that vaccinations for typhus were going on at the camp among the longer-term inmates and that a delousing in August 1942 brought the epidemic to a halt."

`Martin lunges for the gun and they struggle. Josh makes a split-second decision and fires the gun twice. The first bullet tears up the side of Martin's head, the second rips through his grey matter.`

"It is so refreshing," Martin said, "to be able to debate these issues with someone who knows their facts."

"We're not debating anything."

"Aren't we?"

I was still looking at the cardboard box, thinking about the gun inside.

"Let's be clear about this," said Josh. "I am stating facts and observing how you respond to them. We are not debating anything, there is nothing to debate. I'm just interested in your responses, yeah?"

"So you can talk about them with Daniel's ex-girlfriend later."

"Yeah, Anita."
"Anita."

```
Josh props Martin's corpse up at the couch,
puts the Luger down on the floor next to
him and leaves the flat. He runs off into
the night while the neighbours are calling
the police, almost turning cartwheels in
his joy at having rid the world of the arch
deceiver, the nemesis he has come halfway
around the world to . . . ERROR.
```

The scenario wouldn't work, I thought, looking at the shoebox again. It made a nice ending, of course, it all fitted together, but nothing in my life would ever be that easy.

WILTON

Nigel Wilton sat for a long time in his car outside Martin Glass's flat. The conversation inside didn't look like it was about to abate. He shouldn't feel worried. Martin would have to confront worse people than this Joshua Levit, he would have to argue in the face of vitriolic hatred, so he had better get used to it as soon as possible. Martin was naïve if he thought he could talk a man like Levit round. Wilton had seen his type before. They never considered evidence, they would never listen to argument. They were locked in the close-minded, black-and-white view of the past the powers-that-be had forced upon the world.

But Wilton was still pleased that he'd had the foresight to send Levit to Daniel. In a way he was glad that Daniel had brought Levit here tonight. It showed that Daniel was still involved — not yet a convert, not exactly a supporter, but willing to accept that he and Martin had a connection. Wilton looked back at the silhouetted figures in the window of the flat, sitting, talking. Perhaps this conversation would be more for Daniel's benefit than anyone else's. In listening to the arguments and counter-arguments, Daniel Legkov might start to understand his old friend's position, he might start to shake himself free of the knee-jerk rejection instinct he'd been indoctrinated into. It might only be a small victory, but it would be something.

Wilton started up his engine and drove slowly down the street. A small victory, a small hope, he needed to believe it was possible. To convince one Jew, any Jew, of the truth about World War Two, that was all he could ask for. He had tried to reach out to Jews so many times before, only to be rebuffed, insulted, hauled before corrupt and biased courts. He didn't want their hatred, he didn't want to hate them, though they made it hard sometimes. God knows they made it hard.

He only wanted to show them the good news, to let them know that the world hadn't treated them as cruelly as they'd thought. They had not suffered in German hands any more than the Germans had suffered in the hands of the Allies. We are all victims or none of us are, no suffering is special. Was this too much to ask for? Just one Jew, now, at this time in his life, after he had suffered so much? Any kind of Jew would do, any kind at all, just one.

He could show them, Wilton thought as he drove out of Martin's neighbourhood through Wellington's dark, quiet streets. He could show them what had really happened if they would let him, he could lead them back to each other. Anyone who has visited the United States can tell you that you can't take a single step over there without running into a Jew. They were unavoidable, they were everywhere. Wilton knew why that was the case, he had the only plausible answer. There were simply millions more of them than official Census figures showed. Many of the Jews who had supposedly died in the so-called Holocaust had been clandestinely relocated to the US at the end of the war. The Jews now persisted in thinking they were the victims when in fact, proportionally, far more Germans were murdered. They thought their population had dwindled when in fact it had swelled; they lived back to back with the very people they thought they had lost.

In Wilton's dream he is the one who writes the final history, he is the one who makes them see. He will take the Jews and show them that they survived after all, that the dead lived, that all the Jews of Europe were survivors, every last one. He will find families, separated and splintered for generations, and he, Nigel Wilton, will reunite them.

And then people like him will be able to take pride in their countries again, pride in strength and unity and discipline; and the decadence and disorder of the current age will be swept aside, along with every lie about the past. There was no hate in his heart, not for the Jews or anyone else, he felt only love. He would embrace them if he could, if they would let him. He would embrace them all.

DANIEL

"Wartime shortages of medical supplies may have meant that there would not have been enough of the typhus vaccine to go around," Martin said. "This is just a theory of course. But I think it is worth considering,"

I was still thinking about the Luger pistol in the box, trying to make sense of it.

"Franciszek Piper," said Josh. "A Polish historian. He made a demographic study tracing 1.3 million prisoners to the camp over the course of its four-and-a-half-year history."

"I'm aware of Dr Piper's work."

"Camp records only registered 404,000 prisoners from that intake and about 200,000 of those are recorded as having died while in the camp. So we have 900,000 people left unaccounted for."

"Without records we cannot make any definite conclusions about their fate. They might have been interned at the camp temporarily without being registered then moved on to another location. Dr Piper may be wrong in his calculations."

"No one was moved on from Auschwitz," Josh said.

Martin smiled but didn't say anything.

Josh would not be the one to fire the gun, I thought. He was crazy but not that crazy, and in his own way he had too much pride, an odd, injured sense of dignity that would preclude any thought of murder. I would have to think harder.

`You leave Martin's flat late in the evening and drive home, dropping Josh back at his hotel on your way. But, unknown to you both, Nigel Wilton doubles back to the address in his car, hours later. He enters through the unlocked door. All the lights are out, Martin is in his bedroom asleep.`

"Seeing as records are so important," said Josh, "let's have a talk about them. The surviving Auschwitz death books contained death certificates for about 70,000 prisoners. Those books covered the years 1942 and 1943 and show that only about 2000 of those prisoners died of typhus. The largest single cause of death listed on those certificates was 'heart failure'. Over 25,000 of those prisoners apparently died as a result of some heart-related problem. Isn't it plausible that 'heart failure' may have been a code for murder? Especially—" a tremor entered Josh's voice here, he had kept control of himself admirably up till now, but perhaps this was the breaking-point, perhaps he could no longer keep his anger in check, "—*especially* since people under forty, and small children, do not usually die of heart failure?"

`Wilton retrieves his pistol from the card-board box, his Luger pistol. It was never a gift, only a loan, for a time. He takes` a pillow from the couch and proceeds into the bedroom. Martin's sleep is deep, his dreams are untroubled. Wilton covers the barrel with the pillow, then pushes it down to an inch away from Martin's head. He fires twice, the pillow muffling the blasts.

"The contents of those recovered books, whether or not they were accurate, do not fall within the scope of my research," Martin said. "They are incomplete and I am not concerned with the cause of death, only with the disposal of the bodies."

"I've heard enough." Josh stood up from the couch. He tugged his jacket straight around his shoulders. "I don't need any more."

Every cause needs a martyr, a name that invokes a history of suffering and sacrifice. Martin just needed a little push, a little nudge, some small guidance. The book was a start, but this will be his best work. Well done thou good and faithful servant. Wilton leaves the way he came in, now with his hand on the Luger pistol in his coat pocket, stroking its warm barrel gently as he disappears into the night.

I let those thoughts run loose in my head for a little while before dismissing them as well.

"You don't really believe what you're saying," Josh said to Martin. "You can't. You know too much."

"You can't tell me what I do or don't believe."

"You're setting out to deliberately cause harm with knowledge and foresight. That's evil."

"I don't think I'm harming anyone or anything."

"I've heard enough," Josh said again. "I'm going. Don't worry, Big Man," he said to me, "I'll make my own way." Like Wilton before him, he pushed Martin's door back and walked outside, not bothering to close it behind him.

After a minute, Martin got up and slid the door shut. I took the opportunity to sneak another look at the Luger pistol resting safely in its box. I prodded the lid open a little further so that I could see it better.

JOSH

Joshua Levit walked away from the flat and Daniel's parked car, turning randomly at suburban intersections, following unfamiliar paths down dark streets. He wasn't sure if he could find his way back to his hotel in the dark, and he was too wound up to even think about plotting a course. He would stumble upon some familiar part of the city sooner or later. For now he needed to keep moving. Josh had stared into the eyes of his enemy, had questioned him, had faced him down. When he finally found his way back to his hotel he would stay up in his room and write down everything he could remember about his meeting with Glass. He would report to Anita later, tell her about Daniel as well. She ought to know what he was really like, the sort of company he kept.

"No," Daniel had said. "Not like me." Josh was willing to cede that ground now. They had nothing in common, they were not alike. Perhaps having a Jewish parent did not make one Half-Jewish, perhaps there was more to it, perhaps it was more complex than Josh had thought. He was learning more about what it meant to be a Half-Jew. He thought about Steve, wondered what his friend was doing; he would try to call him this evening and tell him that he was on his way back home.

Martin Glass was an evil man. Evil was quite a word to throw around, but Josh felt comfortable using it. He had seen the man, he had talked to him, and there was no other word, no other name for what he was. This must be the end, Josh thought. He'd had the final moment of his Holocaust experience; he had stood eye to eye with evil and looked it in the face. It was not quite the same as the evil of that other age, that older world, but it was as close as he could get, he had gone as far as he could go. "I don't think I'm harming anyone or anything," Martin Glass had said. Another lie. He was harming truth and memory. He was harming everyone who had survived to tell their stories and everyone who had perished. He was harming Joshua Levit.

Josh would have died in the Holocaust. He would have been interned in a camp, swallowed up in the machinery of death. That was what it meant to be Half-Jewish — not quite one thing, not quite the other, but a victim all the same. Daniel would not have died though. He would have found a way out, he would have turned traitor. Perhaps another quality of Half-Jewishness was that one could choose to be otherwise, one could turn from it, reject it. But Josh would have died, he had only survived the Holocaust by being born in another time and place. Josh was a survivor in his heart and mind, that was what gave him strength and purpose. The Holocaust was his and it could not be taken from him — not by Martin Glass, nor by any law of ancestry. It belonged to him, wholly and utterly, and for all time.

MARTIN GLASS

"You can take it out if you like," Martin says.

"What?"

"If you want to touch it, touch it. Take it out of the box."

Daniel slowly pushes the lid back and reaches inside the shoebox. Martin hears his fingers rustle through the wrapping, then Daniel withdraws his empty hand. Martin reaches over and pulls the Luger pistol out of the box himself. "Here," he says, offering it to Daniel, "it's not dangerous," but Daniel doesn't accept the gun.

Martin grins and rests the barrel against the side of his head. He pulls the trigger a couple of times. The internal mechanisms of the Luger make dry crunching noises. "The firing pin is broken," Martin says and tosses the pistol back into the box. "Probably irreplaceable in New Zealand. It's strictly ornamental now."

Daniel nods, he looks distracted. "I'm going away soon," he says.

"Really?" says Martin. "I'm thinking about doing the same." Another few weeks or days perhaps. Time to disappear for a while, time to start a new life. He has done all he can do for now. He has laid down the groundwork, has softened the terrain just a little bit more. Others will follow, in years or in decades.

"There was something I wanted to talk about before I go."

"I can understand that. You want to make a clean break. Tie everything up before you leave. No loose ends or unanswered questions."

"I saw Karen today," Daniel says. "I dropped her off at the airport this morning. We talked about the old flat and everything . . ."

Martin nods. He remembers the way he'd been back then, full of virtuous ideas. Confronting the evils of the past to build a better tomorrow. Learning from history to avoid repeating it. He had read and studied witch-hunts, heresy trials, executions, persecutions, conquests, annexations, every kind of torture, cruelty and murder. He had filled his head with evil in the abstract. Stories and statistics and debate, he lapped them all up, but still remained insulated from it all, kept safe by the barriers of the printed page.

"We talked about what happened. And she said that nothing happened, not really, not anything really bad. She said it wasn't worth thinking about."

Nothing Martin had said could convince Karen about the way things had been. She is well now, she is happy and far away from him. Martin's thoughts on history had their beginnings there, but only took shape later, while he studied under Marion Pryor, and while he travelled in Europe.

"But I've started thinking about it again, I guess. And I'm not sure if it's right any more."

Martin can sympathise. The past is in a constant state of

flux. The pressure is to find the best story, the one we need the most.

"Maybe I've been wrong. Something bad happened. You've always thought that. But now I'm starting to see . . ."

"Can I ask you something, Daniel?" says Martin. "Suppose you're right. Suppose you think I was right after all. Do you try to make amends, do you try to repair it, all these years down the track? Or is this more a 'confronting your inner demons' kind of thing? What changes? What do you do?"

Daniel looks puzzled; he can't quite understand the question.

Remembrance, reverence, our fetishisation of past atrocity — Martin thinks it all just sets the bar higher. Evil is only worth our notice when it surpasses an existing standard and that standard is now so very high. Should he tell Daniel, should he let him off the hook, let him go? Martin is uncertain. Everything could all be torn down, he knows this. We do not need it, it does not help us. What we need is another chance to do right, to think that we can live like good people, incapable of cruelty. Martin has read, he has studied, he has spent his life gazing into the abyss. And, almost to his surprise, it had been the abyss that blinked first.

DANIEL

I took some time to consider Martin's question. He did not seem to be in any hurry to hear my answer — he looked away from me, out through the window, and I imagined that he was searching shadows of the street for the lurking forms of Josh or Wilton. They were waiting for me to leave, waiting to creep back inside and seize the Luger, the firing pin now mysteriously functional, and put an end to this story with one last triumphant act of madness.

I looked at my old friend and wondered how we had come to this point. He had said he would be leaving soon. This sounded like a good idea. Karen had already left, I would go soon as well. We should all be like Josh, I thought. Always moving, never slowing down, never pausing to allow the past to catch up.

`No, you think to yourself. That's not how it's going to go tonight . . . ERROR . . .`

`You sit down next to her and lean close . . . ERROR . . . A cold, nauseous feeling is growing in your gut . . . ERROR . . . She lets go . . . ERROR . . . Everything is wrong here . . . FATAL ERROR.`

I had changed my mind. But those thoughts and vague half-memories would sit in my head like a long-forgotten saved-game file on a dusty hard drive. The data was there, perhaps it had always been there, but so long as nothing forced me to open it then I could just keep moving and leave it all behind. We can all change our minds, over and over again, but nothing in our present lives had to change. I looked at Martin again, and this time he turned in his seat to meet my gaze. It was all his fault. All this past, this history.

"I don't know," I said eventually. "These things just happen, I guess."

"They do," Martin said. He stood up from the couch and after a moment I stood up as well. I wasn't sure if I had given Martin the answer he had been looking for. I had told him that I could keep moving and not think of myself as bad, or worse than anyone else, or even not think of it at all. Karen could deny all knowledge, or claim that she now knew different, and I could know and live with it. I wasn't sure where that left Martin and the knowledge he carried. He would probably agree that all knowledge claims were relative anyway. Whatever happens, no one gets the whole story.

"This Anita sounds like an interesting character," Martin said to me at the door.

"You should look her up sometime if you get the chance. Anita Clarkson. You've got a lot of similar interests."

"I may not see you again," he said at the door.

"Maybe not," I said. And that suited me just fine, it really did. I stepped outside.

"Right then," Martin said.

"Right," I said and he slid the door shut.

```
But later you slide the unlocked door back open and creep into the darkened living room. The battered white shoebox is still on the table; you reach under its lid and pull out the sleek, beautiful Luger pistol. Light shines out from under the door of Martin's bedroom. He has been waiting up. He has been expecting you. Pushing the door open, you see Martin sitting at his desk, his back to you. He is writing something in his notebook.
```

That should have been the end of it. I should have got into the car and driven away. Instead I sat at the wheel for a long time, watching the lights go off one by one in Martin's flat, thinking about what else I should have said, or what I failed to understand. I was still not sure how everything fitted together; I didn't know all the reasons and meanings behind Martin's actions, behind Karen's, behind my own and everyone else's. Perhaps there was no all-encompassing pattern for me to discover. Such things might only exist in the games we play, I thought, because they were the only places where we knew every rule. Outside of them things just happened, and we would put them in whatever order we thought best because we already knew what we wanted to learn from them, and already owned the message we intended to take away.

```
Of course, you think as you start to edge towards him. This is the only possible ending, the only one that makes any sense. How can you have a story about the
```

Holocaust where no one dies? You ease the safety off and place the barrel of the Luger against Martin's head. Your hand falters for a moment, but Martin catches hold of you, pushing the pistol back up into position. It's all right, Daniel, he says. We are all capable of anything. Then his fingers find yours and you pull the trigger together.

RAVINGTON

By the time summer came, Lewis Ravington was feeling confident enough to leave his house, though he seldom strayed too far. He never went into the city any more. Tunnel Press was a thing of the past and his old haunts — the pubs, the cafés, the bookstores and semi-regular poetry readings — no longer held any appeal. Instead he would walk along the beach in good weather, or sit at the window table in a nearby teashop, lingering over a single cup of coffee. But mostly he just stayed at home. The first seizure had been followed by two more in quick succession and he still felt cautious and oddly vulnerable. For a while the doctors had been concerned that he might have had a lesion on his brain (seizures were unusual for a man of his age with no previous history), but every scan had come up negative. In the end Ravington had been diagnosed with epilepsy, and discharged from the hospital. Weak and somewhat dazed, he had spent his days dozing in bed in his Seatoun house or on the couch downstairs, flitting in and out of consciousness.

Eric Stapp and Adja cared for him over the first few weeks, dropping round with bags of groceries, quizzing him about his health, making sure he took the medication the doctors had prescribed. They packed up the Tunnel Press office for him, sold off the remaining furniture, dumped the bookcase of page proofs at the tip. Nigel Wilton had visited him once, in the early days of his convalescence. Wilton was returning to Australia and proposed to take the remaining copies of *Body Disposal at Auschwitz* with him. He would sell them off his website, he had already worked out a deal for distribution with Martin Glass, it would all be perfectly legitimate. Ravington felt like telling him no, there would be no more of this, that the only place that destructive, deceptive book would be distributed to would be a pulping machine. But he had no other way of paying Wilton the money he still owed him from royalties, and he was weak and tired. So Rav nodded his reluctant agreement and gave Wilton and Stapp the keys to his lock-up. He was only human, after all.

For a while Ravington worried about how he would get rid of Eric Stapp. They were mates now as far as Stapp was concerned, and the leader of the NZNS dropped by almost constantly to lecture the still bleary Ravington on the virtues of White Nationalism and read him his poetry. But an opportunity for estrangement soon presented itself, when Stapp broke down one afternoon and almost tearfully confessed that he and Adja were in love and had been sleeping together for a bit over a fortnight. It was a hell of thing to do to another man, Stapp had said, to go behind his back like that. But he hoped Ravington would understand and forgive him. He left that day and did not return. Since then, in his darker, lonelier moments, Ravington would sometimes picture Stapp in a sharp, tight, black SS uniform advancing into a bedroom while Adja reclined naked on the bed, her blonde hair spilling back over the pillow, shouting "Yes, yes!" as Stapp pulled off one of his black leather gloves with a snap. "Fuck me hard and call me Eva!" Generally though, Ravington was not too upset. In some strange, perverse way he almost wished them well.

Free from Stapp's friendship and Adja's companionship, Ravington spent his days alone. As his strength returned, he continued the reading project he had set himself before the first seizure. Manuscripts were still being submitted to the now-defunct Tunnel Press; the lounge was slowly being conquered by piles of paper and the unopened parcels forwarded to his home address. Rav hadn't wavered in his determination to read them all. He would read everything until the packages stopped coming and all the words dried up. Rav now consumed the manuscripts eagerly, without judgment, absorbing all that he could. He still occasionally found a far-right tract in the post, but the more traditional Tunnel Press type of author had also started to trickle back. As the Martin Glass scandal receded into the past, Ravington once again found himself the recipient of poetry, memoirs, New Age philosophy. He couldn't publish anything, of course — he was no longer Lewis Ravington, editor-in-chief. But he read the books and wrote back to their authors.

Ravington's medication worked, for the most part, though sometimes he still had seizures. He fell down in the hallway, in the kitchen; never on the stairs, thank God, though he once burned his face on the bars of a radiator heater in the living room. As time passed the attacks came less frequently, but Rav never quite believed that they would fade away altogether. "Epilepsy"; "epileptic". Falling down and twitching and jerking. Someone with a tendency to fall down and twitch and jerk. The words had sounded so complete before, but Ravington now knew they were empty terms, labels that denoted the absence of any knowledge. Though they described his outward symptoms perfectly, they could not offer any real explanation for the strange crackling darkness that sometimes descended upon his brain. It had a long history and powerful connotations, but the word "epilepsy" was only a medical shorthand for "We don't know what the hell is going on", or "We know what it looks like, but we've got no idea what causes it, or even what it is, when you get right down to it". Naming something did not necessarily entail knowing what it was. The act of naming could only conceal ignorance and make the world seem less uncertain, at least to those who had not experienced the named condition first hand.

And so, because the medical community could offer no reasons for it, Ravington was left to make up his own. Emotional and physical exhaustion. God smiting him because he was bad. His own body rebelling against his general badness. Ravington could take his seizures as a sign. He had to mend his ways. Do no more wrong. Be good. Ravington knew that his potential goodness might turn out to be every bit as insignificant as his general badness had ultimately been. But still, he would try.

Now that he was feeling better, Ravington could get through a manuscript in one day with still enough time to pen a polite 'thank you' to its author and inform them that Tunnel Press was no longer accepting submissions. He would try to mention at least one or two things he had honestly liked about their work. Before his illness, before the collapse of his press, Ravington had often viewed his authors with incredulity. *How could anyone write this?* he would think. He thought he understood them better now. The world had proven itself to be an uncertain place, and new experience could easily undermine long-cherished meanings. The urge to write was a desire to keep something safe in the midst of all this chaos, to set down something solid. This is the way things are. This is how I saw it. This is what the world is like. So when Ravington did stumble upon the parts of an author's work which sounded true to him he tried to let them know that he had seen their world, that for a moment they had shared an understanding of the way things were and how they had always been.

Ravington was not sure if it would be enough to redeem him — he wasn't sure if redemption was possible, even for his own brand of small, inconsequential badness. But his reading had begun as an act of penance and evolved beyond the word into some small good thing in its own right. And when it was finally done he would return to the world, not redeemed perhaps, but ready to live a little longer and to do his best to live well. Maybe he would learn to drive while he was at it. And stop smoking again. He wasn't sure how much this would count for in the scheme of things. Little, perhaps, but not quite nothing. He was only human, whatever that meant.

PART THREE

DANIEL

"Do I know you?" was the first thing Anita said to me when I saw her again. It was almost two years after I had finally driven away from Martin's flat in Wellington, three years since she and I had lived together in London. We met in Krakow, in the wintertime, in an almost deserted hotel in the heart of the snow-bound city.

For a moment I wasn't sure how to answer her. I shook my head and started to back away from her chair, but then her eyes narrowed and she straightened in her seat and said "Daniel". Anita folded the newspaper she'd been reading and put it down on a coffee table. "I didn't recognise you."

I nodded. Outside the sky had already darkened and a light snow was starting to fall. Anita and I were alone in the hotel lounge, surrounded by empty armchairs and couches, some of them covered with dusty white sheets.

Anita frowned, considering me. "You look . . ." she started to say, then stopped and shook her head.

"No, tell me," I said.

"You look better," Anita said.

"Better?"

"Much, much better." And then she smiled beautifully, and stood up to kiss me on the cheek, and to my surprise I smiled back.

Nazi Hunter had been a big success, once it was finally released on the American and European markets. The graphics were gorgeous, the game-world physics impeccable, and its gripping narrative led players into the darkest corners of the Earth in search of the crippled Nazi war criminal who had murdered their parents. The reviewers had labelled the game *ground-breaking* and *enthralling in its scope and creativity*. They had particularly liked the final level where the player engaged in a pitched gun battle against an entire rest-home full of geriatric Nazis somewhere in Brazil. Sales had been high and Styx Softworks were happy enough, despite having to field a rather bothersome lawsuit from the Simon Wiesenthal Center.

I had intended to stay in San Francisco only until my contract ran out and then move on, but *Nazi Hunter*'s success changed things. At Heckle's recommendation, Styx Softworks had offered me a permanent job as a level-designer at their game studios. Since then I had been eating better, losing weight, exercising, spending time in the sun. Californian women offered powerful incentives for self-improvement. For a while I felt like I had become a better person.

"I wish I could go back to my old high school," Logan Heckle once told me after we'd had a particularly successful night on the town. "I wish I could go back there and find myself again, you know? Not me exactly — this isn't a time-travel scenario — but I'd find someone like me, a geeky overweight loser-type, too smart, too interested in all the wrong things. I'd put my arm around his shoulder and say it's okay, I know you're having a hard time now. But outside these walls, in the real world, *we run shit.*"

It was true. The geeks had inherited the earth. In the wake of *Nazi Hunter*'s blockbuster success, Styx had now devoted its considerable resources to accelerating the development of Heckle's follow-up project, which had been given the working title *Simu-Holocaust.* Heckle called it "a stark, frank examination of one of the greatest horrors of history". In the game, the player would take on the role of a death-camp commandant who has to construct and maintain the gas chambers and furnaces, organise the guards and transport trains, and brutalise the inmate population to prevent escapes and uprisings. It would be not only historically accurate, but also a hugely entertaining game of strategy and resource management.

"You have the option of playing as commandant with a conscience, of course," Heckle had told me, while we took lunch at an outdoor café. "You can take the *Schindler's List* approach, and try to save as many Jews as possible — sabotage the German war-effort, do the Righteous Gentile thing — or you can just be a black-hearted Nazi. The player has the freedom. Sure, it's a little edgy, but we should be able to deflect any flak by stressing its educational merits. It's like an act of witness or something. Anyway, it'll be good having you on the project, you being Jewish and all."

"Actually," I said, thinking about Josh and his Half-Jewish advocacy, "just my father is Jewish."

"Daniel," Heckle said, slapping me on the back, "if Hitler would have killed you then it's good enough for me."

The Marxist graphic artist, who had travelled with Heckle and me from Wellington, had converted to Veganism shortly after arriving in San Francisco. Every day, while we worked on the initial level-designs for *Simu-Holocaust*, he had taken time to lecture me on the evils of eating meat. "Speciesism is the epitome of the might-makes-right moral paradigm," he tells me. "Animals are weaker than us and we exploit them simply because we can. Everyone knows about the gruesome slaughter-houses, everyone knows about the cruelty of their living conditions. But nobody cares. Eleven million people died in the Holocaust, but a similar number of animals are killed every day in the United States. Meat isn't murder, Daniel. It's genocide."

In between his lectures, the Marxist graphic artist told me about Morbid's new project, back home in New Zealand. Apparently my old flatmate had made a name for himself in the field of interactive art with a series of completely immersive computer-generated environments. There were no set goals for their explorers to achieve; his worlds had no point or purpose, no beginnings or conclusions, and would be free from the tyranny of narrative for as long as their player-inhabitants could refrain from making up stories of their own. I still felt bad about Morbid sometimes. He hadn't always been fun but he'd never been boring.

"So are you here on your own?" Anita asked me.

"I'm with someone."

"I see."

"But she's sick. Bad flu. Been in bed for two days."

"I'm very sorry."

"Are you here with anyone?"

"No."

"I see."

"My boyfriend is staying in Warsaw, he has friends there. He's been here before, he didn't want to come back with me."

"I've never been here before."

"I know," Anita said. "What are you doing here?"

I was travelling in Europe again because I had reached a kind of crossroads in San Francisco. A slightly larger game company in the Silicon Valley area, one of Styx's competitors, had recently approached me with a job offer, asking me to head the design team on their new 3D adventure game: *Survivor: Belsen.* We had been bouncing emails back and forth about the salary and bonus system for some weeks, and I felt like I needed to take some time off and think things through.

When I talked over potential holiday destinations with a girl I'd been seeing in the Bay area she suggested Europe, even though it was close to December. The girl in question was into "authentic travel", and thought the continent would be better in the wintertime — fewer tourists, cheaper hotels, less hassle. I had agreed, and she set us a three-week itinerary of ruins, cathedrals, museums and galleries.

Paris, Madrid and Barcelona had gone well, and I had just allowed myself to be swept along. In some ways it wasn't too different from travelling between museums and memorials with Anita and Josh and Steve in the UK. Back then, the talk on television and the airwaves had been about weapons of mass destruction, protests against a planned "illegal invasion", and everyone had believed it was really all about the oil. Now the talk was about liberty and democracy for the people of Iraq, the protests were against an "illegal occupation", and everyone still believed it was really all about the oil. Several histories, of conflicting qualities, seemed to have occurred simultaneously while the present remained unchanged.

But by the time my friend and I reached Berlin we were getting tired of each other's company. We had pressed on to Krakow anyway, where my friend caught her flu and I discovered that most sites in the city closed at three in the afternoon as the sun went down. I had cancelled our other travel plans and arranged to fly back to the States early, via Heathrow, and doubted that we would see much of each other after our return. We were staying in a beautiful, rambling art-deco hotel in Krakow's Old City, just opposite Wawel Castle and practically empty over the winter season. I spent my evenings alone, avoiding our room and my friend's sickbed as much as possible, wandering the streets of the Old City until the cold drove me indoors, then sitting at the hotel bar for hours, or reading English-language newspapers in the lounge. And that was how I had met Anita again.

"I was invited to a conference in Warsaw," Anita said. "There's been a lot of interest in my work. I'm only in Krakow overnight. I want to revisit some sites tomorrow."

"More research?" I asked.

"Kind of. There are physical facts I want to check. There's been a recent revival of debate in certain historical circles. Nothing you'd have heard of, not yet."

Anita suggested that we get some dinner together. There was a café she liked, not too far away. "Have you seen my book yet?" she asked, as we left the hotel. "What did you think?"

My brother, Nathan, had sent me a copy of Anita's book a few months ago. *Memory and its Limits*. Memorials and memorial culture in the United States, Israel, Germany, Poland, the United Kingdom. I couldn't bring myself to do much more than skim it; memory was not a subject that had served me particularly well. But I did give the chapter entitled "Dismantling Memory" careful examination. Anita had dealt with "the Martin Glass incident" in New Zealand in some detail. Josh must have kept excellent notes for her.

> At one level Holocaust denial is an attempt to strip Jewish people of the perceived moral authority that now goes hand in hand with historical victimhood by denying that the event which most vividly defines them as "victims" ever occurred. At another

> level, the activities of Holocaust deniers can be seen as an attempt to appropriate this victimhood for themselves. By setting themselves at odds with mainstream thought and historical inquiry they deliberately invite criticism and derision. A "persecution complex" lies at the heart of all forms of Holocaust denial, the small yet controversial history of the Auschwitz crematoria by Martin Glass being no exception.

She had told a good story and it was a rewarding conclusion to reach. But it was untrue in Martin's case, or so I believed. He had vanished not long after I left Wellington. I liked to imagine Nigel Wilton dropping round to see him, only to find his flat cleared out, the shoebox containing his Luger pistol lying abandoned on the floor. I had thought about Martin a lot since I left New Zealand, wondering what he would have made of my life in California, of *Nazi Hunter*, *Simu-Holocaust*, and *Survivor: Belsen*. I had heard that *Body Disposal at Auschwitz* was still in circulation. Nigel Wilton continued to sell copies of it on his online forum. Wherever Martin was, I could imagine him taking a quiet satisfaction in that. When people eventually decide that they have had enough of history, his book will be waiting for them.

Over dinner we talked about Anita's revised American edition and my new career in San Francisco. Anita was familiar with the success of *Nazi Hunter* — she had played it through to the last level herself, but the wheelchair-bound ex-Nazi kept killing her with his mechanical claw arm. I told her about *Simu-Holocaust* and *Survivor: Belsen* and felt a little uncomfortable with the way she laughed.

"Are you still in touch with Josh?" I asked.

"Sometimes," she said. "A little. He doesn't really approve of the new boyfriend." Anita put her fork down and turned her head, looking out the café window into the dark, snow-encrusted street. For a moment her profile struck me as oddly pensive. "He didn't really approve of my book either," she said at length. "It wasn't what he thought it would be, in the end. I don't think he ever really understood what I was doing, he never got what it was all about."

"I know I didn't," I said.

"He settled in London for a while, talked about writing a book of his own, but that didn't work out. Then he went to stay with Steve for a while. Steve's living in Berlin now, and doing really well apparently. Job, boyfriend, all-round happiness, or at least contentment, according to Josh. But anyway, Berlin didn't work out either for Josh. Things weren't the same with Steve, he didn't need Josh any more, not in the way he used to, and Josh didn't stay for very long. Since then I think he's been travelling again, but on his own now. It must be lonely."

For a moment I almost felt sad for Josh, still lost in his world of glass-enclosed museum displays, lists of names and photograph walls. Then Anita asked me what I was doing tomorrow. "You should come with me on my day-trip, if you're not doing anything else," she said.

I didn't say anything. I bent my head and pushed the leftover food around on my plate.

"You must have been planning to go at some point. Just about everyone who comes to Krakow goes to see it sooner or later."

To tell the truth, I hadn't thought about it. Somehow I couldn't quite believe I was so close to the site itself, it was only a few hours away. I knew this and yet I couldn't believe it.

"Come on, Daniel," Anita said, smiling, and reached

across the table to touch my hand. "Let me be your tour-guide."

Buses for the town of Oswiecim left every hour from the central PKS station in Krakow. Anita and I arrived early in the morning to buy tickets, then descended to the basement carpark to board our coach along with a handful of other passengers, clearly tourists like ourselves. The sun had half risen by the time we left the city, but visibility had not improved. From the window of the bus I could barely see the sides of the road, and everything else was lost in a haze of whiteness.

When I had returned to my hotel room the night before, the girl I was travelling with had been asleep. I had woken her as I slipped into the bed and murmured that I was thinking of taking a day-trip, but said nothing about meeting Anita. The girl had nodded — her face was still hot and flushed with fever — and had rolled over onto her side, away from me. By the morning her temperature had dropped a little, but she had pretended to still be asleep while I dressed. We held no animosity, we had not fallen out, but we had lost interest in each other. That was just the way things went.

Next to me on the bus, Anita had taken out her notebook and was reviewing some old entries. I craned my neck round, looking at our fellow passengers; a pair of Canadian back-packers, an American couple in late middle-age, a solitary Asian boy with an iPod. I rested my head against the window and dozed. We made a few stops along the way, picking up and depositing Polish passengers in small towns, but after about an hour and a half the driver stopped the bus, opened the door and turned in his seat to face us. "Museum," he said, pointing to the open door of the bus. Outside the air was freezing but the weather had cleared a little and the sky above was a brilliant blue. The door hissed shut behind us and the bus drove away, weaving into the centre of Oswiecim. The entrance to the museum was not clearly marked, and our fellow tourists lingered for a moment by the bus stop, checking the times for their return journey to Krakow, but Anita led me across the road, to an open wooden gate and a wide tree-lined path. We walked up it in silence, our boots crunching on the snow and frozen dirt. Moving slowly, almost reluctantly, the other tourists drifted away from the bus stop and crossed the road to follow us. After about five minutes the path widened out into a carpark. Beyond it, I could see guard towers and barbed wire.

"Where are we?" Anita asked as we walked.

"We're outside Auschwitz," I said, humouring her.

"Are we?" she asked, smiling.

"We're outside Auschwitz I," I said.

"We're in Auschwitz already," said Anita. "This carpark sits right in the middle of the camp as it stood in 1945." She pointed to a group of pleasant yellow stucco buildings to our right, fenced off by a concrete wall and partially hidden by a grove of trees. "That's the old protective-custody camp right there. The buildings were seized as military quarters for the Polish army and never reincorporated into the camp."

She shook her head. "You approach thinking that you're walking towards an entrance, that you're on the threshold of a horror, but you're already in the middle of it, you've already gone in deep. You don't enter a place like this, you don't pass through a gate or step through a door. You get absorbed before you know it. There's no way to prepare."

The buildings Anita had pointed out to me, the barracks of the protective-custody camp, had been too well maintained and excellently designed to stand as monuments to a mass slaughter. With the crippling lack of housing in post-war Poland they had to be seized for practical purposes. People now lived in the same buildings where prisoners had awaited their deaths. They looked too solid, too much like houses;

their chimneys, large windows and slanted roofs did not fit the image of death-camp barracks.

Anita stopped in the middle of the carpark and drew my attention to a kiosk on the far side. "And that's where the main gate to Auschwitz I used to be, that was where most of the prisoners used to enter, from 1942 to 1945. All this is Auschwitz," Anita said, "but the site isn't effective unless it's contained. They want to give you something tangible, something you can see and explore. But Auschwitz is bigger than this, bigger than you can properly comprehend."

We walked into the visitors' centre, a long narrow building that sat adjacent to the main camp. It looked as if it was half shut up over the wintertime; only a few bored-looking attendants sat at the information cubicles, and the cafeteria and cinema were closed. There was little to see there, but Anita stopped me from moving on. "Still looks like a threshold," she said. "But now we're in deep, you wouldn't believe how deep we are. This building was part of the original camp. It may look like an addition, but it's old and it's real."

According to Anita, the exterior of the building was almost completely intact, but the long hall in which we stood had been constructed after 1945, the building's internal walls having been knocked out to create it. During the war, this had been the entry point to Auschwitz I, and within these walls prisoners had been herded through a series of rooms and stripped of every facet of their identity over the course of an hour. They had been registered and tattooed, robbed of their valuables and forced to undress. Then they were shaved, and washed in showers that stood parallel to a set of gas chambers used to delouse clothes. In another room prisoners were dried, and in another, sets of striped pyjamas were thrown at them, before they were pushed outside. The long hall offering comforts and amenities now occupied the same space where prisoners were once offered their own first taste of Auschwitz.

Outside the visitor's centre we walked down a dirt path to what had once been Auschwitz I's internal gates. I had already seen them in photographs a hundred times over, the tall steel portals bearing the words *Arbeit Macht Frei*. Beyond them lay what was left of the Auschwitz I camp. Three rows of near-identical wooden buildings laid out in a grid. The prisoner barracks and the administrative office. The four infirmary buildings where the weakest prisoners had been selected for death, and the block where sterilisation experiments had been conducted by Professor Carl Clauberg. The roll-call square. The central camp jail (the "death block") and its dark solitary cells. The nearby courtyard where prisoners had been executed, one fragment remaining from the wall against which they had been shot.

Anita seemed to know every building, every doorway and every corridor. She knew how and when and why they had been built, she could describe every change in their routines and functions. She knew what had been preserved since the camp was liberated, what had been destroyed and what had been restored. She could tell me how the museum-camp had been structured and restructured, what had been kept and what had fallen away.

We wandered for hours, glutting ourselves on the site. The cold was pervasive, it worked its way beneath my coat and layers of clothing until my muscles were stiff and sore. The air inside the barracks was like ice. Every now and then we would come across one of our fellow tourists, the Canadian back-packers, or the Asian boy, but we would not look at each other as we passed and walked on deeper into the empty camp. The frozen paths were ours alone, and the snow blankets to either side were crisp, smooth and untouched. "You should see this place in the summer," Anita told me. "It's got a different vibe during the tourist season, believe me."

We finally we came to the traditional ending point for

tours of Auschwitz: Krema I, a squat, dark little building with low sloping roof, its square chimney standing tall and stark against the skyline. I thought back to *Body Disposal at Auschwitz.* Martin had written a lot about the two double-muffle coke-fuelled furnaces installed within it, but very little about the building itself, and its gas chamber was barely mentioned. Body disposal had been the entirety of Martin's subject, the foundation stone of his new history. He had left the question of body production for someone else further on down the track. I thought of Nigel Wilton, still peddling Martin's book over his online forum, and did not doubt that some other writer would eventually rise to the task that Martin had left. The devil was in the details, as they say.

"There's barely anything left of the real crematorium," Anita said. "Though it used to be a sort of unofficial policy to let visitors believe they're looking at a perfectly preserved gas chamber and crematorium, found intact and kept that way since the camp was liberated in 1945."

Though it stood on the site of Krema I, the building we were looking at had been almost entirely reconstructed. According to Anita, the Krema I gas chamber had been abandoned in 1942 and its furnaces dismantled in 1943, most of Auschwitz's homicidal functions having been moved to the Birkenau camps. In 1944 the building was turned into an air-raid shelter and emergency operating room. When the structure was eventually restored, post-liberation, its chimney was rebuilt from scratch and four hatched openings were installed in the roof to suggest the points where Zyklon B would have been poured. It presented a grimly convincing façade, but it was a façade nonetheless, a mere stand-in for its larger brothers, the chambers and crematoria that were now crumbling ruins on the fields of Birkenau. But you could not end a tour of Auschwitz without seeing some sort of gas chamber, reconstructed or not. I watched one of the American tourists wave his wife into position in front of Krema I, then take her photograph with a digital camera.

"I would have liked to have shown you Birkenau," Anita said, as we walked back to the bus stop in the late afternoon. "But the bus between the camps doesn't run over the winter and it's too far to walk now."

We waited for the bus with the two Canadian backpackers. "I saw my family name in that list of names," one was saying. "Freaked me out."

"I know."

"Seriously, I just about lost it in there."

"It was intense."

"Really intense."

"And cold."

"Yeah, it's fucking freezing."

"How long till the bus?"

"Shit, I don't know. Half an hour? There are two different timetables here, I don't know how anything works in this country."

"Wish we were back in Krakow. This cold is too much."

"I'm glad we did this trip instead of the salt mines though. Totally worth it."

"Really intense."

"I can't believe I saw my name though. Yeah, I just about lost it . . ."

Anita slept on the bus ride back into the city, waking only as we pulled into the central station. "An hour till my train leaves," she said, checking her watch. She had already left her bag at the station, so there was no need to return to the hotel. We found a café and sat down for coffee.

"Why did you want to take me there?" I asked Anita.

"It's nice to revisit with someone who hasn't been to Auschwitz before," she said. "It gives me a fresh perspective, reminds me what it's like to be a tourist. And it was nice to see you again, I enjoyed showing you around. Do you understand anything better now?"

I shrugged and looked away, out the window. Across the street crowds of city workers in heavy coats and jackets were hurrying down into the underground bypass that led to the bus and train stations, beginning their evening commute. Everything I had seen that day at Auschwitz I had been neat and compact, I thought. It all fitted together, everything came to a definite conclusion. The whole of the Holocaust, the distances covered, the varying mechanics and routines of death, had been reduced to just one small site, easy to walk around and easy to comprehend. From the portentously symbolic gate to the reconstructed chimney of Krema I, the museum camp had not shown us what Auschwitz really was — it could not, that was not its function. All it could do was show us how we thought and what we felt about what had transpired there. One cannot know the past simply by walking the ground where it has been enacted. All we have are the stories we make as we walk, the contents of our own minds thrown back at us.

"What happened to your friend Martin Glass?" Anita asked me. "His book is still being circulated."

"I haven't seen him since I took Josh to visit him, like you asked."

"I hoped you might know how to find him," she said. "I wouldn't mind interviewing him, directly this time."

"No idea, sorry. And I don't think he's doing interviews any more."

Anita considered for a moment. "Well, it was worth trying," she said at length.

"I'm telling the truth. I've got no idea what happened to him."

"Whatever you say."

I started to laugh. "Do you seriously think I'm protecting him or something?"

"Josh was a little prone to hyperbole when describing their confrontation. I would just like to get a real sense of the man."

"I can't help you with that," I said. "Sorry."

Anita nodded and sipped her coffee. I asked her a few questions about Birkenau but she worked the conversation back towards Martin. "It was a sophisticated book in its way. A very concentrated attack on history which only unravels under close scrutiny. Josh found him a very calculating and tenacious denier. He dodged every counter-fact and rebuttal."

"Really? I thought Josh came off quite well in their little face-off; he surprised me. Tell me, is he still obsessed with that Half-Jewish thing of his?"

"Not quite so aggressively," Anita said. "He told me that he has been trying to find distinctively Half-Jewish sites of persecution in Germany, but I think he's been a little forlorn with the whole idea since he last saw Steve. That visit really didn't go well."

Outside, the sky had darkened and clouded over once again. Light flecks of snow slowly started to fall.

"In certain revisionist circles *Body Disposal at Auschwitz* is being regarded as a seminal work," Anita told me. "It's fascinating how far it's spread."

"So is your next book going to be on Holocaust denial?" I asked. "Is that where this is going?"

"I'm doing some preliminary research," Anita said. "It's a good topic — it hasn't been academically strip-mined, not quite yet. I think it's going to be the next big thing."

"I've still got no idea where Martin is now," I said as she stood up from the table, to go and catch her train. "You believe me, right?"

"Would you tell me if you did?"

"Why don't you let me walk you to the station."

"That's all right, Daniel," said Anita. "I'd rather you didn't."

And then she left, walking out the door into the thickening snow, and that was the last I ever saw of her.

The American girl I'd been travelling with was feeling a little better the next morning. She sat up in bed, ate some toast, and agreed that we should start travelling back to the States soon.

With one more day to kill in Krakow, I returned to the central bus station and bought a ticket back to Oswiecim. The bus was even emptier on that trip, and I was the only person to get off when the driver opened the door and barked "Museum" again. I headed up the path and out the exit on the other side of the Auschwitz I carpark, following the sign with the arrow that said *Birkenau 3km*. I walked past some closed shops and over a traffic bridge, then on down the road, following infrequent signs. The pavement petered out into a roadside track, buried in snow and my progress became slow and plodding.

I thought about Josh as I walked, about what Anita had told me, and I could picture him still travelling between his sites and memorials, alone now, a nation of one, trying to find something in the fragments of the past that would make him complete. He would probably approve if he could see me now, struggling through the snow towards the fields of Birkenau. I remembered him telling me how we were both Half-Jews and that the "halfness" meant something, that it was a viable quality in its own right. I supposed that I agreed with him now, though just in the sense that he and I were both only half-something, both lacking some quality, both somehow incomplete. But I could live with what I lacked, and he could not, and I was not sure which of us was better off for it. I did not like Josh, I hoped to never see him again, and doubted I could ever think of him fondly. But perhaps he was right to be mad, clawing to find a foothold in the past, while I kept moving forward.

Finally, under a low overcast sky, I reached the entrance of Birkenau, Auschwitz II. What was left of the camp's fencing stretched out on either side of me, leading away into the distance, and once I passed beyond it I found few signs and no tour guides or museum staff, just a vast expanse of snow veined with half-submerged train-tracks. Far off in the distance I could make out the weatherbeaten ruins of buildings and chimneys. It would be impossible to see Birkenau the way I had seen Auschwitz I. To walk around it would take days, not hours. The site was not contained, there was no way it could be contained. It seemed to sprawl out in every direction, unmappable, unexplorable, and utterly empty.

I walked out along a wooden ramp, towards the main Birkenau monument. I wasn't sure why I had come here, all I knew was that my visit to Auschwitz I had not been enough, I couldn't leave without seeing Birkenau. Martin had thought the past and present were irreconcilable, that we couldn't live with the weight of history, it could not make us better and had to be lifted. Perhaps that was what he'd been trying to tell me the last time I saw him, when he asked me, "What changes?"

Perhaps he thought he had learned all this from Karen and me, from our remembrances and revisions. That idea had troubled me occasionally over the past two years, but never for very long. I had remembered more about my life, my knowledge was as full and complete as it could ever be, and I had found I could still live with myself, though from time to time that revelation would fill me with a kind of dread. I could keep the weight of my history behind me, I could move so fast that it would never catch up. For better or worse, I was set on my course.

What changes? Not much. I remembered the Latin phrase I had found in Martin's notebook, it had taken me a while to track down the reference. A line from the pinnacle of German literature, from Goethe's *Faust Part One*, written by a devil pretending to be a scholar in a student's book of Aristotle. *Eritis sicut Deus, scientes bonum et malum.* We can be as God, knowing good and evil. The devil's best joke. His oldest temptation.

I wandered on, out past the Birkenau monument and into the snow, towards the ruins in the distance. There was little to see here, Auschwitz II was slowly crumbling away into nothing. But "nothing" itself should not be disregarded and wars can still be fought over an empty space. Birkenau was the prime site of Hitler's Judeocide and yet I had seen a bronze medallion depicting drawn swords, a symbol of Christian martyrdom, attached to the main monument. Anita had mentioned that the building, which was once the *Kommandantur* of Auschwitz, had been converted into a Roman Catholic church.

"Many Poles died at Auschwitz," she had said. "Jews and Gentiles. Poland was almost enslaved by Germany but it endured. So Auschwitz is also seen as a symbol for Polish survival as well as a memorial to the Jews of Europe."

It was difficult for a place to serve as a symbol both of survival and destruction, she had told me, and for years, on the empty fields of Birkenau, Christian triumphalism had been at war with Jewish mournfulness. Visiting the site in 1979, Pope John Paul II had honoured the Polish dead and suggested that the evil of Auschwitz-Birkenau needed to be combatted with a beacon of Catholic piety. A convent of Carmelite nuns was established soon after, close to the perimeter of Birkenau and described by a Catholic charity as "a spiritual fortress and a guarantee of the conversion of strayed brothers from our countries". After five years of complaints levelled by Jewish groups the convent was relocated, 550 yards back from the camp perimeter.

But perhaps the strangest story came when pious visitors started leaving crosses in the ruins of the gas chambers to honour the memory of Edith Stein, a Roman Catholic nun of Jewish origins who had died at Birkenau. Offended by what they saw as a Christian appropriation of Jewish suffering, some Jews erected a large Star of David on a post near the ruins in response. The Christians only left more crosses and a battle of religious symbols ensued. For a time stars and crosses piled up around the gas chamber ruins. The situation was only resolved when schoolchildren of Warsaw erected a large wooden cross with a Star of David in the middle. But did having the star in the middle of the cross mean that Judaism is a mere facet of the much larger religious truth of Christianity? Or does it mean that Judaism lies at the heart of all true Biblical religions?

I could not tell, and I wasn't sure if the question mattered. Birkenau was vast, and if every great basilica of Christianity were to be uprooted and moved to that one site, there would still be infinite space to spare. It seemed to me that one could tear down Jerusalem and rebuild it in the fields of Birkenau, brick for brick and stone for stone, and still not come close to filling the emptiness. Auschwitz-Birkenau could have many meanings or it could have none, but all it meant to me on that afternoon was that there had been a time when we had known good and evil like a god and shown ourselves capable of anything. If Auschwitz had to be a symbol then it could stand for humanity, for no human act could be properly called inhuman.

I stopped walking after a few minutes. I was up to my calves in snow; trying to reach the ruins ahead of me was hopeless. I could now see that they were chimneys, seven or eight or nine of them spotted across the fields, reaching up to the grey sky like stiff bony fingers. My guidebook had told me that I was walking towards Building Section 2 of Birkenau and so I knew I was looking at the chimneys of long-vanished barracks and not those of crematoria, but the sight chilled me nevertheless. One comes to Birkenau with certain expectations and the sight of a chimney is always unnerving.

But I knew that those chimneys could not stand forever despite our best efforts to keep them upright. In time they would topple and, come the summer, long grass would grow over the rubble. Nature could retake Birkenau and maybe, years or centuries from now, people would cross its fields without knowing that those chimneys had once stood there. They might stumble upon a stone, or a slab of concrete, or the piece of a long-rotted cross or Star of David, and wonder what had taken place on the grass where they now walked. I turned away from the chimneys and back towards the gate.

ACKNOWLEDGEMENTS

I consulted a number of sources while writing this novel. Particularly useful were *Images of the Holocaust: The Myth of 'Shoah' Business* by Tim Cole, *Writing and Rewriting the Holocaust and The Texture of Memory* by James E. Young, *The Holocaust and Collective Memory* by Peter Novick, *Denying the Holocaust* by Deborah Lipstadt, *Holocaust Remembrance: The Shapes of Memory* edited by Geoffrey H. Hartman, *A Problem from Hell: America and the Age of Genocide* by Samantha Power, *Fantasies of Witnessing: Post-war Efforts to Experience the Holocaust* by Gary Weisman, *Constructing the Holocaust: A Study in Historiography* by Dan Stone, *Auschwitz, 1270 to the Present* by Robert Jan van Pelt and Deborah Dwork, *Preserving Memory: The Struggle to Create America's Holocaust Museum* by Edward T. Linenthal, *Hitler's Jewish Soldiers: The Untold Story of Nazi Racial Laws and Men of Jewish Descent in the German Military* by Bryan Mark Rigg, and *Reproducing Jews: A Cultural Account of Assisted Contraception in Israel* by Susan Martha Kahn. An earlier version of Part One of *Holocaust Tours* previously appeared in Best New Zealand Fiction 1.

This novel was completed as part of my candidature as a PhD student at the University of Melbourne and with the assistance of an Australian Postgraduate Award. I would like to thank Kathleen Mary Fallon and Anna Livesey for their generous comments and advice. Thanks also to Rosemary DuPlessis, Kate Middleton, Mark Bradley, Harriet Allan, Lesley Marshall, the University of Melbourne English Department, and to Edward Lynden-Bell for *You Killed JFK*.